LORDS OF LONDON ·

Books 4-6

TAMARA GILL

COPYRIGHT

Lords of London
Books 4-6
To Vex a Viscount
To Dare a Duchess
To Marry a Marchioness
Copyright © 2019, 2020 by Tamara Gill
Cover Art by Wicked Smart Designs
Editor Authors Designs
Editor Free Bird Editing
All rights reserved.

ISBN: 978-0-6489312-5-6

TO VEX A VISCOUNT

Lords of London, Book 4

For the past six years, Miss Lizzie Doherty has had exactly zero proposals. Not because she isn't attractive, or from a good family, or doesn't have well-connected friends, but simply because she is poor. Or so the ton believe. Invited to a country house party on a stormy night, her journey takes an unexpected turn when her driver delivers her to the wrong estate. Upon entering the home, she's soon masked and sworn to

secrecy. Never has Lizzie ever experienced such an odd and intriguing event, so she plays along to see where the night will take her.

Lord Hugo, Viscount Wakely lives for sin, for anything scandalous, and for house parties that involve all of those things. At least he used to. But imagine his surprise when his good friends' ward, Miss Lizzie Doherty, an innocent and a successful debutante six years running, arrives at the last debauchery house party he'll attend. Or when an impromptu, scandalous kiss turns his life upside down.

Lizzie decides to stay for the week-long house party. Masks keep the guests' identities secret, but Lizzie would know Lord Hugo Wakely anywhere. And that one impromptu, scandalous kiss tells her that he is the Viscount for her…he just doesn't know it yet.

PROLOGUE

J. Smith & Sons Solicitors, London, August 1812

Lord Hugo Blythe, fourth Viscount Wakely, stared mutely at his solicitor of many years, Mr. Thompson. He blinked, fighting to comprehend the meaning behind the gentleman's words.

Damn my father to hell. Had he not already been dead, Hugo might have killed him himself for playing such a game.

"I'm sorry, but can you explain to me again what the terms are of my father's will? I'm not sure it's making sense to me. You said I must marry within a year? This part I'm a little muddled about." How he dearly wished there really was some confusion on his part.

Mr. Thompson, a stout older gentleman with a receding hairline but honest features, threw him a pitying glance and then stared down at the paperwork before him again.

"The will explains that as per your birthright, you inherit the title of viscount, and Bolton Abbey, along with the London home and the estate in Cumbria and Ireland. However, the dowry your mother brought to the family upon her marriage to your father will revert to her family should you not marry by your thirtieth birthday. I believe that is less than twelve months away."

Disbelief sat in Hugo's gut like a heavy boulder. "Only just. July twenty-third, to be exact," he said, running a hand over his jaw. How could his father do this to him? Of course, they'd had many discussions—very well, arguments—about his dallying and raking about town without any direction toward marriage, but to do this to him, forcing his hand, was beyond cruel.

His solicitor placed down his papers and met his gaze. "I suggest that you find a wife before the end of the next season. If you fail to satisfy that clause, the money will go to your uncle in New York according to your father's instructions. Your uncle has been notified of this condition and is receptive to claiming the money that went with his sister to your father upon their marriage. The clause is quite watertight and cannot be waived. Of course, looking at the financial statements regarding your inheritance, should you lose this money, there will be very little remaining to keep the estates running. You may have to look to leasing them out indefinitely, as you're unable to sell due to them being entailed properties."

A weight settled on Hugo's shoulders and he slumped back in his chair, not having known it was as bad as all that. "Did Father state exactly who I'm to marry?" He'd certainly spoken loudly enough from beyond the grave with his will, he might as well also state who was acceptable.

"As to that…" Mr. Thompson said, shifting on his seat and looking a little uncomfortable for the first time during their meeting.

The weight on Hugo's shoulders doubled.

"Your father has stipulated that not only are you to marry before your thirtieth birthday, but you are also required to marry a woman of fortune, as he did. No less than thirty thousand pounds must be her dowry. Your father wrote that he asks this of you to ensure that the family name, and all those who rely on your lands for their livelihood, are kept secure. He also wrote that he believes you are more than capable of this task, and he wishes you well and every happiness in your future marriage."

Hugo met his solicitor's gaze, unable to fathom what he was being told. He'd thought he would have more time before he settled down. He very much enjoyed being an eligible bachelor, but the select, very scandalous house parties that he was accustomed to would all have to stop if he were to find a wife. How dull. A wife. His life was over.

Mr. Thompson stood, holding out a rolled-up copy of the will tied with dark pink ribbon. Hugo clasped it, the urge to scrunch it up into a ball of rubbish being his first thought.

"Good luck, Lord Wakely. If you have any further questions, please do not hesitate to call on me. I'm at your disposal whenever you need."

Hugo shook his hand, then, swiping up his hat and gloves, strode for the door. "Thank you, sir. Once I have found the poor victim who will become my wife, I shall be in contact."

And she would be a victim, for a marriage made in haste, and solely due to requiring funds, would never be a good match. He'd always admired the love match marriages of the couples with whom he associated, knowing he too would desire such a connection for himself. Just not yet.

He stopped on the cobbled pavement and slammed his

beaver hat on his head. *Damn.* If what the solicitor said was true, and there was no doubt that it was–he had the will in his hands to prove it–then he had to find a wife.

Eleven months approximately before his time was up. Before his uncle made the trip across the Atlantic and took back what was rightfully Hugo's. His birthright.

Well, he wouldn't have it. He would adhere to the clause, but he would enjoy his final year as an unmarried gentleman as well. There was nothing he disliked more than being told by his father what to do. That his sire had managed this from beyond the grave was not something he'd thought the old curmudgeon capable of, but alas, he was wrong.

He swore. Eleven months and then, and only then would he find a willing heiress wanting a marriage of convenience, and be done with it.

In all the past Seasons he'd failed to find anyone who inspired him with anything other than with lust, so, in the next season, he would marry a biddable heiress to secure his properties. A perfectly convenient plan if ever he had one.

Under no circumstances was he willing to lose his lands, have to lease out his estates, and live off meager funds for the rest of his life. His name would be ruined; he'd be a lord pitied by everyone. The Wakelys had never had to ask for money, and he would not be the first one to do so. He shuddered. Oh no, that would never do.

Heiress hunting he would go. Well, in eleven months in any case.

CHAPTER 1

Ten months later. Garden party, London

"It says right here in Pride and Prejudice that a gentleman in possession of a large fortune must be in want of a wife." Lizzie Doherty slapped the book shut and noticed her cousin by marriage, the Countess of Leighton, making an amused study of her. "What are the odds my very sentiments are confirmed in these novels. What do you say, Kat?"

Katherine laughed, shaking her head. "Lizzie, that unfortunately is not always true, and then when it is, the man usually makes the catastrophic mistake of marrying someone they don't care about, or even like for that matter. And you're not a man, you're a woman in possession of a large fortune, if not known within society, and so it's you who is looking for a husband."

Lizzie stared down at Pride and Prejudice, thinking over her cousin's words, which unfortunately her last Season in town had proved correct. Despite her connections, no one had offered for her hand, nor suggested they might, in all the balls she attended. It had even started to frustrate her, and she wasn't normally the type to become annoyed at other people's decisions or actions. But to be a pariah for an unknown reason seemed peculiar. And now, she'd had enough of it.

Lizzie came from a family with great connections, even if they were on the poor side of the Upper Ten Thousand. Her own situation was improved when her cousin Hamish, Earl Leighton, bestowed on her a large dowry some six years ago, which had only grown in value over that time due to his investments, or so he'd told her. She was set to be gifted close to seventy thousand pounds upon her marriage, or her twenty-fifth birthday. A tidy sum any future husband would be happy to receive. If one would only ask her.

Lizzie smiled, giving thanks every day for her mother's decision to send her to town all those years ago to have her Season with Lord Leighton's mother, even if she wasn't the most pleasant woman to be about.

She sighed as her mother came to join them, flicking her fan shut with a snap. "Oh, for heaven's sake, Lizzie, stop sitting here with Lady Leighton and go and stand out on the lawn with the young ladies your own age. You're the epitome of a wallflower at this very moment."

Lord Leighton had thought it best that they keep the fact Lizzie was now an heiress from both their mothers, due to their inability to keep secrets. The last thing they wanted to do was make her susceptible to fortune hunters. And so, at picnics such as the one they were at today, Lizzie had to tolerate her mother's chastisement over her failure to catch a husband. But it was harder than one thought, especially when all the men believed you were poor.

"I see your friend Sally has arrived, Lizzie. You had better go say hello," Katherine said, winking at her.

"I shall, thank you," she said, standing and starting toward her friend. She took in the guests at Lord and Lady Hart's picnic. She had found that a lot of the gentlemen only wanted a rich wife, or worse, were just carousing and seeing if any delectable widows were up for a naughty jaunt in their carriages. Of course, Lizzie wasn't supposed to know what was happening behind the closed doors of the London *ton*, but one would be a simpleton indeed if they thought all those who paid attendance on them, made house calls, and had the best intentions outwardly, were always angels.

A distinct whisper tittered through the guests and Lizzie turned to see Lord Hugo Blythe, Viscount Wakely, join the picnic, bowing to the hosts before walking toward the Duke and Duchess of Athelby.

Lizzie took the opportunity to watch him, not unlike so many other women at this very moment. But when one was faced with the fine, athletic form of Lord Wakely, one ought to stop and admire the view.

His lordship oozed the forbidden deliciousness that she shouldn't know anything about. But if one listened carefully enough at balls and parties, you could always pick up tidbits of information about what society was up to. Who was having an affair with whom, who was a terrible lover or had vices at both table and horses. The things Lizzie had heard her first Season in town, many years ago now, would've been enough to make her mother have a turn of the vapours had she disclosed them.

Now, six years later, she was a well-known wallflower, or at least a debutante too long in the tooth to be considered for marriage. Not that it mattered, due to the sizable dowry she would be gifted either upon her marriage or on her twenty-fifth birthday. And since she was closer to being five and twenty than she was to marriage, the allure of not marrying at all had taken hold in her mind and wouldn't dislodge. There were worse things in life than being unmarried, such as marrying the wrong kind of man, or having a loveless marriage. Marrying a man who sought the comfort of others, even after their marriage vows were spoken. She would rather remain single and become a spinster than make such an unchangeable, catastrophic mistake.

Lord Wakely grinned devilishly toward a group of giggling debutantes, but despite his teasing and mirth, not once did he falter in his gentlemanly behaviour. And yet, Lizzie wondered what was really going on behind his dark, stormy blue eyes. What did he really think about being one of London's most sought-after bachelors? Did he enjoy the attention or merely tolerate it? After all, his lordship even had the ability to make Lizzie's stomach flutter. Her heart pumped faster whenever their gazes clashed.

It was a reaction she'd never experienced with anyone else, in all her years dancing in the ballrooms of London. She'd known him for some years now, her cousin having introduced them during her second Season. Although she couldn't tell what effect she'd had on him, if any, Lizzie had lost her breath a little that day they'd met and never really got it back.

He seemed to have been born with the most luscious dark hair she'd ever seen, His skin had a beautiful olive tone to it, not pasty white like so many English gentlemen. She took a sip of her champagne, having forgotten to go to her friend, and instead remained standing by the cake table watching him. She pursed her lips, wondering if he had any Spanish blood in the family, with a jawline that looked like it could cut glass, not to mention his perfectly proportioned nose.

One day someone would snatch him up, make him fall

desperately in love with them, and how lucky would that lady be. To wake up each morning next to such a man would be heavenly indeed.

Her friend Sally spotted her and waved. Putting Lord Wakely out of her mind, Lizzie joined her just as the woman Sally was speaking to, Lady Jersey, bade her good day.

Lizzie kissed Sally on the cheek and accepted a fresh glass of champagne from a passing footman. "I so wish Mama would stop making me attend these types of events where we're paraded like cattle at Tattersalls. I'm getting too old to worry about men and marriage, and my mother has a tendency to throw every rich youth at my head, even when it's quite obvious I'm too old for them and that they're absolutely in no way interested in me."

Sally chuckled, her eyes twinkling in mirth. "You are not too old. Why, for a man, you're not even considered in your prime. You debuted so young, only seventeen, it is no wonder you're sick of all these games and courtship dances."

Lizzie nodded, agreeing with everything Sally said. Her friend always spoke the truth and without exaggeration. She was truly the best person Lizzie knew, other than her cousin Hamish. "You are right of course. And I will admit the Season is getting awfully stale. I long for adventure. I will tell you this Sally, because I know you're my friend and as silent as the grave, but if I could, I'd purchase a home of my own, move away from Mama, and procure a cat. Or better yet, lots of cats. I will be well satisfied once all of those three things are complete."

Sally shook her head, smiling. "I don't believe you for a second. I know very well there is a certain gentleman who'd change your spinster ideals in a trice should he court you. What a pity he's so elusive, even though quite polite to us young, inexperienced females. Although I did hear a whisper that he's on the hunt for a wife. Perhaps you may be in the running…"

Lizzie laughed, as understanding dawned. She looked around the gardens and found him without trouble, and inwardly sighed at how darling he was in every way. "How handsome he is. Do you think he knows that every woman in London is in love with him? I wonder if he has any Spanish blood in him. He has the most beautiful olive-toned skin I've ever seen."

"Why, yes, I think you're right. From memory I do believe his grandmother was from Portugal. Maybe that's where he inherited his dark good looks." Her friend studied him a moment before she said, "Lord Wakely could pass for a pirate–rugged, sun-touched and terribly naughty, from what the gossip rags state." She grinned, taking a sip of her drink.

"His outwardly features are to be praised, but he is good at heart too. Why, last year he made a sizable donation to the London Relief Society that the Duchess of Athelby and Marchioness of Aaron run. And he always dances with debutantes new to town, and gives them a good start to their Season. He is never unkind. In fact, I've never heard a bad word about him, not regarding his manners or temperament. What a shame there is chatter that he's after Miss Edwina Fox." Just the mention of this debutante made Lizzie's teeth ache. "She debuted this year and is the talk of the *ton* since her uncle is related to the Duke of Athelby. Well-connected and rich…exactly what all young gentleman seek in a wife, is it not?"

"Your final words dripped with sarcasm, Lizzie. Perhaps you should be less cutting when we're in company," Sally suggested. "Are you looking forward to Lady Remmnick's house party? We're leaving early tomorrow morning–father wishes to arrive well before the afternoon. With everyone who's invited, I doubt there will be many left in town."

Lizzie couldn't wait to return to the country, the fresh air, and the horse riding she would be able to do more often. "I am looking forward to it, and I cannot thank your mama enough for allowing me to go under her chaperonage. Although I will arrive the day after tomorrow with my maid. Mama is going home to Bellview Manor and I'll travel onto the Remmnicks' from there."

Sally clasped her arm, walking them about the fringes of the lawn. "I'm so excited to attend. Arthur will be there. Do you think he'll finally ask me to marry him if he can manage to drag me away from Mama for one moment?"

Marquess Mongrove–or Arthur to Sally and Lizzie, since they'd known him since childhood–was the newly appointed Marquess and finally able to decide for himself what his future would be. Not his mother, which Lizzie could sympathize with since she too had an overbearing parent. He'd been a pleasant child and had grown into a lovely gentleman that suited Sally and her honest and obliging temperament. A perfect match for her friend in all ways.

"I'm sure he will. In fact, look at him now pining for you over there under the elm tree. How sad he looks that he hasn't got his love beside him, hanging off his every word and worshipping the ground he stands upon."

Sally slapped her arm. "Stop your teasing." She smiled. "He is lovely though, I must agree, and should he ask me to be his wife, I will say yes immediately and request a very hasty marriage. I'm ready for my life as a wife and mother to start. I see no point in waiting before we say our vows, if you understand my meaning."

Lizzie smiled at the light blush that stole across her

friend's cheeks. "You'll make a beautiful bride and a perfect, loving wife. Lord Mongrove will be lucky to have you."

"Thank you, dearest." Sally threw his lordship a small wave, delighting when he waved back in return. "I simply cannot wait another day, and so I suppose this house party has come at a perfect time. We each need a little diversion from life's trials."

Lizzie couldn't agree more.

"Not to mention," Sally continued, turning her attention back to her, "we'll be away from town and staying under one roof. What fun we will have. And even though my head is already turned, it does not mean you cannot find someone to love."

"There is only one gentleman I want, and he doesn't even know that I exist. I'm simply the cousin of one of his closest friends, unremarkable and forgettable at best. And as I've stated before, I'll not marry anyone simply to procure children and do my duty. Whomever I marry, it will be for love. Such a deep, heart-wrenching, all-consuming love that it will simply drive away all my dreams of my own home, vacant of parents and filled with cats."

"I like this plan. It suits you well, and you know I want nothing but the very best for you," Sally declared, her tone serious.

"Do you know if Lord Wakely is attending the Remmnicks' house party?" Lizzie asked, trying but failing desperately to hide the hope that was in her tone. Oh dear, she really was desperate and pining for the man. If only she could curb her enthusiasm toward him and see other gentlemen for their worth. When there were some, of course.

Sally grimaced and Lizzie had her answer before her

friend uttered a word. "Unfortunately, he's not attending, although I was told he will be in the county attending another event. Not far from the Remmnicks' estate, in fact."

Lizzie bit her lip and wondered what this other event was, and who was attending. The social set his lordship was part of were the elite of society. Only gentlemen of extreme wealth and with very few cares in the world were allowed entry. Gentlemen who loved the frivolities of societal living, and the luxurious lifestyle and loose women that their status afforded them. No rules and no wives allowed.

It was not for the faint of heart, and certainly nothing like Lizzie could ever imagine for herself had she been a man and able to join such an association. Not that she was supposed to know any of these things, but some gossip was too juicy to ignore. "I will not deny that I'm somewhat disappointed by that news, but then he doesn't even know that I exist, so what does it matter which event he attends?"

Sally clasped her arm and cuddled her a little to her side. "Do not be downcast, dearest. There is a gentleman out there with your name written on him. And you shall marry him and love him wildly when you find him."

Lizzie laughed, not even able to imagine such a possibility, but wishing it nonetheless. If only to get away from her mama, who could at times be terribly stifling, sooner than her twenty-fifth birthday. "Only time will tell, I suppose."

Not that she would tell Sally, but Lizzie was content waiting for her endowment from Hamish, because it was far more likely than being noticed by the viscount. If he had any interest in her at all, he would have made his intentions clear years ago.

"It will tell, my dear, and when it does, it'll be a great story to hear."

CHAPTER 2

Kent – two days later

The carriage rocked alarmingly, and Lizzie clasped a strap beside the window with two hands to stop herself from tumbling to the floor. Her maid let out a squeak when once more the carriage slipped on the muddy track, sending them to sway about like leaves in the wind.

"Oh, Miss Lizzie, this is terrible. If we do not arrive soon I fear we'll never make it."

It was a fear Lizzie herself had had multiple times already since they set off from her family's estate early that morning. The weather from the south had come in so fast that by the time they'd left the last inn where they'd changed horses it was too late to go back.

A howling sound whirred through the door and Lizzie shivered. "I'm sure the storm will pass soon. Do not worry, Mary. We'll be there shortly, I promise."

Tears sprang in her maid's eyes and Lizzie looked outside. Night was falling fast and still no sign of lights could be seen, no beacon of safety in this terrible storm.

The carriage rocked to a halt, then dipped as the driver jumped down. Lizzie opened the door and it was wrenched open by the howling wind, hitting the side of the carriage with such force the window smashed onto the carriage seat. Her maid screamed, and she cursed.

"Miss Lizzie, we're at a crossroads, and the storm's blown over the sign showing the direction of Lady Remmnick's estate," her driver yelled, the sheeting rain making it hard to hear what anyone was saying.

She shivered, squinting as the rain pelted against her face. "Go left and we'll hope for the best."

"Right ye are," he said, shutting the door and leaving them alone once more.

Lizzie reached under the carriage seat and pulled out a blanket, handing it to her maid. "Push the glass away with this and we'll try to block the window a little."

Her maid did as she bade, and with a little trouble they managed to keep some of the weather from intruding into the vehicle. Not very successfully though, and by the time the carriage did arrive at the estate, both Lizzie and Mary were drenched and shivering with cold.

A footman ran from inside the well-lit home, a most welcome haven after their ordeal.

Lizzie stepped down and ran indoors along with her maid. Inside, a woman she'd never met before strode toward them, with a calm assurance and grace that was the opposite of how Lizzie looked and felt at that exact moment. In fact, she was pretty sure she was leaving a terrible wet puddle on the mosaic tiled floor.

"Welcome, you've arrived just in time."

Lizzie dipped into a curtsy, wondering where Lady Remmnick was as this woman certainly wasn't her ladyship. A servant walked past with a tray of champagne, and through an ajar door Lizzie spotted guests with masks, even though the lady before her didn't have one herself. "Thank you so much for inviting me, but I must apologize for my tardy arrival. The weather outside is atrocious and we almost lost our way."

"You're right on time. If you follow me upstairs, I'll show you to your room where you can change."

"Thank you," Lizzie said, looking about and taking in the home. The silence was deafening, and she frowned. Normally house parties were lively, with people milling about all over the place. The guests in the adjacent room were oddly quiet. "I'm Miss Lizzie Doherty by the way, and you are? I suspect Lady Remmnick is busy with the guests who are already here."

The woman stopped, placing a finger against her lips and shaking her head in silence. "No one has names here. Not for the next three days at least, my dear."

Lizzie stopped on the staircase's top step, her maid's furrowed brow reflecting her own thoughts. "May I enquire as to whose estate this is?"

The lady laughed, a sultry sound that caused unease to coil through her blood. "That's a secret too, although I'm sure you're only teasing. You received an invite after all. You must have, to be here. The location is secret." The woman paused, turning to face her. Lizzie met her inspection and wondered if she looked as pathetic as she felt standing before this golden goddess. "You did receive an invite, yes?"

"I did, yes, but—"

"Well then, you may follow me and join the party once you've cleaned yourself up. We have recently had running water installed upstairs in every room, so you may have a bath if you wish. The gowns that are suitable for wear are in your armoire, and tonight's color requirement is green, so please use a gown that's appropriate. Your maid will find an appropriate mask in the tallboy."

Lizzie followed without saying a word, her mind a whirr of thoughts. Was this a new event Lady Remmnick had introduced at her house party? The approach was indeed intriguing. Lizzie would go along for now, but when she found Sally she would enquire about the details.

A familiar laugh sounded, and she looked over the balustrade and spotted Lord Wakely coming out of one of the rooms downstairs. His stride and voice were as familiar as Lizzie's own, so she would've known him anywhere, even if right now he had a black mask covering half his face. He was not supposed to be at Lady Remmnick's house party.

Clarity bloomed into Lizzie's mind as it dawned upon her that it was she and not he who was at the wrong house party.

She bit her lip, butterflies fluttering in her belly at the thought of him being here. This must be the house party that her friend Sally had been talking about. The one that was coveted by anyone who was anyone within the *ton*. And invite only.

What was it that everyone got up to here that was so secretive?

"This is your room, my dear."

With a flourish, the woman showed Lizzie into her bedchamber situated at the end of a long corridor. A frisson of excitement ran through her that she was actually here. Even if she wasn't supposed to be. How fortuitous that the current evening's activity was a masquerade.

Lizzie walked into the room and marvelled at the beautiful furniture and decorations throughout. A large bed with a canopy rested before the windows. She'd never seen such a layout before, but didn't mind it in the least. It looked delightful, in fact. There was a large tub for bathing, along with a wash basin and bowl. Two high-backed chairs sat before the fire, with deep green covering that suited the dark wooden floor and the green coverlet on the bed. It wasn't the least feminine, nor overly masculine either. In fact, it was just a perfectly lovely, welcoming room.

"This is quite acceptable. Thank you," Lizzie said, setting down her bonnet on the ladies writing desk.

"I'll have one of my own maids sent up to show your girl what you should wear and when. I will see you in an hour downstairs for dinner."

Lizzie nodded, trying dreadfully hard not to show her nerves at what she was about to embark on. At any time she could be caught and sent home, ruined beyond repair because she had no chaperone present.

As soon as the door closed behind the mysterious woman, Mary turned toward her, her eyes as round as the moon. "Miss Lizzie, ye can't stay here. This house, these guests...well, did ye see the gentleman that was about downstairs? He had a mask on, covering himself for some reason. I have a feeling this party is not like the ones you are used to."

Lizzie looked out the window and a black, stormy night greeted her. Should this party be what she assumed it to be, one of ill repute and debauchery, there was little she could do about it now. She was here whether she wanted to be or not, and there was no way they could leave for the Remmnicks' house party in this weather.

The gale rattled the window as if in agreement and Lizzie pulled the heavy velvet drapes closed to keep it at bay. But she also couldn't help but thank providence that she had arrived on this doorstep instead of Lady Remmnick's. For years there had been rumors–tales of debauchery regarding the parties Lord Wakely attended. Now she had a chance to see for herself what was fiction and what was truth.

"I will bathe and change into what they wish me to wear, put on my mask, and at the first opportunity tomorrow we shall leave. No one will guess who we are if you stay here in the adjacent room, and I'll keep my identity secret. Something I'm guessing they wish us to do, since we're not to use any names at all or show our faces."

"Well, ye can't go about the house as no one. What name shall you use if you're asked?"

Good question. Lizzie frowned. She had always liked Eve as a name, and it would do should she have to come up with something. "If anyone asks, call me Mrs. Eve Jacobs, a widow from Cumbria. That's far enough away that no one would've ever heard of me."

"And your husband died how?"

A light knock sounded on the door and her maid bid another young woman welcome. The young lady showed Mary how to pour the bath and where the linen was kept before laying out Lizzie's dress for the evening and showing Mary where the masks were kept.

Once they were alone again, and Lizzie was undressing for the bath, she said, "A tumor in his belly is what killed my husband. Not that I expect anyone to ask, or that servants would be enquiring about me, but just in case. I'm sure they've seen these sorts of events before, where questions are frowned upon."

"I will do as ye ask, Miss Lizzie. I promise," Mary said, turning off the tap.

The hot water of the hipbath was a welcoming delight after the cold journey they had endured. She sent Mary away and shut her eyes. Images of Lord Wakely filled her mind. His mask made him look forbidden, dangerous, and her nipples puckered in response. She ran the soap over her body, imagining his lordship's hands instead, and a heavy longing ached between her legs. For so long she'd wanted to throw herself at his head and see if he'd have any response to her, such as the visceral response she'd always had with him.

His satin knee breeches and gleaming hessians had accentuated his athletic form. He was certainly not a man who lay about. Much too perfectly shaped for that. As for his coat and perfectly tied cravat, and the pieces of his hair hanging about his mask, she could only agree that what Sally said about him resembling a pirate really did ring true. Maybe he'd plunder her.

She chuckled at her own unladylike imaginings and washed away the soap. In all seriousness, she really ought to take into account what her being here could mean for her future. Her cousin may have gifted her an endowment, but it didn't come without certain obligations that had to be met. Hamish had stipulated that he would speak to whomever Lizzie wished for as a husband, and if he found him genuine, and in love with Lizzie, he would give his blessing on the marriage, and thus pave the way for her to receive her fortune. Should Hamish not come to this conclusion upon meeting her intended, he would not allow the marriage to proceed.

To maintain her reputation, it was essential that no one found out she was here. And if she did approach Lord Wakely, would he have any interest in her? Or would he send her away? Lizzie sighed, touching her lips and wondering if his kiss would be as sweet and all-consuming as she imagined it to be. He was a renowned rake, so he would certainly know what to do…

She threw the soap away, her mind made up. She would go downstairs disguised, and see how the night progressed. The storm made it impossible to leave, but that did not mean she had to spend the night enclosed within her chambers. If Lord Wakely happened to take a liking to her masked self, she would enjoy a stolen kiss or two but nothing else. Never would she put her future in jeopardy. Not when she was so close to having her hands upon her fortune, all for herself and without anyone else lording it over her for the rest of her life.

If she could not find a husband who loved her, she would love all that her fortune could give her instead.

CHAPTER 3

Hugo stood at the piano, listening as their hostess Lady X, as she liked to be known, even though all those in attendance knew she was really Lady Xenia Campbell, a widow whose husband had died during a carriage race. She had chosen a lovely sedate piece of music from Mozart to the gathered throng that did not impinge on or distract from what the guests were discussing. A lover of music, Hugo leaned over the pianoforte and surveyed the room and all the guests who had arrived over the last day.

All of them were up to mischief and wanting to escape the confines of London Society and what was expected of them. All of them wanted to be here to partake in the pleasures of the flesh without censure or guilt. He had attended quite a few of these events over the years, and sometimes even partook in the games that were afoot, but alas this would be his last. After his father's last decree in his will, Hugo had only until July twenty-third to procure a wife, or he'd be without funds to continue the life to which he was accustomed.

His initial reaction to being told what to do had been rebellion, and he'd done everything he could not to look for a wife. But of late he'd felt restless, disillusioned with the games and intrigues within the *ton*. He'd decided that Miss Edwina Fox, an untitled gentleman's daughter with a fortune that would suit the terms of his father's will, would suit his pocket very well. She was honest, not a silly young woman, maybe a little cold and aloof, but marriage to her might be tolerable enough. He did not love her, but he certainly liked her very much. And with the time constraints he was now under, she would have to do. There was little time left to look for another suitable bride.

The parlor door opened, and he wrenched himself upright, almost spilling his whisky as he did so. What the devil was Lizzie Doherty doing here?

His gaze devoured her like a man starved of food. Her dark emerald gown brought out her perfect cream skin and made her fiery auburn hair positively shine. Not to mention her breasts were amply advertised. He shut his mouth with a snap. Never had he seen her dressed so provocatively, presenting herself for the taking. She didn't move, simply took in the room, and the breath in his lungs froze while his blood pumped hot in his veins.

She was magnificent. A small smile tweaked his lips. How could he not admire her being so bold, so brave, when she had one of the strictest mothers in all England?

Hugo took in the room's reaction and frowned, not liking the fact that all the gentleman present were admiring her, some with a hunger that matched his own.

He'd not let any of them touch one hair on her body. She was his, and his alone. If anyone was going to pluck her innocence it would be him.

He took a calming breath, reeling himself back to reality. What was he thinking? He could not touch her either.

To even imagine taking her to bed was such a breach of trust that he'd never be able to re-establish the friendship between himself and Lord Leighton. He fisted his hands, fighting his body that had hardened at the sight of her, even knowing who she was.

Thank the lord for the masks they wore, well-made ones that ensured no one's identity was absolutely obvious. Even if most of the guests knew by now who everyone was, it was not always the case, as it seemed right now with Lizzie. Yes, he'd picked her out, but one was wont to do such a thing when one often appreciated the lithe, delicate, and yet bountifully gifted Lizzie in person.

With a strength Hugo had always known she possessed, Lizzie steeled her back, raised her chin, and met the ogling guests head on.

Lord Finley sauntered up to her, and Hugo ground his teeth. The gentleman had hands as slimy as an eel's skin and was a regular at these parties. Always willing to shove his cock into anything agreeable.

"Friend of yours, sir?"

Hugo turned to his hostess and shook his head. The last person he would tell was Lady X. She was as meddling as his father at times, and he didn't need any more people interfering in his life.

Lady X chuckled as she continued to play. "Miss Lizzie Doherty, I believe. Not that I'm going to tell anyone here, mind you. But I greeted her late this afternoon when she arrived. I've had it from my steward that her carriage was turned about in this afternoon's storm and they arrived here instead of Lady Remmnick's house party three miles away. If she keeps her identify a secret, no harm shall come of her."

So that was how she came to be here. He didn't think Lizzie was into the kind of lifestyle most of the people present enjoyed. Not unless she was living in a world he knew nothing of. "You should've told her to stay in her room and not come out. You know what goes on at these types of parties. Hell, she's a lovely sweetmeat just ripe for the eating."

"And would you like to eat her, my lord?" His hostess grinned up at him, devilment in her gaze. "Something tells me you would."

Hugo wouldn't deny the charge, nor would he answer such a question. Did he wish to eat the delectable little Lizzie? Hell yes, he did…had for a very long time. Over the months that they had been thrown together due to their mutual friendships, and her relationship to the Earl and Countess of Leighton, he'd become quite fond of her. Had she not been a poor relative of the Earl, Hugo would've courted her instead of Miss Fox. He certainly liked her more than anyone he'd ever previously met, and found she brought forth in him a hunger he'd not known before with any other woman.

Certainly, he was too fond to allow her to lose herself to the pretty talk and false promises that the current Lord Finley was no doubt whispering in her ear.

"Do not tell anyone of her being here. I will make certain she returns to Lady Remmnick's house party on the morrow."

Lady X nodded. "I think that would be best."

Hugo strolled about the room, keeping his attention sporadically fixed on Lizzie. How beautiful she looked tonight in her green, revealing empire cut gown. The dress appeared to be a size too small, and her breasts, which had always been generous, filled the top of the garment more than they should. It fell about her slender frame, her silver slippered shoes peeking out from beneath the hem.

Without being obvious, he made his way to Lizzie's

side, although by the time he arrived his patience had waned, just as his temper had spiked at the attention the little minx was getting from those who ought to know better. What was worse was that Hugo knew that even if some of the gentlemen who courted her now were aware of who she was, it would make not one ounce of difference. They would still wish to seduce her, have and enjoy all that she could give them, and walk away leaving her to fend for herself.

He bowed, taking her gloved hand and kissing it in welcome. "I do not believe we've been introduced." Lord Finlay glared at his interruption, but didn't comment, simply stood by, silent.

Her eyes widened, and his interest spiked. Did she know who he was? Would she run away or stay if she did? Lizzie dipped into a perfect curtsy, her rouge-covered lips lifting into a grin. Desire rushed through his veins and without doubt Hugo confirmed his suspicions. He wanted her. In his bed. His and only his. Which, he reminded himself, he couldn't do. He wasn't able to marry a woman with no dowry. Maybe she'd be open to a stolen kiss before he sent her home… It was worth a thought.

"My lord," she said, not an ounce of fear in her voice.

"My lady," he said, although he knew she held no title to speak of. At these parties it had been long agreed that no names should be spoken, and that everyone was a lord and lady in this environment, even if they acted less than the ideal their name would normally be associated with.

"You're new to our gathering. Are you enjoying the night so far?"

She smiled, and there was no doubt left in his mind as to who stood before him. "I am, yes. It's been quite pleasant so far."

Lord Benedict approached and bowed over her hand,

placing a lingering kiss on her wrist. "And mayhap the night will end pleasurably for you too, my lady...should you choose me, that is."

The need to pummel Lord Benedict into dirt on the Aubusson rug was almost too much to resist. But she was new to these events and so every gentleman, and some ladies, would want to experience her mystery. Lizzie's cheeks flushed bright red and Hugo took her arm, steering her away from the party. "Some wine, perhaps," he said, turning their backs on the confounded lord.

"Thank you. I fear I'm not used to such...entertainments."

"So, you've never attended one of these parties before? I thought you were new. I would've remembered you." He was flirting, and her coquettish smile made him want to tease her even more, if only to see more of the same.

"No, never." She took the glass of wine he offered and, to his amusement, downed it almost immediately.

"Refreshing?"

She laughed, placing her glass on the tray of a passing footman before taking another. "In need of fortifying, more like."

Hugo chuckled and nodded in agreement. If the elixir of drink helped her relax in the environment she now found herself, who was he to naysay her? He would however remain by her side and ensure that no harm came to her reputation, and no rake that now graced the parlor went within a foot of her person. Unless it was him of course.

It was the least he could do, being a family friend. Or so he kept telling himself.

SOME HOURS LATER—DELIGHTFUL, exciting hours at that—
Lizzie strolled toward her room, her body very aware of
the tall, masculine frame walking beside her. Hugo stood
back as she came to her door, and Lizzie wished the night
wouldn't end. What would he do if she were to proposition
him? Turn her away, or take her in his arms?

She licked her lips at the thought of being held by him
as she wished. After all the months that she had lusted after
this gentleman, to have him before her, quite alone and
without the worry of being caught since this party was for
the very purpose of being naughty, was a temptation she
wanted to explore.

She reached out and touched the lapels of his coat.
Lord Wakely stilled under her palm. Having watched the
other ladies tonight waltz a dance of seduction with their
chosen gentlemen, Lizzie had picked up on a couple of
ideas. She leaned forward, placing her body scandalously
close to his, and his eyes darkened in hunger.

The entire evening he'd stayed by her side, ensuring
her every comfort was met, so would he now ensure her
every desire was as well? Surely that meant she was about
to be kissed. Her first kiss, and with a man she'd long
admired as well as desired. Not that she was willing to
throw her maidenhead out the window, but a kiss couldn't
hurt.

"I hope you enjoyed your first night?" he asked, leaning
against the door's threshold, his cravat untied and hanging
loose about his neck. She itched to rip it off and slide her
hands over his chest, not just his lapels, and feel the
muscles respond to her touch.

"I did, thank you. It has been quite entertaining and
eye opening as well." Like when she had seen the Countess
of Eden, whose mask had slipped during a passionate kiss
with one of the first gentlemen who'd bowed before her

upon arrival in the parlor. They had all but bundled each other out of the room and not returned. Lizzie had little doubt as to what the couple were up to at this very moment. Heat bloomed on her cheeks and she bit her lip, thanking providence that his lordship couldn't read minds.

"That tends to be the case at these parties." He closed the space even further between them, so that her breasts were brushing his chest and coiling heat to her core. He kissed her cheek and her knees wobbled. Without thought she leaned into the embrace, closing her eyes as the smell of sandalwood intoxicated her senses. Lord Wakely paused a moment, his breath whispering foreign words against her neck.

"Do you attend these parties often, my lord?" The question came out breathless and she cursed knowing he would be aware of what his nearness did to her. Made her want things no respectable woman would dare think of. Made her yearn for a man's touch over that of respectability or propriety. She fisted his lapels in her hands, holding him close.

"This is my last." He kissed the lobe of her ear and she shivered.

"Why is that?" He kissed her ear again and she bit back a moan. Golly he made her ache, made her want so much.

Her attention snapped to his lips. His hand clasped her nape, his fingers tangling into her hair. This was it. Right here and now, Lord Wakely was going to kiss her. Show her everything she'd been missing all these years. Her body shook with expectation and she leaned up on tiptoe to better meet his height.

He pulled back, severing their nearness, and she stumbled a little before righting herself. He watched her a moment, a muscle working in his jaw. "That, my dear, is a conversation best had on another day." He bowed. "I will be across the hall should you need any assistance."

Lizzie watched his lordship run away from her as if she had the pox, his door closing with more force than was necessary. She slumped against the door frame, frowning. Why had he run away like that? These parties were supposed to end with seduction and pleasure, or at the very least a passionate kiss that would make her toes curl in her slippers. Unless he knew who she was and wouldn't touch her because of her cousin Lord Leighton, one of his best friends?

If he did suspect who she was, it meant that his attendance on her this evening had been wholly to ensure she remained safe and not assaulted by the other gentlemen present. Disappointment stabbed her. How mortifying if that were true. And she'd thrown herself at his head like a desperate ninny. Her cheeks burned, and tears blurred her vision.

Mary was waiting for her when she came into her room, and with her maid's help, Lizzie was soon in bed, reliving the feel of his lips on her cheek, and then again on her earlobe. A disturbing little thrum thumped between her legs at the memory and she rolled over, squeezing her thighs together to soothe the need that coursed through her.

How could he bring forth such a reaction within her if she meant nothing to him? Could men have reactions to women in such a way? Did it even matter who warmed their bed, just so long as someone did? If he was never interested in kissing her in the first place, why had he kissed her neck? It made no sense.

Could men be so fickle?

The sound of the pounding rain on the window lulled her for a time, but it did little to soothe her disappointed hopes. When he'd sought her out early in the evening she'd felt such anticipation that the night would end in a kiss. That he would find her interesting and charming. She could only conclude that he knew who she was and was being a gentleman, a good friend to her cousin. The embrace before bidding her goodnight had been a slip in his armor and nothing else. He might even have done it to try to scare her off, tell her without words that this party was not for her and she shouldn't be here.

For if there was one thing she knew for sure about Lord Wakely, it was that he took what he wanted. That he didn't take her was all she needed to know.

Just like her life in London, here at Lady X's house party, she was undesirable. A wallflower destined for the spinster shelf. Well, at least she'd have her cats for company, and bucketloads of money. It was better than nothing.

CHAPTER 4

Lizzie rolled over in her bed and stared at the ceiling of her room. Images of men and women in very compromising positions looked down at her, their smiles and gazes of satisfaction mocking her and her inability to seduce the man she wanted. Had wanted for an age.

Here she was, at the most sought-after party of the Season, and she'd failed to gain a kiss from a man who was famous in the *ton* for seduction. She looked at the discarded mask she'd worn the night before. No one should've recognized her wearing it, but Lord Wakely wasn't everyone.

Did he know who she was? And if so, even though he hadn't kissed her, why didn't he send her packing the moment he realized who graced the scandalous house party? For all his rakehell ways, as a gentleman he would see such a task as only right and honorable.

But he had not. In fact, he'd flirted with her for most of the night. His attentions prior to dinner were telling, as were his hot stares throughout the meal, not to mention that kiss before saying goodnight. Well, a chaste peck against her cheek, her ear, her neck...

She sighed, looking at the curtains still drawn against the morning sun. Getting up, she walked over to them and pulled one back, taking in the landscape before her. This side of the home sported a lawned area that flowed like a green sea into the oak forest a little way away. From here she could just make out the roof of a summer house hidden amongst the woodland. There were many leaves and small sticks lying on the ground from the previous night's storm, and she watched for a moment as a gardener tried to clear away as much as he could.

Sensing movement on the terrace below, she looked down and watched as the very gentleman who haunted her dreams smoked a cheroot while leaning casually against the terrace balustrade. From here she could make very little out of his features, and yet his height and stature gave him away.

He stood outdoors, covered only by a thin white shirt that did nothing to hide his muscular form, which flexed beneath the shirt with the smallest amount of movement. Lizzie sighed, admiring his muscled thighs that today were encased in tan, skin-tight breeches. Not for the first time she was jealous of whoever ended up marrying him.

He walked along the terrace, looking out on the grounds as well, and she realized he wore no boots. She'd never seen a man's feet before, and seeing Lord Wakely's only left her eager to see more of him in a similarly naked way.

She ran her finger along the pane of glass. What a shame it was that men like Lord Wakely were never interested in the meek, mild debutantes who graced Almack's with their parents in hand. Something she was still unfortunately doing, since her mother wasn't privy to her endowment. She only had two more years and the money her cousin had bestowed upon her would be hers, marriage no longer a necessity. Her mother could be told then, when she no longer had any say in her life. Until then, Lizzie was happy to behave, and do as she was told.

Men like Lord Wakely enjoyed women, married or otherwise, such as the ones at this house party. They only wanted their wives to grace ballrooms with elegance and accomplishment that would do their names proud, but never to love and be besotted by them. Unless they were cut from a different cloth, like her cousin Lord Leighton, the Duke of Athelby, or the Marquess of Aaron, who were the exceptions to that rule.

A longing to know what it was exactly that went on between husband and wife assailed Lizzie, and with it an urge to stomp her foot. Last evening she should have pressed him for more, taken what she wanted and be damned the consequence.

She should've shoved her fears aside and kissed him, not concerned herself with what he would say and do. Then, if he had sent her home without touching her, without bestowing her first kiss, well, it wouldn't have been without trying. In any case his rejection of her hurt, but at least if she had been brave she would've had a kiss, chaste as it might be, before she was bade goodnight.

Now, she seemed to have missed her chance. If the rumors were true, he was courting Miss Fox—a woman with ducal titles in her blood, who would bring to marriage numerous estates, and money. Lots of it. Did he care for that woman? Was that why he pulled away? The *ton* whispered that the union would only be a marriage of convenience, but maybe it wasn't. The thought depressed her. She didn't want Lord Wakely to want anyone else.

The memory of his kiss against her neck hinted that the union was indeed one of convenience, which left her wondering why he wanted Miss Fox as his wife. Was his lordship looking to align himself with a woman of wealth? And if so, why? The Wakely family had always been affluent.

If his lordship was in need of funds, and by some miracle he did turn his attentions toward her, it was imperative that he not find out about her endowment. She could not stomach any man marrying her for money alone. Just as her cousin had stated all those years ago, if a man fell in love with her, as poor as he thought her, then he was the man worthy of her heart, and her fortune.

Lizzie sat down in the window nook. After seeing her cousin, the Earl Leighton, marry the love of his life, Kat, she could never settle for a marriage of convenience. No, she wanted so much more than that. Passion was what she desired. Passion and love. And without either of those emotions she would never marry at all, no matter what her mama had to say about it.

A knock at the door sounded and she jumped. A moment later, her maid entered with a breakfast tray laden with delicious food that made her stomach rumble.

Lizzie went about her morning routine, washing and breaking her fast before her maid helped her dress in a cream cotton morning gown with silk ribbons that trimmed the hem. Mary arranged her hair into a motif of curls, and as she pushed the last pin into position, the lady who had welcomed her the day before entered.

Her maid dipped into a curtsy and left to go to the adjacent room, giving them privacy. Lizzie stood. "Good morning, Lady X."

The woman didn't smile, but simply stood before her, hands clasped in front of her, a slight frown line marring her forehead. "I must apologize, Miss Doherty, for I have done you a most grievous injustice and one I shall remedy. I was a little hazy of mind after drinking champagne most of the afternoon yesterday, and I should never have played my little game and allowed you to join us downstairs last evening. Be assured that I'm doing all that I can to ensure your safe passage to Lady Remmnick's house party, which is the location you should have arrived at yesterday afternoon. I promise I shall do all that I can to keep your reputation intact after you leave."

Heat bloomed on Lizzie's cheeks and she cringed at being caught. "It is I who must apologize. I should have told you immediately that I was not whom you expected, and what had happened to us in the storm that ensured our arrival here. I hope I haven't put you out with my attendance. It was not purposely done."

Lady X came over and clasped Lizzie's hands. "You have not put me out in the slightest, but you have put your own reputation at extreme risk. My house parties are not like…well, let's just say, they are wicked. I'm sure you saw last night the happenings and goings on that occur. I thought it would be a lark to allow you one night, and then send you on your way today, but I was wrong. And now my keeping you here as a little distraction for myself may have put you in grave risk."

"Why so, my lady?" Lizzie asked. "We will simply ready the carriage and I shall be on my way. No harm in that."

Her ladyship sighed. "There is a stream that all vehicles in and out of the estate must pass through. It is flooded by the storm, terribly so in fact. Therefore, you are stranded here with us for at least three days. I am so sorry."

An array of emotions ran through Lizzie at her ladyship's words. Lord Wakely had walked away from their interlude. To have to face him again and not be able to leave and hide, to pretend she had never been here and ignore the fact she had offered herself up like a sweetmeat, was mortifying. Then again, another night under Lady X's roof could be her chance to change his mind... He had slipped a little and kissed her neck. Could she get him to do more than that if he knew she was willing?

They were to wear masks at all times, so her anonymity was secure. Even if he did suspect her, there was no way he could prove she was ever here, and she'd never admit it. Not to anyone.

Another night in his lordship's company could be a coup she'd not thought to have. "Will you sit, my lady? There is something I wish to tell you and you may need to be seated to hear it."

The woman raised her brow but did as Lizzie asked. She flattened her hands against her knees once seated on a nearby chair. "What is it you wish to tell me? I'm all ears, my dear."

Lizzie took a breath, trying to calm the nerves that fluttered in her belly. "There is really no polite way of saying what I wish to, so I'm just going to be honest. I'm actually very happy to be stuck here, and even though I know this must shock you, I would like to continue with the party, take part, and enjoy the time that I have left."

Her ladyship's brow rose. "I do not think my house party is the right place for you, my dear. What if it becomes known that you're present? Both of our reputations will be put in jeopardy, yours for innocence lost and mine due to the inability for people to attend incognito." She worked her hands in her lap. "You're unchaperoned and I do not wish to be part of a plot that ends with the ruination of an innocent. I'm ashamed that I even allowed this charade to start in the first place."

"But that is where you're wrong. This is the perfect place for me. If I continue to wear my mask, then no one shall know my identity. And I'm not going to lose my innocence to anyone in attendance, if you're worried about that. There is only one gentleman for me, whom I like more than anyone else. I live in hope you see that his interest will turn toward me too, even though I know I have no chance."

"Is the man in attendance? I really ought to just cosset you away and keep you safe," Lady X said, her gaze weary.

Something in her ladyship's voice gave Lizzie pause and she wondered if the woman already suspected who the gentleman was. Most would after last evening's dinner and the looks Lord Wakely had bestowed on her at times. Glances that were enough to curl her toes in her slippers.

He'd never noticed her in town, or at least she'd never been aware of his notice. "He is in attendance," she said. "The gentleman is a man of the world, has known many lovers, and I have no doubt that if I were not here, he would never look my way. I have nothing other than myself to offer to him, and as it is with most gentlemen of the *ton*, that is never enough. But here, behind a mask, I'm not anyone. It does not matter if I have a fortune or if I don't. It doesn't matter if my family is titled or in trade. The attraction here is based on mutual desire, a connection. I want to experience that and learn all that I can before I have to return to my mother and the life she wants me to lead."

"Hmmm." Lady X tapped her chin. "I will not play coy and deny knowing that you're speaking of Lord Wakely, but it does fill me with some concern. That you like him was obvious last night, and in turn I believe he is quite fond of you too—at least the masked you. But he is a rake, a man who has had many lovers, many who are present at this party. Do you not think it would be best that as soon as I can arrange it, we send you back to the house party you're supposed to be at, and you can start your courtship of his lordship when you return to town? I've never had a guest lose their reputation by being here, and I'm not about to start now. And should Lord Leighton find out you're here he would simply kill me stone dead. I would never recover in society, and neither would you."

"You of all people must understand the restraints that women in our society live by. You would not have started such house parties as these if you did not. Can you not simply for the next few days turn a blind eye? Please, Lady X," Lizzie beseeched.

Her ladyship bit her lip, frowning in thought.

"Do not assume that I misunderstand your concerns, because I don't," Lizzie continued. "I'm simply putting them all aside for a few days. This is my only chance to live a little. Away from everyone. I shall wear my mask and have my maid do me up so I'll never be recognized. I promise you, I shall remain anonymous."

Lady X remained silent, and Lizzie fought not to fidget while she waited for her reply. Would she let her attend the party tonight and the other events like everyone else, or keep her hidden away until she could throw her into the carriage and be rid of her?

"Very well," Lady X sighed. "You may stay, but you're to double your effort in hiding your appearance. An alteration of your voice may be required at times, and whatever you do, do not slip and mention friends or family during conversations." Her ladyship's eyes narrowed on Lizzie. "I am curious to know your age, Miss Doherty. Why is it you're not married yet, my dear?"

"I'm three and twenty." Almost on the shelf by London standards. Not that this was a growing concern for Lizzie; the closer she came to receiving her money the closer she was to escaping her mother, and living a life of her own.

She might do as she pleased then, and the *ton* and the men who'd looked the other way when she passed due to her lack of funds could go hang. Lizzie reminded herself that she must thank Hamish again the next time she saw him for saving her from fortune hunters.

"If you stay, do you mean to try your luck with Lord Wakely? I'm not sure your mama has warned you of the risks that you take should you follow your infatuation. No mask will save you from an unwanted pregnancy."

Lady X's words were blunt, and it was a point that Lizzie would have to take into account. If she stayed, and did try her luck with his lordship, she would just have to ensure it stopped at kissing, and maybe a few scandalous caresses. As much as having a child was something she longed for, she did not want one out of wedlock. "I'll not do anything to risk my virtue, in that respect. I know I'm putting my reputation at risk, but it's a risk I'm willing to take."

The thought of having Lord Wakely hold her in his arms, his delectable, sinful lips taking hers, teasing her and leaving her flesh to burn, her blood to pound in her veins, made her stomach clench in delight. "If I was to try and lure Lord Wakely into kissing me, would you know how I could do such a thing? I've never been kissed before, you see."

Lady X let out a sigh, but a small smile lifted her lips. "I can help you, if only to guide you in what you shall wear tonight, how to seduce a man with your eyes and have him eating out of your hand like a little lost, hungry puppy. But anything further than that I'm not willing to do. Are you in agreement?"

Lizzie nodded. "When can we begin?"

Lady X smiled. "We shall begin right away."

CHAPTER 5

Later that day Lizzie made her way downstairs. Earlier, her maid had delivered a note from Lady X asking for all the guests to assemble in the parlor. The note stated that the guests had two alternatives for the morning's pleasure, that being billiards or charades. Lizzie had already made up her mind to play billiards as she'd never played charades well in her life.

Before entering the parlor she checked carefully that her mask covered her face and nose and only allowed her lips to be seen. Most guests were already present in the room, and thankfully her step didn't falter the moment she spied Lord Wakely sitting on the arm rest of a settee. A beautiful, dark-haired beauty sat beside him, her body turned toward him in open invitation, but his attention wasn't on the woman, it was on *her*...

A frisson of awareness shot through her as his dark, hooded gaze wandered over her, and she sat in between two gentlemen who were only happy enough to have her join their party of two.

Lady X clapped her hands, gaining everyone's attention. Today again she wore no mask, and Lizzie had to congratulate Lady Campbell for not following her own rules regarding anonymity. She supposed it wouldn't work for the hostess to be unknown–too much trouble during the events, for starters.

"As you're aware, today's games are billiards and charades. I have taken the trouble of pairing my wonderful guests with partners I think you shall enjoy. As I walk about the room, when I touch you and then the next person, that is your chosen partner."

Lizzie caught Lady X's mischievous gaze and fought not to smile. Would her ladyship partner her with Lord Wakely? After his refusal to kiss her last night she shouldn't want to be around him again, shouldn't want to give him another chance to right his wrong and kiss her.

But it was what she wanted most of all, nincompoop that she was.

The mask ensured her identity remain secret, and the reminder bolstered her confidence. Unless she told him, he would only be guessing if it were her or not. He could not prove it unless he ripped the mask from her face. He wouldn't do such a thing, so she could either run back to her room and hide herself for trying to seduce him last night, or take the few days she had left here and try to have a little fun with him.

The gentleman beside her leaned toward her and whispered his appreciative thoughts regarding her gown. She'd chosen the blood-red silk empire style dress that was extremely low cut across her breasts. The morning gown she'd worn earlier in her room wouldn't do for this house party. Her poor maid had almost had an apoplectic fit when she placed it over her head, but Lizzie adored it.

Yes, the bust was too low. But if she were to play billiards, and she wanted to seduce a certain viscount who continued to watch her, like the gentleman beside her, the red gown was simply perfect.

Lady X went about the room, touching people on the shoulder. Finally she came before Lizzie, touched her, and then turned and surveyed the room. Lizzie fought back a chuckle as her ladyship strolled before a group of gentleman she hadn't met as yet. The resulting thunderous visage of Lord Wakely's gave her pause.

Did he not appreciate her being partnered with any of them? Did that mean he wished to be partnered with her? Lady X moved on and went toward Lord Wakely. From where Lizzie sat she saw him throw a warning glance at Lady X before she touched his shoulder.

Without moving a muscle, he met her gaze across the room and she shivered at the hunger she read in his eyes. Maybe he wasn't so indifferent after all.

Once everyone was partnered, Lizzie stood and started for the billiards room, not waiting for Lord Wakely. Within a moment he was beside her and placing her arm about his own.

"I gather we're playing billiards then?" he said without looking at her.

"You gathered right. I like the game and play it often, so if we're to play anyone else in our respective games I'm likely to win. How do you play, my lord? Is it adequate?"

"I play adequately at all things," he said, grinning.

She smiled. "Good, because I hate to lose."

The billiards room was as large as a ballroom and sported not one, but three tables. The ten people Lady X had partnered up stood around the centre one, discussing who would play against whom. Lizzie and Lord Wakely joined them and it was soon decided that a couple, who made up one team, would play another couple. Lizzie would go up against the other lady, and Lord Wakely against the other gentleman.

They went to the farthest table from the door and Lord Wakely set about giving them each a cue before placing down the pair of cue balls and one red object ball each. The two men played first and Lizzie sat on a chair with the lady she was to play against. Her female opponent clapped at different times when her partner scored a Hazard or Cannon, but the play was very fierce, both men taking painfully long shots to try to sink a ball or hit each other's. Unfortunately, even though Lord Wakely's effort was admirable, he lost the match.

Lizzie stood, picking up her cue and checking the little piece of leather on the end of her cue was in place to give her enough friction against the ball.

"Better luck next time, my lord," she said, grinning at him. His eyes narrowed and he stayed too close for her comfort, taking hold of her cue and pulling her nearer still.

"Do not crow too soon, my lady, you're yet to prove your worth."

Lizzie clasped her hand about his neck. His eyes widened behind his mask before she whispered against his ear, "I'm worth a lot, my lord. As you will soon find out." Her words were not entirely regarding the game, but herself as well.

She stepped away, checking the placement of the balls and taking stock of her opponent. The poor woman didn't seem to even know how to hit the ball, or hold the cue correctly, and many of her shots didn't go anywhere at all toward her score. Lizzie leaned over the table, took aim, and scored a Canon on her first shot. She looked up and met the gaze of Lord Wakely. He leaned against the wall, arms crossed, but his attention wasn't on the game–it was on her.

Lizzie pushed the distraction that was his lordship from her mind and concentrated. From that point on the contest was really no contest at all. After only minutes, Lizzie sank her opponent's red object ball and finished the game. She clapped, triumphing in her victory. The woman pouted and received a consolation kiss from her gentleman admirer for her effort.

Lizzie placed the cue on the table and went over to join Lord Wakely. She grinned up at him. "Thanks to me, we drew. If you want any tips on playing I'm more than willing to help you."

His lips twitched. "Are you always so amusing?" He led her out of the room and along a large passage that ran along the back of the house. The bank of windows overlooked the rear of the house and the expanse of lawn that surrounded the estate.

"When I want to be, I am. Although my mother thinks to laugh in public is vulgar." A shot of fear went through when she realized that she'd spoken about her family, which she'd promised Lady X she wouldn't do. Her mother was known as one of the worst harridans circulating the *ton*, and mentioning her strict ideals could give her away. If Lord Wakely was even still wondering who she was, of course.

"You're lucky to still have your mother. I lost mine as a young boy. I think I would give anything to hear her chastise me once more." He threw her an amused glance but something in his eyes spoke of pain hidden in their grey depths.

Lizzie didn't know how her ladyship had passed, and she didn't like thinking about Lord Wakely being left motherless as a boy. How sad for him. Her heart gave a little lurch.

"I'm sure your mother would also give anything to be able to do so, my lord. You loved her very much."

He cleared his throat. "I did, but such is life." He seemed to shake himself from the conversation and asked, "Where did you learn to play billiards like that? I think even I could lose to you and I always thought myself adequate enough."

Lizzie preened a little at the compliment. "Father had a table at our home in the country. Whenever my parents left for the Season before I debuted, I would spend the time playing billiards. I used to run competitions with our staff, some of whom are very good players, and I learned that way. It was jolly good fun, and whenever I can sneak out to play when we're home I do so. I usually have to wait for Mama to retire before I can round up the few staff who like to play."

"You play billiards with your servants?" he sputtered, his words laced with shock.

She laughed. "Of course. There isn't much to do in—" She stopped before she gave away where she lived.

He shook his head, chuckling. The sound was deep and sent a frisson of awareness through her. Was he laughing at her second slip of information or at her story itself? That she couldn't answer, and she fought to turn the conversation away from such personal information that could give her away.

She spied a cat asleep in the window and, letting go of Lord Wakely, she went and picked it up, scratching the little animal under its ears before placing a kiss on its head.

"You like cats?" he asked, coming over and giving the animal another scratch.

The black and white moggy purred in Lizzie's arms and she smiled. "I love cats. When I… that is to say, when I can." She had been about to say 'when I come of age'.

48

Seriously, she needed to remember that she wasn't supposed to advertise who she was. "I'm going to fill my house with them. I simply adore them. What about you?"

He patted the cat's head. "I prefer dogs, but I tolerate cats."

Lizzie placed the cat back down where it had been lying and faced Lord Wakely. The question that had been burning in her mind since last night was too powerful to deny a moment longer. "Why didn't you kiss me last night? And I mean really kiss me, like a man kisses a woman in passion."

HUGO FOUGHT to find a grain of truth as to why he'd denied them both what they wanted. The moment he'd seen her enter the parlor this morning, being with her had been all that his mind could conjure. He'd kicked himself for not kissing her, for not giving her what she wanted. He could only blame the last shred of gentlemanly behavior–his friendship with her cousin Lord Leighton–for his actions.

But not anymore. He wouldn't deny either of them what they wanted. In the few moments when he'd thought Lady X would partner her with some other fop, he'd almost had apoplexy before the guests. No one wanted to see a grown man throw a fit over the hostess's choice, but if it meant securing Lizzie as his partner, he was willing to do anything. Even act the fool.

That in itself wasn't normal behavior, not for him, and it was telling indeed.

"I couldn't say as to why I didn't. I wanted to. So much," he said, not able to tell her it was because he knew who she was, and knew her cousin would rip his bollocks from his body should he know he was kissing his relation at a party of ill repute.

But that wasn't the only reason, and this one was the worst of them all. For all of Lizzie Doherty's attributes, she wasn't an heiress and couldn't satisfy the clause in his father's will. Somehow it seemed wrong to kiss her under such circumstances. And even though no one was supposed to know the identity of anyone else at these parties, Hugo would know Lizzie anywhere. Something in the way she trusted him, spoke guardedly with him, told him that perhaps she knew who he was as well.

She leaned back against the wall, reminiscent of his stance as he watched her play billiards. She rocked on her heels, observing him. "Will you kiss me now?"

His body roared with hunger and he closed the space between them without a moment's thought and kissed her. The instant his lips touched hers he moaned. The minute he'd seen her enter Lady X's parlor, he knew they'd end in this position.

Her kiss was untutored, and he clasped her chin, shifting her a little to allow him to deepen the embrace. He nipped her bottom lip and she gasped. It was the perfect opportunity to introduce her to his tongue, which he tentatively touched hers with. In his arms he felt her soften, become pliant. Her hands wrapped about his neck, her body soft and moulded against his.

In this position his desire for her was plainly obvious, but she didn't seem to shy away from it. If anything the minute undulation of her hips told him she was enjoying this as much as he was.

The luncheon gong floated toward them and Lizzie pulled back, her eyes wide with newfound awareness. He grinned. "Did you like my kiss?" he asked, leaning in to bestow another on her before they moved on.

She slowly nodded, her attention snapping to his mouth. What she was thinking was clear to read. It was the same thing he was. How much he'd damn well enjoyed kissing her just then, and not only that, how much he'd enjoyed the morning in her company, playing games and talking about all things, including cats.

He took her hand and pulled her back toward where they came from, heading for the dining room. "Come, we'll sit together for lunch."

CHAPTER 6

L izzie all but floated down the stairs the following day. She'd slept late and broken her fast in her bedroom. The kiss that Lord Wakely had given her had filled her dreams, and today started with the promise of more delicious things to come. Would he kiss her again? She couldn't help but hope he did. At this point in time it was all she wanted in all the world.

The wind howled outside, the storm refusing to dissipate. Lady X had left a note on her breakfast tray that stated the road out of the estate was still flooded, so Lizzie would have to stay another day. It was no hardship, not if it meant that she could continue her seduction of Lord Wakely.

Her stomach fluttered at the thought. If he did suspect who she was, what did that mean for them when they returned to town? Would he wish to see her again, court her perchance?

Lizzie stepped off the stairs and stopped as the man himself strode out of the parlor. He came straight toward her and, taking her hand, towed her in the opposite direction to the room.

"Come, I have a little activity set up for us."

Lizzie fought not to read too much into the fact he held her hand, was seeking her and only her out. They crossed the vestibule and entered a room that would catch the full afternoon sun when it was out. Even with the stormy wet weather outside, the room was still bright, decorated in light pastels and greens.

There were a number of chairs around the room and at each one stood an easel and an array of paints for guests to use.

"I'm going to paint you today," Lord Wakely said, grinning and pulling her toward a chair near the corner of the room which had windows on either side. "Do you paint, my lady?" he asked, helping her to sit and straightening out the folds of her gown to be ready for her impromptu portrait.

"I had lessons as a child, but I was not very good at it. I can sketch better than I paint. Something about mixing the colors just right I could never manage to do well. My paintings all ended up looking abstract and coarse."

"Are you trying to tell me the portrait you'll do of me today will be modern in its appearance?" Lord Wakely sat and positioned his parchment. He gave instructions for how he wanted her to pose and, doing as he asked, she turned her gaze toward the windows and watched the storm bluster outside.

"I am, yes. I'm no Thomas Gainsborough. But I see they have pencils, so I'll forgo the watercolor paint and draw you instead."

He painted her in silence for a time, and for the entire duration Lizzie could feel his gaze, his attention burning against her body like a brand. Every now and then she caught what part of her body he was concentrating on, and her skin heated. "Do you think you've captured the likeness of my breasts well, my lord? You seem quite fixated on that part of my person." She fought not to laugh at his throat clearing. It was very forward of her, but if she was to take this opportunity while she had the guise of anonymity, then she would do all that she could to tease him. Lord Wakely was so very educated in the art of dalliance that it was only during times such as these that she had the slightest chance of matching his skills.

He put the paintbrush down, but she didn't turn to see what he was up to. Her heart thundered in her chest when he stood, tipped her face up toward him, and kissed her. The kiss lingered and without thought she kissed him back. He was impossible to resist, not that she wanted to. She would take all that he could give her while she was under this roof, to a point at least. Her virginity wasn't up for debate.

No sooner had he started their little indiscretion than he sat back down and commenced painting again. Lizzie fought to control her emotions, reminding herself to believe he didn't know who she was and that was why he was interested. The other option—that he did suspect—gave her too much hope, and she wouldn't allow her mind to run away into fantasies of them marrying and having a horde of children together.

"May I ask you a question, my lord?" Lizzie watched an old elm blow in the wind outside and hoped the majestic tree survived this storm.

"Of course." He reached out and adjusted her gown, and she swallowed as his hand lingered upon her leg. "You may ask me anything."

"I'm assuming, by the fact you've not spent any time with anyone else here these past few days, that you're not interested in anyone else. What made you choose me?"

He sighed, leaning back in his chair. She turned to watch him, wanting to see his eyes while he explained his actions.

"I think it was the gown, along with your beautiful fiery red hair. The moment you walked through the door I wanted you in my bed. Everyone else paled in comparison to your beauty. And having spent some time with you, I think you're quite mature and intelligent. So now that I know you also hold those positives...well, I'll not be letting anyone else have you."

"And if I don't sleep with you, my lord?"

He threw her a devilish look. "You may not. It doesn't mean I'll not have fun trying to change your mind."

Lizzie bit her lip. Golly, she couldn't look away from him. Her body burned with unsated need and without thought she stood, walked over to him, and sat on his lap.

"I may be an ugly witch with warts under this mask. You may not wish to sleep with a fraud."

"Are we not all frauds in here?" His hands clasped her hip, hoisting her hard against him. Lizzie could feel his desire for her, and even though outwardly she showed no signs of what he was doing to her emotions, inside she was a riot of feelings and thoughts. "I shouldn't want you as much as I do," he rasped, his eyes dark with desire.

"Isn't that the whole point of this party? To want and then have your desires." Lizzie reached into his hair, loving how it slid soft and silky between her fingers.

"Of course it is, but these parties are not supposed to have conversations as lengthy as we're having. The interactions are supposed to be of other kinds."

Lizzie smiled. "For whatever it's worth, my lord, thank you for keeping me company and being such a gentleman about it all. I know you would expect more from a participant at these events, and although I'm more than willing to try some things, I cannot try everything." His hand idly rubbed her back and she shivered under his touch.

What was it about this man that she reacted in such a way? And what a shame that their interlude would end the moment she left for home. If he did not suspect who she was, she could never confront him in London about their time together. But if he did know who she was, would he seek her out?

"I will never force myself on any woman, so you're quite safe with me. And I'm more than willing to teach you other things you can do with a man without taking him to your bed."

Heat bloomed on her cheeks, but nonetheless she was intrigued. "You can teach me things? Like what?"

He half growled, half sighed. "You do realize that to voice what we can do is torture to a man. It'll make me want you all the more."

"Tell me," she urged, wanting to know everything while he was willing to speak. No gentleman would ever talk to an unmarried woman in such an open and frank way in town. Lizzie had often suspected that her cousin and his wife, along with their married friends, all spoke in this way, but within general society the conversations were, to say the least, not stimulating or very worldly. Boring was a good word to describe them.

"I would strip the gown from you, to allow me to view your exquisite body that's hidden behind all this silk." His finger skimmed the neckline of her gown, his finger tracing the flesh of her breasts.

"I would pay homage to your breasts, taking my time with your nipples." His finger traced one through her gown and she gasped, her hands fisting in his hair.

"Then, as I kissed my way down your body, I would

hook your legs on my shoulders and kiss you down here," he said, cupping her mons through the gown. Lizzie closed her eyes, biting her lips as he kept his hand there, stroking her.

She moaned, and before she knew it he was kissing her, ravishing her mouth. Her own hand covered his, keeping him touching her, delighting in the feeling his touch brought forth in her.

He broke the kiss, his breathing ragged, his lips red from her kiss. "I would take you with my mouth, lick your sweet flesh until you rocked against my face and found your pleasure."

Lizzie shuddered, her body not her own, but all his. "What kind of pleasure?"

"You'll see…" he said, kissing her again and making her forget who and where she was entirely.

CHAPTER 7

The following day Hugo lazed in a chair beside the roaring fire in the parlor, his blood as hot as the wood in the grate. Lizzie was literally driving him to distraction. After their interlude in the painting room the day before, where he'd made her climax in his arms, he'd almost ripped both their masks off and stopped all the pretence. But he could not. She was here enjoying a little freedom that was so seldom given to women of her station, and he would not ruin the time she had left by exposing her. He'd wanted for himself one last foray in debauchery, but he'd never imagined those days would be with Lizzie Doherty, a woman who made him laugh and long for so many things he'd not thought to want.

To have a marriage of convenience now didn't hold as much shine as it once did. In fact, it didn't glow at all.

Her laughter carried to him and he looked up, spying the little minx lazing in the window seat with Lord Finley, the man's hands too close to her thigh for his liking. The seductive determination he read in the rogue's eyes was

TO VEX A VISCOUNT

enough to make him seethe, tempted to pummel him to
dust.

In the few days they had been stuck at the house party,
Lizzie had blossomed into a woman. She should've been
gone from these walls the very next day after her arrival,
but as luck would have it she was stranded here with
them all.

He'd thought she would hide in her room and remain
cossetted away like a good girl. Instead she'd thrown herself
into the party with a gusto that left him struggling to find his
footing. At first, he'd looked at her and had seen a lovely girl,
but now…now he saw nothing but woman, a passionate,
intelligent woman who made his blood pump fast and hard in
his veins. He wanted to be around her, to discuss all manner of
things, and he'd not wanted or looked for such things before.

At these parties, the chase, the lure of having someone
he'd wanted for weeks, was what had made him attend. He
didn't have to worry about courting or conversations, or
enjoying himself with anything other than the pleasures of
the flesh.

But not anymore. Now he couldn't wait to return to
town where he would see Lizzie's face again, this time
without a mask.

Hugo sat forward and all but threw his crystal tumbler
onto the table before him. He couldn't court her unless he
somehow came up with a way to keep his fortune from
going back to his uncle. Lizzie's cousin watched over her
like a hawk, and if he knew what Hugo had already done
with his charge, he'd call him out.

A little voice taunted him that she would never be his,
not as poor as she was, and he could thank his father for
such a fate. There was little chance he could talk his uncle
into allowing him to keep his inheritance, and so because

of his need to find a rich wife, something Lizzie was not, he would lose her.

He looked over toward her again and inwardly sighed. He could've looked forward to having her as his wife.

Lady X clapped her hands, gathering everyone's attention. "We're going to play a game. Ladies, I will ask you to leave the room while the men will stay. The gentlemen will spin a top which has an arrow marked on it. Whoever the arrow lands on will bid a woman enter. You will then be required to partake in the most passionate kiss you can create."

Some of the gentlemen laughed, while the ladies giggled and oohed at the game. Hugo met and held Lizzie's across the room, and determination warmed his blood. As everyone went about preparing for the game, he grabbed Lady X's arm. "Can you ensure I'm paired up with the one I want? I'll be most disappointed if she's saddled with any of the other men here present. They should not be honored with her kisses."

Lady X looked at him with amusement. "Oh, and you should? You must take a keen interest, to ask such a thing from me." She let that little statement hang in the air for a moment before she said, "You may ask, my lord, but I do not have to grant your wish. You'll have to wait and see how lady luck plays her hand."

"I'm sure you and lady luck will ensure it's so." He let her go without another word. With Lady X, no one ever really knew if she would help or not should you request assistance. She was an oddity for certain, but hopefully knowing Lizzie was innocent—so much more innocent than anyone else present—she would look out for the young woman. And by God, if he couldn't marry Lizzie, he'd at least taste her sweet lips at any and all opportunities that arose.

Once the room was cleared of ladies, the men sat about a round card table. Lord Benedict, a frequent guest to these types of events, picked up the top and spun it. It landed on Lord Stratford, a man who'd just come into a large fortune and viscountcy. "Seems you're first, lucky sod," Lord Benedict said, smiling and pushing the young buck toward the door.

A lady in a blood-red gown that dripped seduction stood behind the door when Lord Stratford opened it. There was little hesitation between them to touch, and something told Hugo that they'd partnered up already during the house party. They left the room in a flurry of squeals and masculine laughter.

Gentleman after gentleman spun the little top, and lady after lady came in and within only a few moments left with their partner for the night.

When Hugo was the only gentleman left, Lady X gestured toward the door. "You may as well open it yourself, my lord. I'm sure you'll find the woman you're looking for behind the threshold."

Expectation thrummed through him as he strode across the room and wrenched the door open, only to find no one on the other side. Perplexed, he stood there a moment, before laugher sounded behind him.

"It would seem your quarry has escaped."

He sighed. Why had she left? Well, he could probably guess as to why—she had been waiting to be mauled by the opposite sex, without the certainty it would be him doing the mauling, someone she seemed to enjoy kissing. It was only normal that Lizzie would make a hasty exit.

"So it would seem," he said, strolling from the room and heading toward the back of the house to where the billiards room was located. He would have a hit about for a time, before he retired. He strode past the staircase cupboard, taking no notice of the door being partially opened before a hand reached out and clasped his arm, and tugged him into the small storage room.

Hugo didn't have a chance to react before the softest lips he'd ever felt gently touched his. Desire rocked through him and the breath in his lungs seized. "So, you wished for a kiss after all," he said when she drew away. "I thought when I didn't see you at the door that you'd changed your mind about me."

He felt her smile more than saw it, and, wanting her with a need that left him breathless, he pulled her up hard against his chest. "Can we try that again? Longer this time, perhaps?"

Lizzie ran her fingers up his shoulders and into his hair. "I took a chance and hoped you'd come in this direction. How lucky am I to guess so well?" Her fingers fisted into his locks. "I'm at your leisure, my lord."

No other words were required. Hugo clasped her chin and kissed her, letting her know in no uncertain terms how much he wanted her. She gasped, then her tentative tongue touched his, and he fought for control.

Damn, she was the loveliest woman to have in his arms. She fitted him to perfection, like a pair of perfectly made kid leather gloves. Didn't shy away from his advances and was all too willing participant. His blood pumped loud in his ears and he groaned. How in only a few days had she become his sole purpose? He attended these events to lose himself, to enjoy women who liked games and were free from society's rules while under this roof, but with Lizzie everything was different. His body reacted differently to her touch, her gasps made him yearn to create more. He wanted to please her, make her laugh, and see her bite her bottom lip when he made her embarrassed.

I want her…and not in the biblical way.

"Your kiss is wicked," she gasped, leaning further into his arms, her breasts hard against his chest. Hugo hardened, the delicious ache in his cock fogging his mind. She wanted adventure, not to lose her innocence. He fought his hazy mind to remind himself of the fact.

He clasped her hip and pushed her against the wall. Muffled laughter sounded in the hall outside, footsteps and servants, but none of that mattered. Certainly not at the kind of house party they had found themselves at.

"So is yours. You've placed me under your spell, my lady," he murmured, never having said anything more truthful in his life. Her fluttering hand against his cheek almost undid his resolve to not push her further, demand more of her before they had to part ways, not just here at Lady X's home, but back in London.

"Then do not stop," she said, clasping his lapels and pulling him back to kiss her again.

LIZZIE LEANED up and kissed Hugo, taking all that he offered her. The hardness that pushed against her belly left her in no doubt that he desired her as much as she desired him. Dizzy with expectation and need, she wrapped herself about him, kissing him with as much force as she could.

Having learned a little during their past encounters, she deepened the embrace, taking a little control back, and his gasp against her lips was payment enough. She longed to hear the sound again. Wanted to be the only woman to ever make him in such a state.

She reached down and clasped his sex, wanting to touch him as intimately as he'd touched her yesterday. The delicious ache between her thighs thrummed and the looks between her cousin and his wife became all too clear.

He hoisted her legs about his waist and pushed them closer than they had ever been before. Still, it was not close enough. She wanted him, all of him, and when he undulated against her sex stars fluttered before her eyes.

Oh yes, this was what she desired. Her heart thumped loud in her ears, and she gasped as he teased them both, giving more pleasure than she'd ever thought possible.

"I wish I knew your name," she gasped, kissing him quickly. "I have an urge to call it out."

He grinned, watching her as he thrust against her sex. "Maybe one day we'll be properly introduced."

Lizzie chuckled. How wicked she was being, and how wonderful it was to be in Lord Wakely's arms while being so. He kissed her again with a fierceness that left her reeling and she clasped his shoulders. The sensations consumed her, and made her wonder how she would ever go on in life without experiencing them again.

And then, like the day before, her body took flight and she shattered in his arms, gasping through his kiss as pleasure rocked from her core to spread to every part of her body.

His breathing ragged, he slowly lowered her to the ground and stepped away. She shivered, already missing his heat.

"May I escort you back to your room, my beautiful lady?"

He took her hand, kissing it quickly before laying it softly against his arm. Lizzie bit her lip at the sweet gesture. "I…yes. You may."

THE FOLLOWING morning Lizzie woke with a start when her maid bustled into the room. "Miss Lizzie, the river will be passable by mid-morning, or so the groundsman has stated, so we must pack up your things and be back at the inn post haste before anyone finds out that you were in attendance here."

Lizzie sat up with a start. Leave? She didn't wish to leave this party, not when she could kiss Hugo in dark, quiet cupboards any time she wished, and not have to be concerned about what anyone saw or thought. Not when for the first time in her life she could freely indulge in passion with a man who was so sensually gifted.

Blast it. But then, if she didn't leave her reputation would be in ruins should anyone find out she was here. And she had been here for a few days now. If Lady X's guests had been stranded due to the river being flooded and the roads being too boggy and wet, it was only rational that others from Lady Remmnick's party would travel to check on her whereabouts. Even now there could be a letter making its way to her mama asking if she arrived safely home after not attending their party. She would have to leave, get back to the inn and pretend that was where she had been all the time.

"Of course," she said, throwing her blankets off and rushing toward her maid, who held an emerald travelling gown. She helped Mary get her dressed as fast as she could, then checked the room once they were packed to ensure she'd not left anything behind. It was an hour of madness. Putting on her mask, she left her room, then paused outside her door.

The viscount's door remained closed at this early hour. He would probably not wake for some time yet. Disappointment stabbed at her that she'd never see him in such relaxed circumstances again. The past few days at Lady

X's home had been scandalous, yes, but awfully fun and carefree. The complete opposite to London at times.

Lizzie pursed her lips, unsure when she'd see Lord Wakely again. Would he wish to seek her out even if their paths did cross, or was their moment of madness these past days simply a little fun for his lordship, and now his dealings with her were done?

That was assuming he'd even recognized her over these past few days. He'd never mentioned her name, but something told her he knew who she was. He was friends with her cousin, so it would certainly explain his instant hovering and keeping his sights on her. Maybe the attraction she thought was between them was simply in her imagination, and Lord Wakely had only sought her out to keep her virtue safe from the other rogues present...but not his, it would seem.

Taking a deep breath, she carried on toward the stairs. In the entrance hall Lady X stood smiling, and Lizzie smiled in return. "Thank you for having me, and I must apologize for leaving with such haste, but, well...I'm sure you understand why."

Lady X walked her outside and toward the carriage. "Of course I understand, dear, and as much as I've enjoyed your company, this is not the place for such a lovely young woman as yourself. But I shall see you in town, where we can converse without those silly masks."

Lizzie clutched her ladyship's hand. "I look forward to it." She gave the house, where for a time her dream of the Lord Wakely had come true, one last longing glance then stepped up into the carriage. She steeled herself for seeing her mama once again, and the many questions she would face over her whereabouts these past three days.

Upon her return to town, Lizzie found London and all the society balls and parties the same, if not a little tedious and tame after her exposure at Lady X's house party. In the week since she'd arrived back she'd not seen Hugo at all, although the whispers concerning his courting of Miss Fox had doubled and there was talk of an impending announcement of their engagement. Lizzie pushed the disappointing thought aside, not wanting to think about that. The idea of him with another woman, kissing someone else, taking her to his bed, was unbearable to say the least.

Her stomach roiled, and she took a steadying breath to stem the nausea.

"Good morning, dearest. How well you look today," her friend Sally said, sitting down on a chair beside Lizzie's dressing table and pulling off her gloves.

Lizzie frowned. "What are you doing here so early?" She checked the time. "You're not normally up until after luncheon. You must have something extremely important to tell me to be here at this time."

Sally laughed and then dismissed Lizzie's maid. "You'll never guess who rode back into London on his phaeton carriage yesterday afternoon."

Lizzie shook her head, having no clue who Sally could mean, although a little part of her thrilled at the idea it could be Hugo. She'd thought he was back in town already, and giving her a wide berth, but perhaps he wasn't. Just like the rumors surrounding his courtship, perhaps the *ton* was wrong on both counts. Maybe he wasn't after Miss Fox, and perchance he'd been away, and the *ton* was simply making up stories to have something to talk about.

It would certainly not be the first time such a thing had occurred.

"Who?" she asked, checking her hair and finding the design agreeable and thankfully a little flattering. Mary was becoming a very talented lady's maid.

"Lord Wakely. And there is gossip he's ruined a young, innocent miss and will have to marry her."

"What?" Lizzie stood, causing her dressing table chair to fall over backwards. "When did this happen?"

Sally threw her a curious look. "At a county house party, although the details are very sketchy at present, but la. Imagine if it were true? I wonder who the woman in question is."

Lizzie stared in horror at her friend, hating the fact that this ruined woman could possibly be her. She had been so careful returning to the inn, and had been found later that day by Lady Remmnick, who'd been beside herself with worry. But Lizzie had explained that she could not travel to their estate due to the impassable roads, and their own small river that had to be crossed to enter, so she'd simply stayed put at the inn with her maid.

No one other than Lady X knew that she'd been at the

house party. Did others in attendance guess as to her identity? Did Lord Wakely too know who she'd been after all?

Of course, the first day she arrived, having no idea she was at the wrong location, it was possible someone saw her enter the house before she was escorted upstairs to her room where masks awaited her to hide her identity.

Oh dear, this was a disaster! Her mama would kill her and put her into a nunnery should she find out about her little escapade. Any chance of obtaining a suitable, secure husband would also be lost, never mind finding one who would love her. Her chance of marrying with affection would be an unattainable dream due to her own stupidity. She'd be thoroughly ruined!

Lizzie shook the panic that threatened to take hold. Lord Wakely was a rogue, of that she had no doubt. Perhaps after she left he had found someone else to amuse himself with, and this fallen woman, whoever she was, the poor soul, was an innocent. Lizzie rolled her eyes, knowing full well how absurd that sounded. No, the young woman in this latest scandal was her. She was a stupid fool to delude herself otherwise.

"With the dissolute reputation of the viscount, it could be anyone," she said. "He is a rogue after all. Let us not worry any further about it. I'm sure he'll do the right thing and marry the girl and save her reputation, should he have acted so low."

Sally grinned. "Oh, I cannot wait to find out who'll marry such a man. He is awfully handsome and rich, and no doubt would keep any woman happily occupied I would think."

Lizzie started toward the fire, needing its warmth. "Two nights ago at the theater there talk of his courtship with Miss Fox. The gossip was his uncle in America is set to arrive within the month, no doubt to attend the wedding. I think this new scandalous rumor is a diversion. He's obviously going to marry Miss Fox and add her fortune to his. Maybe they had a tryst and it's becoming public knowledge."

"Maybe you're right. Even so, the next few weeks in town are set to be very interesting," Sally said, her eyes twinkling with mirth.

Lizzie smiled, but pain radiated within her chest. Silly of her, but she'd thought they'd had a connection. His kisses certainly discombobulated her–totally seduced her into the idea of him and her, having a future together. Had she been naive? A silly chit who was imagining more than what was there? Maybe Lord Wakely never knew who she was at all and had simply enjoyed himself with a woman at a party, just as he'd done many times before.

Sally stood and went over to the armoire, flicking through Lizzie's gowns at a rapid pace. "Everyone will be attending the Lefroys' ball this evening, and so too are you. Now," she said, pulling out her favourite gold and silver threaded gown, "this is what you shall wear tonight. The coloring suits your red locks."

"What should it matter what I wear? I have no one to impress." Not anymore at least.

Sally laid the gown on the bed and went in search of gloves. "That has no bearing at all. Everyone who is anyone will be in attendance, no doubt to see Lord Wakely. They'll want to see if his interest in Miss Fox is still founded, or if these new rumors point to another woman entirely."

Lizzie rang the bell for her maid. "Very well, I'll do as you ask, but in all truth, I do not care who his lordship is to be betrothed to. Nor do I wish to see the *ton* take to the fallen woman, should there even be one, and peck her character apart with their elevated opinions."

"Well," Sally said, picking up her gloves and slipping them on, "aren't we cutting this morning? Now, make sure you get some rest today, for tonight shall be a long, exciting time and I expect you to keep me company until the early hours of the morning."

Lizzie sighed. "Since you're so keen on my attendance, I shall meet you at the supper room doors at eight."

"I shall see you then." Lizzie watched Sally turn and leave just as Mary arrived.

"I'm to attend the Lefroys' ball tonight. Please have a bath prepared late this afternoon along with a supper tray brought to my room for an early dinner."

"You do not wish to eat at the ball, Miss Lizzie?"

"I prefer not to eat too much at such outings." And if the nerves coursing through her stomach already were any indication, eating at the ball this evening would be nigh on impossible.

HUGO WATCHED the entrance to the Lefroys' ballroom like a man starved of water looked for rain. For the last week he'd thought of nothing else but Lizzie Doherty and the time they'd spent together at Lady X's estate. Not to mention the delectable kisses she'd bestowed. That the little minx had hightailed it back to London the following day was not what he'd expected to wake up to find, after a very restless night thinking of nothing other than her sweet lips.

He rubbed his jaw, reminding himself it was for the best that she had left. Their interactions had become more and more carnal during the days they were together, and a few times he'd had to restrain himself from begging for more.

He'd left for his own estate the same day she departed, determined to move on with his plan of marrying Miss Fox before his uncle could claim his inheritance. Time was running out for him to find a rich wife, and Miss Fox had shown she was open to such an arrangement. Therefore he'd pushed the idea of Lizzie from his mind. They had been at Lady X's house party in disguise, after all, so he could forget the fact he'd known who she was the moment she'd walked into the parlor that day. He'd made no promises, no declarations of undying love.

Whatever love was.

A vision in gold came into view, laughing at something her friend was saying before she curtsied to their hosts and entered the ballroom. His heart did a little tumble in his chest as he took her in, relishing every move, every gesture she made while unaware of his notice.

Taking a sip of brandy, he ignored the tittering about him over his latest scandal. Well, two scandals in fact, but with his reputation, they were nothing new. If the *ton* actually *knew* whom the lady was he was supposed to have ruined, it would be different. How delicious they would find such information. Not that they would care that he hadn't ruined her at all…although he couldn't deny that the thought had crossed his mind numerous times during their few days together.

Never had he felt such acute disappointment as he had the morning he'd woken up and found she'd left the house party. The whole day had turned for the worse from that point on. He'd ordered his manservant to pack his things, and by luncheon he was on the road heading back to his country estate.

He had stayed there for a few days, catching up with his steward and ensuring everything was in order before he headed back to London to see out the end of the Season.

Not to mention securing Miss Fox and her thirty thousand pounds before the end of the month.

Now the vixen named Lizzie Doherty glided straight past him without so much as a by-your-leave, and his annoyance doubled.

Not only at her, but himself. He should be glad she wasn't demanding anything of him, allowing him to court Miss Fox and solve all his financial woes. That she did not seek him out left him contemplating the fact that she'd never known the identity of the gentleman who'd kissed her senseless at Lady X's party.

The idea that Lizzie would kiss any man in such a way made his blood run cold. His resolve to remain distant from her, leave her to her own devices, warred with his desire to speak to her again. To be near her and hear her laugh. Her cousin, Lord Leighton, was one of his closest friends, so it wasn't entirely foreign for them to be thrown together at a ball. The *ton* wouldn't read anything more into his being polite to his friend's cousin.

Hugo watched her. She was so very pretty and it was a pleasure to see her once more without a mask. Her laugh caused warmth to course through his blood, and her vibrant eyes simply lit up a room. But she wasn't for him. He needed to marry an heiress with a substantial dowry, and he had to do it soon.

Unfortunately, Lizzie Doherty was a poor relation to Earl Leighton, and because of it, each year she did not find a husband left the possibility of her gaining one decreased. Hugo understood why his father had stipulated such a clause in the will. His father knew of his lifestyle, endless lovers, and spending of funds on the things he valued—horses, gambling, and trips abroad. But now his vices would stop him from pursuing the woman whom he was certain suited him most in this society. Now his own foolhardy past meant Lizzie Doherty was lost to him and he'd have to marry the cold, aloof Miss Fox.

And he *would* marry her, because that was all that was open for him, what he had to do to secure his tenant farmers, his employees across his many estates. Even so, the slow burn that grew as he watched Lizzie wouldn't abate. It hadn't dimmed in the few days since he'd seen her last, and something told him it would not, no matter how much time passed. She'd ignited a fire in his blood that he didn't want to step away from. But how could he have her when taking her as his wife would mean losing everything?

He pushed the problem away to think about another day.

It was a selfish, ruinous, bastard thing to do, but he wanted another taste. He wanted her in his bed, writhing in pleasure. He wanted to kiss every inch of her silky white skin. Suckle her nipples until they coiled into hard little peaks that begged to be licked. Hear her moan his name as she found pleasure on his cock.

He pushed away from the wall and followed her toward the end of the room. She stood with her back to him, gentlemen and women friends surrounding her, and their conversation carried to him as he came closer. Discussions over the latest on-dit.

Him.

He grinned as the conversation halted–all but Lizzie's, that was. Unable to deny himself the feel of her again, he slid his finger along her spine as he came to stand beside her, his own body hiding his inappropriate touch.

"Good evening," he said, catching Lizzie's startled eyes with his own. "You look very beautiful tonight, Miss Doherty." He bowed, clasping her hand and kissing it.

A deep blush bloomed across her cheeks, and he stood back, inwardly laughing that she could kiss him with such passion only a week before, touch and talk to him openly, but feel embarrassment now. That was if she'd even been aware of who he was at the house party.

But something in her manner right now told him she knew he'd been the one with her in the country, and that he knew in return who the vixen was that tortured him with the memory.

Others about them greeted him while some of the ladies present tittered and pulled out their fans, waving them in front of their faces. He turned toward his quarry and gestured to the dance floor. "I believe the next dance is to be a waltz, Miss Doherty. Will you do me the honor?"

She cast a nervous glance at her friend Sally, before nodding, her eyes as wide as saucers. "Thank you, yes."

Hugo led her onto the floor as the previous dance ended. The tremble in her hand gave away her nervousness, and he pulled her closer than he ought. The few days apart had been as long as he'd ever remembered time being. So now, having her in his arms, about to dance a waltz, where they could talk...left him discombobulated to say the least.

Somehow the little wallflower looking up at him with trepidation had captivated his soul.

"Do you like to dance, Miss Doherty?"

She nodded. "I do, yes, when I'm asked." The dance started, and they glided their way about the room. The ball was a crush, but even with the multitude of guests, Hugo didn't miss the curious stares that were being thrown in their direction.

"I do not believe there is a man present who wouldn't wish to dance with you."

She arched one brow, her gaze weary. "You have never asked me before. One might wonder why you would do so now?"

He started and almost lost his footing. She was right too, much to his annoyance. He'd not danced with her before, even though they were often in each other's company. "It's a lapse that I intend to remedy from tonight onward."

"Really," she said, looking over his shoulder. "And why is that?"

He slid his hand a little further down her back, settling it just above her buttocks. He met her gaze, wanting to lose himself in the deep blue depths of her eyes. "Because after what you did with me under the stairs at Lady X's house party, there is little else I think about, other than being with you. Near you. Kissing you until we're unable to stand even that."

Lizzie gasped and stumbled. Hugo hoisted her back into the correct position and continued the waltz. "I see the disguise I was made to wear didn't work with you." She sounded annoyed and he chuckled.

"While I do believe others were unaware of your true self, I was not fooled, no. But then again, I have known you for some time and would recognize your delectable figure anywhere, I should imagine. And your hair, which is a shade not often seen in the *ton*."

"You, sir, are being very forward, and I must admit, rude. You shouldn't speak about me in such a manner."

He scoffed. "Why should I not? What I say is the truth." He pulled her into a tight turn. The memory of having her up hard against the wall, her lithe body full against his, undulating in its own course to gain pleasure, bombarded his mind. He groaned at the thought.

"Are you unwell, my lord?"

"Hugo, please. And no, I'm not unwell, but that does not mean that I'm not in pain." Excruciating pain, and thankfully the waltz still had some music movements to go to save his reputation. The last thing anyone here present needed to see was his engorged cock standing to attention.

"Oh really, and what kind of pain are you in, *Hugo*?" she accentuated his name, mocking it slightly, and the devil sat on his shoulder.

"Do you really wish to know, *Lizzie*?" he asked, accentuating her name in turn. She didn't answer, merely raised her brow.

"Very well, Miss Doherty, I shall tell you. I'm in pain, you see," he whispered, "because from the moment you kissed me, for the handful of days we've been separated, you, my dear, have been the single object of my thoughts. I deliberate on you constantly, longing for a kiss as sweet and thrilling as the last, and I have no shame in admitting that I want you." He leaned closer still to ensure privacy. "I want you in my bed."

He was going to hell for saying such things. Wanting a woman he could not have, not unless she miraculously became an heiress or his uncle refused his mother's money. Neither were a possibility and he shouldn't be here, giving her hope, but he also had to know if what they shared was real, not a figment of his imagination. Was Lizzie Doherty the first woman he actually cared about?

LIZZIE SHUT her mouth with a snap. He wanted her in his bed! Oh, how scandalous and so very tempting. She grinned up at him, having not thought he'd be so honest with her, but loving the fact that he was. "You wish to ruin me, my lord?"

"Hugo. And yes, thoroughly."

His lordship pulled her into a turn before they headed back down the long ballroom floor. For the last several days, being apart from Hugo had been torturous for her as well. Her body seemed no longer her own, and now in his arms, warmth and throbbing expectation hummed through her blood, and other places as well.

But to walk down this path meant ruination, especially as he'd made no promises to her. Had not offered for her hand in marriage. She would be best to keep him at a distance, see if his desire for her led to more, before allowing anything life altering to happen. Still, that didn't mean she couldn't have a little fun with him in the interim. A stolen kiss here and there never hurt anyone.

"After this dance, *Hugo*, go to the top of the staircase and turn right, then follow the corridor to the very end where you'll come to a room on your left. Enter it and wait for me there."

His eyes widened, and a little triumph blasted through her that she'd been the one to shock him this time.

"And what do you intend to do with me once we're in this room?"

She ran her hand over his shoulder, halting it close to his nape. "Everything. I intend to do everything with you."

As luck would have it, the dance came to an end, and, curtsying while Hugo bowed, Lizzie took her leave of him. She rejoined Sally, who was in a deep discussion about the terrible storm that had come through while she was attending a country house party, the very one that ensured Lizzie had arrived at the wrong location.

"Sally, I have a slight headache and I think I shall return home if you are in agreement. I'll take the carriage and send it back for you for when you're ready."

Sally frowned, taking her hands. "Are you alright, my dear? Do you wish for me to attend you? I do not mind."

Lizzie waved her friend's concerns aside. "No, you stay and enjoy what's left of the ball. It's just a headache, and it will pass. I shall see you tomorrow." She headed toward the entrance hall and had a footman collect her shawl before waiting for the carriage to arrive.

It wasn't long before she was helped up into the equipage and they pulled away from the front of the house and were on their way. What happened next was all a blur, but before the carriage had gained too much speed the door swung wide and Hugo threw himself across the floor before her slippered feet.

"What are you doing?" she gasped, watching as he rolled over, sat up and slammed the carriage door closed. He was rumbled from his little escapade, and when the carriage slowed to stop Lizzie called out to the driver to carry on.

"You're running away from me. Yet again." He looked up at her from the floor, his hair askew along with his cravat, which drooped significantly, leaving his delicious neck visible.

"As much as I enjoyed our time at Lady X's, Lord Wakely, I'm not going to be an easy conquest for you." Despite the fact he was being absolutely adorable by chasing her down, barrelling into the carriage and scaring her half to death. He looked a little shocked by her declaration, and she laughed.

"Where's the fun in an easy conquest? I do not mind chasing you about London if every now and then you throw me a little crumb. Say, a kiss every now and then."

He came and sat beside her, and nerves skittered across her skin. He was so imposing, so worldly, and she was neither. Why on earth he was even in her carriage sitting beside her, she couldn't fathom. The viscount was courting Miss Fox. Cunning and cold was what the *ton* termed the poor woman, even though she was in no way poor. Still, why did he want her?

"Why are you here, Hugo?" she asked, not wanting to be anyone's toy, no matter how well they could distract her with a kiss. She would marry for love and nothing else, and as far as his lordship knew, she was penniless—not something men of their sphere wanted anything to do with. So why did he?

He studied her for a minute, the carriage rocking them gently, the flickering lights of the street lamps illuminating his seriousness every so often. Lizzie didn't say another word, just waited for whatever his answer would be.

"I like you, more than I ever thought I would. Yes, we've known each other in passing due to your cousin, but I've never really seen you before. I feel that in the time we spent together, without society's rules, my eyes were opened and…well, I see you now."

"I will not sleep with you. I will never be another one of your conquests, no matter how much I may have enjoyed our time at Lady X's estate."

He took her hand, pulling her toward him. "When you kissed me, you seemed to have woken me from a dream. An endless cycle of nothings. When I'm near you I feel a sense of calm, but also madness. I knew that if I did not see you again, I would surely become insane."

"You tease, my lord," she said, pulling away. "I do not like games where I'm the playing piece."

"I never tease, no matter what you may think of me or have heard. I always say the absolute truth."

He frowned, and she wondered what he was thinking. If she wasn't a game to him, what was she? Did he even look at her as a prospective bride or was he simply infatuated with her after their weekend at Lady X's house party? Lizzie didn't know the answer to her questions. Was she willing to place herself into a situation where she could be hurt? Not just her heart, but also her reputation. She'd always liked Lord Wakely, and should she allow him to remain close to her, could he possibly fall in love with her and offer marriage?

It was a risk, certainly, but meeting his dark blue-gray gaze, she already knew she would risk everything if it meant she could possibly have this man in her arms as her husband.

"There are rumors about town that you're about to offer marriage to Miss Fox. Is it true?" She had to know, but when he sat back, his attention turning to the streets of London outside the carriage window, a rock of doubt wedged in her stomach.

"Society would have you believe I'm always courting some debutante or matron of the *ton*. But society can go hang, because it's you I want to be close to. Let me, for the remainder of the Season, be with you as much as we can."

Lizzie caught his eyes, willing herself to believe what he said was true, and yet a small part of her wondered at it. Even though she'd seen him at balls and parties with Miss Fox, dancing more than once with her, escorting her to plays and the opera with her parents. Everything pointed to an understanding, and yet, here he was, beseeching her to let him court her.

"I will not deny that I enjoy your company, and you may dance and speak to me at any of the balls or parties that we find ourselves at, but anything more than that, I must decline. If you prove yourself worthy, if what you say is the truth and you're not courting Miss Fox, then by the end of the Season, we'll know."

A muscle worked at his temple and a deafening silence filled the carriage. Had she insulted him? Possibly, but right now she had to think of herself, and the fact that Lord Wakely was a rake could ruin her chances of ever finding a man who'd love her for who she was, not what she had.

Not to mention her cousin would not bestow her dowry if she was a fallen woman. Two years and she could live however she liked. Wherever she wanted. To risk her future, whatever direction it moved in, even for a few delightful, very naughty kisses under a staircase was a risk she wasn't willing to take. Not yet at least.

He rapped on the roof and the carriage pulled to the side of the road. "I would never wish to do anything that would cause you harm. In light of what you said, we shall go on as before, friends who socialize. I will not ask any more than that from you even though right now"—he leaned in toward her—"I want more than anything to kiss you."

He was so close that the whisper of his breath flittered across her lips. Without thought Lizzie dampened them and delighted in the fact his attention snapped to her mouth.

"You wish to kiss me?" she said, her words but a whisper, but even Lizzie herself could hear the desire echoing in her voice. Need pulsated between them, invisible and yet linking them like a piece of string. He was so dangerous to her plans. Men like the viscount only had liaisons, married for what they could gain for their pocketbook, not what they could gain for their heart. If she married, and that was a very big if, her marriage would be a love match, and nothing else would sway her. If not, she would die an old, rich spinster who had travelled the world and adopted as many cats as her porter could carry.

"More than anything, but I won't." He sighed, then pushed the door open and stepped from the vehicle. "Are you attending the DeVeres' ball tomorrow evening?"

Lizzie nodded. "I am, yes. Lord and Lady Leighton are chaperoning me. Mama has caught a cold and wishes to remain at our country estate for the time being."

He bowed, shutting the door with a thud. "Well then, I shall see you there. Goodnight."

She called out for the driver to drive on. Oh, what was she going to do with him? However was she supposed to remain chaste, when simply one look from him and she melted like Gunther's Ices on a hot summer's day?

"Goodnight Lord Wakely," she said, laughing when he yelled out on the street "Hugo" before the equipage turned a corner and she lost sight of him.

CHAPTER 9

Lizzie stood beside Sally at the DeVeres' ball and watched as Lord Wakely danced a minuet with Miss Fox. What a beautiful woman she was–tall, dark, her skin as flawless as milk. And yet when one came close enough to her, there was no denying that her eyes were as cold as ice.

For a moment she wondered if she'd made the right choice telling his lordship that they could remain friends, but that was all. If he didn't offer for anyone before the end of the Season, then she would know his words were true and maybe they could start anew.

The Marquess of Mongrove bowed before her friend and soon they were off, dancing the minuet as well. Lizzie stood alone for a time before her cousin Lord Leighton joined her, with his wife Katherine by her side.

His lordship offered her a glass of champagne, which she took gratefully. "You look awfully downcast, my dear. Is something the matter?" he asked, frowning a little.

"In all honesty, I am troubled." And if she didn't speak to someone about it soon she would drive herself insane with her own second guessing.

"What is it, Lizzie?" Kat asked, pulling her toward a small settee that sat along the wall and getting her to sit.

Lizzie took a fortifying sip of her champagne. "I'm sure it has not escaped your notice that no one is courting me. I fear that unless they know of the fortune, my circumstances will not change, and I do not know what else to do. I don't want a fortune hunter, but I also don't want to marry in my dotage." The minuet finished, and Lizzie spied Lord Wakely escorting Miss Fox to her parents, who seemed all too eager to have him with them again.

"As I said six years ago, a man who marries you without a dowry will be marrying you because of how much he loves you, not your pocketbook. Trust that the right man will throw all else aside to have you as his wife. You're worth more than your fortune," Lord Leighton declared, gaining a small smile from his wife.

"I agree," Kat said, taking her hand. "And I must admit that it makes no sense that you've had no callers. Why only last week Lord Lumley enquired about you, and from what I know of that gentleman, he has a fortune of his own."

Lord Leighton stared down at them, a scowl on his face. "Now that you mention it, it is very odd, is it not? Six years since your debut and not one offer. Let me make some enquiries into this and see if I can find out why you're not marriage material."

Lizzie gasped, having not expected her cousin to be so blunt.

"Hamish, that was unkind. Apologize to Lizzie."

His wife's words seemed to pull him from his thoughts and he met her gaze. "Oh, I am sorry, my dear. I didn't mean to make you upset. But women marry men all the time without fortunes, and your family is well connected, so it cannot be that reason. So, there must be something else that's impeding your options."

Lizzie shrugged, then looked up to see Lord Wakely talking to a group of young bucks, one of them Lord Lumley, who her cousin had just mentioned. Hugo met and held her gaze across the ballroom floor, and she shivered. He was so very intense, his eyes all but screamed with heat, and from where she sat even she could feel the warmth.

She tore her gaze from Lord Wakely. "Promise me that if I do not find the right man to be my husband, you'll allow me to do whatever I want with my fortune. After six years gracing Almack's wooden boards, I think it's the least you can promise," Lizzie said, only half joking.

Lord Leighton bowed, grinning. "You may, my dear. I would not deny you your wish."

Lizzie caught sight of Lord Wakely excusing himself from his friends, before he strode purposefully toward them. Butterflies took flight in her stomach and she nodded in welcome. He bowed, taking her hand and kissing it lightly.

"We meet again, Miss Doherty." His lordship shook Lord Leighton's hand and spoke quickly to Katherine.

"Good evening, Lord Wakely. I see you've dragged yourself away from your friends long enough to speak to us. How fortunate we are," Katherine said, grinning up at the gentleman. Lizzie smiled, liking the fact that Kat only spoke the truth, even if it was blunt.

"Ah yes, I have been busy, but I'm here now, and with permission from both you and Lord Leighton I would like to ask Miss Doherty to supper."

Lord Leighton gave his consent and Lizzie stood, seeing no harm in it. They were to be friends after all, she reminded herself. "I would like that, thank you."

Lord Wakely took her arm and they made their way toward where others were going to dine before the other half of the ball commenced. He sat her hand atop his arm and placed his firmly on top, eliminating any chance of escape. Not that she was looking to go anywhere.

Lizzie took in his very fine assortment of clothing that from memory covered a very hard, well-defined body. His black satin knee breeches and white stockings accentuated his legs. His dark blue superfine coat with tails showed off his considerable strong shoulders that could lift her without a moment's hesitation. And had done so beneath Lady X's staircase before he had hauled her up against the wall.

He glanced down at her and held her captive with his eyes, and she fought to remind herself why she'd told him they were to remain friends until his sincerity was proven.

A discreet cough brought Lizzie to a halt, and she dipped into a curtsy when the Duchess of Athelby stood before them, an amused lift to her lips. Sally's mama stood beside her grace, the ladies' inspection of Lord Wakely thorough. Both women were formidable influences within the *ton* and over the past few years Lizzie had come to rely on the duchess's advice whenever she needed a different opinion.

"Your Grace, Mrs. Darwin, you know Lord Wakely. He was just escorting me to supper. Would you care to join us?" she offered, not wanting them to think any more of her being with his lordship than they probably were already. They were friends, and would remain so. The fact that they had shared a passionate kiss meant absolutely nothing.

He bowed, but never ventured to take his hand off hers on his arm. The duchess gave the clasp a marked stare, before raising one perfectly groomed eyebrow.

"Lizzie, I'm so glad to see you tonight. It has been too

long. I hope Lord Wakely is being a considerate escort to supper. I would hate to hear otherwise," the duchess said, her words friendly but with a thread of steel lingering within the tone.

Lizzie waved the duchess's concerns away. "Of course he is. We were just talking about how the DeVeres have the best lobster patties available during supper, and how we should rush to ensure we don't miss out."

"I'm sure you have nothing to concern yourselves with. Supper hasn't been announced yet, so you're a little early." The duchess waved a fan idly before her face and Lizzie wished she had one in her keeping, since her cheeks were decidedly warm and getting warmer by the minute.

Mrs. Darwin turned her attention to Lord Wakely, her eyes narrowing in thought. "I heard about town the oddest rumor about you, Lord Wakely. That you're about to be married and that your uncle is already crossing the Atlantic as we speak. Is there something you wish to tell us? We would so love to be the first to know."

Hugo tensed under Lizzie's hold, and not for the first time she wondered herself if he was in fact courting Miss Fox whilst also paying attention to her. But then, they were friends. Perhaps he simply liked her company, since they seemed to get along well enough when together. She had no claim on him, even if she'd dearly love to have one if he were to prove worthy.

"I am not engaged, nor is there any understanding. I'm simply enjoying the Season and looking forward to my uncle's visit. As you know, with my father's death twelve months ago I've had no near family remaining in England."

Lizzie felt a pang of sadness toward his lordship at his reply. She too had lost her father, and even as meddling and annoying as her mother was, at least she still had one parent left. Was Lord Wakely lonely? Was that why he sought the company of parties of Lady X's caliber, where he knew he would have good company both in public and private?

"I'm glad that your uncle is coming," the duchess said sincerely. "We look forward to meeting him when he eventually arrives."

Mrs. Darwin smiled at Lord Wakely before saying, "We missed you at Lady Remmnick's house party, but on our return to London we stopped at a delightful inn and I thought I saw you changing horses. Were you nearby?"

His lordship threw Mrs. Darwin an amused glance and heat rose on Lizzie's cheeks. "I was in attendance at another house party, yes. I hope you found the break from London to your satisfaction?"

The duchess's attention snapped to Lizzie and she raised her chin, not wanting to look as guilty as she felt.

"It was very enjoyable. And your house party, my lord?" the duchess asked, watching them with such inspection that Lizzie couldn't help but feel the duchess knew something was being hidden from her.

"It was most enlightening and pleasurable, your grace." Lord Wakely's clasp on Lizzie's hand tightened, and it shot heat straight to her core. She swallowed, fighting the need to flee, to run away from all these questions.

"Shall we find a table, Miss Doherty?" his lordship asked.

The duchess and Mrs. Darwin moved aside, and they moved on.

"What a stroke of luck that we ended up at the same house party. Did you enjoy the festivities as much as I did? I never asked before." His whispered words tickled the side of her neck, reminding her of his kisses upon the very spot.

"I may have," she answered honestly. In fact, the few

times she'd spent in Lord Wakely's arms were something she was never likely to forget. Even now, the pull to be alone with him, kiss him again, touch him and enjoy every nuance that made up who he was, was almost impossible to ignore.

The viscount laughed, covering it with a cough. "*May have?* Are you trying to tell me my seductive wiles are lacking? If so, we can remedy that. You only have to say the word and I'm at your disposal."

Lizzie schooled her features to be less shocked. She bit her lip as the overwhelming feeling she was playing with fire and with a man who was too worldly for her rushed to the forefront of her mind. "Another time perhaps. I see the lobster patties are available tonight. You did mention before that you're desperate to have some again," she said, dissembling.

He pulled her to a stop and caught her gaze. The heat that resonated from his attention made her tremble. What was it about him that brought forth these wonderful but odd emotions to riot inside? His chiseled jaw, perfect olive complexion, and dark hair made him one of the most heart-stopping rogues in the *ton*. And right now his attention was fixed on her. Lizzie swallowed, her gaze sliding to his lips.

"I will hold you to that statement, Miss Doherty."

She nodded, unable to do anything else. How did one answer such a declaration without giving away just how much she wanted him to hold her to it? And if he did not, she would hold herself to honor what she'd said. For if one thing was certain, she would kiss Lord Wakely again if it were the last thing she did.

CHAPTER 10

House calls were not something Lord Wakely did. Ever. And yet the following afternoon, Hugo found himself standing before Lord Leighton's townhouse, about to be ushered indoors to partake in an hour of frivolous discussions about nothing of particular interest, other than Miss Doherty, who was of very particular interest to him.

Somehow after their time together in the country she'd awoken a part of him that he'd never thought existed. He was a viscount with a terrible reputation. If he had any desire to hold onto his fortune, he ought to be knocking on Miss Fox's door right at this very moment and courting her. But he could not pull himself away to do so. There was something between him and Lizzie, more than a physical attraction, although that was certainly there as well.

She made him laugh, found situations amusing just like himself. Was happy to have a bit of fun. Her attendance at Lady X's house party was proof of that, but also, the day they'd played billiards, she'd not acted the retiring lady who couldn't possibly play a game generally only men would partake in. Not only had she stepped up to the competition, but she'd been an exceptional player and had looked delightful bending over the table.

Lizzie had a direction for her future. Whether that included a husband would be anyone's guess, but something told him she would be perfectly capable of living the spinster life and becoming quite fond of it. Miss Fox had never been very particular toward him–she showed as much interest in him as he did in her, and it gave him pause. Lizzie had showed him there could be so much more between a husband and wife, which drove home just how much he'd want his marriage to resemble that of his friends' love matches.

He needed to kiss her again, if only once, to know if his desire for her was simply a one-off emotion or if each time they kissed he'd want nothing more than to do it again.

If what he suspected was true, and Lizzie would suit his character much better than Miss Fox, he would petition his uncle to forgo the inheritance that was set to revert to him at the end of July. Surely the love his uncle had for his sister, and for her child, would outweigh his need of money.

Hugo rapped the knocker on the front door and it opened without delay. He strode into the entrance hall, handing the footman his coat and gloves. An elderly butler stepped forward and bowed.

"Lord Wakely, if you would be so kind as to follow me, the at home is being held in the front sitting room today."

Hugo followed the old retainer, bracing himself for a flurry of gasps and gossip when he entered the room. The butler announced him, and Hugo halted just beyond the threshold as an army of startled female eyes, gaping mouths, and amused expressions met his appearance. He took in the room, seeking out Miss Doherty, and inwardly cringed at seeing her mother seated beside her. When had she returned to town?

Hugo steeled his resolve. He'd faced worse challenges in his life—a room full of women and a bedevilling mother was nothing to be terrified of.

Mrs. Doherty stood and curtsied. "Lord Wakely, welcome. Please, come be seated by us," she said, gesturing to a vacant chair before them.

Hugo did as she bade, welcoming a cup of tea that Miss Doherty handed him, her small smile of welcome warming his blood.

"We're very happy you decided to join us this afternoon, are we not, Lizzie?" Mrs. Doherty said, sitting back down and smiling between them both.

Lizzie took a sip of her tea. "You are most welcome, Lord Wakely." Her welcome was benign enough, but Hugo could hear that she actually meant her words and was pleased to see him. A little warning bell went off in his mind that he was toying with her, giving her false hopes where there might be none, and yet he couldn't stay away from her. He'd never reacted to anyone in the way that he reacted to Miss Doherty. No matter the consequences, he had to see if their chemistry was a figment of his imagination or something he could discuss with his uncle, beseech him to leave Hugo with the funds that should rightfully be his in any case. If his uncle would allow him to choose a wife he felt some affection towards, not one who had a fortune and would marry him before the month was out.

"Did you enjoy the ball last evening, Miss Doherty? I heard this morning that it ended after dawn."

Lizzie laughed, and her eyes brightened with amusement. "I did, my lord, and I can assure you, as I was one of the last to leave the entertainment, that it did indeed end as the sun kissed the morning sky."

"You did not stay, Lord Wakely?" Mrs. Doherty asked.

Hugo shook his head. "Alas no, I had another engagement to attend." And not one that he wished to elaborate on here and now, or ever, if he were honest.

Lady Leighton came over and stood behind Lizzie's chair, joining their conversation. "You attended Miss Fox's soiree, I understand," she said, her words tinged with an edge of reproach.

Hugo smiled, taking a sip of his tea. "That's right, and the event was overcrowded. I did not stay long." Only long enough to dance with Miss Fox and then depart. Lady Leighton watched him, and he fought to remember if she had been in attendance. Did she know he had danced with Miss Fox? He was a cad, keeping his options open in such a way. Panic tore through him that what he was doing was wrong. Not just to Lizzie, but to Miss Fox also, and he couldn't continue down this line of untruths.

If he told Lizzie his predicament, would she understand? If only he could get her away from here, talk to her privately.

"If you would excuse me. My friend Sally has just arrived, and I need to speak with her."

Hugo stood when Lizzie did and, bowing, watched her leave him with her mother and cousin by marriage. He placed down his cup of tea, not wishing to stay with Lizzie occupied elsewhere. "It is time I left as well. Thank you for the tea, Mrs. Doherty, Lady Leighton. I shall see myself out."

"Good afternoon, Lord Wakely," her ladyship said, her tone no better than before.

Hugo left, and while making his way to the entrance hall found Lord Leighton hanging about the staircase. "Hugo," he said, coming over and shaking his hand. "It's good to see you. Come, I need to speak to you. We can talk in my library."

"Of course." Hugo followed, wondering if Hamish's wife's cold manner toward him was the reason for this sudden tête-à-tête. Hamish gestured for him to sit and Hugo made himself comfortable. Thankfully, instead of tea, Hamish handed him a glass of brandy before seating himself behind his desk.

"I won't mince my words, as I'm sure you're aware of why I asked to talk to you privately today."

Hugo took a sip, not willing to give way that easily, although Hamish was one of his oldest friends, so he wouldn't dissemble for long. He wouldn't lose his friendship over the predicament that his father had placed him in.

"You've been seen a couple of times around Lizzie, and your appearance here today makes me wonder what your sudden interest is about. Are you courting her?"

Hugo ran a hand through his hair, searching for how best to explain himself. "In all honesty, I'm not sure why I'm here at all. And I'm sorry if that offends you, I mean no disrespect, but when it comes to Miss Doherty I can't seem to keep away. Even though a marriage between us may be impossible."

The earl leaned back in his chair, his stoic visage giving away little other than annoyance. "You can never marry her why?"

Hugo sighed, hating his father more than he ever had before in his life, and there were plenty of times he'd hated the man dreadfully. His father had never taken to him as a child. Hard and painfully correct in all things, he'd pushed Hugo to do as he did. Of course, Hugo had never taken after his father, had been a free spirit like his dearly departed mama, and had rebelled. So much so that his father had won the final battle and ripped his inheritance away from him in his final blow from the grave.

"You know my uncle is on his way to London. Well, everyone in London believes it's so he may attend my wedding to Miss Fox, who I'll apparently offer to very soon. That is not the case. He's arriving to take control of the money my mother brought to her marriage to my father. My sire has felled his final blow against me from six feet under and stipulated in his will that I'm to marry within twelve months, and to an heiress of no less than thirty thousand pounds. If I do not, the money goes back to my mother's family. I only have a few weeks before the deadline, and because I've not married as yet, my uncle now assumes that I will not—hence his arrival."

Lord Leighton let out a whistle, his eyes wide in shock. Hugo nodded. "So, you see, I shouldn't be here and yet I also cannot stay away."

"Lizzie is my cousin, and under my charge whenever her mother leaves town. Katherine and I care for her deeply, look out for her just as if she was one of our own children. You know she has no dowry and therefore cannot meet the stipulation in your father's will." Lord Leighton stood, coming around the desk and taking his glass. He refilled them both before handing his back to him. "As much as I sympathize with your predicament, I cannot allow you to continue to court Lizzie, or give her any hope. She deserves a marriage of love and I'll not have her marry anyone, not even you, my friend, if there is no affection. You may be as you've always been—distant friends, people who move within the same set—but do not venture any further from those rules. I would be most displeased if you did."

The thread of steel in his friend's voice brooked no argument. Hugo could understand. Hell, should he be in

Hamish's situation right now, he would say the exact same thing. But the thought of removing himself from Lizzie's sphere, courting Miss Fox, and entering a marriage of convenience wasn't what he wanted. Not anymore. "Of course, I shall do as you bid. Allow me some grace in pulling away from Miss Doherty. She's innocent in all of this, and if I can I will try to limit the hurt I may cause by ceasing my interest." The thought of not being near her left a hollow void in his gut.

"Of course. I wouldn't expect anything less. Now," the earl said, downing his drink. "I had better make an appearance at my wife's at home or I shall be in the doghouse."

Hugo stood, placing his crystal glass on the desk. "I'll see myself out."

He left, climbing up into his carriage that stood waiting at the front of the townhouse. This was for the best. Lord Leighton was right, and he'd been wrong in his dealings with Lizzie Doherty. It was a cold comfort knowing he would never hold her in his arms ever again.

⚘

A WEEK LATER, Lizzie hadn't seen or spoken to Lord Wakely. Not since she saw him leave her cousin's townhouse looking like the sky had fallen and he was trapped beneath it. Katherine had let it slip that the viscount had spoken to Hamish prior to leaving, and not for the first time she wondered what that conversation was about.

They were friends of course, so it could've been about anything, but something told her it had involved her. And whatever her cousin said had made Lord Wakely leave in much lower spirits than when he'd arrived.

Tonight she was attending the Duncannons' annual ball. Across the room she spied her friend Sally, who waved and started toward her, weaving through those who stood between them.

"Lizzie, how lovely to see you again. I had hoped you would attend tonight. The gossip throughout London is all about Lord Wakely and his sudden arrival at Lady Leighton's at home last week. He left just as I arrived. How long did he stay for?"

"I have heard I'm the latest on-dit, and truly, he didn't stay long enough to cause all this drama. And since his departure, we've not seen him again," Lizzie said, hoping to put to rest any gossip, although by the curious looks she was gaining from those in attendance tonight, her wish didn't look to be coming to fruition.

"Come and sit, it'll be more comfortable a little away from this terrible crush." Sally pulled her toward a couple of vacant chairs and sat, tapping the chair for Lizzie to do so also.

"I heard that the viscount came and spoke to you and no one else, and that after he left he was seen entering Lord Leighton's library. Do you think he's going to offer for you?" Sally clasped her hand, her excitement over the prospect of Lord Wakely asking for Lizzie to marry him too much to stifle.

"Sally, I need to tell you something, but you must promise not to tell another living soul. Ever. If you speak a word of what I'm about to tell you I will be ruined in society forever."

Sally's eyes widened and for a moment she didn't say a word, before she crossed her fingers. "I will never tell anyone. Not that I need to promise such a thing, as I would never break my trust with you, but you may be assured I promise never to tell another living soul."

Satisfied, Lizzie ensured they were alone before she told her friend all of what had happened at Lady X's estate–how she came to be there and what happened over the ensuing days. Never had she seen her friend without words, but it would seem that after hearing every little detail Sally Darwin was totally mute.

"Say something, please, anything. Your silence concerns me."

Sally let out a sigh before she said, "And now that you're back in London, what is it exactly that's between you? He's most definitely seeking you out, but you do know that he's still being seen in the presence of Miss Fox? I don't have to tell you that Lord Wakely is known within the *ton* as a bit of a rake, easily led and not the most trustworthy when it comes to the female sex."

"Lord Wakely and I have decided to remain friends and that is all. I'm mindful of him, do not despair, I'm not blind. Especially with his courting of Miss Fox, which was quite ardent prior to what happened in the country between us. It leaves me wondering if he's in need of funds."

"He's wealthy though, my dear, so that cannot be the reason. He either wishes for more coin to add to his coffers or perhaps he holds some affection for her." Sally frowned toward the dancers and guests milling about them. "Or there is something we do not know and that he isn't telling anyone. I did hear that his uncle is coming over from New York. Maybe something is afoot in his family."

Lizzie couldn't help but chuckle at Sally and her wayward thoughts. She had always had a great imagination and saw possibilities of things where Lizzie could see none.

"Whatever it is, I have no dowry, and although my cousin is titled, my own family line is not. Unless someone falls in love with me, I will not marry." And when that special someone did fall in love with her, then and only then would they find out just how wealthy she was. Otherwise she would gleefully buy her own townhouse, take in any stray cats that needed a home, and be quite content with the situation.

"Whatever has happened between you, either in the country or now back in town, the one question you should be asking yourself is if you like him enough to try and help him on. Turn his attention to you fully, so that he'll forget Miss Fox and her fortune and want you instead. It's happened before–it can happen again."

Lizzie doubted it would happen to her, but the thought had crossed her mind. How she would love to have Lord Wakely to wake up beside every morning, be the whole center of his affections. She sighed. "And if I throw myself at him and he still marries Miss Fox? What then?" Well, then she'd be unmarriable. Was the risk of being in Lord Wakely's arms again worth it?

Sally clasped her hand, gaining her attention. "No one need ever know you set out on this course. Not if you're careful. Lord Wakely could be the other half to your soul. Don't you think seeing if that is true is worth the risk?"

Lizzie didn't know what to do. It was such a gamble. Could she encourage his lordship into kissing her again, being more than friends as they had agreed? Remembering their time at Lady X's, and then again when he was in the carriage with her in town, something told her it wouldn't be that hard at all.

"He is rumored to be arriving tonight. A perfect opportunity to put your plan into action."

"Your plan," Lizzie said, smiling. Hope blossomed within her and excitement thrummed in her veins at the thought of seeing him again. "Do you know what, Sally? I think I shall throw caution aside and see what will happen.

I'm sick of sitting about, waiting for my true love to find me. Maybe he needs a little help. A little push."

Sally nodded. "I agree. And if I'm not mistaken, your quarry has just entered."

Lizzie bit her lip, looking toward the ballroom doors. Lord Wakely stood on the threshold, bowing to their hosts, and all she could do was take in his glorious beauty. His dark, wicked looks, his striking height and immaculate evening dress. Nerves pooled in her stomach. It was one thing to kiss a man with a mask on, thinking no one would know who you were, but it was another thing entirely to kiss him without any pretence. But if it meant that she would kiss Lord Wakely and possibly find he was the man for her, she would. It was a pleasurable sacrifice she was willing to commit, and maybe even commit tonight.

HUGO SURVEYED THE DUNCANNONS' ballroom floor and spotted the very bane and sole center of his attention sitting next to her closest friend. Both women seemed to be enjoying the ball, but their conversation appeared to be keeping them separate from everyone else and, if anything, appeared a little secretive.

Hugo found himself grinning and making his way into the room. He started in Lizzie's direction, wanting to see her again no matter that only a few days ago he'd promised Hamish he'd stay away. But tonight Lord Leighton was attending another ball, and therefore wouldn't know Hugo was about to ask his cousin to dance.

He bowed before Lizzie and Miss Darwin, who stood and curtsied. "Good evening, Miss Doherty, Miss Darwin. I thought I might ask Miss Doherty to dance. The waltz is up next." Hugo held out his hand, waiting for Lizzie to take it.

She looked at it for a time, her eyes wide, before placing her hand in his, allowing him to escort her out onto the ballroom floor. The room was a crush, and instead of going out to dance, he led Lizzie toward the terrace doors. With so many in attendance, very few paid them any attention of the direction they were heading. Before anyone could take note he whisked Miss Doherty outside, to stroll along the flagstone courtyard.

The night air was warm and in the distance the sounds of London and its life echoed through the night. Other couples strolled as well, and Hugo led Lizzie away from them to ensure privacy.

"I have not seen you for some days and I apologize for that. My time has not been my own with my uncle's expected arrival some time in the next few days. There are other things that have taken up my time, but I had to see you again." How he wished he could tell her why he should not be before her, wanting her as much as he did. He fought not to lift his hand and place a little strand of her hair off her cheek. He wanted to touch her, kiss her, make her his.

"The Season is busy, you don't need to explain anything to me." She took a couple of steps away and studied the shadowed garden before them. A bird cooed in the dark and a small smile lifted her lips. How beautiful she was. How had he never seen it before? If only he'd not been so involved satisfying his own pleasures, he might have made Lizzie his wife years ago and his father would never have done what he did.

"I want to kiss you," he blurted out, unable to take his words back. Nor did he want to. They were the truth. He wanted her, and upon his uncle's arrival he would beseech him to ignore his father's will, allow Hugo to keep his inheritance and marry Miss Doherty who had not a penny to her name.

She didn't turn to look at him and her strong resolve made him adore her even more.

"I want to kiss you too. In fact, I've thought of little else since I left the house party."

Her words were a blow to his gut and he moved closer, sliding his hand along the balustrade to the point where they just touched. The moment his finger touched hers it shot a bolt of longing so strong and fierce it threatened to knock him off his feet.

Hugo looked behind him and noted there were fewer couples than before, but the terrace doors remained open and hundreds of people were only a few feet from where they stood. Anyone could walk out at any time, and yet, he had to taste her. His body was blocking a lot of the guests from seeing Lizzie. Maybe a chaste kiss would be possible, if they both desired it.

"Kiss me," he said, laying his hand atop hers, linking their fingers. "No one will see."

Lizzie glanced behind him and then, when he thought she'd thought better of his idea, she leaned up and quickly but quietly kissed him. The chaste touching of their lips wasn't enough, and even though he tried to deepen the embrace, she pulled away, again checking to see if anyone saw.

That there were no cries of scandal told Hugo no one had witnessed them.

"Tell me something, anything, to stop me from ruining us both and taking you in my arms in front of all the *ton*." Hugo straightened, holding his arms behind his back.

"What would you like to know?" she asked, tilting her head to one side.

"Everything I do not know already."

She turned and leaned against the balustrade, watching him. "Well, I'm on the shelf, but you already know that. I'm three and twenty and have very little to recommend but myself. I enjoy horse riding and travel, and I volunteer at the London Relief Society for the Duchess of Athelby and their set. I have no siblings and my mother is controlling and pushy. Not that I should speak about my parent in such a way, but yet it is true. I love cats and will tolerate dogs."

Hugo barked out a laugh. "How can you only tolerate dogs? They are the best of company. They never judge, and will give unconditional love."

"Hmm." She shrugged. "But they're awfully pouty, I find. Always wanting affection and reaffirmation about what a good boy or girl they are. Whereas cats, well, they're independent, strong, wilful, and do not care what anyone thinks. I suppose I strive to be very similar to the species. I no longer wish to care what anyone thinks of me."

"Really?" Hugo wagged his brows. "Is that true? For some, should they know we're outside having an indiscreet tête-à-tête, would have a lot to say about you. In fact, you'd probably end up in one of the gossip rags that will come out next week."

"I'm willing to risk all if it means that I get what I want." She met his gaze and the dark determination in her blue orbs fired his blood. Did she mean him? Did she wish to fight for him?

Her words strengthened his resolve to beseech his uncle to leave his mother's money well alone so he could marry her. The idea of starting a life with a woman who not only stimulated his mind but his body calmed his soul.

"My horses are in need of a good run. I'm taking the

gig out tomorrow, a couple of hours in the country to see how they perform. Would you be willing to accompany me?"

"Alone?" she asked.

He nodded. "If your mama will allow."

"There is no impediment if you have a driver and groom with you to act as chaperones. Mama will approve such an outing."

"Eleven then," he said, watching as she pushed away from the balustrade and headed back into the ballroom. He followed her progress, enjoying what he saw. Tomorrow he would have her to himself for a couple of hours, where they could talk freely and maybe continue the delightful kissing that had brought them together to begin with.

CHAPTER 11

Lizzie woke with a start, and sitting up, she jumped out of bed. The day trip into the country with Lord Wakely beckoned and she couldn't wait to see him again.

Last night, after she'd kissed him, chaste as it was, she was left longing for more, and with the realization that she wasn't willing to allow his lordship to marry anyone else but her. The uncontrollable feeling of floating whenever she was about him, the desire to see his eyes darken in hunger, was something she wasn't willing to lose. Not to a Miss Fox and her thousands of pounds in any case. That woman could marry whomever she pleased, and it did not please Lizzie for her to marry Lord Wakely.

At the allocated hour she paced the hall of Lord Leighton's home, watching the traffic for his lordship's gig. Right on time, his driver accompanied by a groom pulled up before the steps with four matched horses. The gig was not any run-of-the-mill vehicle, but a barouche box.

After helping her climb up, he gave her a small blanket to place over her legs, and they were soon heading out of

London on the great north road. If only they continued on the road, they could travel all the way to Gretna Green.

What a delightful adventure that would be.

"Are you well, Lizzie?" he asked, throwing her a small smile.

She reached up to hold onto her bonnet. "I am. Very well, thank you. I'm also very excited about our outing today. Thank you for inviting me."

"My pleasure," he stated, meeting her eyes.

"So, where are we going today? Is there a plan?" On the seat opposite them sat a basket, and she hoped that it held a picnic. How wonderful if he'd thought to do such a thing. She'd never had a picnic before with a gentleman.

"We will drive a little ways, to let me see how my matching pair go under the guidance of another, and if we find a nice place to stop, we'll have a picnic. I hope you're not averse to eating outdoors."

Lizzie shook her head. "On the contrary, I love doing things like this." She looked about for a time, before saying, "Are you looking forward to your uncle arriving? You said he was due any day."

He didn't reply at first, but kept his attention on the scenery. Then he said, "In all truth, my uncle's arrival isn't a happy prospect. He's here to ruin me, if I'm to be honest with you."

Lizzie gasped, having not expected that answer. Did he really mean what he said? His uncle was coming to ruin him? What did that even mean? "I don't understand, my lord. Why would he wish to do that? Wasn't he your mother's only brother?"

Lord Wakely sighed, rubbing his jaw, which Lizzie noticed had the slightest shadow of stubble. Her hand itched to feel it, to see if it would prickle against her palm, but she did not. First she wanted to know what was going on.

"He is all that I have left of family, but it's not his fault he wishes to ruin me." His lordship paused for a moment, the line between his brow deep and furrowed. "My father, as you would remember, passed away just under twelve months ago. When alive, it was no secret within the *ton* that we disagreed on many things, one of which was my life-style. I wasn't the best-behaved gentleman running around London."

He threw her a bemused glance, and Lizzie chuckled, having seen that herself. She'd also pined over Lord Wakely while he'd enjoyed his life to the fullest, often dreaming she was his quarry, to be flirted with and seduced. "I have heard of your antics."

He turned and grinned at her before looking back to the driver as the man maneuvered the carriage to the side of the road to allow a mail carriage to pass in the opposite direction. Their driver yelled out a salutation to the other driver and then pulled back into the centre of the road.

"What I didn't know was that my father would strike at me one final time, from the grave. He stipulated in his will that I am to marry within twelve months of his death, to an heiress who comes with a minimum of thirty thousand pounds. If I do not, the money my mother brought to the family upon her marriage will revert to her brother living in New York. And, as you can see," his lordship said, gesturing to himself, "I have not married, and my time is almost up, hence my uncle's imminent arrival."

Of all the stories that Lizzie had heard, she'd not expected this one. Lord Wakely would not be penniless unless he married an heiress, however he would find it hard to keep up his present lifestyle without selling off some of his property. Well, at least it explained why he'd been courting Miss Fox these past months, even if sporadically. And why he was reluctant with her, only too willing to remain her friend and nothing else. There would be many reliant on Lord Wakely for a living, not just the servants who worked in his homes, but also those who worked his lands. The loss of his mother's money would be devastating for so many. Even so, Lizzie was an heiress, not a penniless miss. But Lord Wakely did not know her secret, so should he choose her in light of his current situation, it could only mean one thing. He cared for her. A great deal.

"Why are we out driving together then, Lord Wakely? Shouldn't you be with Miss Fox instead? She after all meets your father's last wish." Lizzie kept her eyes on the road, wondering what he'd say to her statement.

"I ought to be, yes, but I'm not, and there's one simple reason why that is so."

At that she couldn't continue looking away. Gazing up, she met his gray orbs and lost herself in their depths. "And that is?"

"I don't want Miss Fox."

His words rocked through her and she clasped the seat to steady herself just as a large drop of rain fell and splashed on her cheek. The single drop was soon followed by a deluge. "Oh my God, Lord Wakely, it's pouring." Lizzie laughed as they were soon drenched, her perfectly coiffured hair now limp about her shoulders, her day gown of light blue muslin soaked and clinging to her like a second skin. The driver pulled up under some trees and Lord Wakely asked his groom to help him with the barouche's collapsible hood. He cursed when the blasted thing wouldn't budge.

"It's stuck," he said, looking about for other shelter.

Lizzie held her shawl over her head, but it too was soon soaked and of no use.

"Over there," he yelled through the rain. "I see a barn." Lord Wakely turned to the driver and groom while opening the carriage door. "I'll take Miss Doherty over to the barn to shelter from the storm."

"Right ye are, my lord," the driver said, nodding slightly.

The barn was a large wooden building with two double sliding doors at its front. Inside, stacks of hay lay about from last year's crop. A few pigeons flew about as she entered, otherwise the space was free of animals.

Lord Wakely joined her, taking off his coat and hanging it from a nail he found on the wall. "We'll stay here until the rain has passed and then I'll return you to town. Your mother will not be pleased you're returning damp." He slid the doors shut, cocooning them in the dry space.

Lizzie laughed. "Damp? I'm drenched through." She went up to where the hay was stacked and sat, pulling off her half boots and stockings to dry. "The storm must have been behind us. I never saw it coming."

"No," he said, coming to sit beside her, taking the opportunity to pull his boots and stockings off as well. "Will you call me Hugo like you did before, when we're in private? I'd much prefer it to my lord or Lord Wakely."

Chilled as she was, warmth ran across her skin at his request. "I would like that. You may call me Lizzie in return."

He reached up and pulled a piece of hay from her hair, throwing it away. Their gazes locked, and no matter how much she tried Lizzie couldn't look away. Unlike the first time they kissed, the lead up to this one seemed like an excruciatingly slow dance.

Hugo leaned down and, clasping her jaw, kissed her. His lips were soft, and although they were cold from the rain outside, with one touch any trace of chill fled. Lizzie kneeled, running her hands over his shoulders to clasp about his back. She kissed him back with all that she was, showing him with her touch that she was his match in every way.

His kiss deepened, and Lizzie matched his desire. How she'd wanted to be with him like this again, how for night after night she'd lain awake with images of being in his arms, having his mouth hot and passionate against hers.

Her skin heated, her cold damp clothes forgotten as his hands skimmed down her back. "Touch me," she gasped through the kiss.

He pulled her hard against him, and, still kissing, they flopped onto the hay. Hugo lay beside her, his hand running over her waist and down over her hip, sliding around to clasp her bottom.

Lizzie gasped as he lifted her leg and laid it over his, placing him so very close to her aching core. Wanting to feel him, all of him, she shuffled closer and the hard line of his desire pressed against her abdomen, so solid and big that she couldn't help but wonder how it all worked. Wanted to know with a desperation that matched her desire.

He clasped her hand and took it down between them to lay it on himself, his dark hooded eyes watching her. The need coursing through her was addictive, and at that very moment Lizzie understood that Lord Wakely was for her. Only with him did she trust enough for such kisses, such touches. Never before had she reacted to any gentleman the way she reacted to him.

"Touch me as well," he begged, his voice hoarse with need.

She did as he asked, taking his hard member into her hand through the fabric of his breeches and feeling its length. He pushed it against her hand, moaning against her lips as he kissed her with a ferocity that left her breathless. "Do you like that, my lord?"

He growled, nipping her lip. "You can see that I do."

Heat pooled between her legs and following his lead she clasped his arm that gripped her leg and put it against her most private of places. A place that no one but him could touch. She ached with the need of him, to stroke and slide his hand, give her pleasure just as he had at Lady X's house party.

He gathered up her gown, pooling it against her stomach, and then without hesitation, without caution, laid his hand against her mons. Lizzie shut her eyes as unbearable pleasure ran through her. He stroked her flesh, teasing her with a tentative touch that wasn't enough. She needed more, beyond anything she could ever understand.

"Touch me like you did at the house party, Hugo." She wrapped her hand about his member, squeezing it a little, and he gasped. "Make me feel what you did before."

"I want you. I want you so much," he said, sliding his hand between her wet folds, circulating his thumb on a spot that made her blood turn to molten lava. She moaned, kissing him, increasing her own touch. She broke away to look down at his breeches, then, ripping at the buttons on his front falls, reached in and touched his flesh.

His skin was so soft, like velvet, and he was hers. All hers. The smallest amount of liquid pooled at the tip of his phallus and she wiped it off with her thumb. His fingers undulated against her core and she moaned, wanting more. Her skin burned beneath her wet gown. Her breasts ached, her breathing shallow as he continued to tease her.

"This isn't enough," he gasped, pushing her onto her back and coming to kneel between her legs. Lizzie licked her lips, wanting him with a need that frightened her. She didn't want to think about the fact that she could lose him if he decided that money was more important than his feelings, and yet she could not push him away.

"I'll not ruin you. I promise. Just trust me."

Lizzie watched as he pushed his breeches down. His manhood jutted out, long and thick, and she swallowed. A part of her wanted to run, get away from such a sight, and yet another part of her wanted nothing more than to see what he would do with it.

He came down over her, placing himself against her flesh, and then he slid, sending stars to form before her eyes. The little bead of moisture she'd felt before mixed with her own desire, teasing them both toward a climax she longed to feel again.

How was such a thing so enjoyable? She spread her legs wide and, wrapping her arms about his shoulders, kissed him deeply. He moaned, and wanting more she pushed against him, undulating and seeking her gratification.

"Oh yes, Hugo," she gasped as spasms of pleasure thrummed through her core and throughout her body. With every push against her flesh another bout of fulfilment went through her and she moaned.

His kiss turned scalding and Lizzie didn't shy away from his frenzied state. She wanted him to be crazy for her, to want her as much as she'd always wanted him. He gasped, calling out her name as heat speared across her belly.

They lay spent in the hay together for some time, their breathing laboured as they tried to regain their equilibrium. Hugo slumped beside her, and after a little time pulled out his handkerchief, wiping away his seed. He gathered her dress and settled it back over her legs.

"It's official, I now am a rake of the worst kind."

His voice held no amusement. Lizzie turned toward him, taking in his profile as he stared at the barn's roof.

"I don't know about that. There was nothing bad about what we just did. If anything, it makes me want to do it again." Her voice even to her own ears sounded sleepy and satisfied. And she was both, wanted nothing but to cuddle up next to him, breathe him in and sleep.

He shut his eyes. "Please forgive me, Lizzie. I should never have done such a thing to you."

The thought of him doing it with anyone else irked her, and she pulled him over to look at her. "I'm not a child, Hugo. I may be inexperienced but I'm not such a naive fool not to know what we did was a normal and pleasurable thing a lot of couples do. Though I know we are not a couple, and I allowed you privileges that are ruinous in the eyes of society. You did not ruin me; there is no risk. So please don't wreck what just happened between us because you think I'm upset or violated in some way, because I'm not."

"I know you're not naive, but I do not want to hurt you." He leaned over and kissed her. "I cannot promise you anything at the moment and therefore I should not have touched one hair on your body."

"And yet, I'm so very glad you did." Lizzie smiled, clasping his jaw and running her hand over the prickly stubble. "You never did tell me what you're going to do when your uncle arrives. Are you going to talk to him about the will?"

"I am," he said, taking her hand and kissing her palm with little pecks. "I will ask him to reconsider taking the funds and instead leave them in the estate, allowing me to therefore marry whomever I choose."

"Do you think he'll agree?" And if he didn't, what did that mean for her? With very few words she could relieve

Hugo of all his troubles, especially as it looked as if he wanted her and not Miss Fox. The words hovered on the tip of her tongue that she was an heiress, that if he married her all his financial woes would be moot, but she did not.

To tell Hugo her secret would be breaking a promise to Lord Leighton, her cousin and the man who had enabled her future to be so secure in the first place. He'd made her promise not to let anyone know of her change in fortunes. He wanted to ensure that should she marry, the man would be worthy and in love.

But it was not only because of her cousin that Lizzie remained quiet. Her parents' marriage had not been a happy one, often plagued by frequent arguments and unbidden loathing. If she married Lord Wakely after telling him of her inheritance, how would she ever really know he married her because he loved her and not because he simply desired her more than Miss Fox? His choice was not easy and she wished she could help him, but this was one decision he would have to make on his own.

"That I can't tell you, but by God I hope he does. I couldn't stomach lo—"

Losing you. He didn't need to finish what he was saying for Lizzie to hear the unspoken words.

It was not too much to ask, and if they were meant to be together, she had to be patient and wait, allow Lord Wakely to realize that a life without love was no life at all. One could not buy happiness, and as the author of Sense and Sensibility advised herself, happiness in a pocketbook should not outweigh that of the heart.

CHAPTER 12

Hugo sat on one side of the desk at J. Smith & Sons Solicitors, listening as his father's final will and testament was read out loud to him again. This time in the presence of his uncle, his only remaining living relative. Not that the man cared for the sentiment–he'd been cold from the moment he arrived, and it didn't bode well for Hugo's strategy.

In appearance, his uncle was the male version of his mother, and it made Hugo nostalgic for her. Not to mention she would be appalled that her husband had done this to their only child. After today, if his uncle did not refuse to take the inheritance, Hugo would have very little to live on, or to keep his three estates running. Did his father not think out his final blow? To be so reckless with the lives of their tenants and their servants was reprehensible.

Hugo shook his head as the clause ordering him to marry an heiress was read aloud. He should have married as soon as he'd heard the will almost a year ago. Had he done so he wouldn't be sitting here today, on the brink of losing everything other than his title. His father might have stipulated for him to marry, but Hugo had wasted the past year with recklessness and endless enjoyment. This was as much his fault as anyone else's.

Mr. Thompson pulled off his pince-nez glasses and placed them on the mahogany table. "Now that you've heard the will and the stipulations, we may proceed."

Hugo's uncle leaned back in his chair, steepling his fingers. "I'm sorry that your father has placed you in this position, Hugo, I really am. But your family across the Atlantic is also in dire need of cash. I thought that you would've married by now and my trip over here wouldn't have been necessary, but I cannot deny that I'm happy you have not. I will be enforcing the clause and claiming the money Elizabeth was given as her dowry upon the marriage to your father."

The blow was like a quick uppercut to the nose. He fought not to cast up his accounts with the realization of what was about to happen. "Uncle, please. There are many who work for my estates, both as servants and tenant farmers, and their families. If you enable my father's clause to stand, if you enforce it, my suffering will be nothing compared to theirs. They will lose everything."

His uncle snipped the end of his cigar off and lit it, taking great puffs of smoke. He shrugged. "And I'm sorry for them, but I must think of my family, and the people who work for me."

"Could you compromise?" Mr. Thompson suggested. "Receive only half the funds so Lord Wakely can continue to run the estates?"

"No," his uncle said, shaking his head. "I'm not willing to compromise. I'm sorry it has come to this, Hugo, but you've had twelve months. Your father wrote to me explaining what he'd done, and while it may not be fair, your lifestyle has been frivolous to say the least. A point proven yet again by the fact that you've had nearly a year to marry and void this clause and you've not done so. Have you even found a woman whom you'd like as your wife? Have you even been looking?"

Hugo leaned back in his chair. He could feel his temper rising and took a couple of deep breaths to calm himself. "I think you're forgetting the clause that I'm only to marry an heiress."

"Are there not plenty of those about town?" His uncle dabbed out his cigar. "I'm sure you could marry some chit who's after a coronet and can offer blunt in return."

The image of Miss Fox came to mind, the very woman who could do exactly that. The thought left Hugo cold. He didn't want Miss Fox. In fact, he didn't want to marry a woman simply because she had money. "Of course there are women about town like that." But he didn't want one of those. Hell, he'd resigned himself to do just that so he could save his tenants and employees—a noble sacrifice—but then he'd gone and kissed Lizzie Doherty, and she'd opened his eyes to how great a sacrifice his actions would be. He wanted to marry a woman who was kind, passionate, and caring. One with whom he could converse and laugh freely, someone with whom he personally melded. He wanted her.

His uncle stood. "I'm sorry, my boy, I know you wanted the meeting today to go a different way, but alas it will not. I'll not change my mind, so I suggest you marry a rich debutante sooner rather than later, for you only have a week left before I claim the money. If you need me for anything, I'm staying at the Grand Hotel in Covent Garden until I sail on the first of the month."

Hugo watched him leave, and all his hopes along with them. "Well, that puts paid to that," he said to Mr.

Thompson, meeting his solicitor's gaze and hating the pity he read in his visage.

"I'm sorry, Lord Wakely. I know this wasn't what you wanted to hear."

"No, it wasn't." He rubbed a hand over his jaw. Whatever would he do? However would he manage the estates without sufficient money? Without funds, it would be impossible to maintain the estates and provide a living for the tenants and staff. And with the homes entailed, he wasn't able to sell them. They would, over time, simply rot.

"If I may be so bold as to ask if you've considered an heiress? A wedding can be arranged in under a week if need be. You may best your uncle yet and keep your money while satisfying your father's last request."

"By marrying an heiress, I will lose the woman I do care for. A woman who deserves so much more than what I've given her." He was to meet Lizzie tomorrow, and the thought of telling her the outcome of today's meeting left an unpleasant taste in his mouth. Although they had not spoken of marriage, the affection he felt for her, the hints he'd given to her, would no doubt have alerted her to his wanting more. And now he could give her nothing, for he was ruined. She deserved so much better than him.

Hugo stood, taking his gloves and walking stick from a waiting clerk. "Thank you, Mr. Thompson, for your assistance today. I'll see myself out." He left, and, making the street outside, stood for a moment in the warm afternoon sun. Still, he was chilled. What was he going to do? Could he place Lizzie before all who relied on him for their livelihood? Would she even marry him knowing all that he stood to lose?

He hailed a hackney and called out his address. He needed time to think about it all, to figure out what his best course of action would be. His steward was also arriving today to discuss the financials of his estates. Once that was completed he would know the best way forward, but whether the best way for the estates would also be the best way for him was yet to be seen.

LIZZIE SAT atop her white mare, quietly watching the other riders on Rotten Row. Some were enjoying a slow canter, while others, like her, were simply sitting, watching, waiting... She spied her groom waiting patiently a little way away from her, and frowned.

Where was he? She looked about the park again but couldn't see Lord Wakely approaching either on foot or horseback. She checked the time once again and her stomach knotted. Lord Wakely had sent a missive to meet him here–had something happened to him? He was over two hours late.

She turned her mare toward the northern gate. She would return home. Maybe there was a missive waiting for her. A reason as to why he hadn't come.

The thought crossed her mind that it had been a deliberate snub, and she shook it aside. She didn't want to think like that. It was neither helpful nor nice, and until she knew for certain, then and only then would she worry about it.

But upon returning home and finding no note, she couldn't help but surmise his meeting with his uncle and the solicitor the day before had not gone well. Which meant Lord Wakely had a decision to make. Marry Miss Fox and her thousands of pounds, a marriage of convenience and little affection, if any. Or, he could marry her, a woman whom he believed to have no dowry, but would love him unconditionally until the day she died. If only he'd prove his worth and choose her.

The thought again crossed her mind that she should tell him she would have enough dowry to satisfy his father's will, and therefore no money from his estate would be lost to his uncle. Hugo did care for her a great deal, and maybe more than she believed. He wouldn't be struggling with his choice if he did not. Maybe she ought to bring it up with her cousin Lord Leighton and seek his counsel. See if he thought it time that Lord Wakely knew the truth, especially in light of him being on the brink of losing his inheritance.

There were so many people reliant on Lord Wakely's estate. In total he would have hundreds of people, with hundreds more counting their families, who needed employment, and who would suffer if they were to lose their positions. Knowing all this, surely Lord Leighton would reconsider his decision on keeping her status as a wealthy woman secret. The last thing Lizzie wanted was to be the cause for so many people suffering when she had the power to stop it.

She thought back to their times together. Other than not turning up today, he'd never done anything that would give her any cause for alarm. He was attentive and trust-worthy. Surely knowing she was an heiress wouldn't be the sole reason why he would offer for her. She usually had a good understanding of people's characters, and Lord Wakely's, for all his roguish past, was good-natured and honest.

❧

LATER THAT AFTERNOON Lizzie sat before her cousin Lord Leighton in his library. He idly flicked through some papers and she waited patiently, her mind a whirr of thoughts over how to go about explaining this predicament so that she might change his mind regarding the secrecy about her dowry.

He placed the papers into a folder, then, clasping his hands on his desk, gave her his full attention. "Sorry, Lizzie. I just had to finish that piece of business. Now, what was it you wished to talk with me about?"

Nerves pitted in her stomach and she pushed them aside. Her cousin would see sense, he was a good man. She was sure of it. "I wanted to speak to you about a gentleman whom I believe I would like to consider marrying. And before I tell you who it is, I need you to promise me you'll not get angry with me. He's probably not who you thought I would look toward to be my husband."

Lord Leighton leaned back in his chair, crossing his arms. Lizzie ignored the fact it was a defensive stance and instead steeled herself to remain calm and discuss the situation like the grown adults that they both were.

"Who is this gentleman?" he asked, his voice weary.

"The gentleman is Lord Wakely." At the mention of Hugo's name, Lord Leighton sat bolt upright in his chair, his eyes wide in shock.

"Hugo? You cannot possibly be serious. What on earth makes you believe he's even looking for a wife? He's not exactly the most settled gentleman in London. If anything, he's quite the rogue."

"I know all about his past. You've been friends with him for years, and I'm not blind. But he is looking for a wife, and I believe should he know of my financial situation he would offer for me."

"You mean he would marry you if he knew you were rich. Absolutely not." His words brooked no argument and Lizzie took a calming breath.

"Listen, there is more to the story than that. Let me explain."

"Well, I certainly hope you will, for as it stands right now my answer is not to agree to whatever you're going to ask me."

Lizzie threw him a quelling look and continued. "The reason his uncle is here is because of his father's will. His sire had included a clause in his will that Lord Wakely was to marry within twelve months of his death, and also to an heiress of no less than thirty thousand pounds. If he does not, his mother's dowry money will revert to her American family. But you see," she continued, "he's been courting me, believing I have no dowry, and now he's conflicted. I could remove that conflict from his life. If I told him of my fortune, he would not be struggling with his choice, for I believe he would choose me."

"Over Miss Fox I gather, if the talk through the *ton* is any indication."

Lizzie nodded. "Yes, that's right. Lord Wakely has so many people relying on him, so many staff and dependents. If he were to lose his inheritance, then with what would he run the estates? If he married me he would adhere to the clause, and therefore no money would be lost. I want to tell him, Hamish. Will you give me permission?"

Lord Leighton rubbed his jaw while he thought about her request. "As much as I would like to say yes, Lizzie, I cannot. I know Lord Wakely, very well, and if he really wanted to marry you he would find another way in which to raise the money required to run his estates. Surely marrying an heiress is not his only option."

Lizzie frowned, wondering if he had considered other ways. "Even if there was another way, he's left it a little late now. He's to marry before the end of the month. And if he's not married, he loses that money. I could stop that."

"But why should you be his saviour? He's in this situation because of the way he lived his life, something he knew his father loathed. As much as I care for Lord Wakely, and would help him if I could, I cannot allow you to be the reason he remains one of the richest men in England. Lord Wakely should have other means of income—investments, art, anything that is not entailed that would help him marry whomever he wanted."

Lizzie bit back the tears that threatened as her future with Lord Wakely vanished before her eyes. She sniffed and Hamish shifted in his chair.

"I'll tell you what, I shall speak to him, see what we can figure out. Maybe he's not tried any other options, or not thought of them. I want a good marriage for you, my dear. I've seen too many unions within the *ton* that are toxic and barely civilized. Your parents' marriage was one of them, as if I need remind you. Katherine and I love you, and want the man who marries you to love you unconditionally, not because of how much money they gain from the union."

Lizzie pulled out her handkerchief and dabbed at her nose. "Just because Lord Wakely would marry me because I had a fortune, does not mean that he does not care for me. Love me even. He's responsible for so many. The choice would not be easy. I would think should you have been in the same situation with Katherine, you would've faltered too. I know how much you care for your tenant farmers, your staff. Can you honestly tell me that you would not marry for money to keep all of that side of your life safe?"

He cringed, meeting her gaze. "You forget I married a woman who wasn't my social equal. I broke all the rules to have Katherine by my side and I would do it all again. But as a business owner with estates such as I and Lord Wakely have, these are businesses, they are homes entrusted into our care for the next generation. I expected to run those properties, put into place secure investments, and have the best stewards around so I never needed to marry an heiress to keep it all safe. Lord Wakely has not done that, and now he is paying the price. You said he's had twelve months. Pray tell me, what has he done in that time to shore up his homes so that he could lose the money and still marry you?"

Lizzie stared at her cousin, her mind conflicted over what to do. "I do not think he's done anything, my lord." All hope fled, and she didn't think she could feel any more dejected than she did right at that moment.

"Neither do I." Lord Leighton stood and came around the desk, pulling her to stand. "I promised you six years ago that I would ensure you married a man who would love and cherish you always. I will speak to Lord Wakely and see if he's worthy of you. Maybe he does have other plans you're not privy to. If he does, I'll give you my consent. If not, then I'm sorry Lizzie, but I cannot give you away to such a life. I will not release your inheritance simply to line an impoverished man's pockets."

CHAPTER 13

Later that night Lizzie ordered a bath and then declined going out with Lord Leighton and Katherine, who were attending a private dinner. She dismissed her maid for the night, wanting to soak in the bath and plan. How could she show Lord Wakely that they were perfect for one another?

After her conversation this afternoon with her cousin, all hope of a life with Hugo seemed to have disappeared. But that did not mean she could not try one last time to have him offer for her, penniless as he thought she was. She couldn't tell him the truth, Lord Leighton had not allowed that, but perhaps if he was with her again, he would tell her of his plans to secure his estates and those who relied on him that didn't include an heiress.

Her fingers tapped the side of the bath and, knowing what she would do, she stood and dried herself quickly. She dressed in a simple gown with buttons at the front, one she could manage without a maid, and pulled on the darkest cloak she owned.

Opening her bedroom door, she checked for servants,

and seeing none, scuttled across the hall to the stairs, stopping again to check who was about. Hearing no one and assuming that the staff were eating their supper, she went down the stairs and started for the back of the house. The back parlor had doors that led out into the yard and a side gate that she could use to slip out.

It didn't take very long to reach Lord Wakely's house, as he lived within a couple of blocks, and in this part of London, with many couples out walking just as she was, Lizzie felt reasonably safe. Just like her cousin's home, Lord Wakely had a side alley that one could access the backyard through. Coming to the wooden gate, she checked her surroundings then pushed it open, closing it quickly behind her.

The house was dark apart from a couple of lamps burning in the upstairs rooms. Movement behind a door that led out onto a small balcony and the silhouette which Lizzie would recognize anywhere told her it was his lordship.

She pursed her lips, surveying the home. There was no way she could climb up to his floor from the outside, so she had to find a way to sneak in from below. Pulling her cloak tighter about her neck and ensuring the cape covered her hair, she inched her way across the garden and toward the back door, of which there were two. One led into the kitchens, if the sound of clanging pots and loud chatter was any indication. Lizzie took her chances on the other door, and sagged in relief when she turned the handle and found it unlocked.

Stepping into a darkened passage, a door slammed somewhere close by. She froze as panic seized her that she would be caught. The sound was followed by silence, no hurried footsteps or staff talking amongst themselves, so she continued on.

Walking quickly through the hall, she came to the servant's stairs and ran up them toward the first floor. Exiting through a door, she came to a shadowy, sparsely lit hall. She tried to gauge her whereabouts, based on when she'd looked at the house from the outside.

It was not easy as most of the rooms' doors were closed, bar one that was slightly ajar and had the faintest flicker of candlelight peeking out. She took a chance and tiptoed up to the door, her stomach in knots over what she was about to do, what she was about to offer Lord Wakely.

Would he send her away? Would he take her in his arms and tell her his absence today was a mistake? She wasn't sure how his reaction would play out. Reaching the door, she peeked through the gap to see his lordship shirtless, clad only in tan breeches. He was sitting at the end of his bed, flipping through a document of some sort. He was completely lost in his own thoughts, the frown lines between his brows indicating that whatever he was reading was complicated or troubling. Her need to go to him doubled. She'd never seen him look so wretched, and if she could she'd put a stop to it tonight.

She entered the room and shut the door quickly, the snip of the lock loud in the otherwise quiet space. The shock on Hugo's face was comical and her lips twitched.

"What are you doing here?" he asked, the papers in his hands dropping to his feet as he stood.

Lizzie swallowed, fighting to bring forth all the determination she'd felt coming over here. Tonight she would have Lord Wakely if he'd allow, and with any luck he would realize that what they had between them wasn't like anything he'd encountered before. It was so for Lizzie at least, and she was willing to risk her reputation to be with Hugo if it meant that she could win him.

Never before had she wanted anything as much as she

wanted the man who stood before her, his mouth agape, his chest rising and lowering rapidly with every breath. Should she not win his heart, it was not for want of trying, and she wouldn't win another's after tonight. If Lord Wakely turned her away, she would wait out her time, accept her fortune, and leave London. Travel the world, go to Italy and buy an olive farm, and adopt stray cats just because she could.

"You didn't arrive at our ride today. I was worried."

He cringed. "I'm sorry, Lizzie. The meeting with my solicitor didn't go well and I forgot. Do you forgive me?"

She strode over to him and pushed him back onto the bed. He bounced, his eyes widening in surprise. She took charge and, steeling her back, climbed onto the bed and straddled his waist. "There is nothing to forgive. And as for what I'm really doing here, well," she said, sliding her hands over his muscular shoulders and enjoying the feel of his skin beneath her palms, "I'm seducing you, my lord."

If she thought she'd shocked him before it was nothing to how he looked now. Totally flabbergasted and without words he stared up at her, before his face darkened in hunger and he flipped her over, pinning her to the bed.

She squealed, having not expected the move, and her stomach clenched in delicious tremors. Ever since their first kiss she'd dreamed of being with him so. Of touching him, kissing him, without the threat of interruption.

"You have no idea how much I've wanted you beneath me, just as you are now." He bent down and kissed her, a sweet, soft melding of lips that left her following him as he pulled away. Wanting more of the same, not less. Never less. "Before we go any further, tell me why you're here. I need to hear it."

Lizzie shivered at the deep, tightly harnessed need she

heard in his voice. She wanted to break that control, see what he was like in his full, wild glory.

"I'm here because I want to be with you. I want you to make love to me." *Love me as I love you.* Heat bloomed on her cheeks and she bit her lip, hoping he wouldn't push her away. That she hadn't been wrong in what she knew to be between them.

He leaned back, running his finger over her cloak, untying it from her neck and pushing it aside to lay about her like a halo. "I shouldn't allow this. You're a maid. I'd be the worst rogue to walk the earth to have you like this."

Lizzie studied him a moment, waiting to see what he would choose. It had to be his choice. She would not beg.

He frowned, shutting his eyes. "Damn it, Lizzie, but I cannot stay away." He slid one hand down her legs and clasped the hem of her gown, pushing it up to bunch at her waist. "I want you naked beneath me. I want to see all that you are. I will, however," he said, throwing her a mischievous grin, "allow your silk stockings to remain."

Heat pooled at her core and she writhed, needing him to touch her. "How very naughty of you, my lord."

"Hugo, please. No titles between us. Not ever again."

Lizzie was only too willing to do as he asked, and in a flurry of movement he had divested them both of their garments. The clothes lay pooled about the bed, and Lizzie chuckled as he came back over her, his hair askew, his eyes bright with expectation.

She fought to control her body, that no longer felt like her own. The touches he bestowed as he stripped her naked left her aching, and not for the first time she clenched her thighs if only to give herself a little relief.

The hair on his chest tickled, the skin on his back was warm and smooth, and he had the most intoxicating smell of sandalwood and something else that was solely Hugo.

He kissed her deeply, seducing her with his mouth, and she gave way to the sensations, the want she had for him.

So this was why her cousin's wife always looked at her husband with such love and reverence. Why their marriage was a loving and obviously passionate one. Hugo lowered his head to her breast, taking one nipple between his lips before licking it with sweet teasing. She moaned, her fingers spiking into his hair to hold him against her. "That's wicked, Hugo."

He blew on her nipple and it puckered at the chill, before he licked it once again. "I want you so much it hurts. From the first moment I saw you enter Lady X's parlor I knew I had to have you. That I wanted you and would never allow another to touch one hair on your pretty head." He placed a soft kiss against her lips. "But are you sure, Lizzie? There is no coming back from this action should we proceed. You will no longer be a maid."

She cupped his cheek, the prickling of his stubble rough against her palm. "I no longer care about being a maid. I've wanted this too for so long, much longer than you'll ever know, and there is nothing in the world that will stop me from what we're about to do."

"You've wanted me for some time?" He rocked against her core, spiking need throughout her body.

"Oh, yes," she gasped, not entirely in reply to his question but also due to his actions. "I noticed you long before you ever noticed me."

"Hmm, you may be wrong about that."

She ran her hand against the nape of his neck and pulled him down to her. "Really? Tell me then."

He stared at her a moment before a mischievous smile tweaked his lips. "The only reason I did not act before now was due to my friendship with Lord Leighton. Of all the people in the *ton*, he knows of my past, my indiscretions. I knew he would not look favourably on my courting of you. But when I saw you at Lady X's, all bets were off."

Lizzie lifted her leg to sit up against his hip. The action brought him closer to her and desire ran hot through his gaze. Warmth pooled at her core and she longed for him to continue what they'd started. "They like you, in spite of your rakish tendencies."

A muscle worked in his jaw and he stared at her a moment. "Lord Leighton will never forgive me for what we're about to do."

"He'll never know," she said, sliding her hands down his back to clasp his buttocks. She pulled him against her, helping to dispense some of her need.

He swore, sucking in a startled breath. "True," he managed.

And with those words he settled against her fully, and with painful care guided himself into her. The sensation was odd, but not wholly unpleasant. Her mother had spoken of searing pain, and tedious annoyance until one ripened with a child. But this, this right now with Hugo, was anything but tedious, anything but painful.

It was delightful.

Taking a deep breath, Lizzie tried to relax and understand the fullness, the sensations that were swarming through her body. Hugo did not rush her. With perfect care, he allowed her to get used to his size before pulling out a little, only to then thrust back within her.

The dance made her crave him even more, and she soon found herself moving with him. He kissed her throughout and she gasped when pleasure thrummed at her core.

"I do not want to hurt you, Lizzie." His voice sounded strained and she shook her head, words eluding her for a moment.

"You're not hurting me." She kissed him deep and long, sliding her tongue against his, the kaleidoscope of feelings he brought forth almost too much to contain. "Keep going. Don't ever stop."

He pushed deeper, and she moaned, her body breathless, a light sheen of sweat chilling her skin. His actions became frantic, harder, more demanding, and yet something was missing. It was like a peak was out of her reach, teasing her close by before floating away.

"I feel…I want…oh dear, I do not know what I want," she gasped as he continued his onslaught of her emotions.

He leaned down, kissing her ear. "You desire pleasure. Not that you know what that is yet, but I'm about to show you." He slid his hand between them and touched her mons. With each thrust he flicked across her flesh. He owned her. At this very time Lizzie would allow him to do anything he pleased if only he would never stop.

What was he doing to her? This love making was more intense, the sensations more vivid than when they were together at Lady X's. It was as if she could shatter into a million pieces and still remain whole. With one last flick, he thrust into her hard, and the peak she had climbed but never assailed crested. She tumbled into unimaginable pleasure, calling out his name as wave after wave flowed through her.

There were no words for the delectable tremors and pulsating thrums that overtook her body. Hugo gasped out her name, kissing her as his thrusts, hard and constant, battered her body. But before his release, he pulled out, stroking himself above her belly. Lizzie watched enthralled as he found his release outside of her, and she couldn't stop herself from reaching out and touching him, sliding her hand about his shaft and helping him find his pleasure.

Their eyes met and held, and with his look Lizzie

tumbled over into love with him. There would never be anyone else but Hugo for her. They were simply meant to be.

He flopped beside her, then, reaching over to the bedside cabinet, he grabbed a discarded cravat and wiped her belly clean. "I do apologize, it can be a messy business."

She didn't care about any of that. All she cared about was when they would meet next. Hugo seemed to be thinking the same.

"When can I see you again? I do not think I can go a day without being near you," he stated, throwing the cravat onto the floor.

Lizzie rolled over and snuggled against his chest. His arm circled her shoulder and kept her close. "I'm attending the Ramsays' masquerade two nights from now. I'm dressing as Queen Elizabeth with a blue satin mask if you wish to seek me out."

"I will find you."

Her heart warmed at his words, and as the clock chimed the late hour she sighed, sitting up. "I need to go before I'm missed. Will you help me dress?"

He slid his hand over her bare back, following the line of her spine and making her shiver. "I would like you to stay."

Lizzie turned to look at him and grinned. "I think we both know that cannot happen, but we'll meet again. In two days in fact, and I shall reserve the first waltz if you wish."

Hugo sat up, pushing her hair over her shoulder to pool across her breast before kissing her nape. "I should not miss it for the world."

CHAPTER 14

I f Lord Wakely was a rogue, Lizzie most definitely was fast. She grinned and continued her stroll through Hyde Park, her maid a short distance behind her immersed in a booklet about the different plant species found in England. Lizzie looked up between the green leaves of the trees, and breathed deep the fresh air and warm dappled sunlight. From the moment she'd left Hugo's bed the other night, the world had seemed brighter somehow, more alive and vivid.

And she was a fallen woman, well and truly, and for some illogical reason she was pleased by the knowledge. Maybe because after what they shared they were a little more even in their knowledge. The fact that she'd seduced *him* in the end too had taken the choice out of his lordship's hands. Seizing what she wanted had brought pride to her soul. Never before had she been so bold or determined, and now that she'd lain with Hugo she wanted nothing more than to do it again.

Be damned the consequences.

"Good afternoon, Miss Doherty. How providential to run into you here at the park."

Butterflies took flight in her stomach and she clasped her abdomen to calm her nerves. "Lord Wakely," she said, dipping into a curtsy. "It is lovely to see you again."

Although they would see each other this evening at the masked ball, the last two days had been endless. Lizzie had debated seeking his lordship out once more, but in the end decided against it. Even if they were lovers, she didn't wish him to think she was so desperate for his touch that she couldn't wait thirty-six hours. She needed him to want her as much as she wanted him. He was the one who needed to fall in love with her, ask for her hand in marriage, and somehow come up with a plan that would solve his money troubles without having to marry an heiress.

"Are you looking forward to the ball tonight, my lord?" A wicked gleam entered the viscount's eyes and Lizzie chuckled.

"I am. *Very* much so." They walked on and the answering smile from Hugo told Lizzie he understood her meaning. She leaned toward him to ensure privacy. "Where shall we meet?"

His eyes warmed with appreciation and desire. He placed her hand atop his arm and continued to stroll. "Sir Ramsay's home has two servant staircases. Use the one closest to the ballroom. If you go into the entrance hall, under the guise of using the retiring room, and turn toward the back of the house, the staircase is to your right. I will wait for you on the stairs."

"And then what?" Lizzie met Hugo's eyes, and the heat she read in them left her in no doubt as to what they would do after that. Although she would like to hear it nevertheless.

"I shall lead you up to one of the guest bedrooms,

where I shall strip every article of clothing from your person. I shall kiss every inch of your body and bring you to pleasure using nothing but my mouth," he whispered against her ear, the breath of his words making her shiver.

Heat suffused her cheeks, but she dismissed her embarrassment, too enthralled with the thought of what he was going to do. What could he possibly mean? She thought on his words a moment and couldn't figure out what it meant, but even so, it would prove to be a delicious night if he made her feel anything like she did two nights ago.

"Is what you're saying even possible?" She had to know, wanted a visual to look forward to until they met this evening. And Lord Wakely could kiss very well, his mouth was most talented, so he probably could do what he promised if he remained determined.

"You shall be pleasantly surprised by what my mouth can do with the help of my tongue."

Oh, my...

"And in return you shall pleasure me with yours if you like."

Lizzie shut her mouth with a snap as a myriad of thoughts entered her mind. And if her thoughts were correct, well, how scandalous. How cocooned she'd lived, having no idea that couples even did such a thing.

She checked to see the location of her maid, sighing in relief when she found her engrossed in her book and a safe distance away from them. "How is that even possible?" she whispered, intrigued.

"Think on it and tonight you can tell me if you figured it out." Hugo stepped back and bowed. "Until this evening, Miss Doherty."

Lizzie curtsied. "Good day, Lord Wakely." She watched him walk away, annoyed a little at his refusal to tell her what she wanted to know. He looked back at her and grinned over his shoulder, and excitement thrummed through her blood. Tonight couldn't come soon enough. Turning about, she summoned her maid to return home. She needed to take a bath and get ready. And maybe sneak down to the library and try to find out for herself what Hugo meant about the pleasure a woman could give a man using her mouth. There had to be something to explain his cryptic taunt.

BY THE TIME HUGO ARRIVED, the ball was in full swing and the room was full to capacity. The hundreds of wax candles above the ballroom floor were surrounded by a smoke haze thanks to the men who were enjoying their cigars and cheroots, discussing politics or horses while watching the dancers and society at play.

Being sociable wasn't on Hugo's mind this evening, but having Lizzie again was. It was all he'd thought about the last two days. After seeing her this afternoon he was without doubt that he cared for her more than anyone ever in his life. He longed to talk with her, to walk as they had in the park, to confide and trust in her, not just have her warm his bed.

But as to actually marrying her, he was still undecided. So much hung on his decision. He now had only days left before he would lose his mother's fortune, leaving him with little to run the estates. Miss Fox strode past him, her black silk gown and mask suiting her dark nature. She nodded her head in greeting and he bowed, watching her. If he married Miss Fox all his troubles would be over. He would keep his fortune, and his estates would be safe. But Lizzie would be lost to him. He ran a hand over his jaw. There had to be another way to keep his estates afloat. But how?

Never in his life had he hated his father as much as he hated him now.

He spied his quarry in a sapphire gown, the blue of her mask bringing out the color of her eyes. The large ornate collar and her red hair made it easy to figure out he'd found his queen. She stood beside her mother, who had obviously decided not to wear a costume. The small upturn of Lizzie's lips told him she'd spied him as well, and warmth spread through his blood. Without delay he headed in her direction.

He bowed before them. "Good evening, Mrs. Doherty, Miss Doherty," he said. "I wonder, Miss Doherty, if you would care to dance. I believe the next set is to be a waltz."

"I would love to dance, thank you, Lord Wakely." Lizzie took his arm, not giving her mother any consideration as he led her out onto the floor. He twirled her into his arms just as the music started, she laughed at being handled so.

Lizzie was the most delightful creature he'd ever met, carefree and honest. Panic seized him at the thought that he adored her and yet might not be able to keep her for himself. Not if he couldn't find a solution to his problem.

She fitted him so perfectly, in so many ways, that he couldn't help but wonder why it was that he'd never really seen her before. Before his father had passed. Had he done so, had his sire seen him marry, he would never have punished him with the clause in the will that now stood. He would've been happy for Hugo, happy the title had a future and the possibility of heirs. In all truth, the reason he was in this predicament was solely due to his own self-ishness and refusal to grow up.

"Has anyone ever told you, Lord Wakely, that you dance divinely?"

He maneuvered them around other couples with

expert ease. "They may have, but yours is the first opinion that I've cared to hear."

"You flatter me, my lord." She smiled up at him. Something in his chest ached and he couldn't help but grin back at the little minx.

"I do flatter you because you deserve to be flattered. Tonight, tomorrow, and all the days that follow." Her startled expression caught him unawares, possibly as unaware as his own words. Next he'd be quoting poetry and writing love sonnets to her. The idea didn't wholly disgust him, and that in itself was telling.

Shit, he cared for Lizzie, more than he'd ever cared for anyone. The overwhelming need to know that she was well, happy, and safe overrode all his other concerns, even those regarding his estates and tenants. How would he ever give her up simply so he could keep his fortune?

"You should not say such things, or I'll start to think you're a romantic like Lord Byron."

He pulled her closer than he ought, fighting the urge to wrench her hard against his chest and never let her go. "Not ever will I be as bad as Lord Byron."

Lizzie moved perfectly in tune with him, and the feel of her silk gown sliding beneath his hand reminded him of their night of passion. Her gloved hand on his shoulder tightened a little and he met her gaze, wishing he could drown in her deep blue eyes.

"Shall we agree that after the next set we shall reacquaint ourselves in the location discussed?" she said, her eyes bright with mischief.

Hugo cleared his throat as lust roared through him. "I...yes."

She all but purred in his arms, and the knowledge that within the hour they would be pleasuring each other made the short sixty minutes seem too far away. He slowed them as they turned at the bottom of the ballroom floor, before making their way up along the other side. "I don't believe I've told you how very beautiful you look this evening."

"You just did." Lizzie laughed, a throaty, seductive sound that made him harden in an instant.

"Before I have the urge to place you on my shoulders and carry you out of here like a caveman, tell me what you've been doing the last two days, other than the time we met in the park of course. I'm hoping you've been a little more productive than myself. I have struggled to have coherent thoughts since you left my bedroom."

"Is this your way of telling me that you've missed me, my lord? You do know that for a man of your reputation, you're putting it in danger by saying such things. Anyone would think that you longed to see me again. That you cared."

How true that was. Lizzie was the only thing that had occupied his mind for the past two days. In fact, before he espied her in the park he'd even considered sending for his stable staff to prepare two horses, so they could go riding. It was only luck that he'd come by her in Hyde Park.

He watched her as they danced and the thought of her being married to some other gentleman made his guts clench. She would never do for anyone else, since she fitted him so perfectly. And yet, while he wished she could be his, if he made it so, he would lose everything. His tenants would lose everything.

He scoffed and pulled them into a tight turn, knowing how unfair and selfish he was being. To give hope where there was none was not something he should do, and yet he could not help himself. He didn't want to give her up. Didn't want to be in this position.

"What are you scowling at, my lord? You seem very fierce at the moment."

Hugo shook his thoughts aside and made himself more congenial. "Tell me more about you. I want to know everything."

She sighed, possibly in relief, and threw herself into the new topic. "Well," she said, frowning a little in thought, "I enjoy horses and riding more so than I like being out in society. That was always Mama's idea, and her desire to find me a good husband. I hate seafood but love sweets. I enjoy shopping, and going to horse races. As you know, I want to travel to Italy one day, possibly even live there for a time."

"I have been to Rome. It's a wonderful city, full of history, and the streets smell of olives and herbs."

She chuckled. "It doesn't smell like that, you made that up."

He laughed. "I did, it doesn't smell the best, but it is old. Ancient, in fact. You will love it when you get there, which I have no doubt you will accomplish one day."

"What else can you tell me about it? I'd love to know."

For the remainder of the dance Hugo told Lizzie about his entire trip abroad and the wonderful people he had met along the way. He spoke of the ruins of the Circus Maximus, the Colosseum and the gladiatorial bouts that had occurred there, how unbelievably majestic it must have been to see it during its glory days. Of the beautiful villas, and the bathhouses, some of which still ran today. As they talked, their discussion turned to other subjects, that of books and what authors they enjoyed, including one in particular that they did not agree about.

"She's not at all writing a sensible story. I highly doubt the Bennett sisters would've found such high and well-connected marriages in real life."

"I'm not titled, although I do have a gentleman father, may he rest in peace, and a cousin who's titled, and yet here I am, talking to a viscount. And," she added, looking about them, "from the annoyed glances I'm getting from some of the ladies present, I can only assume they're put out with me taking up so much of an eligible man's time."

"You deserve my whole attention." It took all of Hugo's control not to lean down and kiss her. Warmth spread through his chest and he could barely wait to have her alone.

Everything that Lizzie and he had spoken of was intelligent and noteworthy. They had not agreed on everything, and she did not shy away from telling him her opinion, or when she thought his was misplaced.

Hugo had never been able to stomach the idea of a wife who had no independent thought. He doubted that Miss Fox would even care about his opinion or giving hers. Her interest in him had never been anything other than an alliance—a contract.

In the weeks since they'd returned from Lady X's house party, Lizzie had become a woman who demanded his respect and admiration. The dance came to an end and, taking her hand and placing it on his arm, he started back toward her mama. "It's eleven o'clock. In fifteen minutes, meet me in the stairway as planned."

She nodded but didn't reply, simply curtsied and rejoined her parent. Hugo lingered for a couple of minutes before heading toward where they would rendezvous. Excitement thrummed through his blood at having her to himself, alone and away from the *ton*'s prying eyes. Very, very alone, where they could get to know each other a little more, but in the biblical sense.

LIZZIE SLOWLY WANDERED over toward the ballroom doors, and when she was certain no one was watching what she was doing, she exited the room, walking quickly toward the servant's stairs where Hugo said he would be waiting.

Finding the door that was made to look like the wall, she pushed it open and slipped away, shutting it quickly and standing there a moment to adjust her vision to the darkened space.

She stifled a scream when he stepped out of the shadows and wrapped his arm about her waist, taking the opportunity to kiss her softly. Lizzie threw herself against him, her body tight and longing for more. It seemed like weeks since she'd been with him intimately, not only a couple of days. The man was addictive and she was sorely suffering cravings when not around him.

"Where to from here?" she whispered when he finally broke away.

He pulled her toward the stairs. "Follow me." They travelled up two flights of stairs before Hugo peeked out into the hall and, seeing it clear of anyone else, pulled her into a room across the way and locked the door.

It was a guest chamber, clean but sparsely furnished. An emerald duvet sat on the bed, and the curtains of the same color hung across the two windows that faced the square. There was a chaise lounge before the unlit fireplace.

"Come here," Hugo said, his voice deep, his eyes warm and inviting.

Lizzie's body didn't feel like her own and she all but thrummed with pent-up excitement as she walked over to him and wrapped her arms about his neck. "What do you plan on doing with me, Lord Wakely?" she asked, although she had a fair idea just what he was going to do with her, and she couldn't wait for the pleasure of it.

"I want you to lie on the bed and lift up that beautiful gown so I may kiss you to climax."

Oh my… Without delay, Lizzie did as he bade. Her gown was heavy but with Hugo's help she soon had it ruffled up about her waist. The cool night air kissed her skin and she shivered. He kneeled, then placed his large hands on either side of her legs and pushed outwards, his eyes dark with need and admiration.

Never had she been so exposed, so vulnerable, but even so, she trusted him, knew he would never do anything that she did not want.

He pulled her toward him, placing her mons right before his mouth.

"You're so beautiful," he said, running his finger over her flesh, paying homage to her nubbin that she now knew existed after their previous encounters, and knew just how pleasurable that part of her body could be.

"Stop teasing me, my lord. I cannot bear another second." If he did not touch her soon she would expire. And then his hot breath moved up her thigh with slow tenderness before his lips kissed her *there…*

Lizzie sucked in a breath, unsure as to what she was feeling having him do what he was. The sensation was odd, but when he flicked her with his tongue she couldn't halt the moan that slipped free.

Heat spread across her cheeks and she closed her eyes and allowed herself to just enjoy, forget the embarrassment at being so open to him, under his complete control, and simply give in to what his fabulously clever mouth could do.

Her hands speared into his hair, and she found herself undulating under his touch. How would she ever live without such tactile contact with a man after experiencing such rich pleasures? The thought of Lord Wakely doing this to another woman left her emotionally spent and she pushed the vision away. He was hers, she was sure of it. Such passion and joy was surely uncommon, only happened between couples who cared for each other deeply.

His pace, his ardent response between her legs increased and she shut her eyes, reveling in his touch. "Hugo," she gasped as he slid one long, strong finger into her heat. The sensation of his touch and his tongue was too much and she shattered in his arms, allowing the pleasure to rock through her over and over again as he kissed and drew every last ounce out of her body.

He came over her, his gaze serious. Laying beneath him, Lizzie's bones resembled jelly and she wanted nothing more than to sleep, to curl up in his arms and be with him like this forever.

She reached up and traced his lips with her finger. "Such a wicked man with such a clever mouth."

He flopped beside her, leaning up on one elbow. The sound of voices carried to them from the passage outside and Lizzie stilled. Hugo sat up, pulling her skirts down quickly and fixing his cravat.

"I saw Lizzie went this way, Mrs. Doherty. If you'll follow me."

Lizzie met Hugo's eyes, all traces of pleasure gone.

"That was Lady Leighton and your mother. You must return to the ball and say you stepped outside onto the terrace for air. Tell them you were feeling unwell and needed some time away from the crush of the ball."

Lizzie nodded, standing and fixing her gown some more before checking her hair was back in place. "I'm sorry I couldn't… In any case, goodnight, Hugo."

He pulled her to a stop when she stepped toward the

door, and cupping her cheek he kissed her. "Goodnight, Lizzie. We will meet again."

She nodded and slipped away, returning to the ball the way she'd escaped it. Oh yes, she would see him again. Again and again, if only he would choose her.

CHAPTER 15

Hugo sat at his desk and glared at Lord Leighton, one of his oldest and closest friends. But after today that was in doubt, and especially after what he had just said. Hugo would be lucky if the man didn't pummel him to a pulp.

"Katherine saw you, and had it not been for her quick thinking Lizzie's mother would've entered that room and seen who knows what. How dare you disobey me after I told you to stay the hell away from my cousin!"

Hugo had never seen Hamish so angry, and should he find himself in Lord Leighton's situation he could understand his temper. However, Hugo could not help what he'd come to feel for Lizzie. He could no sooner stay away from her than the sea could stay away from the sea bed. It was impossible.

"Do you love her?" Hamish asked him, his eyes as hard as his tone.

Hugo shifted on his chair, having not thought whether what he felt for Lizzie was love. He certainly cared for her a great deal, wanted only the best for her, but love? That he couldn't say. "I don't know what I feel for her, but what I do know is that I have a decision to make, one that is not easy. I care for Lizzie, more than I thought I could care about anyone in the world, but I don't believe it's love." The words spoken aloud rang an alarm in his mind and he frowned. Denying the emotion seemed wrong, didn't sit well with him, and his stomach turned.

"Then tonight at our ball you will announce your betrothal to Miss Fox. She will be in attendance and it would be the perfect location to tell the *ton*. Lizzie no doubt will be upset, but at least she may retire to her rooms, away from prying eyes and gossiping tongues."

"I will not do that to her so publicly. How could you ask such a thing of me? Do you not care for your cousin at all?"

The fury on Hamish's visage gave Hugo pause and he wondered if he'd pushed the earl too far. "I love my cousin, and care for her a great deal, have cared for her for the past six years. Had you not been a blind fool you might have seen her pining after you all these years, but you were too busy dipping your wick about town and now it's too late. You told me yourself of the financial predicament you find yourself in." The earl paused, taking a calming breath. "You had twelve months to look into other options to secure your estate. Such actions might have given you the ability to marry anyone you wished and whenever you wanted. Tell me, what have you been doing with your time, Hugo? Because to me it looks like you've been a sloppy viscount."

"I've been a fool, I know that now. I should have done more than to decide to marry an heiress to solve my problems. But I never banked on Lizzie being as wonderful as she is. To have her I must lose everything, and yet I find myself not wanting to make the decision either."

"Lizzie cannot help you with your financial difficulties, therefore you need to choose. You either offer for Miss Fox and her thousands of pounds or you offer for my cousin. But I will not allow you to tamper with her emotions any longer. She deserves a man to pick her, to love her for who she is. Are you that man, Hugo? Are you willing to risk all that you have, to have her in your life?"

Hugo swallowed, unsure what he wanted. Oh, who was he kidding? He wanted Lizzie, in all the ways a man wants a woman, and a husband wants a wife. But by doing so his tenants and the servants at his country estates would be unemployed overnight. Their livelihoods gone without notice. He could not do that either. Hamish had said he'd been a sloppy viscount. Well, at least there he might be able to make amends for his wrongs.

Lizzie deserved more than what he could give her. He could give her affection, passion, but little else. They would be forced to live in London, with no country estates, no house parties, and their living would be frugal—the servants in town would have to be minimal. He could not do that to her. She deserved to be lavished with beautiful things, treated and pampered like the goddess she was.

"I will tell her I cannot marry her."

Disappointment crossed Hamish's face and Hugo looked away, not wanting to see reflected in his friend's eyes the dissatisfaction that he himself felt. "No, you will not. You will write a letter right now and I shall deliver it to her. If I know my cousin, and I do, very well, she will try and persuade you otherwise should you not offer for her. I cannot allow her to do that. The man who marries her, if she ever marries, will be worthy. You, Lord Wakely, are not."

Hugo nodded. There was no point in trying to dissuade the earl. He pulled out a piece of parchment and scribbled as best he could a note to Lizzie. A note that he knew would break her heart when she read it. He signed it then folded it and sealed it with wax. "Tell her I'm sorry."

Hamish snatched the note out of his hand and strode to the door. "On reflection, you're disinvited to the ball this evening. I do believe it will be many years before we'll be friends again. Good day."

Hugo stared at the door for some time after it slammed closed. What had he done? His guts churned with the knowledge that Lizzie would read his note, be crushed by his words. He stood and poured himself a brandy. He was a bastard. She would never forgive him. She would never be with him again, and rightfully so.

How was he ever to survive it? That he didn't know, and right at this moment in time he wished he would not. Death was better than this wretched, self-loathing emotion he now had coursing through *h*is blood. The *ton* had always thought him a cad, and now he'd truly earned that name. For the first time in his life, it was true.

LIZZIE SAT in the coach as it rumbled toward Lord Wakely's home. After reading his missive, she'd scrunched it up and thrown it in the fire. If he was going to break her heart, he could damn well look her in the eye and do it. Not hide behind a letter and have her cousin deliver it for him.

The coach rocked to a halt and she jumped out, not waiting for the driver. Without knocking, she opened the front door and let herself in. The butler, on his way to meet the viscount's guest, started at her intrusion and mumbled something about her not disturbing the viscount as he wasn't receiving guests, but she pushed the library door open and slammed it in his face without care.

"What the hell do you think you're doing, Hugo? You think you can write me a letter and I'll just scuttle away like a good little girl?"

His eyes wide, he looked up from the chair before the fire and Lizzie could tell from his bloodshot eyes that he'd hit the brandy. "Lizzie. I—"

"Don't you Lizzie me. How dare you treat me with so little respect. I think after everything we've done, all that I thought we felt for one another, I deserve more than just a note." She took a calming breath, not wanting to lose control of her emotions, although that may happen anyway as her eyes already stung with the threat of tears.

"Your cousin wouldn't allow me to see you."

"You have no right to blame Hamish. He has nothing to do with this. You could've said no to that. You could've said you wanted to speak to me. Explain why you would sleep with a woman, open your heart to her, only to discard her without a backward glance."

Hugo stood, coming over to her. He went to take her hands and she slapped him, hard. He reeled and she swallowed, the sting of her palm nothing to the sting of tears in her eyes. "I loved you." She shook her head, not believing this was even happening. "I thought you loved me too."

"Lizzie, I cannot marry you. I lose everything, the people who rely on me lose everything. I could not care less about having nothing, but I do not want that for you. As for my employees, they do not deserve to suffer because of my father's spite and my inability to toe the line. I have to give you up, for I have nothing. I'm damned if I do and damned if I don't."

"You have shown lack of character when it was needed most. I will never forgive you for this."

"Lizzie, please," he begged, stepping toward her.

She held up her hand, halting him. "You don't even want me enough to try to find another solution. You've known of this predicament for a year and yet all you have done is taken the easy way out. Do not think for one moment I do not understand how important your estates are, the people who work both on the land and within your households, because I do. People need employment, a safe place to live. However, I also believe that fighting for love is important. I have never felt for anyone, have never allowed such intimacies with anyone else before in my life, such as I have with you. You're the man I wanted to marry, have children with, love and cherish for the rest of my life. But you're not willing to fight at all for any of those things. Instead you've chosen the cold and aloof Miss Fox and her thirty thousand pounds."

Hugo stared at her, offering no words, no excuses, or alternatives for how they could turn this all about. Lizzie shook her head, unable to believe that after all they had shared, they were even in this situation.

"Should I take a husband I want him to fight, not just for me, but for his responsibilities. A real man would've looked into every possibility he could to secure his properties, not sleep his twelve months away with anyone who would warm his bed. I'm just ashamed that I've enabled myself to be one of your many doxies."

She turned and he didn't try to stop her. She steeled her back, not wanting to know what that meant. She supposed it meant that they were really through, that he would marry Miss Fox and she would go home.

"I'm sorry," he whispered.

"Go to hell, you bastard."

LIZZIE MADE it all the way back to her room at her cousin's house before she crumbled into a fit of tears. At some point Katherine brought up tea and scones, but Lizzie didn't want any of it. All that she'd wanted was lost to her, and some heiress would claim the prize.

She had hoped, had prayed, that Lord Wakely would see her self-worth, not what her worth was to a marriage. How wrong she'd been. She had risked everything, had ruined herself by sleeping with him, only to have him discard her due to her lack of fortune.

She threw a pillow onto the floor. Of course she could see why he'd chosen Miss Fox. To be responsible for so many and have the threat that they would be left without any security wasn't anything even she would allow. But why hadn't he thought of another way? Like Lord Leighton had suggested, why didn't he look at other options so he wasn't left with only one: Miss Fox?

Lizzie didn't think she could ever hate anyone in her life, but right at this moment she hated Lord Wakely. Well, she would show him. If he thought she would skulk about London heartbroken, she would not. On the inside she might be broken, but on the outside she would be a rod of steel–strong, unbending, and hard. And no man, not Lord Wakely or any other, would ever break her in two again.

CHAPTER 16

Hugo wasn't sure what had come over him, but after seeing the hurt he'd caused to Lizzie, for the past two days he'd set about righting his wrongs of the past twelve months. That included a trip to his solicitors, and a hasty summons to the three stewards who looked after his various estates.

Tomorrow night was the Keppell ball, where for the first time since Lizzie had walked out of his life they would both be in attendance.

"Tell me again what isn't entailed and what I can sell. I know the properties are entailed, of course, but what's within them that I can be rid of? If I'm to marry Lizzie Doherty, penniless as she is, then I need all the funds I can get."

Mr. Thompson shuffled his papers and pulled out a list. "Between myself and your stewards, you could lease out Bellside Manor and Neverton Hall, leaving Bolton Abbey as your only country estate. At least for the next ten years. With the income those estates would yield, and if you gave the gentlemen who leased each property a lengthy contract to live there, the estates would be kept up and not fall into disarray."

Which would also see him save funds. "And the paintings? Which ones are able to be sold to a collector or museum?" Across all his estates there were numerous paintings, some that would have to fetch a hefty price. He would be sad to see them go, but not as sad as he would be to see Lizzie removed from his life forever.

The memory of her features crushed with hurt haunted him and would not dissipate. He shook the thoughts aside. He would fix this problem. What he'd failed to remedy in twelve months he would repair in two days.

"We were able to find six paintings: two large classical Titians, a Botticelli, a pair of Canalettos of Venice, and a Raphael portrait. I have offered them up to be auctioned privately, and if sold at their estimated value, they will almost put you back where you were financially had you never lost your mother's fortune."

"I never lost her fortune, my father simply gave it away," he reminded the steward. "And the London townhouse? Would I have to lease that out also?" Hugo asked.

"We've looked at the sums, and if you agreed to lease it out every second Season, it would place you in a more solid position. You have fourteen carriages across the three estates that you could sell, and the horses of course. If you were willing to part with them."

"Leave enough cattle for the carriages and servants to use, my hack of course, and the new carriage I recently purchased, otherwise auction the horses at Tattersalls and sell everything else. We won't be needing them all," Hugo said, relief unlike any he'd ever known flowing over him. He would win Lizzie back yet, and now that he could offer for her without the burden of his staff and employees losing their positions, there was no moral impediment to him asking for her hand.

Sorry, Father, but you will not best me yet.

Hugo stood, shaking hands with his solicitor and stewards in turn. "I must apologize to you all for making you pull these figures and an account of my property within the time that I've given you. I will be a more attentive landlord in future, better than what I have been in any case. I intend to go on as I am now. A viscount in name and in character."

"Very good, my lord," Mr. Thompson said, smiling.

Hugo nodded and left them to their work. Now he was ready for the Keppells' ball. He just had one more call to make before the evening. One more loose end to tie up.

❦

LIZZIE STOOD to the side of the ballroom at the Keppells' ball, Sally standing beside her, her friend's thunderous gaze fixed on the Viscount Wakely and his dance partner Miss Fox.

They made a beautiful pair, and Lizzie hoped they both tripped and fell over. With that lowering thought she schooled her features and smiled at Katherine, who stood a little distance from her, but always with a watchful eye on Lizzie.

The deadline for Lord Wakely to marry was nigh and it was rumored tonight that they would announce their engagement that evening. The end of July was only days away after all.

"I cannot believe he has treated you so poorly and then has the audacity to show his face in public."

Lizzie threaded her arm with Sally's and hugged her a little. "I was the one who treated myself with so little respect. I should never have done what I did." Not that she'd told Sally of everything that had occurred between herself and Lord Wakely. Not even Katherine would ever know how far Lizzie had gone.

Even so, she'd been a fool. She had been the one who had stolen into his home, seduced him. She shook her head, hating the fact that she'd looked like a desperate fool. If only she could tell everyone she was an heiress, a woman who would from this time forward make her own choices, mostly that of being a spinster. A cat lady who would relocate to Rome, as she'd dreamed.

As the dance ended, she caught Lord Wakely's gaze. She flicked her attention away and fought not to glance back, to see if the longing she read in his dark orbs was a figment of her imagination or was actually present.

"Look how cosy Lord Wakely is with Miss Fox's parents. How ill they appear. I swear if they were not distantly related to the Duke and Duchess of Athelby the *ton* would turn their backs on them."

Lizzie didn't bother to look. She didn't wish to see in any case. As for her friend's claims, she doubted that would occur. As far as the *ton* knew, nothing untoward had occurred between herself and Lord Wakely. There was no reason to turn their backs on him, and even if they did know, it was she who would suffer the scandal. She would be the one shunned and excluded forever and a day.

The next set of dancing began and Lizzie took a glass of champagne from a passing footman. Maybe if she drank a little more, this night would not be so painful to be a part of. The dancers went about the quadrille, but then a disturbance had them pausing and within a moment the orchestra stopped and all eyes turned to what was happening in the middle of the room.

The sight of Lord Wakely standing in the middle of

the ballroom floor, absent Miss Fox, gave Lizzie pause. What was he doing? She frowned as it soon became obvious to all that his attention was fixed on her and no one else.

The weight of a thousand eyes turning toward her hit her like a club and she raised her chin, not wanting to succumb to hysterics over what Lord Wakely was about to do.

"If I may have your attention, ladies and gentlemen," he yelled over the exuberance of the guests. "There is something I wish to declare before you all."

"Oh dear God," Sally muttered beside her, and Lizzie completely agreed with her words. What on earth was he doing?

"Some weeks ago I met a woman who embodied all that I wanted in a wife. A woman of strong character and substance. A woman who made me want to be a better man. And at a time when I needed to prove my worth, I let her down. The words may not have been spoken, but I broke a promise to her, and to myself."

Lizzie felt Katherine's comforting hand as she came to stand beside her. Lizzie couldn't move, couldn't form words, even though her mind raced with the shocking reality of what Lord Wakely was doing.

"Many of you knew my father, and know that in his final years he and I did not get along. So much so that in his will he demanded I marry an heiress within twelve months of his death or I would lose my mother's fortune, which keeps my estates running. I have not fulfilled that promise as yet, nor will I."

The silence was replaced with gasps for a time. The *ton*'s attention turned toward where Miss Fox had been standing, but was now vacant. Had she gone home? Lizzie turned back to Hugo, unwilling to hope, and yet

TAMARA GILL

her body thrummed with the possibility he was about to choose her.

Her…over fortune…

Her eyes stung and she sucked in a shaky breath.

"I'm sorry, Lizzie Doherty, but I cannot live without you. And if that means we will live without luxuries, without grand estates and trips abroad, then that is what I want. For I want you. Just you and nothing else."

Lizzie let go of Katherine's hand and walked as steadily as her shaking legs would allow. She came to stand before him, meeting his gaze, unable to believe what he was saying was true. It was too wonderful, too much.

"Do you mean it? Really mean it?"

He nodded, cupping her cheeks. "I have found another way to enable us to marry. Your words to me two days past shamed me, and you were right to do so. I have not been thinking and I did take the easy way out. But it was not the only way."

Lizzie cleared the lump in her throat. "And Miss Fox? What of her?"

"I spoke to Edwina and, as I suspected, she held no tendre toward our union. She has released me, although she did state that because there was never really an understanding, she wasn't sure why I sought her opinion over my choice."

"I appreciate why you did it, and I'm glad you did. It was the right thing to do." His thumb brushed her jaw and she leaned into his touch, having missed it dreadfully.

"I love you, Lizzie. I love you and no one else." He paused, taking one hand and kissing it. "Marry me, my heart. Be mine."

Lizzie nodded through a flood of tears, then laughed as he bent and kissed her, the *ton* and the startled gasps all forgotten as they sealed their fate before them all. He picked her up, hugging her close.

"I do love you. I'm sorry, my love. Please say you forgive me."

"I forgive you." She hugged him tighter still. "I love you too. So much."

Hugo let her down slowly, then pulled her toward Hamish and Katherine, where they were standing with Sally. The smile on her cousin's face told her she would have no argument with him in relation to marrying Hugo.

"Before we celebrate with my family, there is something you must promise me," Lizzie stated, pulling Hugo to a stop.

"Anything. I'll promise you anything," he said ardently and without hesitation.

"That is all I want. Your promise for anything."

"You're being very secretive, Lizzie darling," he said, kissing her hand once again.

She shrugged. "All in good time, Lord Wakely. Good things come to those who wait. And I think we've both waited long enough."

EPILOGUE

Lizzie breathed in deeply the dry heat and the air that was fresh and warm. Under the Tuscan sun she lay on a blanket, Hugo placing an olive on her tongue every now and then as he read the paper beside her.

They had purchased the small chateau during their honeymoon, which was mostly spent abroad. And now, whenever the chilling, damp English weather became too dull and cold, they travelled to their Tuscan home and enjoyed all that it had to offer.

"I see Miss Fox is a widow only two years after marrying that decrepit old duke."

Lizzie grinned, rolling over to lean on Hugo's legs and use them as a pillow. "Katherine wrote to say that Miss Fox is not the least heartbroken at his death, and with an heir secured, she's enjoying widowhood very well."

"I should imagine she is, and how could anyone blame her? The duke was old enough to be her grandfather."

Lizzie shuddered and rolled over to straddle Hugo's lap. "You seem very interested in what Miss Fox is about. Do you regret your choice?"

Hugo threw the paper aside and hauled her hard up against him. "Regret my choice? Regret choosing the woman I love, even if she did lie to me about being well-dowered?"

She chuckled, remembering poor Hugo's face in Lord Leighton's library the afternoon after the ball at which he'd so publicly declared himself. The mute shock that followed the declaration of how much she was worth. Worth waiting for, he had said, and she had hoped he was right, for he was certainly worth fighting for.

"I'm so happy, Hugo. If I was to die right now I'd know I lived well and loved with all my heart."

He kissed her and she wrapped her arms about his neck, never wanting to let go.

"I love you too," he said when finally they pulled apart.

"I don't believe I actually said I love you just before, but if you insist, I love you too. Shall we return inside, husband?"

He waggled his brows and she grinned. "Are you going to love me some more if I say yes?" he asked.

"Maybe. You'll have to find out."

Just then the meowing of one of their children sounded and Lizzie reached down to pick up Puss, the pure black kitten that had wandered into their yard some weeks before, and who had fast become part of their family. She kissed the adorable ball of fur, smiling at the purring that was as loud as its meow.

"How many does that make now?" Hugo asked, patting the kitten.

"Seven in total, but they're good at catching mice, and they're no trouble. You don't mind, do you darling?"

He shook his head. "I don't mind, no. You forget you told me of your plans to become an unmarried maid with an abundance of cats. I can tolerate the little furballs if it's what you want, and I get to have you instead of spin-sterhood."

"I think really I have gained a good bargain with marrying you, Lord Wakely. I get my cats, I have my Italian sky, and I have you. I want for nothing."

"Me too." He kissed her again and she sighed as he deepened the embrace before one little black paw touched their cheeks. They pulled away, both looking at the culprit who didn't like not being the centre of attention.

Ah yes, life was positively perfect. And tomorrow, when Lizzie wrote her monthly letters to London, she would write to Lady X along with Sally and tell them all her news, including the surprise that she was bestowing on Lord Wakely tonight, of another addition to their family, but this time, one that came without fur.

TO DARE A DUCHESS

Lords of London, Book 5

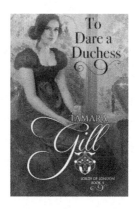

After five long years trapped in the country, newly widowed Nina Granville, Duchess of Exeter, has returned to town to start over. But it was here she committed an indiscretion—one stolen night of pleasure —that would threaten all she holds dear if revealed.

. . .

Byron always loved Nina from afar—until the house party that turned his world upside down. Guilt saw him flee England's shores, and Nina wed to a man old enough to be her grandfather, but now the handsome rogue is back...and ready to claim what is his.

Yet Nina has kept a secret from Byron, one that could threaten their sizzling attraction and sever their longstanding friendship forever. With Byron's brother determined to reveal the truth, Nina must use her power in the ton to ensure her secret is kept safe. Even at the expense of love...

PROLOGUE

Edwina Granville, Duchess of Exeter, sat in a carriage on her way back to Granville Hall, a large and imposing estate that resembled a castle. With its impossibly high walls and turrets, and its location on top of a steep hill, the only architectural elements missing were towers and spiralling staircases. The building loomed over the town of Minehead, Kent and looked as superior as the duke she'd just married.

From this day on, now that their vows were spoken, this was her home. She looked back out the window and watched the church disappear from view, her parents still standing outside and greeting the few guests who had attended from London.

A rumbling snore sounded from beside her and she turned to see the Duke of Exeter asleep, his head lolling about and his mouth drooping as if he'd had a stroke. She sighed, having not thought this would be her husband at the end of her second Season, but here she was, a duchess and wife to a man who was old enough to be her grandfather.

Her stomach roiled at the idea of bedding him, but she would bear it, and she would tolerate it with a formidable strength, because that was her duty, what she'd been brought up to expect upon entering the marriage state. The carriage lurched as it started up the steep hill toward the Hall. Edwina, Nina to her friends, would play the obliging, attentive wife for one reason and one reason only.

Because anything was better than to be seen by the man she loved as a pitiful, sad gentlewoman who had lost her head with the worst outcome. She narrowed her eyes, fisting her hand in her lap as she recalled the reason she was in this predicament.

Mr. Andrew Hill, a gentleman who had made her believe she meant more to him than she truly did. A bastard and flirt if ever there was one, and a man whom she should've stayed the hell away from. But she did not, could not if she were honest with herself. And now she was married to a duke, would have his children and be an upstanding woman of rank whenever they travelled to town.

Nina supposed she should feel guilty marrying a man she did not love, but she could not. The leech beside her was only too willing to marry a woman so many years beneath him in age it ought to be illegal, but her money and her family made her too much of a temptation. So when he'd offered, in her desperation about being slighted, she'd said yes. The one saving grace, she supposed, was the fact that the duke already had a son. One who was older than herself, which made for awkward meetings, especially because his wife, the marchioness, hated Nina with more passion than she loved her husband.

Nina stared at the grey velvet upholstery seat across from her. The decision to marry the duke had been made with such haste on her part, she hadn't considered in depth what it really meant for her.

Her time in London would now be curtailed somewhat, due to the fact the duke disliked town so much and left the entertaining to his son. A silver lining, perhaps, to the awful situation in which she now found herself. At least she wouldn't have to face the man who'd ruined all her dreams, and her in the process. Wouldn't have to face Society and their snickering snide looks because she'd sold herself into a loveless marriage and to a man twice her age.

The way she had fooled herself that she would be different from her parents, that she would have a grand love match when she took her vows, now mocked her to her core.

Nina sighed, staring down at her fingers. She would miss her friends, and one more than most. Byron, twin brother to Andrew, the blaggard who'd taken what he wanted with no iota of remorse. A man who could up and announce his engagement to someone other than herself could never really have cared for her. She would miss Byron though. He had left for the continent before her wedding and she wasn't sure when she'd see him again. She hoped it would be soon, but she wouldn't fool herself. She would probably never see him again.

CHAPTER 1

Kent. Five years later.

Nina sat on a blanket on the lawns behind Granville Hall and watched as Molly and Lora ran about chasing their wolfhound, Bentley, who was three times the children's size. The dog had been Molly and Lora's constant companion since the day they were born, and even though their grandmother worried and fretted about the young children being bitten, or worse, mauled by the large animal, Nina knew Bentley would never hurt them.

But she could not guarantee the dog wouldn't hurt others if he thought they were a threat.

Molly laughed, rolling onto the ground, and Nina chuckled when Bentley sat on Molly's back, holding her down. Lora tried to shift the dog off her sibling, to no avail.

"Mama, I'm stuck," her daughter yelled, her sweet little voice full of mirth.

She shrugged, shading her eyes to keep watch. "You

seem to have lost this war, Molly. Maybe a treat for Bentley since he's the victor I think."

The mention of the word *treat* had Bentley trotting over to her, and she clasped the wolfhound's face, kissing the bridge of his nose. "Off to Cook. Go see what Cook's made you."

Molly and Lora squealed their excitement and started for the back of the house, running as fast as their little legs would carry them, but not as fast as Bentley who'd already disappeared from view. Their cook Mrs. Jones would have an abundance of treats both for the dog and the children. Nina stood and shook out the blanket, ready to go indoors now that the sun was getting lower in the western sky.

How she would miss this estate. But it was time for her to return to town, take part in a Season and help pave the way for her children in the years to come. Not that she was looking for another husband—one had been plenty enough, and a loveless marriage was not an easy life to lead. And there was no reason why she should look for another man to warm her bed. She was wealthy in her own right, owned multiple homes, and was about to embark on a new direction here in her home county of Kent. Even so, as busy as she was with the planning of her village school, she missed her friends—in particular her cousin's wife, the Duchess of Athelby, whose letters had become more and more insistent she return to London.

And so she would, and for the first time since having the children she would leave them here in Kent. To do so had not been an easy choice, but with their studies, and her desire for them to breathe fresh country air instead of the coal-clogged air of London, it would be better this way. Of course she would return home at times throughout the Season to see them.

"Your Grace, an express has arrived from the Duchess of Athelby. It is on your desk in the library."

"Thank you, I'll be in directly."

The maid bobbed a curtsy and left her. Nina started for the terrace doors that led into the Hall's abundantly stocked library. The room was lined with mahogany wooden panels and book shelving. Books from all over the world stacked the walls from floor to ceiling. A pair of buttoned leather chairs sat strategically before a window, grabbing the light from the outdoors. A fire burned in the grate, warm and inviting. Going to her desk that sat in the center of the room, Nina picked up the missive and broke the ducal seal. She skimmed the note, clasping the desk for support as the safe little world she'd made for herself dissipated before her eyes.

DEAREST NINA,

I feel I must warn you to prepare yourself for your return to town. Mr. Andrew Hill has returned from Ireland to have a London Season and is married, as you know. You must expect to see them both. I'm so sorry, dearest. I know this is not the news you would want from me. I shall see you in a few days.

Darcy.

NINA SCRUNCHED up the note and fought not to cast up her accounts. Andrew was back in town! Oh dear lord, no. Of all the Seasons she was to attend, he would have to choose this one as well. To see him again after so many years, to hear his voice, the sound of his laugh, the smell of his skin... However would she bear it? However would she remain civil and not slap his deceiving, lying face?

She remembered back to the night of her shame. The

details were so clear it was almost as if it had happened yesterday. Having snuck into Andrew's room in the middle of the night, taking advantage of his inebriated state and seducing him wasn't the proudest moment of her life. But he'd been so caring, so loving toward her that evening, that she was sure he would offer for her. He had not. Instead the rogue had announced his betrothal the following morning to a Miss Fionna O'Connor, and had ripped her heart right out of her body.

Nina immediately acted like the silly youth she was at the time, and had given in to what her parents had always wanted for her—a grand match. And so within an hour of Andrew's announcement she was engaged to a duke and would move on from being the dutiful daughter to the dutiful wife.

A light knock sounded on the door and a footman entered, bowing before her. "Lunch is served, Your Grace."

"Have it brought in here, please. I have some correspondence to attend to that cannot wait. Also, send a note to the stables to have them prepare the carriages for my return to London three days from now. And send in my maid, please."

The footman bowed again. "Yes, Your Grace."

Nina walked over to the fire and sat on a leather wing-back chair, staring at the flames licking the wood in the grate. Her decision to leave Molly and Lora behind was even more sensible than before. The girls had features that were so similar to Andrew's she was certain that if he ever got a glimpse of the children, he would know they were his. He was a proud man, or certainly was when she'd known him last, and he would not care for them being under another man's name when they ought to have his.

She clasped her hands in her lap to stop them from

shaking. If she were to survive the Season, survive seeing the one man in the world whom she'd loved with such passion, with her whole heart, she would need to get a better hold of herself.

Andrew Hill broke her heart once. He would not have that power again.

THE SEASON in town was not something Byron Hill thought he'd ever have to endure again. And yet here he was, back in London, fiancée in tow, and about to enjoy these last few months of the Season before he married Miss Sofia Custer.

She was not the type of woman that he'd ever thought to marry. Sofia was from a family of miners—hardworking, honest people who had enabled her every desire in life. The Custers owned practically all the copper mines there were in England, and as their only daughter Sofia enjoyed the luxuries that such a life brought her. She was a little immature, he supposed, and used to getting her own way, but they got along well enough and it was time he settled down to start a family of his own.

Byron stood out front of White's and kicked his heels waiting for Hunter, the Marquess of Aaron to arrive. The gentleman was already five minutes late and if he didn't arrive soon the footman standing out front of White's would move Byron on.

A hackney pulled to a stop and Hunter jumped down, coming toward him with a smile. "Byron, how good to see you again," he said, clasping his shoulder and shaking his hand.

Byron smiled back, delighted to see his cousin again

too. "It's been a long time. Too long." And yet in a lot of ways, not long enough.

"Let us walk toward Hyde Park and catch up. The weather is congenial enough."

Byron couldn't agree more. The day had dawned warmer than normal for March, and after his long voyage back from the continent, a stroll sounded just the thing. "Tell me everything that has happened since I've been away."

Hunter laughed, his cane tapping a crescendo on the cobbled footpath. "I could ask the same of you. I hear you're to be married. I met Miss Custer two Seasons ago, before the family travelled abroad. She seemed very pleasant and intelligent. I'm assuming by the fact that Byron Hill, an eligible bachelor if ever there was one, is marrying you've found the love of your life?"

The bold question caught Byron off guard and he balked at the idea of answering his cousin. There wasn't any love between him and Sofia, even though they did get along very well. Byron hoped that in time perhaps their mutual like and respect would grow into deeper, meaningful emotions, but that would take time.

"It is not a love match, no. I leave those emotions to you and Cecilia." He ought to want more for Sofia, and himself, but to love someone again? No. He gave his heart away many years ago and had never really got it back.

The memory of Edwina Fox, now the Duchess of Exeter, a woman who only had eyes for his twin brother Andrew, made his teeth ache. To this day the memory of them together, of watching them at balls and parties dancing and laughing at mutual jests, made Byron's blood boil. He pushed the recollection away, not wishing to feel melancholy when being back in town was a good thing. It was time for him to move on, marry and settle down.

His cousin had a whimsical look on his face before he said, "I'm not ashamed to say that I love my wife, adore her beyond what any respectable gentleman should, and I would not change my situation for the world. But are you sure you wish to partake in such a union? If there is no love, there is no guarantee that there ever will be, and to marry someone is a lifelong commitment. I do not want to see you make a mistake, Byron."

"I made my biggest mistake many years ago. This is merely a trifling matter." The declaration simply slipped out and he was unable to rip it back. "Apologies, Hunter, it seems London has many ghosts that want to come back and haunt me."

His cousin threw him an assessing look. "How is Andrew? I understand he returned from Ireland last week."

"He did, and Fionna accompanied him. They will be returning to Ireland after my marriage and the Season's end." They came to the corner of Upper Brook Street and Park Lane, and crossed the street before heading into Hyde Park. In the distance they could see a group of children running in the direction of the Serpentine. Women strolled and rode in carriages along with a few gentlemen who preferred horseback. The park was full of London society out for their daily dose of gossip and exercise.

They started along the Broad Walk both lost in thought for a time and content with silence. It was one of the things Byron loved most about his cousin—they didn't always have to fill the silence with meaningless chatter.

"Now that you're back in England and Andrew resides in Ireland most of the time, have you taken over the London townhouse?"

Byron nodded, watching two boys run about as their nurse kept watch over them from under a large oak tree. "I have. I'll make it our home until we find something closer to Sofia's family in Cornwall." Which was a long way from London, and just as he liked it. He didn't wish to be anywhere near the city where he could run into Edwina at any given moment. Not that she was aware of his feelings —she'd only ever had eyes for his brother and never gave Byron a second glance.

"The townhouse will suit you very well, and with Andrew staying there for the Season at least, it'll give his wife and your future one time to acquaint themselves."

"Very true," he replied, having not given the situation much thought. As it was, Byron wasn't certain Sofia would get along very well with Andrew's wife. Fionna O'Connor came from titled stock in Ireland, and to have a future sister-in-law who hailed from mining stock wouldn't reflect as well on Fionna as she might like. He would have to ensure that she didn't put on any airs to cause offence to Sofia.

"I'm attending the Tattersalls auction on Thursday. Would you care to join me? With none of us living in England for some years now, we have no cattle. The mews is empty, save for the carriage that is stored there. I would like your opinion on a grey mare that I spied for Sofia, if you're available."

"I shall drop Cecilia off at her charity meeting and meet you there."

"Is Cecilia still very much occupied with the London Relief Society? Having children has not slowed her down?" Byron asked, smiling in fondness as he thought of the woman who had captured, and saved, his cousin. What a remarkable woman she was—always helping others, kind natured and loving. Hunter was a very lucky man indeed.

"I very much doubt anything will ever slow Cecilia down. She's simply marvellous. Speaking of marvellous things, the London Relief Society is holding a charity ball Saturday next. We're holding it at our home and would love for you to attend. Do you think you're free?"

And so it would begin, the whirl and madness of the Season. Even if this was only a charity ball, it was the start of many. But then it would be good for his fiancée to meet his extended family, and maybe Sofia would like to volunteer with the charity organization. "We would be honored to attend," he said sincerely.

Hunter chuckled, throwing him a bemused glance. "You may regret those words, cousin. A charity ball it may be, but bring your pocket book. Cecilia and the ladies who volunteer will be collecting donations and they'll not let you leave without some sort of monetary contribution."

Byron smiled. "Duly noted. I shall not forget." They started back toward the park gates. Would Nina be at this charity ball? Byron cursed his own longing at wanting to see her again, glimpse her from afar, while also praying that he wouldn't. He took a fortifying breath. He would have to be stalwart should he see her. One thing he never wanted Nina to know was how her marrying someone else had almost broken him in two. *Had* broken him in two, and he was still mending the fracture.

CHAPTER 2

With his fiancée on his arm, Byron walked up the steps to the London home of his cousin Hunter, the Marquess of Aaron, and waited in line to be received by their host and hostess for the evening.

The line was long, and already the charity ball was looking to be a crush. It would seem that Cecilia had fitted perfectly into the marquess's exalted status in society and made it her own. Just as she should, for Bryan had never met a kinder woman.

Meeting the marquess and marchioness, Byron introduced Sofia, and kissed Cecilia in welcome. His brother, who was standing behind him, did the same for Fionna and then they entered the ballroom. The large, rectangular room glowed with candlelight, and already some couples were dancing. Byron took in the room, having not expected the grandeur of the spectacle to cause a twinge of nostalgia to hit him. The last time he'd been in a ballroom he'd been a green lad, still wet behind the ears and eager to live life to the fullest in London, or at least that was how it seemed. In truth it had only been five or so years, but much had changed since he'd left. He wasn't the green, malleable man he once was. No longer did he allow others to dictate his life or tell him what to do, or how to act.

Andrew took Fionna out to dance and Byron turned to Sofia. "Shall we dance also, my dear?" he asked, glancing over her shoulder when a vision in red caught his eye. He stilled, his arm held out to take Sofia's, and the breath in his lungs seized.

Edwina Fox. Damnation, it was her.

Sofia nodded. "Thank you, yes."

Byron shut his mouth with a snap and schooled his features into an expression of indifference. For all that he and Edwina shared, she wasn't privy to the secret he carried, and never would be if he could help it. Only his cousin Hunter—who came across Byron the morning after Byron's error of judgement and demanded he tell him the truth—knew his secret. And he would keep it that way until he was dead.

Byron started toward the dance floor, but before he could take two steps, Edwina's attention strayed to where he stood and he read the moment she recognized him. Somehow, even though he was a twin, she'd almost always been able to tell him and Andrew apart. Maybe it was the single dimple on their cheeks, on opposite sides, but he wasn't smiling right now.

She started toward them, her beautiful, warm smile just for him. Or at least that was what he told himself before he reined in the idiocy that tended to come to the fore whenever he was around her.

"Byron," she said, coming up to him before leaning up and kissing his cheek. "I'm so glad you're here this Season. It has been too long since I saw you last."

The intoxicating scent of jasmine was like a physical blow to his gut. The years of not being near her—not being able to smell her sweet scent, hear her voice or view her beautiful face—almost felled him like an old oak in a storm.

He stared at her a moment, unable to do anything else. Christ, she was beautiful—her dark hair the color of the night sky, her perfect creamy complexion, and her laughing blue eyes. Not to mention the adorable dimples on her cheeks that he'd kissed and kissed again after their one night of sin.

"Your Grace, how lovely to see you again." His voice was formal, lifeless even, and Sofia stared up at him with a look of confusion on her face. He gestured to his fiancée. "Your grace, may I introduce Sofia Custer, my betrothed."

Edwina smiled as Sofia bobbed a small curtsy. "It's lovely to meet you, Miss Custer, and congratulations on your engagement. I had heard you were engaged and I'm glad to hear it is so. I'm very happy for you and Byron."

Byron swallowed the bile that rose in his throat at having Edwina so very close to him, and yet never had their distance been so far. "Is His Grace here this evening?" Asking after Edwina's husband made Byron want to snarl. He'd hated the curmudgeonly old slime who preyed on young women of fortune. Edwina was his latest victim.

Edwina frowned. "No, my stepson the Duke of Exeter is here. Maybe you have not heard, but my husband passed away some years ago now."

"I had not heard," he managed to stammer out, the room spinning. She was unmarried? A widow? "If you'll excuse us, Your Grace, I promised Sofia the next dance." He dragged his fiancée out onto the floor and lined them up with the other couples setting up for a quadrille.

"What an interesting and enlightening meeting that was," Sofia said, smiling across at him.

Byron didn't see anything at all amusing in what had just happened. If anything, never had he ever been in more pain. He thought he'd prepared himself to see her again, watch her dancing with her husband and enjoying the Season. He had not been prepared to see her unmarried.

"You think so?" he said, throwing himself into the dance with more zest than was necessary, hoping Sofia would change the subject.

"I do. You have friends in high places, Byron. I'm surprised you never mentioned before that your cousin is a marquess or that you are friends with a duchess."

Friends with a duchess. How he wished that were true. Of course it was in a way—they had once been the best of friends—but he'd wanted so much more than that. Since he and his brother Andrew were twins, with looks that replicated the other to perfection, he'd never understood why she'd gravitated toward Andrew and not him. Andrew was by far the more sedate and gentlemanly of the two of them, more willing to listen to and care for others. While Byron… well, he enjoyed life, the outdoors, and riding, and not just in regards to horses. He was the wild one, he supposed, and mayhap it was not what she was looking for at the time.

And now it was too late.

His fiancée linked arms with him, peering up at him. "I'm not blind, Byron. I saw the way you looked at her. You cared for the duchess once. Maybe even still do."

If there was one good thing about his understanding with Sofia Custer it was the promise they'd made each other to be always honest. No matter what that honesty may cost. But could he be truthful on this? He didn't wish to hurt her, but the laughing gaze she looked up at him with told him she wasn't the least piqued over his reaction to the duchess.

"I did care for her. Once. But that is long over now." He twirled her through one of the steps. "I'm willing to put the past behind me, be friends with the duchess. She seems amenable to the idea, and with her alliance, and that of my cousins, you'll have a good position here in Society. We will have friends who'll support us."

Sofia shrugged. "I care little for this Society. Once we're married, we'll travel back to Cornwall and you'll help father run the mines, just as we agreed."

"Of course," he said, bowing as the dance came to an end. "Shall we return to Hunter and Cecilia? I'm sure they would love to catch up with you some more and get to know you better."

Again Sophia shrugged, seemingly little interested in his family.

Was she angry at him? Was she jealous after all regarding Edwina? He supposed there was a chance that she liked him more than they had admitted to, but then they'd had so little time together he really didn't think that was possible. You couldn't be jealous of someone you hardly knew and who hardly knew you in return. When they'd met abroad in Rome, while Sofia was visiting the continent with her family, they'd enjoyed each other's company. He'd taken them to the sights of Paris, of Rome and Florence. They had always had something to talk about, but having returned to London, that carefree life had ended and with it their conversation had dried up. He'd proposed to Sofia after a wonderful day boating off the coast of southern France and it had seemed the perfect end to a perfect day. He was of an age where he longed for a family of his own, to have a wife and not a mistress, and Sofia suited that role very well. But upon returning to

England and the realities that came with that—his town life and her Cornwall one—their compatibility wasn't as good as he thought.

When they returned to his cousin, Cecilia greeted Sofia warmly and asked if she would like to join her for a turn about the room. A sliver of relief shot through Byron when the ladies walked off into the throng of guests. That in itself was telling of the emotional bond between them, which was very little.

"You are as pale as a ghost, cousin. Is your cravat too tight, or is your dear fiancée not too pleased with how you reacted when you saw Edwina Fox?" Hunter threw him a bemused glance, and Byron cringed.

"You saw that, did you? I'd hoped to mask my features before she noticed, but alas it seems I was unsuccessful."

Hunter took two glasses of whiskey from a passing footman and handed one to Byron.

"I have not forgotten what she meant to you. Edwina, I mean. It's been many years since you've seen her—it is any wonder that you reacted so? I'm sure it was like seeing a ghost. But remember, cousin, Nina doesn't know it was you in that room that night and so you need to be careful around her. Your mannerisms will give you away and she will start to wonder why it is that you act so strangely around her person."

Byron conceded Hunter's point. The memory of that night was so vivid in his mind it could've happened only yesterday, not five years ago.

The night of the Duke and Duchess of Athelby's annual ball, that was held that year at their country estate, had started like all of the events Byron had suffered through. Edwina Fox, as she was known then, had been enjoying her second Season in town, being courted by many, but had somehow managed to be known as cunning and cold, certainly when it came to her admirers. All her admirers but one—Byron's brother Andrew.

During her first Season she'd managed to slip the snare of Lord Wakely, who'd been rumored to marry her, but then he'd up and married Lizzie Doherty and so Edwina was free to do as she pleased.

His brother had always been sweet, polite and kind to the opposite sex, and Nina, like all the debutantes he'd ever met, loved to be admired and cherished. Byron knew the game his brother was playing—make many fall, play the admired gentleman the matrons of the ton adored, all the while courting someone out of the London elite set.

On the night of the ball and the day after his sibling had arrived at the estate, Andrew had come to him with a request. "Brother, I'm happy to have caught you before dinner. Would you mind if we swapped rooms this evening? The bed in my room is too hard, and I know you don't mind mattresses to be so, so I was hoping to swap."

Byron had rolled his eyes at his brother's problem. Typical of him to complain of the littlest troubles in life. "We're here one more night. Can you not put up with it?"

Andrew made a show of rubbing his back, and Byron should have guessed then, at his brother's terrible acting skills, that he was up to no good. "Please, Byron. I'll talk to our valets and have them move all our things. I cannot bear another night on that bed."

Byron cursed under his breath. "You've only slept on it one time as it is. Surely it's not too much of a hardship."

"I get no rest in it. You don't mind hard mattresses, please swap," his brother begged. "My back is already troubling me and it's only been one night, as you said."

"Fine," Byron said, not wanting to be bothered by such a petty problem. "Instruct your valet to change our rooms."

Andrew smiled, his relief evident. "Thank you, brother. I'll direct Walter to pack up both our things."

"You do that, and soon. I'm tired after my journey here today and a hard mattress or not, I'm looking forward to going to bed tonight."

CHAPTER 3

Byron stood at the base of his bed, staring at the vision that was Edwina Fox who'd entered his room not a moment before, shutting the door quickly behind her. Clad only in a dressing gown with a shift beneath, the cotton was so sheer that Byron could see the outline of her person in the light from the fire burning in the grate.

Holy bollocks, what is she doing here?

He'd headed to bed early after being the last to arrive for the Athelby ball held that very evening, taking a bottle of the duke's best whisky to his room to help him sleep. Just as his brother had informed him, the bed was terribly hard, so the liquor should help somewhat.

Nina snapped the lock on the door closed and he swallowed, blinking to clear his blurred vision. This was not what was supposed to happen. Nina loved his brother, not him. Had she had a change of heart? Had she finally seen his worth? He drank in the vision that was her, her hair cascading down her back, her long dark locks curling a little around her angelic face.

Hell, she was pretty. So beautiful and sweet. And damn

it all to hell, he wanted her. Had wanted her to be his for so long, and here she was, finally after all the years they had been friends.

"Hello there, are you surprised to see me?" she asked, taking a step toward him.

Byron stepped back, the edge of the bed hitting his knees. "Yes. Yes, I am," he stuttered, shaking his head. "Edwina, you should leave. You being here is a mistake and one I do not wish for you to regret."

She closed the space between them and he had nowhere to go, unless he flopped back onto the bed. As she came toward him he fought not to notice how the light of the fire outlined her long, slim legs and the curvature of her waist.

She looked up at him uncertainly. "Don't send me away," she beseeched him. "You know I want you. We've been friends for so long, I have known you for an age. I want to kiss you. Let me."

Kiss her? Dear God, yes.

She leaned up, trying to capture his lips, and he clasped her shoulders and pushed her away. "Listen, Nina, are you sure? There is no turning back from this. One taste of you and I'll want you forever."

She shook her head, her dark locks bouncing with the effort. "I'm sure. Please kiss me and make me yours."

Byron debated with his own moral code. She was a maid, but then she was only asking for a kiss. What was the harm in that? He stared down at her, reading the longing in her stormy blue eyes, and his resolve to deny her crumbled.

Her hand slid against his bare chest, and he cursed the fact he'd stripped off his shirt after partaking in too much drink. Her touch seared his skin and left him burning wherever her palm moved.

The room spun a little and he clasped the bed for support.

"Just a kiss and I'll sneak back to my room. No one ever needs to know."

Byron shut his eyes for a moment, not wanting to look at her, for he knew that if he did, he would crumble and do what she wished. Her beguiling tore him in two, and the years of denial, of always being on the sidelines, never the one that she wanted, rose to the surface and crashed all his defences. He could not deny her anything. Not even a kiss.

He caught her gaze. "I will kiss you. But only one."

She nodded, her eyes brightening with awareness and expectation. The smell of jasmine wafted from her hair and he shut his eyes, reveling in the essence of her.

Just before they kissed he took in her features. She had the most beautiful, perfectly arched brows. Lips that begged to be kissed, so plump with the slightest rosy hue. Her eyes were closed, her lashes perfect arcs against her cheeks. He placed a small kiss upon her nose, another on a cheek, and then kissed down to her chin, working his way around her jaw, wanting to savor the moment and not rush his time with her. The one and only kiss he would have with Nina.

She sighed, the whisper of her breath making his blood pump hard in his veins, and he took her mouth in a searing kiss. Her hands reached about his neck, holding him against her. Her breasts pushed upon his chest and he swore he could feel her heart pumping as fast as his own. The fluttering of her tongue touched his and his control snapped. He hoisted her against his hardened sex, desperate for her and unable to deny the feel of her lithe body in his arms.

He ground her against him and she moaned, a deep seductive tone that he wanted to hear again and again. She undulated in turn, seeking her own pleasure, although she would not know just how it could be between a man and woman, not yet at least.

"Take me. Make me yours. I want you."

He tumbled them onto the bed. His hands without thought fought with her shift, wiggling it up her body to pool at her waist. She wore nothing beneath, and he swore. He wanted to kiss her mons that glistened in the firelight. Hear her moan his name. Make her climax under the touch of his lips. He wanted to do everything with her. One night would never be enough.

A little voice warned him against this course. It was wrong, what he was enticing her into. Edwina was a virgin. This action could ruin her chances of a good match, but the idea of her being with anyone else pushed away his guilt. He wanted her to be his, had been patient waiting for her to notice him. And now she had. He could no sooner push her away than he could push the sun away from the day.

He kissed her again and she sighed as he settled between her legs.

"Oh, Nina, you have no idea how much I want you. I've wanted you for so long it hurts."

Her fingers slid into his hair, pulling him down for another kiss. Her wish was his command—in her arms he would do anything she wanted, give her every desire if only she'd let him.

She lifted her legs, locking them about his hips. He took his cock in hand and guided himself into her hot, wet core. Blast she felt good, tight and warm and so deliciously wet. He gasped as he sheathed himself fully, her sharp intake of air holding him still a moment as he allowed her to familiarize herself with their joining.

"Are you well, Nina? I'm sorry I hurt you," he said,

kissing the lobe of her ear. She relaxed in his hold and he fought not to continue. He wanted her with a desperation that could make him careless, and he didn't want that for her. He wanted her to remember this night forever. Wanted to be all that she desired and more. To be the beginning of them.

She clasped his face with her hands and met his gaze. "Don't stop." She nodded. "This is what I want."

And it had been what he'd wanted from that night on, right up to now as he watched Edwina, now the dowager Duchess of Exeter, talk with a group of ladies beside the ballroom floor. But fate the following morning had played its joker and he'd lost the game.

His brother came up beside him, joining in his conversation with Hunter.

"I must admit I'm pleased to be back in town," Andrew said, pulling Fionna closer to his side. "We should return more often, my dear. I'd forgotten how fun London could be."

She agreed amicably, and Byron fought not to roll his eyes at the banal chitchat his brother had with his spouse. Since their marriage five years earlier, his brother had become the most boring man on earth. Not that he hadn't been before. Really, Byron still could not understand the attraction that the women of the ton had for him.

"I saw you talking to the duchess. Is Edwina well?" Andrew asked, meeting Byron's eye.

"Very well, I can gather. She too is here for the Season," Byron said, trying to keep his composure when around the one woman who could discombobulate him at any given moment. He rubbed a hand over his jaw, his attention snapping back to the duchess. She cast a glance in their direction, and excusing herself from the group she stood with, started toward them.

Hunter cleared his throat, and Byron reminded himself that she did not know the truth. Didn't know it was him in her bed that night, not his brother. Unfortunately he had only found out that was who she'd thought he was after they had slept together. After walking Nina to his door and checking that the passage was vacant of guests he'd wished her goodnight, only to hear his brother's name whispered against his ear. Having his heart torn from his chest would've been less painful. He knew in that moment what a colossal mistake she had made, and he as well. That a night where he'd thought of nothing but beginnings would be only the end should Nina know the truth. Not that it mattered, for the following day both Nina and Andrew had made their choices and he was left with nothing.

Byron looked to his brother and didn't miss the flicker of fear that entered his sibling's eyes. He ought to be afraid too. Hell, they both should be if Nina were ever to find out the truth. The whole truth, some of which even Byron would never forgive himself for.

NINA CAME to stand before the two brothers, marvelling at how similar they both were, identical in fact, and yet the years had not been kind to Andrew. He'd rounded in the five years since she'd seen him last. Whereas Byron had aged well, like a fine wine just ripe for the picking.

Nina checked herself. Such thoughts were not appropriate, and Byron was her friend. To have such a visceral reaction to him was not what duchesses did, no matter how much she wondered what lay beneath his superfine coat and perfectly starched waistcoat and shirt.

The men bowed and Andrew's wife made her a pretty

curtsy, one that she didn't return. They didn't deserve such respect, or at least her husband did not.

"Duchess, how very well you look," Andrew said. "It has been many years."

The reminder of what they had done together prior to the years passing them by shot a blast of annoyance through her blood and she fought not to throw her glass of champagne over his head.

Not that she desired him in any way anymore. His treatment of her had put paid to such sentiments, but still, that did not mean she would allow him to enjoy his Season without a little payback.

"Some may say not long enough." An uncomfortable silence ensued and Nina smiled up at Byron. She'd started to wonder what it was exactly that she'd liked about Andrew in the first place. For a man to treat a debutante in such a deplorable manner, in light of what they'd done, made him no man she wanted to be associated with. "Are you here for the Season staying at your townhouse?"

"We are, Your Grace," Fionna said, smiling a little. "We hope to hold our own ball a little into the Season."

Nina had to concede that Andrew's wife was pretty, even though the last time she'd seen her, she'd been almost sick at the news of her engagement to the man who'd deflowered her the night before.

"How very lovely. I'm sure it'll be a great success."

"Please allow us to offer our condolences on the passing of the duke. His son has inherited the title I presume?" Andrew asked, his tone that of disinterest, which was exactly what Nina was feeling right at this moment.

"Matthew has inherited the title, and he and his wife are also in town this Season, although they spend most of their time at the estate in Derbyshire."

Byron frowned. "I thought the duke's home was in Kent."

"It was," Nina said, "but that home wasn't entailed and George left it to me, so it's where I live. I also have a town-house on Berkley Square all to myself, which is one small comfort." Considering she'd married the duke without an ounce of attachment and that she'd then allowed him to believe the children she gave birth to were his.

"How are the girls?" Lord Aaron asked. "I understand they're staying in Kent while you're in London."

Nina had decided that, but when the time had come to part she couldn't leave them behind and so she'd bundled them up and brought them with her. "I was going to leave them in Kent, but decided against it. They're in London with me, and enjoying all the museums and parks that we don't get at home."

"You're a mother?"

The blunt question that came from Byron wasn't what Nina expected and she glanced at both brothers, hoping they would not pry too much into her life. Andrew certainly had no claim on her anymore, or her children, even if he was the father.

"I am—two girls, and my sole reason for living. They are simply my heart."

"How old?" Byron asked, his voice hoarse.

Nina wasn't willing to tell them anything further and she smiled in welcome as Cecilia, Lady Aaron joined them. Nina kissed her cheeks in welcome.

"How lovely to see you again, Cecilia. I've been meaning to write, and I hope Darcy has maybe told you what I wish to do."

Cecilia nodded, going to her husband and linking arms with him. "She has, and I think it is the most marvellous idea."

"What is the idea?" Lord Aaron asked, throwing a curious glance at his wife.

"The duchess has purchased a vacant building in the village near her estate and she's going to make it into a school, and, for the children who require it, a place to live. We have two other schools based in the country, but this is our first in Kent. I'm so very excited about it."

Byron's betrothed joined them. Her long golden locks that sat high atop her head made her appear older than she was and her white muslin gown had a pretty pink ribbon at the waist. Coming up to Byron, she wrapped her hand about his arm. The familiarity between the two twisted something within Nina and for a moment she simply stared at where they were joined.

Miss Custer dipped into a curtsy, but her inspection of Nina seemed less than enthralled. "It's lovely to see you again, Your Grace," she said banally. "What is it that everyone is talking about?"

Cecilia caught Miss Custer up on their discussion about the new school, but even with this subject Byron's betrothed looked less than interested.

"I think it's just what is needed if we're to fight the divide between the classes," Nina added. "It is very hard to better oneself, but this new school will enable girls and boys to become whatever they wish, if they have the determination to do so."

Miss Custer scoffed. "I shall not be offering to put one up in Cornwall. We would lose half our workforce in the mines in a day should we do so. We rely on the youngins working for us." Sofia chuckled at her own statement, as if the poor and needy were something that one ought to find funny.

Nina fisted her hands at her side. "You believe that allowing children to work underground, inhaling air that is no good for their lungs, stopping them from possibly doing other employment that would certainly give them a longer, more satisfying life, is a bad thing?"

"I do," Sofia said, meeting her gaze. "Someone has to do the job and the children are most capable. I think your idea, no matter how revolutionary, will never happen."

A shiver stole down Nina's back at the coldness she read in the woman's eyes. No matter what Sofia said or what Nina did, they would never be friends. The dislike oozing from the woman towards her was palatable. Not to mention anyone who thought it proper to allow children to work in mines was no friend of hers.

"I disagree, Miss Custer, and I hope to see the end of children working in your family's mines. Children deserve so much more than what we, our society at large I mean, give them."

Sofia took a sip of her wine but didn't say anything further.

Their set fell into awkward silence and Nina couldn't help but narrow her eyes at the little Cornish chit. She especially wanted to say more to Miss Custer about her atrocious beliefs, but she did not. She was Byron's betrothed, and Byron was her friend. She would not embarrass him no matter how much she detested his future wife.

Fortunately Nina was then asked to dance by the Duke of Athelby and the night progressed well, save for the little hiccup with Miss Custer and her archaic views. She suppered with Darcy and discussed the plans for her new school, making her wish the Season was coming to an end, not just beginning, so she could go home and start the building work on her new property.

Byron came to sit with them during the repast. Darcy

excused herself and Nina turned toward her old friend, glad to have some time alone with him.

She touched his arm lightly. "Have I told you how very happy I am that you're back in England? I thought for a time that you would never return."

He nodded slowly in agreement. "The draw of the sunshine simply was too much to deny."

Nina laughed, a sound she'd not heard often these past years, unless she was with her children of course, who always made her happy. "Come, Byron, even I know your words reek with sarcasm." She took in his features, his strong jaw and straight nose. Dark brown orbs the color of cocoa. How was it that she'd never looked at him with anything other than friendship? He was certainly handsome, just as handsome as his brother once was, but maybe a little more wild. Was that the reason? Andrew had always seemed responsible, careful, and trustworthy. How wrong she'd been. All the time she'd been holding onto Andrew, placing him on a pedestal, hoping their union would be a love match, he'd been looking at someone else.

"I glad we're alone, Byron, because there is something that I want to discuss with you."

"You can tell me anything. What is it, Nina?"

His use of her name warmed her from the inside out. "The history between your brother and I…I do not want it to come between our friendship. You've always been there for me. My friend and rock. I have missed you these five years."

"I missed you too." He cleared his throat and took a sip of his wine. "Nothing will come between us. I will fight for our friendship no matter what obstacles we face. I promise you that."

"Well, let us hope there are no more obstacles and that we can move forward. I knew seeing Andrew with his wife would be difficult at first, but now after seeing him again, viewing him without the haze of adolescent idiocy, I simply cannot understand what I liked about him. He's a little vapid, don't you think?"

"Too true," Byron said, his eyes alight with mischief. "To be honest I could never understand what you saw in my brother either. And I love him, I do, but I never thought his character suited yours. I know you were known as a little cold and aloof during your first Season, but to me you've always been warm, funny, all too willing to laugh. I always thought you should marry a man who tested you, loved you wildly, and honored you. Andrew was never that."

The breath in Nina's lungs seized and she found herself entranced by Byron's eyes. How well he knew her, behind the façade she once hid behind. How had it been that he saw all that she was and could offer and Andrew had not? She sighed, supposing when one was looking at marrying someone else, their attention wasn't as focused as one thought.

A fluttering settled in her belly and she looked down at her champagne glass. Why was she reacting to Byron in such a way? For one, he was betrothed, and second, she was not looking for anyone to marry. Especially not one of the Hill brothers. No matter how much she loved her friend, she would not walk that road again. For the first time in years she was happy with who she was, a mother. The girls needed her and would need her guidance even more as they grew into young women. Being independently wealthy with her own estates afforded her a freedom most women could only dream of, and she wasn't willing to give that up, especially not to another man.

"I hope I have not offended you, Nina, with what I said."

She shook her head, smiling to put him at ease. "Of course not. I think what you said was lovely and I thank you. I know we'll always be friends, and I wanted to ensure that stayed so. As for me and your brother, well, we will never be friends again."

Nina read the understanding in her friend's eyes and she was thankful he was back in town. They used to have so much fun together, and with Byron back her Season would have another element of joy.

"I can understand your stance regarding my sibling, and I know there is no point in trying to change your mind. So," he said, holding out his hand, "shall we dance instead?"

She slid her gloved fingers into his hold, grinning. "I would love to."

CHAPTER 4

Byron strolled into the breakfast room the following morning and was glad to find Andrew there alone. He served himself up a couple of veal and ham pies, along with poached eggs and a piece of toast, before sitting. A footman poured him a coffee and Byron took a moment to gather his thoughts.

Andrew folded the newspaper he was reading and placed it beside him on the table, dismissing the servants from the room. Byron glared at him across the mahogany space and Andrew looked at him in surprise, no doubt wondering what had put his mood out of sorts.

"The night that you told me to stay in your room at the Athelby's country estate, due to your hard mattress if you recall, tell me that Nina turning up was not orchestrated by you," Byron said, watching his sibling. "Tell me that you did not know she was going to enter your room and offer herself like a sweetmeat on a plate."

Andrew's eyes widened and Byron knew his summarisation of his brother had been correct. He had set him up!

Had known that Nina was coming to his room, and had deposited Byron there to face her instead. Made Byron believe she had been there for him, while all the time she was there for his brother. "You bastard, Andrew. I ought to get up right now and pummel you to a pulp."

Andrew placed his coffee down with enough force for the liquid to spill a little onto the white tablecloth. "What if I did know? It is too late to change things now. I wanted to marry Fionna and Edwina stood in the way of that." His brother shrugged and a red haze closed over Byron's vision. "I was surprised by her blatant dislike for me last evening–it was more than I expected from a woman who'd simply been told that I wouldn't marry her. She seemed scorned to me."

"That's because she was scorned. Scorned by you. The following morning she arrived downstairs to find you announcing your betrothal to Miss O'Connor. What did you expect from Nina? Joy? Congratulations? You do not deserve anything from her."

Andrew studied him a moment and Byron fought to keep his hands unclenched. The silence was long, and when he met his brother's hardened gaze he knew Andrew had figured out his secret. "You slept with her, didn't you? She arrived at my room, thinking it was me, and you took advantage of that. She thinks I slept with her the night before I announced my engagement to Fionna."

Andrew ran a hand through his hair and for a moment Byron's calm and patience cracked a little. "I thought she was there for me. How did you know she was going to come to your room?"

His brother shifted on his seat, adjusting his cravat. "She sent me a missive that day, saying she wanted to talk in private. I could not meet with her, obviously, and I suppose I panicked. The bed was hard, I will admit Byron, and so us swapping rooms was necessary for me to sleep, but I did not think she would follow through on her plan. I seem to have been wrong."

"You were bloody well wrong alright. She thinks you slept with her the night before your betrothal. She doesn't know it was me. This can all be laid at your door, you damn fool. Why would you not just send her a note stating your affections lay elsewhere? Do you have no conscience?" His brother was a coward and damn it to hell, how would Byron ever gain Nina's forgiveness over this mess.

"I cannot have my wife hearing that I supposedly deflowered a virgin before asking for her hand. Fionna would never forgive me," Andrew said, standing and letting his chair fall back against the floor.

Anger thrummed through Byron's veins and he fought not to lose his temper. "I swapped rooms to allow you to sleep. I did not know she was going to arrive at my door and ask for things you damn well know I'd longed to hear from her for years. You played me and Nina to gain your own happy ever after."

"And during all the time she was in your room, can you honestly say that a name wasn't uttered? Did you not wonder at it, Byron?"

Byron swallowed the bile that rose in his throat. He had not wondered. Being so caught up in the delight of having her in his arms had made him incapable of clear thought. He'd truly believed she was there for him. What a fool he'd been. And the moment she'd whispered his brother's name just as she left, a little piece of him had died.

"I did not think my blood could use me in such a way. I will not be fooled twice, brother." Byron stood, taking a calming breath. "I must tell her the truth of it."

Andrew gestured with his arms, knocking over the

remainder of his coffee. "Of course you need to tell her. Edwina woke the following morning and watched me announce my engagement to everyone at the house party, all the while thinking we'd made the beast with two backs the night before."

Byron stormed over to his brother, ready to rip his damn head off. His sibling stumbled back and fell over his chair, landing with a loud thump on his ass. "If your precious Fionna finds out how you used Nina, courted her and flirted with her during her two Seasons, then you deserve her wrath. Tricking your own brother to save your own hide, well, you have lost any respect I once held for you. I will allow you to stay here for the remainder of the Season and then you shall return to Ireland and stay there. You do not deserve me as a brother, or Nina as a friend."

"Who do you think you are?" Andrew yelled, pointing a finger at him. "You could've offered for her. Why did you not make an honest woman of your precious Nina? Instead, you allowed her to marry a man old enough to be her grandfather."

Byron clenched his fists. "You damn well know I came downstairs only to find both of you engaged and basking in the grand matches you'd made. I couldn't say anything to Nina. She would've been ruined, and as much as she loved me as a friend, she was infatuated with you. It would've broken her heart, and she'd already had that broken seeing you engaged to Fionna. I could not break it twice in one day."

How he'd wanted to go to her that morning. To take her in his arms and tell her to marry him instead. That he would make her happy, keep her safe, and give her all that she wanted in life. A part of him had been a coward, scared to lose her even as a friend should he tell her the truth, but no longer. He would tell her now, and be damned the consequences. And he would tell her soon.

Andrew stood, dusting down his buckskin breeches. "I will accept my part in this sorry mess, but now you must tell her the truth. I'll not have her believing it was me who took her maidenhead."

Byron thought over how he would even begin to tell Nina. When she knew the truth of that night she'd never speak to him again, and the idea of the severing from a woman who had always been his friend, a woman whom he'd fallen in love with that Season all those years ago, made him want to retch. He swallowed. "Of course I'll tell her the truth. But this isn't something that you can just blurt out to anyone at any time. I wronged her. You wronged her. And this will devastate her."

Andrew snatched the paper from the table and started toward the door. "It needs to be done, and soon. I'll give you the time you want, but don't drag it out simply because it'll be hard for her to hear."

Byron watched his brother leave, resisting the urge to throw a plate at his head. Andrew had always been a heartless prig, only worrying about his own hide in any situation. In the five years since Byron had seen him last, his sibling had not changed one bit for the better.

Byron sighed, righting his brother's chair and looking over the mess of the breakfast table. He sat back down before his now cold meal. He picked up his fork as his mind turned to what he would have to do, and how Nina would handle hearing the truth. No matter how much he'd loved her, how much he'd longed for her, it was not him she'd wanted. He should've known the night she came to his room that she was mistaken, that they were both under miscomprehensions.

The cost of that night would be greater than he'd ever

imagined, and possibly too much for a friendship to recover from.

NINA STOOD on the steps before the Hill brothers' London home. Not a location she'd thought she'd ever grace again, and yet here she was. She rapped on the door using the iron knocker. She looked out onto the square and smiled at a couple of passers-by before the door opened and a footman greeted her.

"Mr. Byron Hill, please." She handed him her card. "Tell him the Dowager Duchess of Exeter is here to see him."

The footman bowed, stumbling over his words to grant her entrance and do as she asked, before he disappeared into one of the rooms leading off the foyer.

The quickened steps on parquetry floor sounded before Byron came out of a room, smiling in welcome.

"Your Grace, how wonderful to see you again. I hope everything is well."

Nina smiled at her old friend, again so very pleased he was back in town. "Everything is well, but I was hoping you would accompany me today. I'm purchasing the desks that are required for the school I'm opening in Kent, and I'd like your opinion on them."

He threw her a dubious look. "Are you sure you wish me to accompany you? The Duchess of Athelby or Marchioness of Aaron may be better suited, since they already run two schools here in town."

She clasped her hands before her and fought to ignore the fact her pulse quickened at the sight of him. Why was it now that she found her dearest friend so very alluring? Was it simply because he was betrothed and therefore not a suitor she could have? Or the fact that she'd loved him as a friend for years and was only now seeing him for his worth?

It could also be both…

"Darcy and Katherine have given me the name and address of their supplier and he's expecting me, but I'd like the company. Men, as you know, sometimes find it hard to be fair when dealing with women."

Byron called for his coat and cane and took them from the footman when they were fetched. "I would love to join you, of course. I just assumed a duchess would have servants who would do such tasks."

"I do have them, but it's something I want to do. I may be a duchess, but that doesn't mean I sit at home lording it over everyone else. How boring my life would be if that were the case."

"And let's not forget you're a mother now, something I simply cannot imagine. You must let me meet your daughters. I'd so love to get to know them."

"I'd love that too. We'll have to ensure you meet before you head to Cornwall. Living in that faraway county, we'll never see you." And if lady luck were on her side, Byron wouldn't recognize the fact the girls looked nothing like her husband but someone else entirely.

He stared at her for a moment before clearing his throat and gesturing toward the door. "Shall we?"

They made their way to her carriage, which sat parked at the front of the townhouse. Byron took her hand, helping her up the step. The feel of his strong touch, even through her kid-leather gloves, left her mind reeling. She would have to get hold of her emotions, of her reactions to him. Acting like a lovesick ninny would never do, especially now that he was engaged to another.

"The location is not too far. Thank you for coming. It

gives us more time to catch up." She settled onto the squabs, aware that her carriage was probably a lot grander than what Byron had, but other than looking about the equipage with delight, he didn't comment on the opulence.

"How many desks are we purchasing today?" he asked.

Nina was glad the conversation had diverted in a practical direction—it saved her from asking him what he loved about Sofia Custer. After their conversation last evening, Nina couldn't find a lot to like in the woman who agreed with child labour.

"One hundred. I've seen some desks that have a little lid on them that opens and allows the children to keep their chalkboards or lunch beneath it. It's most revolutionary and the design I'm most interested in."

"A hundred desks will cost you."

Nina barked out a laugh. The cost was the least of her problems. "I'm an extremely wealthy woman, Byron. You needn't worry I'm spending my pin money."

His cheeks reddened and he leaned forward, taking her hand from her lap. "Apologies, Duchess. That was very crass of me. In fact, I don't know why I mentioned it. I suppose out of concern and friendship."

Nina squeezed his hand then broke the contact. Why was it now that he discombobulated her so? He never used to. "Where did you go after the Athelby house party where we saw each other last? Your brother hightailed it to Ireland and he never gave me a forwarding address for you. I wanted to write, tell you everything that had happened, but I didn't know where to send the missives."

He glanced out the window, the muscle on his temple working. "That day, that we parted, I'd prefer to forget. I slept late and came down to a house in uproar, or at least in jubilation uproar. My brother engaged to Miss

O'Connor and you engaged to the Duke of Exeter. I thought I was living in an alternate universe."

Nina had often felt the same. Her hasty decision to accept the duke after hearing the news of Andrew's engagement had been financially rewarding, and the duke, no matter how much older than herself, had not been unkind. But if she had her time again she would not have done it. She would've ruined herself, publicly declared that Andrew had deflowered her, and demanded he marry her. Not that their marriage would've been any good under such beginnings, but the fact that he could do such a thing to her and then marry someone else still irked. How could anyone be so heartless?

"I will not insult you by declaring that I loved the duke and didn't want another, for you know that would be a lie. I married the duke because Andrew broke my heart, foolish and young as it was then, but nevertheless he did, and I wanted to prove to him that he was not the only one who could be so unfeeling, so cold and aloof. I suppose I really did live up to how people viewed me after all."

"I'm sorry about my brother and his actions toward you."

Nina scoffed. What would Byron think if he knew the whole truth? That Andrew hadn't just broken her heart, but had ruined her. Looking back, she knew she'd been fortunate that the duke had asked for her hand. Had he not, she would've had to tell her parents that she was with child once she realized the truth herself, and that the father was a married man. Such news would not have been welcomed by her parents or by society at large.

"Not as sorry as I am that I fell for his pretty words, but," she said, wanting to end this discussion, "let us discuss my new venture and the Season ahead of us." She didn't want to spend a moment more thinking about

Andrew Hill or his treachery. She wanted to look to her and her children's future, the future for all the children she'd help with her school in Kent.

Byron's lips lifted into a small smile. "I heartily agree. Now, tell me where exactly this school is going to be. I'll need to know so when I get back to town I can order and send books down to you. A school is nothing without a library."

Warmth spread through Nina and she felt an over-whelming urge to hug him. "Your generosity will not be forgotten. Thank you, Byron. You're too good."

He threw her a wicked grin, and for the life of her she could not look away. The pit of her stomach clenched and the carriage suddenly seemed awfully small and confined.

Byron cleared his throat, and she was glad of the distraction. "Have you been a member of the London Relief Society for long? How did you become involved?" he asked, the tension of the moment relieved by his genuine interest in her work.

"The Duke of Athelby is a relative, and I knew Darcy was involved for some years. My husband didn't like coming to town much, so I would often visit the small village at the base of our home in Kent. Even in a quiet village I could see that there were children without schooling, children without proper care or food. I want to change that. Help where I can."

"You always did have a heart of gold. Your daughters must be very proud of you."

Nina smiled thinking of her girls. "I hope they are, or they will be at least when they're older. I want them to be strong and kind women. Women of power who want to make a difference in the lives of others."

"You'll be wanting the vote next," Byron said, grinning at her.

Nina sighed. He'd been her friend for so many years, and they had always got along so well. To be around him for more than snippets of time would be no hardship. It was certainly something she would enjoy on a daily basis if she could. "I hope one day that we do have the right. It is only fair and just that women have what men have, and have the same opportunities as well. I want that for my girls and I'll not apologize for my opinions."

"I wouldn't want you to," he whispered, meeting her gaze.

She chuckled to hide the rioting emotions he seemed to conjure in her. "I'm glad you're back in London. Thank you for coming on my jaunt today."

"What are friends for if not to help each other?"

Friends... The word echoed through her mind. Did she want to only be friends with Byron? She studied him as he looked out the window at the passing streets of London. Her attention travelled over his attire. His suede buckskin breeches required no padding on his muscular thighs. His shoulders were broad and his black greatcoat only made him look larger, more dangerous and brawny. They had always been the best of friends, but now, seeing him with Miss Custer, she wasn't so sure she liked the idea that he was destined for another. Didn't want to imagine him beside his wife in the privacy of their room, his body hers to enjoy, to run her hands over and play with. Miss Custer's and Miss Custer's alone.

Just as Nina had made a mistake with Andrew, she now realized she'd also made a terrible error of judgement with Byron. But what to do about that error? Not since her youthful folly with Andrew had she felt this desire to be with a man, but she was certainly feeling it now with Byron. Should she dissuade him from marrying Miss Custer? Or should she acknowledge the fact that they were only ever meant to be friends and nothing more?

Surely if they were meant to be together fate would've stepped in years ago and showed its hand. It had not. Even so, Nina debated with herself over what she wanted and what was right, and at this very moment in time, the selfish part of her wanted Byron for herself and Miss Custer could go hang.

CHAPTER 5

Two nights later Nina attended the Duke and Duchess of Athelby's annual ball. Their London home was one of the capital's finest, and just as the house was magnificent, so too was the decoration and floral arrangements that Darcy loved to have throughout the ballroom.

Entering the room, one would've thought they had stepped into a forest landscape. Somehow Darcy had brought the outdoors in, and with the terrace doors open at the end of the room, had the floor not been parquetry but grass, one would've thought it was outside.

Nina dipped into a small curtsy and kissed the duke and duchess in welcome. "You've outdone yourself, Darcy. How beautiful this ballroom is."

Darcy smiled, pride alight in her eyes. "The large trees that I've used are the ones that I'm sending to Kent to be planted in your new school grounds. The transport is booked for two days from now, so I thought I'd make use of them. I hope you like my donation to your new venture."

Tears blurred Nina's vision at the generosity of her

friends. "Thank you, I'm overwhelmed by your kindness. The children will love them and I shall have a plaque made up so they'll always remember who gave them such magnificent oaks."

Darcy squeezed her hand. "My pleasure, and please, go in. I'll catch up with you shortly."

Nina joined the throng, and seeing Katherine, Lady Leighton standing alone she started in her direction. "Katherine, so lovely to see you again," she said, coming to stand beside her and taking a glass of champagne from a passing footman.

"Duchess," Katherine said, dipping into a curtsy. "I heard you were back in town and joining in more with the London Relief Society. I'm very happy we'll be seeing more of you. We need more members, particularly women that hold a position of rank, to be active in charity. More people notice our cause, I think, when women like you take part."

"I heartily agree and will do all that I can to make a difference." Nina had met the countess during her first Season, as she was related by marriage to Lizzie Doherty, who had married the man Nina had been courted by that Season, Lord Wakely. Thankfully they were now happily married and living abroad. Nina thought back on that Season for a moment, realizing she seemed to be a beacon for gentlemen who ended up marrying someone else.

The thought left her uneasy, as if there was something possibly wrong with her. She had been cold and aloof that first Season, but only because she loved Andrew Hill and didn't want to marry Lord Wakely. But then Andrew had slept with her and chosen another only hours later. Maybe there was something that others saw in her that she wasn't aware of. Something negative.

"I understand you have two daughters, Your Grace. They're twins, are they not?"

The mention of her daughters, whom she'd tucked safely into bed not an hour before, made her smile. "They're five now and very active. Already they love stories and going out in the carriage. We're going to Hatchards tomorrow. I know they may be a little young, but I think they'll enjoy the outing in any case."

"You could take them to Gunter's for ices afterwards. I know my children enjoy such treats."

For a time they discussed their children and the antics that they sometimes got up to, before Nina glanced across the ballroom floor and spotted her daughter-in-law, the Duchess of Exeter. The scowl on Bridget's forehead as she made her way over to them made a feeling of foreboding lodge in Nina's abdomen. She steeled herself for the confrontation that was without doubt soon to follow.

"Your Grace," Lady Leighton said, as Bridget reached their side. Nina raised her brow and fought to bring forth a welcoming smile for Bridget, who still had a face that was set in stone.

"A school, Nina? If it were not embarrassing enough that I have a mother-in-law who is younger than myself, now we have to live with the knowledge that you're opening a school in Kent. How could you do this to the family?"

Nina rolled her eyes. Bridget was a short woman, especially compared to the duke, who was a good foot and a half taller than her. She also was full figured and her gowns seemed too frilly, too pretty for a woman of her age. No matter how many times Nina had tried to help her gain a little fashion sense, she seemed stuck in her debutante years when her mother used to dress her up.

"There is no shame in helping those less fortunate. My

opening a school will not bring embarrassment to the family. However, your public airing of your disdain for my venture may. Perhaps you ought to call the day after tomorrow and we can discuss this in private."

Bridget had the smarts to look about and see a few of the guests watching them. Her cheeks reddened. "I will not call—we have nothing to say. But if you think you're going to open a school, I want to notify you that this will not happen. Not while I'm the Duchess of Exeter."

"Well, my dear, I'm the dowager Duchess of Exeter and I do not answer to you. Now run along. This conversation has concluded." Nina lost all pretence of calm and glared at her daughter-in-law. The woman was as nasty as her husband, who had also never approved of the duke marrying her. Not that Nina cared a fig what either of them thought, but it vexed her that Bridget would snarl at her in such a public place. That she would not stomach.

"I will call tomorrow after all," Bridget said, turning away.

"You may call tomorrow but we'll not be home. I said the day after tomorrow."

Bridget didn't bother to reply, just huffed off, and Nina took a calming breath when she lost sight of her in the throng of guests.

"I'm so sorry, Your Grace. I've never seen anyone react to charity in such a negative way. Is the duchess always so toward you?" Lady Leighton asked.

Nina took a sip of her champagne, knowing she may need a few more tonight if Bridget was present. "She's always so. No matter what I do or say it is never good enough for them. As you may have heard, the duke was quite a lot of years older than me, and they never approved. They thought I married him for his money, but it was in fact an equal arrangement, both in financial and emotional terms."

"I hope you don't find my next question prying, and please tell me if I've overstepped my mark, but I understand that you've kept the estate in Kent and the duke gifted you his second London home. Do you think the current duke found the terms of his father's will too generous, and so they intend to strike at you in any way they can?"

Nina shrugged, having had the same thought many times. But what was done was done, and the current duke knew very well that Nina had brought a fortune to the family, a portion of it allowing him and Bridget to live very comfortably. If they had any smarts between them they ought to be polite, and leave her well alone.

"Possibly, but the Kent estate was not entailed, nor was the London home. It used to be the duke's mistress's home, not that the ton knew since it's located in Mayfair. The duke and duchess may harbor some anger over losing those properties, but it's not as if they don't have many more to keep themselves occupied. The duke had multiple estates in England and Scotland."

Lady Leighton chuckled. "Then they are simply spiteful and I shall not venture to invite them to any future events at our home. And I shall talk to my friends as well and ensure they feel the coldness that can be heaped on people when they mistreat someone who does not deserve it. You opening a school is a wonderful thing, and if the current Duchess of Exeter did something similar, maybe her life would be more fulfilled than it is right now."

Nina doubted much could fulfil the duchess's life, but she nodded in agreement in any case. "I'm sure you're right."

They were soon joined by Lord Leighton, who whisked

his wife out for a waltz. Nina stood alone, content to observe the guests and enjoy her champagne. Tomorrow couldn't come soon enough, and she looked forward to spending time with her girls.

"You seem lost in thought, Duchess. I hope the ball isn't boring you too much?" Mr. Byron Hill said against her ear, sending a delicious shiver down her spine. She stepped away, giving them distance and praying he hadn't noticed her reaction to him.

"Simply watching and thinking. I'm taking my children out tomorrow and I find I cannot wait. I've been so busy with the Season that they're woefully overdue for an adventure."

"That sounds like a wonderful idea," Byron stated.

He smiled, and the gesture made the small dimple on his left cheek stand out. Nina stared at it for a moment, knowing both brothers had one but on opposite sides of their faces. The night she'd slept with Andrew she could've sworn it was on the left, not the right side of his face...

"Duchess, are you well?" Byron reached out and touched her arm and Nina shook the thought aside. Now she was being silly, her memory playing tricks on her.

"I'm perfectly well, thank you. Tell me, where is your fiancée tonight? I have not seen her."

Byron rubbed a hand over his jaw, looking out toward the throng of guests. "Her father summoned her back to Cornwall so she'll miss the remainder of the Season. We're to marry in the church in her village, so I will travel there once the Season has come to an end."

Despair swamped her at the mention of Byron leaving and she took a moment to steady her emotions before she said, "And so we shall never see you again. Please do not become a stranger like you did these past years. Now that I have you back, I'm loathe to lose you again." She stared up at Byron and read the awareness that flared in his eyes. She shouldn't say such things, not to a man who loved another, but she also couldn't help herself. If only she'd seen him sooner. Had seen his worth before his course was set.

He tore his gaze from her, the muscle in his jaw flexing. "We have the Season, my friend. Let us make a promise to enjoy it together as much as we can, before I'm to Cornwall and you're back to Kent on your new adventure."

Nina held out her hand. Byron looked at it for a moment before chuckling and clasping it firmly. His hands were so very large compared to her own, and the idea of them holding her, pulling her close, giving her pleasure rocked her to her core.

He shook her hand once. "Deal, Duchess?"

"Deal," she said, letting him go. "That is one understanding I'm willing to enter into."

BYRON WALKED about Hatchards holding the new poetry books that the desk clerk had notified him of their arrival while he sought out other reads. The bell on the door chimed, followed by the sound of excitable children's voices. He looked up to see the dowager duchess of Exeter and her two daughters enter, the children's nursemaid following close on their heels.

He caught hold of the shelving and stared at Nina, taking in her beauty that was amplified when around her two children. The little girls took after their mama, dark haired with just the slightest curl. They ran past him and he stared after them. They were adorable. He ought to feel annoyed, slighted, that Nina had children with a man who'd not been worthy of her affection, but he could not. Nina didn't deserve his wrath. She'd been the one he and his brother had wronged, even if Byron didn't know of his wrongdoing at the time.

He needed to tell her the truth, and soon, but it wouldn't be easy. In fact, it would be one of the hardest things he'd ever do in his life.

"Byron, I forgot how much you loved reading, even though you used to feign disinterest whenever I caught you in the library."

He bowed, taking Nina's hand and kissing it. He lingered longer than he ought and then caught himself, stepping away. "You always knew me too well."

She walked about him, running her finger along the spine of the books he was perusing. "Poetry still. Anyone would think you have a heart that longs for romance."

He swallowed and hoped the heat spreading up his neck would not settle on his face. "I do not read love poetry, and you know it." He smiled down at her and she chuckled, heading off in the direction of her girls.

"Come," she said, gesturing for him to follow. "Come meet my daughters."

Nerves settled in the pit of his stomach, but he followed, wanting to meet them but unsure if they'd like him or not. The idea flitted through his mind that the girls could've been his had he fought for her the morning she announced her engagement to the duke.

The two girls sat on the floor near a front window, laughing and giggling at a book their nurse was reading to them. They were simply the most perfect little cherubs, and the pride he saw in Nina's eyes said that she thought the world of them.

"Darlings, come meet my friend, Mr. Byron Hill. Our families were friends and we grew up together. Mr. Hill and I have been the best of friends ever since."

The two little girls looked from their mama to him, and

studied him in great detail. Their eyes were the same color and shape, their hair tied up in pink ribbons, and their rose-colored frocks were identical.

"They're beautiful, Nina," he whispered, taking her hand and squeezing it a little. Then he kneeled before them and held out his hand. "How do you do, Lady Molly, Lady Lora. I'm very pleased to meet you at last. Your mama speaks of nothing else."

The two girls chuckled, the sound so like their mother's laugh, but younger. "You're not supposed to talk about us all the time, Mama. Not at balls and parties. You're supposed to talk about the weather, or the latest gowns," Lora said.

Nina nodded, looking very serious all of a sudden. "You're quite right. I shall ensure I follow those rules from this day forward."

Lora nodded, seemingly pleased with her instruction on proper etiquette. Byron fell in love with them on the spot and couldn't stop taking in their sweet little features that were so like their mama's.

"Do you like books, Mr. Hill? We're picking out some new ones today," Molly said.

"You like to read then? I'm very pleased to hear it. I love reading also." Byron stood marvelling at them.

"We do like reading, sir. We especially like it when Mama is home and reads to us. She makes the funniest sounds with some of the stories she reads to us," Lora said mischievously.

Nina chuckled and Byron didn't think he could've loved a woman more. He remembered the exact moment he had fallen in love with her, the year before her first Season. They had been riding horses at her parents' country house and she had come off, landing hard in a puddle of mud. Most women in her situation would've screamed at the ruination of their gowns, or about the silly horse that had not behaved, but not Nina. She had laughed, laughed so hard that tears had slipped down her muddied cheeks. She'd slapped the puddle, dirtying her gown more, and Byron had laughed along with her. Had fallen in love on the spot and had never fallen out of it.

He ran a hand through his hair, reminding himself that he was engaged, that he cared for another, but even he knew that wasn't the absolute truth. He was marrying Sofia simply because she was willing and her family were looking to climb the social ladder, which he could help with. He may not be titled, but his cousin was a marquess, and he was a wealthy gentleman. Their daughter and their family would be elevated by the union.

But there was no love. No affection. In all truth, had they not been caught up with the beauty of southern France, the aquamarine water that had lapped at their boat lulling them into false ideals, they probably wouldn't have become engaged.

Being here and now with Nina, standing before what his future could be if only he tried to win her love, won out over his desire to settle. How could he allow Sofia to marry a man who loved someone else? That would not be fair to her or him, and their marriage would not be a happy one should he allow the façade to continue. He'd wronged Nina once, but he would not do it a second time, and he would not wrong Sofia either. It was time he stopped making mistakes.

"Those are the best stories of all. Now, I shall leave you to find your books." Byron bowed toward the duchess and moved off to search for more reading material, but his mind was a whirr of thoughts about what he had do to and how he would do it.

Sofia and her family would not be pleased, and he may

have to offer some sort of financial settlement to get out of the contract. If Sofia wouldn't let him break the agreement he wasn't sure what he would do. Surely since there was no love, she would not be so upset. Annoyed maybe, but not enough to hold him to his promise.

He cringed.

"Byron, are you well? You seem troubled."

He didn't turn toward the duchess. They were in a secluded part of the store, hidden by bookcases. The sound of customers talking whispered to them, but still, they were alone. Quite alone…

"I'm well. You should return to your children. We'll have time to see each other at the Duncannons' ball this evening." *Please leave. Leave before I take you in my arms and kiss you like I've longed to do for five years.*

Her hand settled on his arm and he stilled. How he missed her touch. It was a form of torture and pleasure all in the one moment. Too much and yet not enough.

"We're going for ices, Byron. Join us. The girls would love for you to come." She paused for a moment before she added, "And so would I."

He turned and faced her, and his gaze shifted to her lips and wouldn't budge. He wanted to kiss her, he wanted her and no one else, had done so for too many years to count. The air in the secluded space they found themselves in thickened, and as if sensing the possibility of them being more than friends, Nina stepped away, starting back toward where her daughters were sitting.

"I will not take no for an answer, Byron." She gestured for him to follow and he could not deny her anything.

Their time at Gunter's was a trip worth taking. Over the hour he sat with Nina and the girls he learned all about their hobbies. Molly enjoyed her pony, while Lora loved dogs and especially the family wolfhound named Bentley that she spoke incessantly about, saying sweet things about how he would be terribly sad and missing them since they were at Gunter's and he was back at the townhouse. Molly had persuaded her mama to allow her to bring her pony to London with them, and before Byron departed, he agreed to take her riding, and to meet Bentley as well. Lora wouldn't have it any other way.

The duchess walked him to the pavement while the girls finished their ices. Byron hailed a hackney before turning to her. "Thank you for allowing me to meet your daughters, and for the ices. I had a wonderful time."

She looked up at him. Her hair was more natural today, loosely tied atop her head with a few wisps floating about her face, framing her perfect features. He fisted his hands at his sides before he did something stupid like reach up and clasp her jaw and kiss her.

"I'm glad you met them. It was time you did."

Byron nodded and bowed, then turned to go. She clasped his arm and he halted, loathing himself for the way his body all but jumped out of his skin each time she was near.

"I will see you tonight?" she asked, her voice cautious.

"You will," he said, and was relieved when she released his arm so he could go. Should he look at her now, turn and face her, there was little chance he would hold onto his morals, to his promise to Sofia, and not take the duchess in his arms. A place she belonged and nowhere else. He would make plans to travel to Cornwall. He needed to speak to Sofia and, if necessary, make a monetary settlement to her family for the wrong he was about to inflict on them. But he could not go on and not be true to himself. He was still in love with Nina, of that there was no doubt. Once he returned to town he would pursue her, make her see that it was him all along who was made for her. That he was the man she'd always loved, not just as a friend.

He waved to the duchess and banged on the roof to notify the driver to drive on. The awareness that was mirrored in Nina's eyes told him, more than ever before, that he may have a chance to win her. That she too had sensed the change in their comradeship, and that the friendship they'd always had had now altered into something so much more.

Nina sat on a settee that had been placed on the terrace of her London townhouse and watched the girls run about the lawn, Bentley never far behind them. Their giggles and squeals of delight made her laugh, but her mind was elsewhere. Was in fact in Cornwall, where Byron had travelled the day after they met for ices at Gunter's.

He'd never said a word about it at the ball that same evening. She bit her bottom lip, not for the first time wondering what he was doing there. Of course she knew he was seeing Sofia. Would he return to town as a married man?

Andrew too had left for a country house party—odd, for it was still early in the Season—so she couldn't ask him what he knew of his brother's sudden departure.

The book she was reading by Frances Burney had not gained her attention and she placed it on the chair, sick and tired of herself and her muddled thoughts. What did it matter if Byron married sooner than he'd planned? Maybe he'd been missing his fiancée, and wanted to see her again.

Perhaps he would return to town with her accompanying him.

All the images those scenarios brought forth in her mind left little ease and she frowned, cross at herself and at him for reasons she wasn't really ready to admit to.

"Your Grace, the Duchess of Athelby to see you."

"Bring her to the terrace, thank you," she said to the footman.

Nina sighed in relief at the distraction. Anything but to be tormented a moment longer by her own musings. She stood, and smiled as the duchess stepped out onto the terrace.

"Nina, how lovely to see you," Darcy said, kissing her cheek and sitting on the vacant settee beside Nina's.

"You too. I'm so very grateful for your company. As much as I love my girls, I'm simply torturing myself with my own mind and need a friend to confide in. Your arrival is timely."

The duchess reached out and placed a hand atop hers. "Whatever is the matter, dearest? You seem quite agitated."

"That's because I am. I don't know what's wrong with me. I feel sick to my stomach. I want to get in a carriage and see something that is bothering me for myself and then decide what to do. I want to wish away coming back to town. I want…"

"You want what?" Darcy asked, her brows raised.

Nina met her gaze and read the amusement twitching her lips. "I…" She shook her head, not believing she was going to say what she was. "I want… I want Byron Hill to be mine and not Sofia Custer's. I want him with everything that I am, and I cannot have him. We've been friends for so many years, so much has happened."

"You have not… Not when he's still betrothed to Sofia, I hope."

"No, of course, not," Nina said, her cheeks heating. "But I wanted to. So many times I've wanted to throw myself at his head. You knew years ago I was fixated with his brother, but I wonder at that now. I question my motives there. Andrew had always been the polite, safe sibling if ever one was to marry into that family, and so like all the ladies, I focused my attention on him. But it was Byron that I laughed with. Who I danced with, who went riding in the park with me. We read books and sought each other out at balls and parties. I wonder now if it was Byron I always loved, and wouldn't admit to it. I chose the safe option, when I really should have gambled my heart on the brother who was wild, fierce, and passionate. The last I'm yet to explore, but I want to. I want to so much it hurts." There. She'd said all that had been plaguing her, and damn the consequences. If she were an unlikable woman then so be it.

Darcy gasped, her eyes bright with comprehension. "Well, that is something to have bottled up inside yourself. And I promise your secret is safe with me, always. But he's engaged, dearest. There is little chance that will change. What options do you have other than to love him from afar?"

Nina flopped back onto her chair, checking the girls' whereabouts and seeing they were digging in Mr. Gregory's rose bushes. The head gardener would not be pleased. "I have no options. I will not come between anyone, least of all my dearest friend's choice of bride. Even so…" She sighed. "I've been such a fool when it came to him. I see that now and unfortunately it is too late."

"Did I ever tell you that the duke and I were once best friends too? Many years ago, before his brother passed away. But then he changed, became jaded and opinionated toward everyone, and we didn't like each other much for some time." Darcy was quiet for a minute, watching Nina's girls before she turned and met her gaze. "And yet now he is my husband, I adore the ground he walks upon and he too me. Life has a way of figuring itself out. Until Mr. Hill is married, there is always a chance."

Nina wished she could tell Darcy the whole truth—that the girls were really Andrew Hill's, not the duke's, and should Byron find out, he'd never forgive her. Even with her choices as limited as they were after Andrew proposed to another woman, Nina should have told Byron of her troubles. He would have helped her, she was sure.

"Perhaps you are right. I simply will stop worrying until I see him next. He may have visited his betrothed and nothing more."

"Do you know when he's due back?"

Nina shook her head, having not heard a word from him. "No. He's been gone some weeks now. Maybe he's decided to stay in Cornwall and not return for the Season?" The idea shot panic through her and she clasped her stomach to stop its churning. She really needed to seize hold of her emotions, or when she did see him next he'd read her like a book. He'd always had the ability to know what emotional state she was in at any moment.

"Nina, he'll return. I think the best thing you could do is to see what has happened while he was away and decide your next step from there. If he's married then there is nothing you can do, but if he is not, well, there is time. Not that I would suggest you step between them, as that would never do, but to simply see what has occurred and decide your own path. Do not forget there are many other eligible gentlemen in town who'd love to court you."

The very idea roiled through her like a poorly tasting

wine. "I didn't come back to town to find a husband. That Byron returned was simply a stroke of good luck. The idea of being courted by any other men does not interest me."

Darcy sat up, clapping her hands. "You need a diversion. Something fun and a little risqué."

The idea was not uninteresting, and Nina turned her full attention toward the duchess. "What kind of diversion?"

"I have a friend, someone I've known for many years, who holds little outings for members of the *ton*. You dress up as a woman of little means—perhaps how scullery maids may dress when they go out. We take a carriage to a less refined locale in London, but a safe one I should stress, and you enjoy a night in a tavern like the common man. I've taken part in one previously, before I married the duke, and it was such fun. He will insist on accompanying me this time, but you will enjoy yourself. You drink at a bar! If you can believe that. We may gamble and dance. Let me organise this for you and our friends and we'll make a night of it."

Nina had never heard of such a thing, but it did sound like a laugh and she so needed to laugh again. To enjoy one night where she didn't have to be the grand dowager duchess, the epitome of standards. What a fake she was half the time, and the *ton* had no idea.

"I will do it. Say it will be soon. I need a diversion."

Darcy stood and held out a hand to pull Nina to stand. "I will return home now and make the arrangements. Wait for a missive from me and that will explain all."

BYRON MADE it back to London late four weeks after his departure. The sojourn to Cornwall had been a welcome reprieve from town life, but the termination of his betrothal to Sofia had not been easy or well received. Which, he mused, was understandable.

He sat outside the Duchess of Exeter's London home, where most of the windows glowed with the flickering candlelight inside. Another carriage pulled up before his and the sound of laughter and animated conversations floated on the air.

The front door of Nina's home opened, and he watched as a scullery maid walked down the steps. Yet there was something about the maid that gave him pause. Her gait wasn't that of a woman who served her betters—this woman sauntered with grace, her chin held high and her posture perfect. The weathered gown went some way to disguise her, and yet he would know Nina anywhere. And right now, Nina was going out dressed as a servant.

Why the hell would she do that?

She jumped up into the carriage and Byron ordered his driver to follow them. They made their way out of Mayfair and toward Southwark before pulling up before the Talbot Inn. His own equipage pulled up across the road and Byron watched as the Duke and Duchess of Athelby exited, along with Nina. Within a minute another carriage arrived, this one bearing his own cousin and wife along with the Earl and Lady Leighton.

Byron shut his mouth with a snap, having not the slightest idea what his cousin was doing there dressed as a man of little means. Had they all lost their minds? He glanced down at himself, his highly starched cravat and perfectly pressed waistcoat. He could not enter the tavern dressed like this—he would be set upon within the first few minutes.

Ripping off his coat, he flung it on the seat across from him, before untying his cravat and loosening a couple of buttons at his neck. The waistcoat soon followed, and then he jumped out of the carriage, pulling his shirt out of his buckskin breeches. Ruffling his hair, he ordered his driver to return home, then headed toward the tavern.

No doubt he still appeared well-to-do, but it was better than a gentleman who looked ready for a ball. The tavern door tinkled as he pushed it open, and he glanced up to see a little brass bell. The room was hazy with smoke, and the stench of male sweat permeated the air.

He came up to the counter and ordered a beer before scanning the space, trying to see Nina and her friends. He heard her laugh before anything else. Moving his attention along the bar, he spotted the group standing before the bar almost at the other side of the room, each with a beer in their hands.

Byron smiled. The group of friends really did look ridiculous, but he supposed it was an escape from their lofty reality. If only everyone in such establishments could have their escape, then head back to their opulent lifestyle and houses.

Nina spotted him as he made his way over to them. Her eyes brightened with pleasure and hope spiralled through him that she liked him as much as he liked her. God, he hoped that was true. After the atrocious month he'd spent traveling to and from Cornwall, he wasn't sure he could stomach Nina turning away from what he was sure they had.

The possibility of a future.

"Byron," she said, coming over to him and wrapping her arm about his own, then pulling him toward their friends. "We're so glad to see you. Have you just returned to town?"

"I have." He nodded, taking in her beauty that was not dimmed even in the worn, tattered clothing she had on.

Her face was a little flushed, whether from the warmth inside the tavern or his arrival, he wasn't sure, but he hoped it was the latter.

"You travelled to Cornwall, cousin. I hope everything is well with Sofia?" the marquess queried.

At the mention of his betrothed—now his former betrothed—Nina pulled her arm free. She picked up her glass of beer and took a sip. Did she not like the mention of Sofia? Was she jealous, perhaps? That he didn't know, but before the night was over he certainly wanted her to know the truth of his situation as it now stood. Maybe, finally, she would look at him and see *him*, and no one else.

"Sofia and her family are all in good health." Byron took a glass of beer from the Duke of Athelby, thanking him.

"When will the wedding take place, or are you here tonight to tell us you're already married?" the Duchess of Athelby asked, looking between him and Nina. Did Darcy suspect something concerning him and the duchess? His reaction toward Nina, as though his skin sizzled and his heart wanted to jump out of his chest, was certainly obvious to him—maybe it was noticeable to others too.

"I'm not married." He met Nina's eyes, wanting her alone. Where they could talk.

Unfortunately as the night wore on they didn't have any opportunity to be alone. Their antics took them to two more taverns before they eventually called it a night and hailed hackney cabs to take them home. The couples bundled themselves into individual vehicles, and finally Byron and Nina were the only two left waiting for the next hackney to drive past.

"I'll return you home to ensure you arrive safely, Your Grace," Byron said. "If you're in agreement, of course."

She threw him a grin, her eyes sparkling from too

much beer and spirits, but never had she been so beautiful to him. Somehow in her plain gown, her hair lying about her shoulders, and limited jewels, she was the Nina he knew before their very first Season. The carefree, happy girl who blossomed into a beautiful woman.

"Aya, is that a duchess? Oy, lads, we 'ave a duchess over here." Byron turned to see a group of men come from a darkened alley beside the tavern. Slowly, he reached for the small folding pen knife in his breeches pocket that he carried with him always, and held it beside his leg, not wanting to show the assailants that he was armed. Little as that arming was.

"We want no trouble, lads. This woman isn't a duchess, but only a duchess to me. My pet name for her, if ye know what I mean." Byron tried to sound like the men, and hoped by their hesitation that maybe his foolery tricked them. His hope was short-lived when one of the men at the back of the group stepped forward.

"Ay, they 'ave money. Look at her earbobs. They're a pretty set that would feed us for a year I'd say."

Byron turned to see Nina and cringed as the single diamond on each of her ears glistened beneath the street lamp. "Paste, boys. We canna afford anything else, and it was a present to my wife. Dinna take them from her."

The men glanced between him and Nina, before two drunk gentlemen stumbled out of the inn, defusing the situation. They took one more look at the earbobs and turned toward the tavern's door. "Right ye are. No hard feelings, cobba. We'll leave ye to yourself."

Relief poured through him and he reached for Nina, pulling her into his arms. Her body shook against his, and he tightened his hold, rubbing his hands along her back to try to fight away her fear.

"It's alright, Nina. They're gone now." A hackney

turned up the road and Byron hailed it, bundling her inside and calling out the direction for home before anyone else could accost them. Had the men attacked, Byron wouldn't have known what to do. One against seven was too much for any man, and the men from this part of London did not play fair. More than likely someone would've been killed, possibly him or Nina.

Byron sat beside her and pulled her into the crook of his arm. He inspected her, if only to ensure she was unharmed, and she glanced up. Their gazes locked, held, and for the life of him he could not look away. He wanted her more than air right at this moment, and it would be so easy to lean in and take her lips, kiss her until they lost themselves in each other.

"You'll be home soon. There is nothing to fear now," he whispered, clasping her cheek. Unable to stop himself, he leaned down, wanting to kiss her, show her there were other things to think about, more pleasurable things, than thugs in the cesspit of Southwark.

She wrenched herself out of his arms, sliding toward the window. "You should not do that, Byron. We're friends and you're betrothed. I'll not be part of a scandalous affair even if I am a widow and can do whatever I choose."

He ran a hand through his hair. Damn it, in his fear he'd forgotten to tell her his news. "When I said earlier tonight that I'm not married, what I really wanted to say was that I've dissolved the marriage contract. There is no longer an understanding between me and Miss Custer."

Nina stared at him with the widest eyes and he fought not to smile at her shock. He supposed such news wasn't what she or anyone would expect to hear.

"You're not marrying Miss Custer?"

"No, I'm not. The contract between our families was never a match made out of love or affection. They wished to increase their foothold within society. I had a marquess as a cousin and I needed to marry. It was time that I settled and started a family of my own. We met abroad and I am fond of Sofia, but mild friendship was only ever the depth of the emotion that passed between us."

Not expecting it, he gasped as Nina shifted back beside him, clasped his jaw and kissed him. Hard. He moaned as her mouth opened to his, her tongue sliding against his own and sending heat straight to his loins. He wrenched her onto his lap, taking her mouth in a punishing kiss. With every nip, every slide of his lips against hers, the entanglement of their tongues was punishment for not wanting him. Of choosing his straightlaced brother over him and this passion that fired between them.

Nina tasted of beer and spirits, a unique sweetness, and he couldn't get enough. Her hip settled against his sex and whether she knew it or not, her small undulations rocked him with pulse-pounding desire. He wanted to bury himself inside her. Push her, take her until they both shattered into a million pieces of pleasure.

The carriage rocked to a halt and somewhere in the recesses of his mind he heard the driver jump down off the box to open the door. He set Nina on the seat beside him. Their breathing was ragged, Nina's eyes full of unsatisfied need that he too could understand.

The door opened and without a word Nina stepped down. He watched her go inside her home, then gave the driver the new address. Hell…that kiss. That kiss everything he'd always wanted, and it would be the first kiss of many if he could persuade her.

He'd always known there was unfulfilled desire between them, and that kiss proved it. But did it mean that Nina would give him a chance? That he wasn't certain, but he was sure as hell going to find out.

CHAPTER 7

The following week Nina stood with the Duchess of Athelby at the Keppells' ball and watched Byron from across the room. He was standing with his cousin the marquess, and both appeared quite engrossed in their conversation.

After their kiss last week in the carriage, Nina had done everything she could to avoid him. Not because she didn't want to see him, for she did, more than anything else, but because her infatuation with her best friend wasn't something she'd thought would ever happen. Not to mention that loving the two brothers made her look flippant and easy to lead.

She hated to imagine what their set would think if they heard whispers about an affair with Byron. They would probably think she had moved on to the other sibling simply because she had not gained the other's hand in marriage all those years ago. Nothing could be further from the truth. Byron, for all his wild nature, was a kind and generous friend and her affection for him had changed over time, moved on from benign camaraderie to something so much more.

Nina turned her attention away from Byron, her mind a whirr. She wanted him, but that did not necessarily mean to have him as her husband. To marry again wasn't something she wanted to do, certainly not at this moment in time. She was happy to be a mother to her girls, the master of her own domain. To become someone's chattel, no matter how much she adored Byron, wasn't a situation she strived for.

Would Byron be happy with a love affair and nothing more? He'd broken off his betrothal for her, when all was said and done. For her to turn about now and say he could share her bed but not her life seemed cruel, a waste of his love. He wanted a wife, children of his own. So much more than she was willing to give.

"What is wrong, Nina? You seem very distracted," the Duchess of Athelby said, catching her gaze.

She was distracted. More than she had ever been before. With Byron her body came to life, he made her laugh, made her smile. He made her happy, but would she make him so? "Is it so obvious?"

The duchess chuckled. "To me it is. To others, probably not. You've always been the best of friends with Mr. Hill. You've not been so obvious in your study of him to be noticeable by others, but I know how close you two were in the past, and how close you've become this Season with his return to town."

"He's no longer engaged. His trip to Cornwall saw him end his association with Miss Custer. From what I can gather they were not pleased, and given the situation I'm surprised that there isn't more talk about it in town."

"There isn't talk because he's the marquess's cousin, and they're friends. Mr. Hill has friends that include us, dukes and duchesses and the like. I doubt there would be many who would naysay him, but there is an undercurrent of scandal, never doubt it. Some homes will never forgive him for abandoning Miss Custer."

"What are your thoughts on the matter? Are you so very angry at him? At me?"

Darcy studied Byron for a moment before she shook her head, smiling a little. "No, I'm not angry with either of you, and we shall stand by you both as your friends. You know I was married before the duke to a man I'd prefer to forget. Such marriages, ones made out of duty and even boredom, never thrive. I would not wish that for Mr. Hill and I certainly never wished it for you. You above anyone else in our friends set would know what it is like to marry a man that you do not love."

Nina knew only too well what that was like. It was a form of torture. To have them touch and kiss you when you were not physically attracted to them left you feeling dirty, assaulted even. As kind as the duke was, she did not like him in a romantic light and it caused their times in private to be very awkward and quick.

She glanced over to where Byron was and saw that he and the marquess had moved on to another set of gentlemen, one of them Darcy's husband the duke. "I think Mr. Hill ended his understanding with Miss Custer because of me," Nina said, relieved to have said aloud to a friend what had been bothering her for a week. If the *ton* found out there was something brewing between them so soon after his understanding had ended with Miss Custer, there would be rampant speculation and gossip. Her stomach twisted into knots.

"What makes you say such a thing? From what Cameron has told me after speaking to Mr. Hill, there wasn't any affection with either party. The Custers may be put out now over the situation, but when they see Miss Custer marry a man she truly loves, I think they'll see the sense behind the decision."

"I hope so," Nina said, greeting two elderly matrons who walked past them. "But there is something else I need to speak to you about. I feel I can't disclose this to anyone else, since it's of a delicate matter."

"You can tell me anything, my dear. I'll never break your trust."

Nina pulled Darcy to a more secluded part of the ballroom and they sat in a vacant settee. She took a fortifying breath before she said, "On our way home last week from our outing in Southwark, we were accosted by a group of thugs before hailing our hackney."

Darcy gasped, and Nina clasped her hand. "Be assured all is well, and Byron was able to convince them to leave us alone. But I was very upset. I thought we were in trouble that was beyond our scope to get out of. In the carriage on the way home, I don't know whether it was because I was upset, or whether it was because Byron wanted to comfort me, help me over the ordeal, but..." She paused for a moment as her body reacted to the memory of his kiss. Of how everything bad that had happened to her up to that moment disappeared and it was like the sun came out and all would be right in the world. "We kissed. Actually, it wasn't a kiss. It was so much more than a kiss." She closed her eyes, wanting to do it again, if only to see if the emotions he brought forth in her were real. Never had she ever had such a reaction to a man, not even Andrew, and she'd thought herself in love with him.

Byron was her oldest, dearest friend. To feel passion in his arms wasn't what she expected at all.

Darcy grinned. "How very interesting. You enjoyed Mr. Hill's kiss then, my dear?"

Nina clasped her abdomen as butterflies fluttered in her stomach at the memory of it. "I did. So much. His kisses are as wicked as his past escapades were and I find myself now wanting to be alone with him again. When he told me that his understanding with Miss Custer was at an end, I didn't feel what one ought to feel for a friend— sadness, wanting to comfort those that are hurting. I wanted to fling myself into his arms and tell him to have me. To take me instead. And, well, I'm pretty certain that's exactly what I did."

Darcy chuckled and as a footman walked past, the duchess procured them a glass of punch each. "What do you think Mr. Hill thinks of the kiss? Do you believe him to be in agreement with your emotions over the embrace?"

Nina nodded. "I believe so, but I've been avoiding him. You know how much I wanted to marry his brother Andrew all those years ago. If I turn my attentions onto his sibling, I appear like a fool. Someone who cannot move on from their first infatuation. Not to mention I never thought to marry again, and Byron wants a wife, a family. I'm not certain I want to give up my freedom just yet."

"You are not under any time restraint, Nina," Darcy said, matter of fact. "People change in time. What you once liked you can hate in the years to come and vice versa. In time you may find that marrying Byron is exactly what you want, or you may both agree that your time together must end. Nothing is set in stone. Let your emotions guide you and I'm sure you'll do what is right."

Could they go from being friends to lovers? There was no doubt in Nina's mind that was what she wanted. She wanted Byron with a need that surpassed any she'd ever felt before. What she felt the night he'd kissed her scared her and tempted her at the same time. She could not walk away now, not when they were both free to do as they pleased, without seeing if there was a possibility for them.

"Do you think it scandalous of me to want him, more than a friend would want another friend? I want," she said, lowering her voice to a whisper, "for him to share my bed. I'm wicked I know to say such things, but I need to tell someone, or I'll simply burst and shout it out loud across the room."

Darcy laughed, sipping her punch. "While I agree with your choice, I would advise that vocalizing that across the room would be a bad idea." She smiled. "Talk to him. Tell him what you want and see what he wants in return. You're both adults. You're a widow. It's not against the rules for you to break them a little. If you're discreet."

Excitement thrummed through Nina's veins at the thought of having Byron in her bed. She looked up and caught the very man who occupied her thoughts watching her. Heat coursed through her veins and she could not look away.

Tonight he wore a superfine coat that fit his muscular figure to perfection. His cravat was perfectly tied and show-cased his tempting chiselled jaw. His dark, heated gaze seared her with intent and she licked her lips, parched all of a sudden.

Her attention slid over his form, his broad shoulders that tapered down to a narrower waist. He was a muscular man—she imagined horse riding helped keep him toned—and she couldn't help but think of what he would look like naked. It was odd to think of Byron in such a way, but now after their kiss, she did little else.

"I will talk to him. We cannot go on as we are now."

"No," Darcy said, her tone laced somewhat with sarcasm. "I fear if you did continue on in the same way as you are now, the attraction you two have for each other will be known all around London. Why, even now, Mr. Hill watches you with the intensity of a man very much smitten. Some may even say wantonly."

Nina knew all about lust—or she'd certainly learned it after kissing Byron. Not even with Andrew had she ever wanted him as much as she wanted Byron. How strange that her body knew her true feelings before her mind did. Byron had always been the gentleman she wanted, she just never realized it before now.

"I will behave and be less obvious in my admiration of the gentleman. And I think," she said, standing, "I shall seek him out now and have our little tête-à-tête. Thank you for listening, Darcy. I appreciate it."

Darcy waved her thanks away. "The pleasure was all mine. I wish you well."

Nina bit her lip, smiling. "I wish myself well too."

Byron had watched the Duchess of Athelby and Nina talking privately, and he would've given anything to hear what their conversation involved. The hairs on the back of his neck prickled and he couldn't help but believe that they were talking about him.

His discussions on the other hand involved politics, horses, and the latest scandal rocking the *ton*. He'd debated excusing himself and going to Nina and asking her to take a stroll about the room, but instead he headed outdoors, wanting a little fresh air.

The cool night air was refreshing after being inside among a kaleidoscope of scents, and he headed to the end of the terrace and stepped down onto the gravelled path leading across the lawn.

The Keppells' home backed onto Hyde Park, and he

strolled toward the little gates he knew the yard held. He would take a few minutes to regain his composure. The longer he watched Nina, the more his body reacted to her presence.

She consumed him, and yet over the past week she'd done everything in her power to avoid him. Did she regret their kiss? Was she sorry for allowing him his advances? Damn, he hoped not.

He ran a hand over his jaw as the iron gates came into view. They were locked. He stopped when he reached them, staring at the park beyond, its dark space as bleak as his own future if he did not convince Nina to be part of it.

"Byron," someone called out. He turned, his heart thumping loud in his chest at the sight of Nina walking purposefully toward him.

"Whatever are you doing out here? I saw you leave and in these slippers I wasn't as fast as you on the gravel."

He chuckled, coming to stand before her. "I needed to clear my head. A lot of scents inside." Although that was only half the reason. His true reason was standing before him, looking up at him with the biggest, bluest eyes he'd ever known. How he adored her. Her kind heart, her friendship, that she was a wonderful mother to her children.

"Yes," she said, walking past him a little to stare out at the park. "I'm sorry I've been avoiding you. I've not wanted to, but I needed to clear my head over…well, you know. What happened in the carriage."

He came and stood behind her, so close he could smell the jasmine in her hair, and yet he did not touch her. He fastened his hands at his side to stop himself. "When we kissed," he whispered against her ear.

She shivered and wrapped her arms about her waist before she turned to face him. "Yes. When we kissed and the friendship we've had with one another changed forever."

"Has it changed forever?"

He swallowed the panic, hoping she was not about to cut him free, tell him that their embrace was a mistake. It was not an error of judgement for either of them. They were made for one another. In time he would gain her love and then he could tell her the truth of their night together all those years ago. Now wasn't the time, but he would be honest with her when she was ready to hear such honesties. Truths that would not be easy to endure.

He was being selfish in his secrecy over the night his brother had tricked them both, but he needed time to win her love. After the years that had separated them, only now were they gaining their friendship back, becoming closer with every moment they spent together. He wanted her to know his heart was true, loyal to her, when he revealed the truth. To have her repudiate him was not an outcome he could bear.

Neither of them were to blame for what had happened —that deceit lay entirely on his brother's soul—but even so, the truth would hurt Nina, and he was loathe to do that to her. His fear that she would cast him aside, that it may cause him to lose her forever, wasn't to be borne. He would tell her the truth, and soon— just not yet.

"Of course it has changed, Byron." She stepped closer still, her arms unfolding to wrap about his waist. His body sagged in pleasure and he shut his eyes for a moment, reveling in the feel of her so close to him again.

He wrapped his arms about her back. "Tell me how."

She grinned up at him. "After our kiss the other night, I've done little else but think of you, and if you're willing, I'd like for us to be lovers."

The breath in his lungs seized and he took a moment

TAMARA GILL

to gain his equilibrium. She wanted to be his lover. Hell yes, there was little else he wanted in return. To be with her privately, to spend time alone, was what he longed for most. Not just to have her in his bed, but to also enjoy her company. To talk, laugh, and play just as they did prior to her first Season.

He missed such days, and he'd missed her. She was giving him this chance, and he was not about to bugger it all up. He would love her, adore her, just as she should always have been loved and adored, so much so that she would never want him to leave.

"I would be honored. You have no idea how much I've wanted to be with you like that."

"You have?" she asked, grinning up at him.

Under the moonlight he could make out the slightest blush. Was she a little embarrassed to have asked him to take her to his bed? Possibly, but what a strong, independent woman she was to have done so. It only made him adore her more.

"You must know that the whole reason I asked to be released from my understanding was solely due to seeing you again. I couldn't marry Sofia when I wanted another woman altogether." Not just in his bed, but in his life. And now that Nina had given him this opportunity there was little chance he would let her go without a fight.

She reached up and wrapped her hands about the nape of his neck, playing with a little strand of his hair. "You've been my best friend for so many years. How do we even start such an affair?"

"Like this, my darling," he said, leaning down and kissing her softly on the cheek. He kissed his way to her ear, paying attention to just below her lobe after she shivered a little in his arms at his touch. She was so soft, pliant in his arms, and had she not been tightly enfolded in his embrace, he could not have believed his turn of fortune. "And this," he said finally, kissing her lips.

She leaned up against him, her breasts hard against his chest, and she let out a little mewling sound that went straight to his groin. She opened for him like a flower in the sun and he kissed her deeply, savouring every moment, wanting more with each second that passed.

To kiss a woman with passion, a woman whom one had respected and cared for, for so many years, made the embrace different somehow. More meaningful, intimidating even. To lose this, to have her walk away when their love affair was over, simply wasn't an option. Not for him in any case.

She met his kiss with as much fire and need as his own and something squeezed in his chest. He understood the danger of kissing a woman one had an emotional relationship with. It could lead to more than simple affection—it could lead to love.

The idea didn't scare him as much as it once might have. Not with Nina at least. With this woman in his arms, he couldn't imagine anyone else who could take her place. Nor did he wish to. And if that meant that he was falling in love with her, then so be it.

He was a man in love, well and good.

CHAPTER 8

Nina lay upon her bed the following morning and stared at the ceiling. Her maid had been in earlier and drawn open the curtains, and the dappled sunlight streaming through the windows gave the room a warm, summery glow.

She grinned, her stomach turning in knots over what had happened at the Keppells' ball the evening before. The kiss she'd shared with Byron had been better than their first, and they had made plans for him to come to the Duke and Duchess of Athelby's intimate dinner this evening.

She sighed and rolled over, staring out the bank of windows that ran the full length of her room. When had she become so infatuated with him? When had he become the sole reason to attend parties and events? If she were honest with herself, the week she'd not seen him after their first kiss had been torture. She'd wanted to see him every second of every day. To take in his athletic figure, admire his sweet nature and devilishly naughty antics. He was an alluring man.

I wonder what he'll be like in bed...

The naughty thought made her grin. Tonight after dinner she may find out, if she were game enough to allow him to stay.

There was a light knock on her door and her maid bustled into the room. She bobbed a quick curtsy. "Good morning, Your Grace. The Duchess of Exeter is in the downstairs drawing room and she's saying she's not leaving until she has seen you. She seems quite agitated, Your Grace."

Nina sighed, cursing her vexing daughter in law to Hades. It was just like Bridget to arrive and ruin her good morning thoughts about a certain Byron Hill.

She dressed quickly in a light blue morning gown and joined the duchess downstairs. "Good morning, Bridget. To what do I owe the pleasure of your company so early today?" Her tone was polite, but edged with sarcasm. She checked the time, and seeing the early hour, fought to deny herself the right to tell the duchess to leave and come back again at a decent hour.

Bridget sat on the settee before the unlit hearth and glared at her. "There is talk of you about town. Talk that will impact my family and children. I'll not have it, Edwina. You need to leave for Kent, and soon."

Nina raised her brow and rang the bell, then ordered tea from the footman who entered. Only when he left the room did she reply to Bridget. "I beg your pardon, Duchess, but what makes you think I have to do anything that you tell me?" She sat on a nearby chair and folded her hands in her lap, lest they be used to strangle her daughter-in-law before her.

"We know about your less-than-proper marriage to the duke, and now there is talk you have a lover. It's embarrassing that you would stoop so pathetically low as to chase the brother of the man who denied you all those years ago."

"Who told you this falsehood?" Nina asked. How did Bridget even find out about her association with Byron? She had been very discreet and only spoken to Darcy about it, and the duchess would never break her trust.

"I need no one to tell me what I saw with my own eyes last evening. You, chasing after a man like a Covent Garden whore."

Had Bridget seen them kiss in the garden? Nina ignored her cutting remark and took a calming breath, feigning innocence. "You mean Mr. Byron Hill, I presume." Just the mention of Byron's name made her heart leap in her chest. "That I'm making a spectacle of myself by seeking him out. Have you forgotten that we have been friends since well before our first Seasons in town? That I practically grew up with him? Of course I gravitate toward him. He's the best person I know."

The duchess's cold eyes narrowed into annoyed slits. "He devours you with every glance. It is obvious to every one of our set that you're infatuated with each other, probably already lovers. Which considering your past does not surprise me or the duke."

If the duchess's words were meant to make Nina rethink her relationship with Byron, it had the opposite effect. If anything, the idea that Byron devoured her each time he looked at her filled her with unsated need.

The tea arrived and thankfully it gave Nina a moment to compose herself. How dare Bridget chastise her in such a way. She was a widow, a financially independent one at that. She may do as she pleased, and damn anyone who had a problem with her choices.

"He may wish to court me, and should I take him to my bed, I can assure you that I will be discreet."

Bridget gasped, her show of shock and outrage more emotion than Nina had ever seen her exhibit before in her life.

"How could you! How could you sleep with a man not your husband?" The duchess levelled a finger in her direction, stabbing it into the air. "You're a harlot. You should not be in Mayfair, but in Convent Garden where all the other prostitutes hire out their services."

Anger snapped through Nina. "Do not criticize me for being a woman of independent thought and needs. And never accuse me of being a whore, when your husband no doubt takes pleasure in the arms of such women on his nights in the slums." Nina felt a pang of guilt when Bridget's face paled at her words, but then the memory of her toxic daughter-in-law's accusations pushed that aside.

Bridget's face contorted into something ugly and mean. "We know the girls aren't the duke's. How my father-in-law fell for such a ruse I'll never understand. Years ago you were rumored to be days away from announcing your engagement to Mr. Andrew Hill, but then overnight you were engaged to my father-in-law and Mr. Hill was betrothed to Miss O'Connor. You understand hasty marriages always make one question the validity behind them. Yours is no different," she said with saccharine spite.

Nina scoffed but her blood ran cold at the mention of her daughters and the fact that Bridget and the duke thought they were not George's. Did others suspect? And now with her renewed friendship with Byron, it may give such rumors even more fuel. But then, what of it? No one could prove the girls were not George's and there was nothing wrong with being friends with Byron. Even if their attachment had grown to feelings far beyond friendship. She would not cower to the woman before her—a nasty, vindictive, unhappy woman. Nina would not allow the duchess to ruin her life. Not now that she'd finally got it back and was the master of her own domain.

"Get out and do not come back here again. Neither you nor the duke are welcome in this home, which I might remind you is mine by law. You have no claim on me, or my estates. You have no right to speak my daughters' names. Do not take me for a fool or a woman who will stand for such insults. I have friends too, Bridget. Friends who would cut you out of society without hesitation should I mention this conversation."

Bridget stood, all pretence of civility gone. "I have friends too, do not forget. As for these rumors, I do not want them out in Society any more than you do. I have children who will suffer from this scandal should it get out. I suggest you end it with Mr. Byron Hill before you're caught and there isn't anything anyone can do to help you."

"I neither need nor seek your help. Leave. Now."

Bridget strode out the door and Nina picked up her cup of tea, taking a sip. What a toxic witch. She thought about Bridget's words regarding her and Byron and wondered if they were too obvious in public. Did he really look at her like he wanted to devour her whole?

A grin tweaked her lips. Yes, yes he did, and she adored that it was so. But she would adjust how she reacted to him in public if only to keep her girls away from potential scandal. She would never wish to sully them because she could not control herself when around Byron.

BYRON COOLED his heels in the Duke and Duchess of Althelby's drawing room while they waited for dinner to be announced. His cousin had garnered him the invite to this private dinner hosted by the duke and duchess, and he was beyond grateful. The night was young, Nina would arrive soon, and there were limited people about, meaning he could monopolize her time and be with her. Possibly take her home and snatch a kiss or two.

The blood in his veins warmed at the thought as he listened to the marquess and duke talk about a horse going up for auction at Tattersalls that they both wanted, while keeping his attention on the drawing room door.

He didn't have to wait long. The breath in his lungs seized at the sight of Nina. Tonight she wore a gown that was pure perfection, hanging from her light frame without a flaw. The green muslin dress hugged her breasts while hinting at her shapely waist and hips. The sheer material was light in color but the undergarment was a deeper shade, making the gown shimmer with each step she took.

Byron caught her gaze and smiled. A light blush stole across her cheeks and he fought not to go to her so soon. To not be too obvious in his interest.

"She's a very beautiful woman," his cousin said, leaning toward him to ensure privacy from the other guests besides the duke.

The duke chuckled, lifting his glass in salute. "She's related to me. Good looks are a trait that we're all blessed with."

The marquess scoffed. "Darcy is beautiful. You, on the other hand, I'm certain she took pity on and nothing more."

Byron chuckled as the duke tried to argue the point but then had to concede that Darcy was indeed beautiful and he was lucky to have her as his wife.

"So," the duke said after a moment, "will Nina be the next Mrs. Hill, good man?"

Byron hoped that would be so. He'd like nothing more

than to have her as his wife. The affection he felt for her had long ago changed from friendship to so much more. His feelings were so much stronger than what he felt for her five years ago. He'd loved her then, but he adored and loved her so much more now. Seeing her as a woman, a kind, intelligent lady, who no matter her status, cared for and loved her children, put them before anyone else, made what he felt for Nina beyond anything he'd felt in his youth.

"If she'll have me, of course I'd marry her. But whatever this is between us is also very new. I do not want to rush her." He needed Nina to love him before he offered for her hand. Not because he needed the emotion to be said between them, but because without love there was no chance that she would forgive what he'd done all those years ago. Or at least, what his brother had ensured he'd done without their knowledge.

Without love he would have no chance of gaining her forgiveness. His brother last night had accosted him in the library, demanding he tell the duchess the truth of their situation. Byron would do so, and soon.

"I think she'll have you, if her admiration of you when she thinks no one is looking is any indication." The marquess grinned at him, taking a sip of his whisky. "Have you spoken at all about the possibility of a future?"

Byron nodded, finishing his drink. "We have, and we're willing to try and see. I know she's very independent and focused, especially on the new school, but I would like to help her with the school. I'd do anything to spend time with her."

The marquess slapped him on the shoulder. "Good man, you're in love with her."

The word *love* echoed in his ear and yet it did not scare him. Why not admit to one's feelings when they were true?

He did love her, had loved her for years—she simply wasn't aware of the fact. But she would be soon. Now that they were going to be lovers, he would show her every moment of every day when they were together how much he adored and valued her.

"Yes, I am," he admitted, smiling a little. "Now if you'll excuse me, I'm going to go dare a duchess to do the same."

He left the duke and marquess chuckling behind him as he went in search of Nina. He found her sipping a glass of champagne alone beside the fire, lost in thought.

He lifted her gloved hand and kissed it gently, lingering over it a moment to savor the feel of her again. "Good evening, Your Grace. You're very beautiful this evening, but I should imagine you already knew that."

Nina grinned at him, taking back her hand. "Why thank you, Mr. Hill. How very kind of you to notice."

"I notice everything about you," he whispered, coming to stand beside her so that they could talk a little more privately.

"I've missed you." His arm at his side, he reached out using the cover of his jacket and her gown to clasp her hand. Their fingers entwined and it was the most erotic move he'd ever made in his life. Of course he'd slept with women before, but to touch her in such a clandestine way, to hold Nina and no one else, even if it were only her hand, sent shocks to his heart.

He loved her possibly more than she'd ever love him. The thought gave him pause. He could be hurt by adoring her so. She was yet to learn the truth of their one night together. He hated that she would be wounded to know that his brother had tricked them both into being in the same location, under false comprehensions where neither one of them could take back what had happened. But to not take the risk of loving this woman, to have her as his, to marry and wake up next to her for the remainder of their days, was worth any risk to his heart.

She didn't pull away from his touch, and the look she bestowed on him radiated need and longing.

"I've missed you too. I also wish to speak to you about something, but not here. Will you escort me home later this evening? We need to be alone for that conversation."

"Of course," he said without a thought. A small frown line sat between her eyes and he wondered what she was thinking about. Was something worrying her? "Tell me, please, that what you wish to talk to me about later today does not involve you telling me that we cannot be together. I could not bear such an outcome. Not after the other evening."

She shook her head, a few wisps of hair about her face bouncing with the movement. "It's not that. I promise."

"You seem a little down, Nina. Are you certain you want to wait until later to talk about what's bothering you? I'm sure we can find somewhere private after dinner."

The butler entered the room and, bowing to the guests, declared dinner served. The select group of guests made their way to the dining room on the opposite side of the house, and Byron found himself seated beside the Duchess of Athelby. He would've preferred to be seated beside Nina, but Darcy was lovely company and always good at keeping the conversation interesting if not amusing.

The first course came and went with general conversation and on-dits about the *ton* and what people were planning to attend during the coming weeks. Byron listened and kept watch on Nina, who was seated on the opposite side of the table and further along. Her conversation with his cousin the marquess seemed pleasant, but there was little doubt that something was on Nina's mind and it was troubling her.

"Is everything well with Nina, Mr. Hill? She seemed a little distant before we came in to dine," the duchess said as she continued her meal.

Byron sighed, having himself been pondering that question. "I'm to escort her home this evening, and she mentioned that there is something that she wished to speak to me about, but wouldn't tell me what that was. I hope she is well. I do not like to see her so distracted."

"I should think not." The duchess threw him an amused glance. "Come, Mr. Hill. It is obvious to all of us here, your friends I might add, that you're smitten with Nina. And why would you not be? You've known her for many years, were the best of friends prior to her marriage to the duke. When you have a connection with someone that is linked and fused in friendship, it is sometimes a natural progression into love."

Having taken a sip of his drink, Byron coughed, almost choking on his wine at the duchess's bold words. "You have a lovely table decoration, Your Grace," he said, hoping that his change of subject would be hint enough that he didn't want to discuss him and Nina any further. What was between him and Nina was private and very, very new. He didn't want their friends to become too involved when he himself was still navigating their blossoming relationship.

"Very well, I will drop the subject. But as for Nina's difficulties, I think you'll find that she is having problems with her daughter-in-law, the Duchess of Exeter. I heard a rumor today that the duchess is quite put out about Nina opening a school in Kent, and I also heard your name mentioned."

"What?" he said, adjusting his tone when the Duke of Athelby looked down the table and met his gaze. "I beg your pardon, Your Grace, but why would anyone be talking about me? I'm no one of importance."

"You are a dowager duchess's best friend, you're male, and she's a widow. There is talk."

Byron cringed. Of course, the meddling Duchess of Exeter was causing trouble for Nina because of her association with him. Well, he wouldn't have it. How dare anyone try and tell them that they could not see each other, or be friends. Now that he was at liberty to do so, he would court Nina, or anyone else for that matter, if he wished to, and no vicious gossiping witch would tell him that he could not.

"Thank you for letting me know. I'll be sure to adjust my behaviour when next we're seen together in the *ton*."

"You would stop courting Nina? You cannot," Darcy said, throwing him a glance as arctic as her husband's just before.

Byron chuckled, slicing into his beef with more force than was necessary. "Oh no, I'm not adjusting my actions to be less noticeable, but to be more so. I'm nothing if not stubborn when told that I cannot have what I want. And between you and me, Duchess, I want Edwina and I will prove to her that she wants me as well. Not just as a friend, but as a husband."

Darcy patted his arm, smiling. "I knew I was not wrong about you. I have faith that you will succeed."

Byron looked down the table and caught Nina's eye, smiling. He would succeed. Failure in this situation was not an option. "I have faith that I will as well."

CHAPTER 9

On the way home from the Duke and Duchess of Athelby's dinner party, Nina sat beside Byron as they made their way through the Mayfair streets toward her townhouse. Her driver would take Byron home after she was delivered safely to her door. She frowned, staring out at the streets beyond, wondering how to tell Byron about her dreadful daughter-in-law's accusations today.

How humiliating that she would have to tell him such things. How awful that the *ton* was gossiping about them like they were having a clandestine affair, which they were not. Not yet at least. If she were going to be accused of something she at least wanted to be guilty of it.

"I wanted to talk to you in private because today I had a visit from—"

"I know who visited you today, and you do not need to explain anything. We're going to ignore the duchess and her viperish tongue and do as we please." He took her hand, unbuttoning her glove from her elbow down before sliding it off. A shiver stole through her body at having him so close to her again. Just the two of them with no one else about to distract them or stop what was inevitable.

"I don't care if we're fodder for town gossip. All I care about is you."

His words were like a repairing elixir, one she'd needed from the moment Bridget had stormed out of her parlor this morning. "Because I threw myself at your brother all those years ago, now it looks as if I'm throwing myself at you. She labeled me a harlot. Someone who cannot let go of the past."

Byron shifted closer to her, wrapping his arm about her shoulder and pulling her in close to his side. "We were the best of friends long before you fell for my brother, which I do believe was nothing but a passing youthful fancy that you grew out of. What we have together, what I feel for you, do not let some nasty, unhappy duchess ruin. I will not leave you alone, I will not leave again, if that is your fear."

Tears prickled in her eyes, and she blinked to clear her silliness away. Byron reached up and wiped a stray tear from her cheek, and she sniffed. "I'm sorry. I don't know why I'm being so emotional over what Bridget said. I shouldn't let her get to me in such a way, but she made me feel cheap. Made me believe the *ton* would look down on my girls for my allowing a gentleman to court me."

"No," he said, shaking his head. "You are a beautiful woman, too young to be a matron, and too sweet to be seen as anything other than wonderful. Your children would want you to take a chance, to possibly find love. I want you to take that chance with me." Byron studied her a moment and she wondered what he was debating saying. "I—"

"What?" she asked when he didn't say anything further. "Tell me what you were going to say."

He clasped her chin, lifting her face up as if he were

about to kiss her, but instead he said, "I've always adored you. When I saw you with my brother all those years ago it used to drive me to distraction. I would act out, create scandals, gamble and drink, flirt with young and old. And it was all because I wanted you and you were looking the other way. I thought that if I created enough noise you would see me. It should have been me you married. Not Andrew and not the Duke of Exeter, but *me*."

The breath in Nina's lungs seized and a little piece of her died at knowing that he'd longed for her, but in her youthful idiocy she'd not seen him as anything other than her friend. How could she have been so blind?

"I see you now," she said, clasping the lapels of his jacket. She fisted her hands about the fabric and pulled him close. "And I'm not looking in any other direction than you."

Byron growled and took her mouth in a searing kiss, one that she matched in every way. The carriage rumbled along the gravel road toward her townhouse, the London *ton* and its many entertainments passed them by beyond the carriage windows, and still the kiss continued…

With each stroke of his tongue, each nip of his teeth, the lure of them solidified within Nina and she never wanted to let go. Oh, she saw Byron now, he was all that she did see and it was an image she'd be loathe to part from. A man of honor, a man capable of loyalty, friendship, and love. A kind, passionate soul who was a match for her in every way.

The thought that should he know who the father of her girls really was lingered in the back of her mind, but she pushed it away. Surely he would forgive her for the false-hood, understand that she'd had little option but to marry the duke when Andrew had abandoned her after their night together.

She kissed Byron with all the passion she could muster, and after weeks of being near him again, of watching him, longing for him, the ferocity with which they touched was enough to singe her skin.

"Touch me," she begged when his hands stubbornly refused to move from her cheeks.

She clasped his hand and placed it upon her breast, moaning at the pure delight that his touch evoked. She'd wanted him to touch her there, ached in the dead of night for him to fill and inflame her.

His hand cupped her breast through her gown, and sliding his hand over her puckered nipple, he rolled it between his thumb and forefinger. "You're so beautiful, my darling. I never wish for this night to end."

Nina threw her head back as his other hand slid down her back, pulling her closer still. He kissed his way down her neck, the touch of his tongue gliding over the lobe of her ear making her gasp.

"You tease," she said, laughing a little. "I don't want you to tease me. I want you to take me to your bed."

He nipped her shoulder, kissing down the front of her chest, before he sat back a little, his hand going to the top of her gown and slipping it down to reveal her breast. The cool night air kissed her skin, and for moment she watched Byron as he gazed at her, the need and hunger in his brown orbs making the ache between her thighs double.

"So exquisite." He leaned down and kissed her nipple, a soft, closed-mouth kiss before his tongue darted out and he licked it once. "Do you like that, my love?"

She nodded, unable to form words as she watched him pay homage to her breast. He kissed her nipple again, this time opening his mouth. The heat of his touch seized her and without thought she clasped his head, holding him against her as he kissed and suckled her breast.

"Byron," she said during a moment of clarity. "It's not enough. I want you."

The carriage rocked to a halt, and for a moment Nina couldn't gauge where she was. Byron fixed her gown before leaning over and opening the door, then stepping down to help her alight.

"And you shall have me, Duchess, but not tonight. There are too many eyes about for me to come to you now. But I will come to you soon and we shall be discreet. I will not put you at risk of scandal. No matter how much I want you right now."

Nina didn't move from the carriage seat, partly because she didn't want to leave, and party because she wasn't sure her legs would carry her. He threw her an amused smile and held out his hand to assist her.

Reluctantly, she clasped it, thankful for the help. Coming to stand before him on the footpath, she looked up and met his eyes. The unconcealed hunger that she read in them left her nerves trembling through her body. His dark locks, a little mussed from their activity in the carriage, made her want to reach up and pull him down for another kiss. To discombobulate him as much as he had thrown her.

She touched her lips, having never had such passion before in her life, and while she understood that whatever was between them was at its beginning, she worried for when it would end. She didn't wish it to end. Something told her that having Byron Hill in her bed would be an adventure she'd crave to repeat. Would be enough to tempt her to forget her ideals of living alone for the rest of her life, content to be a mother only, and throw caution to the wind and place herself into the hands of a man. A husband.

"Goodnight, Mr. Hill," she said, stepping toward the front steps of her home.

Byron reached out and took her gloveless hand, kissing her fingers gently. "Goodnight, Your Grace."

Nina sighed, watching as he strode the couple of steps back to the carriage and jumped in. The door to her home opened, but she didn't move, simply watched as Byron's carriage pulled away into the London traffic. The sound of Molly's sweet voice sounded behind her and she turned to see her daughter standing on the staircase inside.

"Molly," she said, coming inside and handing a waiting footman her coat. "Whatever are you doing up? You should've been in bed hours ago." She reached down and picked her daughter up, and carried her upstairs.

"I had a bad dream, Mama." Molly paused, taking her in. "You look pretty, Mama. I like your dress."

Nina smiled, kissing her sweet cheek. "Thank you darling, but tell me what happened in your dream," she said, cuddling her close.

"A monster. Behind the curtain. He wanted to eat me and Lora."

"Aww, my poor little poppet. Just remember, my sweeting, that dreams are only figments of our imagination, and although they can be scary, they're not real. And Mama's home now. I'll not let anything happen to you."

Her daughter looked up at her, rubbing her eye—a sure sign she was beyond tired. "Will you sleep in our room tonight, Mama?"

Nina made for their bedroom, which was on the same floor as hers as she refused to have them too far away from her. Entering the room, she smiled as Lora sat up in her bed, seemingly wide awake as well.

"How about instead of me sleeping in here, you girls

come and sleep in my bed? It's much bigger and we can have a little catch up if you like. Would you like that?"

The girls squealed with delight, and Molly wiggled to be put down. Both girls grabbed the small dolls they had on their beds and followed Nina to her room. Nina had her fire stoked and the children settled into her bed before she joined them. Nina ordered breakfast for all three of them in her room the following morning before dismissing her maid. Then she jumped into bed between the girls and wrapped her arms about them both.

"Mama, do you want to know what my dream was about?"

"Of course," she said, and listened to Molly describe the monster who'd hidden behind the curtains. Nina took in her children's features as they chatted about the dream and how they would kill the beast that scared Molly. They were so like Andrew in looks, it was no wonder that Bridget had concluded they were not the duke's. How Byron had not caught the resemblance baffled her, but perhaps he'd not seen the girls enough. She would have to tell him the truth before he guessed himself.

With their dark locks and lithe figures, that alone put them apart from the duke. He'd been a short, round gentleman of very little height. The girls were thin and tall for their age. Not to mention there was something about their eyes that echoed Andrew's family. Even Byron had the same almond-shaped eyes as his brother, and the girls did too.

She would have to tell him, before they went any further in their relationship together. He deserved to know the truth before they started a love affair on a foundation of lies and deceit. Byron deserved better than that.

CHAPTER 10

B yron called on the duchess late in the afternoon two days later, bringing a posy of yellow roses, which he knew had always been her favorite flower. He was ushered into the front parlor and found her seated before the unlit hearth, reading a book.

"Byron," she said, standing and coming over to greet him.

He kissed her cheek before they sat back down on the settee.

"Tea, please, and please close the door on your way out," Nina said to the footman. He bowed and did as she bade before she turned her attention back to Byron.

Today she wore a morning gown of bright canary yellow, a color that suited her. She looked like summer and spring rolled into one and he wanted nothing more than to kiss her as if they were already married.

"You look beautiful today, Nina. You should wear yellow more often." Her cheeks flushed and she leaned back into the settee, studying him.

"I've not seen you in two days. I had started to wonder

if I had frightened you away." She chuckled, then leaned forward and kissed him. Her lips were soft and warm, and his need of her increased.

Since their parting the other evening he'd thought of little else other than having her in his bed. He longed to be the one and only man she desired, wanted, and loved, and he would do everything in his power to have her love him. For there was little doubt in his mind that he was well and truly, deeply in love with his best friend.

"You would never do so. I've thought of you constantly too."

She nodded, but something in her eyes gave him pause.

"Is there something wrong, Nina? Please tell me. I never want to see you unhappy." He took her hand, reveling in the fact she had no gloves on and he could feel her, her warmth and delicate fingers.

"I haven't been honest with you, and I fear that what I'm about to tell you will hurt you very much. So much so that whatever this is between us now will end."

The pit of Byron's gut churned with fear that he knew what she was about to tell him. Or at least what she thought to be the horrible lie that sat between them.

"Go on," he managed to say, bracing himself to listen to her side of the story.

She adjusted her seat, folding her hands in her lap. "You know that I threw myself at your brother, but what you don't know is that I offered my body to him the night before he asked Miss O'Connor to be his wife. An offer he accepted."

She stared into the fire, and he wished he could rip away the pain that he could read in her dark orbs. A pain that he had inflicted on her, if not on purpose.

"I lost my innocence that night, and the following morning I woke to the news that he'd offered to Fionna and they were to be married in Ireland, where her family were from. I debated going to Mama and Papa and telling them what I'd done. I knew they would force his hand. And with the Duke of Athelby my cousin, I could've used his social standing to make Andrew marry me. But I realized I couldn't marry a man who'd sleep with an unmarried maid, and then turn about only hours later and offer to someone else. Such a man was not worthy of my hand."

Byron clenched his jaw closed, his mind and heart arguing over what he ought to do and what he would do. Should he tell her the truth, that it had been him, he'd lose the opportunity to have her love him. To choose him. But to not tell her that it was him in her bed that night, not Andrew, railed at his conscience.

"The duke offered for my hand when he caught me distracted in the music room and I said yes without a moment's hesitation or emotion. I understand if this information is too much for you to bear, and if you wish to remove yourself from my life."

Byron shook his head, tipping up her jaw so she would look at him. The unshed tears that he saw swelling in her eyes broke his heart. He was a bastard to have done this to her. But no matter how much he wanted to tell her the truth, the words would not form. She would not forgive him should he say he'd thought she'd come to his room for him. That she'd finally realized the friendship they had was also a romantic one. The idea that she would not believe that Andrew had tricked them both and that he would lose her because of it made his throat tighten in fear. Selfish as it was, he could not lose her now, not when he'd only just won the woman he'd always adored.

"This does not make me think any less of you. To have married the duke, to have sacrificed yourself to a man you did not love, makes you honorable." Something that Byron had not done. If he could go back he would've fought for her, told her the truth of that night. Outed his brother for the instigator he was. But they could not go back, they could only go forward. "You are to be commended, nothing else."

She searched his gaze, her eyes brightening with hope. "You do not hate me."

"I could never hate you, Nina. Ever."

She nodded, reaching out and clasping his hand just as the door opened and a footman came in carrying a tray of tea along with some steaming freshly baked scones.

Nina waited for the footman to leave before she said, "Thank you, Byron. I do not know what I would do without you. You're so very understanding toward me, especially since I ruined myself with your brother and now I'm wanting to ruin myself with you."

His body had a visceral reaction to her words and he wanted to haul her onto his lap and kiss her senseless. "You're not ruined," he said, tugging her over to him. She came willingly and he stared at her a moment, basking in her beauty before he leaned down and kissed her.

The touch fired his blood. Nina clasped his face, kissing him back with a need that matched his own. After wanting her for so long, he wasn't certain that they could come away from this embrace without going further. And he wanted to go further, so much further.

Nina broke the kiss and straddled his legs, her gown pooling at her waist. The warmth of her body rocked against his as she kissed him again. He wanted to love her again. Had longed for and dreamed of such a moment for years. To have her want him, not his brother, but him, left him breathless. He needed to hear his name on her lips.

She moaned as he pushed her against his sex, teasing them both. "Please tell me you're not going to scuttle away this time and leave me desperate for your touch for another day. I do not think I could bear that again."

He chuckled, rubbing her against him again. "You enjoyed our time in the carriage, I take it. Did you like the touch of my mouth on your breast, suckling you, teasing you with my tongue?"

She closed her eyes, her sex pressed hard against his and making his control waver. No one would be scuttling anywhere. If anything, he would take Nina here and now, on the settee, and be damned anyone who interrupted them.

"Yes," she gasped through their kiss. "I want you, Byron. Here. Now."

Her words lit a fire in his blood and he reached down between them, all pretence of restraint, of taking his time to savor the deliciousness of her gone. He ripped his front-falls open, and opening her pantalets, he guided her onto his cock.

She stretched over him, then slowly sank down until she took his full length, and he groaned. Her warmth wrapped tight about his member and he took a calming breath, not wanting to lose control of himself like a green, untried lad.

Her hands spiked into his hair and she clasped him tight, and with slow, delicious torture she lifted herself a little before lowering herself once again.

This time she gasped out a sigh of pleasure and he held tightly against her hips, trying in some way to gain control of not only her movements but his as well.

"You're so beautiful," he said, kissing her soundly. Her tongue meshed with his and with each undulation, whispered sigh, and decadent kiss his control wavered on a cliff's edge.

"Oh, Byron." She held onto him tighter, her movements more frantic and deep. At this time he tried to deny himself his pleasure, wanting her to release first, to orgasm while fucking his cock. Just the thought of it made his balls ache and he reached to touch her mons, flicking her little nubbin as she rode him hard.

"Let go, Nina," he begged, the sound of his name on her lips, not anyone else's, making it impossible not to lose control. She was everything to him and he would do all that he could to ensure she enjoyed their time together, whether it be under intimate circumstances such as this, or when they were in company.

She kissed him hard and he moaned as she tightened about him, her climax strong and pulling him toward the same conclusion. He lasted as long as he could bear, before his balls tightened and he came hard and long into her heat.

She sank against his chest, their breathing rapid as they both came back to reality. Thankfully no one had entered while they were engaged in the middle of the afternoon with such acts. He ran a hand over Nina's back, simply touching her, reveling in the fact that she was in his arms finally.

"Nina," he said, waiting for her to look at him. She released a contented sigh and lay her head on his shoulder, staring up at him.

"Yes," she said lazily.

He watched her for a moment, emotions swelling up inside him so much so that he could no longer hold them back. "I love you. I've always loved you."

Her eyes widened and she sat up, looking at him as if he'd grown two heads. He grinned. "You're shocked, I can see."

"Well," she mumbled, "I am, yes. We've been friends for so long and, well, I have always loved you too."

"Not in that way." He shook his head, clasping her face in his hands. "I love you as a man loves a woman. As a husband ought to love his wife. I love you so much more than a friend loves another friend."

He didn't expect her to say it back to him. In time he hoped that she would, but no longer could he go on without telling her how he felt. He'd made many mistakes when it came to them, but he would try and go forward without any. That would also include telling her the truth of them all those years ago. It was time Nina knew the truth, and he could only hope to God that she would give him the chance to atone for his hand in his brother's scheme. Forgive him his part of the sin.

NINA CLASPED BYRON'S CHEEKS, wishing she could tell him that she loved him too, but she could not, when she'd only told him half the story. To admit to marrying the duke out of spite was one thing, but then to allow her husband to believe the children in her belly were his was a shame she could not bear to voice aloud.

Byron may love her, and she adored him in return, but to keep the truth from someone, to not allow Byron's brother the opportunity to know his children, even if from afar, was a shame she carried with her every day. There was no certainty that Byron would forgive such duplicity, even if she and Andrew had done wrong by each other all those years ago. To hear such truths now would ruin what they'd just shared, and selfishly, she didn't want to have that conversation now. In time she would, just not yet.

She wiggled off Byron's lap and set her gown to rights, watching him out of the corner of her eye as he did the same with his buckskins. He stood, so tall and strong, with his chiseled jaw and his dark, intense eyes staring at her and making her stomach twist in delightful knots.

"Dine with me tomorrow night," he said. "Alone, just the two of us. I want you to myself."

"Where will we dine? You're staying at your family home in London, where I'm sure I need not remind you that your brother and his wife are also staying."

He placed a stray piece of her hair behind her ear and sighed. "They're out that evening, and will not be back until the early hours of the morning. Come to dinner," he persisted, throwing her a glance that was pure imploring. "I shall have Cook bake up your favorite dishes."

Nina chuckled, stepping against him and wrapping her arms about his waist. How lovely that they could be like this. Tactile and open with their thoughts. And soon she would be open to him about her daughters. "Very well, I shall come. What time do you wish for me to arrive?"

"Eight will do perfectly," he said, kissing her softly. "Tomorrow. Eight." He stepped away and started toward the door. "Sharp."

She watched him go, then looked down at the little table before the settee realizing they'd not taken tea or eaten any of the scones that had been brought in. She rang the bell and ordered a bath. There were no entertainments that she was to attend this evening, which gave her time to think about when and how she would tell Byron the truth.

His reaction to knowing that Nina had slept with his brother had gone better than she'd thought. Some men would never forgive such a thing, but then, Byron had always been different. Open minded, caring toward her, as a best friend ought to be she supposed.

He'd always been her knight prior to the years that they had been parted. It should not come as any surprise to her that he would support and understand why she'd done what she had, and forgive her actions.

It gave her hope that he would forgive her keeping the fact the girls were Andrew's children from his brother. She left the parlor and started up the stairs, the sound of her daughters' laughter in their room bringing a smile to her lips.

She would hold onto the fact that Byron would accept her truth when she told it, and not fret about it now. Tomorrow she had a meeting with the London Relief Society and needed to get an early night. She checked in on the girls, wishing them goodnight before heading off to her own room.

Dinner tomorrow evening would be delightful with Byron, and her stomach fluttered with the knowledge she would see him again. He was the very best of men, and if her reactions toward him told her anything, she was falling in love with her best friend too. No, she wasn't falling in love with him. She had fallen in love.

CHAPTER 11

Byron sat in the library and watched as the clock ticked slowly toward the hour Nina was to arrive. He downed his brandy, running a hand through his hair. His brother, damn the man and his meddling wife, were running late and had not yet left for their evening engagement.

At this stage there was a chance they would all cross paths in the hall. The knocker sounded and Byron swore, standing and adjusting his cravat he headed out to the entrance to greet Nina.

She came into the house, untying her cloak and handing it to a waiting footman. Byron's step halted and for a moment his ability to speak evaded him. She threw him a knowing smile, before stretching out her hand for him to kiss.

"Good evening, Mr. Hill. I hope I'm not late for our dinner."

He shook his head, lifting her hand, but instead of kissing the back of her glove, he turned her hand over and kissed her palm. She took the opportunity to touch his cheek, before he wrapped her arm around his and started toward the dining room.

"Dinner will be served directly, so I thought we'd skip pre-dinner drinks and proceed straight in to dine."

"Are you eager for dessert, Mr. Hill?" she asked, grinning mischievously up at him.

Oh hell yes, he was eager. And once the dinner was served, he had full intentions of dismissing the staff and having her alone for the remainder of the meal.

"Your Grace?"

Nina halted at the dining room door and turned startled eyes up toward his brother, who stood at the top of the stairs.

"I did not know Byron was having company tonight, ah…" Andrew gestured with his hands, "with you. I did not think you would ever grace our home again."

Nina raised her chin, and the cool glance she bestowed on his brother would be enough to halt any ideas of friendship, if that was what he was aiming for. "Byron and I were friends long before I set my sights on you, Andrew."

Byron bit back a laugh at his brother's shocked countenance, but he stilled when Fionna came to stand beside her husband, taking his arm and walking down the stairs.

"Let us leave them, Andrew. It seems the rumors about the duchess are true."

Byron covered Nina's hand on his arm with his own. She'd always had a quick temper, and on hearing such slander he doubted she'd allow the slight to stand. "You owe the duchess an apology, Fionna. You know as well as Andrew that we've been friends for many years. Our dinner this evening is nothing but a dinner between friends."

Nina chuckled, looking up at Andrew and his wife. "They would not know what friends are, Byron. Just as rumors circulate about me, they circulate about you too, Mr. and Mrs. Hill. And let me tell you that you're known as the most boring couple in London this Season. Maybe you should refrain from insulting your betters and try to have a little fun before you return to Ireland. In fact," Nina continued, stepping away from Byron and heading toward the dining room. "I don't believe I've ever seen either of you smile. Some would think you do not like each other very much."

"Edwina, how can you be so cutting?" Andrew demanded, taking his wife's arm and assisting her down the remainder of the stairs.

Nina shrugged. "I speak as I find. Good evening," she said, walking into the dining room.

Byron glared at his brother, who glowered back. He sighed when the front door slammed shut. Taking a deep breath, he joined Nina. After having the servants bring in the three courses, he dismissed them for the evening.

"I apologize, Nina. I thought they would have been gone by eight. Had I known I would've sent word to halt your arrival."

She shook her head a little, spooning out a bowl of turtle soup for herself. "While I'm sad that we obviously cannot be civil to one another and at least pretend to get along, I can understand her hatred of me. I'm sure Andrew told her that he once courted me."

Byron nodded, but even to him it was noncommittal. His brother had told Fionna that he had courted Nina, but not that she'd propositioned him, and that her husband had agreed to the proposition, only then to trick Byron into swapping rooms with him, allowing Nina to turn up at his suite thinking he was Andrew.

What a wicked mess they'd all made of their lives, the lies that they lived with and tried to keep from one another.

"Let us not talk of them any longer. I understand you had a meeting today with the London Relief Society. How did that go? Have you made any more progress on your school?" he asked, giving Nina his full attention.

"The meeting went well. We're thinking that some of the older children—those who wish to learn how to work in stables or around horses, or do farm work—could start schooling in Kent with me. A program of sorts to have the children move out of the city to pursue another line of work if they liked. Of course we'd still have the learning of numbers and letters, but we also need to look at schooling as a pathway into their future. A stepping stone that will lead them in a direction of secure employment, away from the vicious and sometimes nasty temptations of London life."

Byron watched her mouth as she spoke about the children she would help, her ideas and dreams for her school. An overwhelming sense of respect and pure adoration thrummed through him. How could she be so wonderful? How lucky he was to have been given a second chance with her.

Their dinner came to an end, and she sipped her port, watching him over her glass. "You're very quiet, Mr. Hill. Have I talked you mute? I know I've been very vocal in my ideas. I hope I haven't bored you this evening."

He chuckled, placing down his own glass of port. "You've not bored me. On the contrary. If anything, you inspire me to do better." And he would, if she would let him help. He'd marry her tomorrow and follow her to the ends of the earth helping as many people as she wished, if only she'd say yes to being his wife.

"You shouldn't say such things. I may take you up on your newfound inspiration and have you help me."

"Merely name what you wish and I shall follow your command."

"Really?" She grinned mischievously. "So," she said, pushing back her chair to come and stand before him. "If I were to ask you to take me to your room, lay me down on your bed and make love to me, you would?"

Every cell in Byron's body hardened at the thought and he swallowed. He reached out and ran his hand over her hip, the silk of her gown no impediment, allowing him to feel every curve of her perfect form.

"I would." He met her gaze and she stepped between his legs, running her hand into his hair, fisting it a little. "I would do anything for you, Nina."

Her fingers tightened as she leaned down and kissed him. He'd thought the kiss would be full of fire, hunger, all the things he was feeling right at this time for her, but instead, it was slow, an exploration and sweet seduction that had he been standing would've brought him to his knees.

He stood and swooped her up into his arms, smiling at her little squeal of laughter, before leaving the dining room and heading for his bedchamber.

"I don't believe I've ever seen your bedroom before, Mr. Hill. How very scandalous of you to carry a woman who you've had over to dine up to your bedroom. What will the servants have to say about this?"

"I don't give a damn what anyone has to say." And luckily enough, to prove his point they passed two footmen on the upstairs landing, their widened eyes proof that he would have to offer for Nina, and soon. Not that he'd not intended to do exactly that. In fact, now that he had her here, it was the perfect time to ask her to be his always.

One of the footmen scrambled to open his bedchamber door, and thanking the servant he kicked it shut with his foot, placing Nina on his bed. Then he went back over to the door and snipped the lock before turning to watch her.

"Undress, Duchess," he said, pulling his cravat from around his neck. He stayed by the door, content to watch as she reached behind her back and started removing her gown. He divested himself of his clothing, strolling slowly toward the bed as he watched her slip the gown over one shoulder then the next before wiggling out of it on his bed.

Her sheer shift allowed him to see her bountiful breasts and the darkened tone of her erect nipples that poked outwards and all but begged him to kiss them. And before this night was over he would kiss them, and every inch of her body.

"And now the shift, Duchess. I want you naked and I want to see you strip before me."

She raised her brow, and he wondered if she'd take a dislike to his orders, but instead of disobeying, she reached for the ties at her neck and pulled them loose, allowing the shift to gape at her front. Just as she did with her gown, she slid it off one shoulder and the next before it too pooled at her legs on the bed. "The correct term is dowager duchess, just so you know."

Byron ignored her jibe, too taken by having her fully naked before him. Not since the day they had slept together all those years ago had he seen her such. He'd often tried to imagine the sight in his mind over the years, and sometimes he'd been successful in remembering, but nothing was as wonderful as seeing Nina in the flesh, her bountiful body his to love, his to adore.

He walked to the bed, reached out and ran a finger down the middle of her chest. Slowly he traced the soft skin on her stomach, before letting it slide to touch her navel. "You're so beautiful. You make my heart hurt."

She shivered and he stepped closer still, smelling the jasmine scent she washed her hair with always, the clean scent of lavender soap on her skin.

"You make mine hurt as well."

He kissed her, slowly lowering her to the bed and settling between her thighs. She kissed him with such tenderness that he thought he may die of happiness. For the love of her.

NINA LET GO of any inhibitions or concerns about what anyone would think of their relationship and simply enjoyed having Byron above her, kissing her, stroking her with the sweetest, lightest touches that drove her insane with need.

She wanted him with an intensity that scared her, and wrapping her legs about his waist, she urged him to have her. Inch by delicious inch he slid into her, filling and inflaming her more than he ever had before. Something had changed between them. Somewhere between their love for each other as friends it had blossomed into lust and soul-changing love.

Nina met his eyes as he pushed into her, clasping his face to pull him down for a kiss. "I love you too, Byron," she said, moaning as he flexed his hips and shot a bolt of pleasure through her core.

He continued to tease her with slow, agonisingly good strokes, each one teasing, tempting her a little closer to release. He was a wicked, wonderful man, and her heart burst with affection for him. She would make him marry her if it were the last thing she did before returning home at the end of the Season.

Byron was hers and she was his and there was little anyone or anything could do about it.

He lifted her hips, changing the angle to their lovemaking, and she cried out his name as wave after wave of pleasure rocked from her core to every part of her body. Byron's release followed and they crumpled into a heap of arms and legs, content to remain joined, but simply lying beside one another, lightly stroking, sleeping when they wished.

"Nina, you've been my friend for so long. These past weeks have been the happiest of my life and I want it to continue." He pushed her hair away from her face, placing it over her shoulder. He stared at her a moment, and she had an inkling where this conversation was headed.

She lifted herself to lay over his chest, to see him better. "I know, it's been the same for me too."

His thumb ran down her cheek and across her bottom lip. "Marry me."

She grinned, unable to hide her delight at his question, and why would she want to? She loved him as well. Wanted him as her husband for now and always. It may not have been her plan when coming to London this Season, but plans change, and so too would her life, for there was little chance she'd ever say no.

"Yes," she said, smiling through the flood of tears that threatened. "Yes, I will marry you, my beautiful, wonderful friend."

Byron rolled her over onto her back and she chuckled at his delight. "I'm going to spoil you and your girls for the remainder of my life."

A lump formed in her throat at his sweet words regarding their future and that of her girls. "Call on me tomorrow evening and we'll dine again, but this time with the girls and give them the news. If you could arrive a little before dinner, say six, there are a few things I want to discuss with you."

"Nothing serious, I hope," he said, kissing her gently.

Nerves pooled in Nina's stomach and she shook her head, hoping against hope that what she would tell him about her daughters wouldn't end with him rescinding his offer of marriage.

"No, nothing terrible I assure you. Simply legalities regarding our forthcoming marriage."

"Very well, I shall see you then. Now," he said, rolling onto his back and pulling her into the crook of his arm. "Tell me everything that I missed while I was away. I want to know everything about you and your daughters before we tell them the news tomorrow."

Nina threw herself into the conversation, only too happy to change the subject of what she would have to disclose the following night. She pushed away her nerves at the thought that Byron may not be able to stomach the fact his future stepdaughters were also his nieces. She reminded herself that his love for her, their history as friends, would make him forgive her, see that it wasn't entirely her fault or something that was planned. That it was simply the result of her hasty decision to throw herself at a gentleman when she was a young and foolish debutante.

BEFORE DAWN, Nina wrote a note to Byron and left it on his pillow, before dressing and sneaking downstairs to leave. A footman stood at the front door, even at this early hour when she'd hoped no one would be up.

"Can I help you with anything, Your Grace?" he asked, opening the door.

"Would you hail a hackney for me, please?"

She waited inside while the footman went to fetch her a cab, and a moving shadow in the corner of her vision almost gave her a heart seizure before she realized it was Andrew standing at the library door threshold.

"May I have a word, Your Grace," he said, turning to walk back into the room.

The footman came inside and she asked him to hold the cab for her before going into the library and closing the door. This was the first time she'd been alone with Andrew since the night they'd spent together. She was pleased to find that being before him, alone and in a shadowed room, she didn't feel one titbit of emotion toward him, except for disappointment. He was no gentleman in her book and hadn't been for many years now.

"Sneaking out, are we?" he said, raising his brow.

With him standing before the lit hearth, she could see the slight shadow of stubble on his jaw and his mussed hair. He still looked to be wearing the same clothing from the night before and she wondered why he wasn't upstairs, with his wife.

"What do you want, Andrew?" she asked, her words blunt and without any niceties, because of course he deserved none.

"I don't want anything from you, but I can assume that for you to still be here at this early hour of the day, you and my brother must be courting. That you've forgiven him his actions all those years ago and are willing to move forward together as a couple."

Nina frowned and narrowed her eyes at Andrew, trying to gauge if he were simply making trouble or if he was referring to something that she didn't know.

"We are engaged, not that it has anything to do with you. You lost the right to have any opinion in my life years ago. Not that I need to remind you of what kind of blaggard you are." The worst kind any young woman could have the displeasure of meeting.

He chuckled and her temper snapped. "You dare laugh at me, after what you did? I'm sure your wife doesn't know the truth of that night."

Andrew stared at her for a moment and then laughed harder. "And I can assume by your accusations that you do not know the truth either, my dear." He sighed, and not that she wanted to see it, but pity crossed his features before he said, "We never slept together, Nina. If you knew me at all, which you did not, you would know I wasn't capable of ruining an unmarried maiden without offering marriage. As much as I knew your feelings toward me were more than what I could offer you, I also knew my brother was infatuated with you and so I played a little trick on you both."

Dread formed like stone in her stomach and the room spun. She slumped onto a settee and fought to breathe. "Are you telling me that it was Byron who I slept with all those years ago and not you? How could you do that to me? You knew how I felt about you."

He shook his head, coming to sit at her side. His breath reeked of spirits and she shuffled away a little so as not to smell him. "I knew you were in love with me, or at least what you thought love was at that time, and no matter how many times I tried to dissuade you, you never got the hint. And so I found an alternative solution." He chuckled and she swallowed the bile that rose in her throat. "The look on my brother's face the following morning when he found you engaged to the duke was a moment I'll never forget. I knew my plan had been successful, that you had acted the whore and bedded him, and then you broke his heart. How sad for you both."

"But that means…" Nina's stomach lurched and she clasped her chest. "Oh dear lord. That means…"

"What does it mean?" he asked, flicking a piece of invisible lint from his rumpled coat.

"All these years I'd thought it was you. That you had slept with me to only turn around the next day and offer for someone else. But it wasn't you. Your brother, he didn't tell me it was him instead of you." Nina couldn't get the words out, so lodged were they in her throat. Had she called out Andrew's name that night? That she couldn't remember, but if she had, Byron had not corrected her on it. How could she ever forgive such duplicity? "You bastard. You swine. How could you do that to me, or to your sibling for that matter? Do you have no conscience at all?"

Andrew sighed, staring at the fire. "I suppose I do not, but it has all worked out well in the end. You're engaged, as you said. No harm done."

No harm done! The man was mad.

"Since my arrival in town I've been beseeching Byron to tell you the truth," he continued. "I knew you loathed me, and that has caused tension between my wife and myself. She suspects you're angry with me for something, but she doesn't know what. I don't want her to hear the false statement from you that it was I who took your virtue, when it was not. But Byron has not done what I wanted him to do, even though he's had multiple opportunities to do so."

Nina fought not to cast up her accounts. Byron was the father of her children. Did he suspect? He would be a simpleton indeed if he'd not at least had the thought once. She certainly would have, had she been in Byron's shoes.

"After this day, we will never speak again. Had you done the right thing all those years ago and told me that you loved another, I would've been hurt, yes, but I would've moved on, just as many young debutantes do every day. Your hand in this is just as prevalent as your brother's, and I'll never forgive either of you."

She stood, swiping at her cheek and hating the fact she was crying in front of a man whom she really wanted to hit.

Andrew stood, swaying a little. "Had I had the inclination I should've stepped aside years ago when I knew that Byron adored you, but I did not. I liked the attention, you see. A young foolish pup wanting to rub it in my brother's face that I too could woo women, take what I wanted. That Season was jolly good fun, you must admit."

Nina started for the door, the pain of the truth ripping her in two. Byron had seduced her under false pretences. Friends to the very last did not do such things to one another. The memory of that night, of what they had done…how he had kissed every inch of her body, kissed her in places she'd not known possible. She cringed at the horror of it all. Oh dear God, she would never forgive him. How could he break her trust in such a manner? People who love one another, as Byron stated he did her, did not do such things.

She wrenched the door open and started for the entrance, the bang of the door as it hit the wall inside the parlor loud in the early hours.

"Nina?"

Byron's voice at the top of the stairs only made her stride faster. Not waiting for the footman, she ran for the carriage that waited outside. She heard Byron call out her name, the sound of his footsteps audible even from outside. "Berkley Square, and hurry." She climbed up into the carriage, settling back into the seat and not looking back at the house as the carriage pulled away at a clipping speed.

She would confront Byron—there was no doubt that such a conversation would need to be had—but she needed time to think through what she would do. How she would handle knowing a truth that changed so many things in her life. Who she loved, who she trusted, who her children's father was.

A sob escaped and she clasped a hand over her mouth to try to calm herself. How could the brothers have done such a thing to her? It was truly the cruellest trick anyone could ever play, and to think her best friend, the man she loved, could deceive her in such a way made it even more so.

No sooner had Nina arrived home than the sound of banging on the front door alerted her to the fact that Byron had followed her there. She went into her study, pouring herself a good drum of brandy, and noted the time. It was still very early, and the girls wouldn't be up for some hours. Perhaps it was best she tell Byron what she thought of his duplicity now, while she was still seething and hurt from the news.

After they parted this day, she would return to Kent and forget she'd ever been fooled by the Hill brothers. Andrew said he'd played a trick on both her and Byron, but was that so? Or did Byron realize early on in her arrival to his room that night that she was there for Andrew and take advantage of the fact? The sound of mumbling in the hall filtered to her, followed by determined footsteps upon the parquetry floor.

The door to the study opened and Byron came in, closing it behind him just as quickly. He held out his hand, in supplication she supposed, but it did little to cool her temper.

"Nina, let me explain. Please, my love," he said, coming to take her hand.

She slapped his arm away, going over near the desk to put space between them. "Explain then. Explain to me how you slept with me all those years ago, allowed me to believe you were Andrew, when all the time you knew that it was you in my bed. That I had given myself to the wrong brother."

His shoulders slumped and she fought the little shred of remorse she felt for him.

"I have no excuse, there is none. But please know I had no idea you would ever come to my room. I didn't know that you had propositioned my brother. He merely asked me to swap rooms due to the bed being too hard, otherwise I would not have been there. I'd loved you from afar for so long, I thought you being in my room meant you'd finally seen my worth. I thought you were there for me." He paced on the opposite side of the chaise lounge, his hands gesturing with each word. "I couldn't believe my turn of luck. That you were before me, offering to love me, and I could no sooner turn away air." He shook his head, seemingly lost to the past. "When I saw the hope, the desire in your eyes, I truly believed it was for me. So I gave you what you wanted."

"What I wanted? I never wanted to be tricked! I never wanted you."

He cringed and she hated she had to hurt him, but the lie that she'd not been privy to pushed her remorse aside. "Nina, please, I loved you even then. I've wanted to tell you for so long, but how do you tell someone such a thing? It was not our fault it happened, it was Andrew's."

She glared at him, wishing him anywhere but here. "You didn't have to deceive me. You could've declared your feelings toward me years ago. Andrew may have tricked me into going to your room, but surely you must have known that my character wasn't fickle. That I truly thought myself in love with your brother. That I wouldn't change my mind overnight and throw myself at your head."

He shook his head, dejected. "I was blinded by hope. I thought finally you had turned your sights onto me. I was mistaken."

Her temper soared, and she fisted her hands at her side. "The difference between you and me, Byron, is that I was honest. I went to the room thinking it was Andrew's chamber. The following morning you realized your mistake and still you kept the truth from me. Do not try to fool me into thinking you're innocent in this. That it was a silly error that we should all move on from."

"I wish it were so simple, but I have no excuse and you know that. I adore you, I've loved you for years. I hated that you only saw my brother and not me." He gestured to his chest and she swallowed the tears that threatened to run unheeded down her face. "But you never did. You only saw perfect, placid Andrew. I knew the mistake we'd both made when you left me that night—if you remember, you whispered Andrew's name in my ear." He placed his hand on his heart. "I swear, until that moment I thought you were there for me. By the time I realized your mistake, it was too late. I planned to court you after that, thought through the rest of the night how I would make you mine, seduce you if I had to, but you accepted the Duke of Exeter's proposal and I never had a chance."

She turned her back on him, her blood hot with anger and pain. "You have no idea what you've done." Her voice cracked and she heard him start toward her, but she moved out of his reach.

"I know what I've done, but surely nothing was so lost

that we cannot move forward with this. I want a life with you, Nina. I want to be there for you and your girls. I want to help you with your school. Let me. Forgive me, please," he begged.

"I cannot." She shook her head, unable to voice the words she must. She sniffed, wanting to flee but knowing she could not. "I have not told you everything. There is more to this sorry tale that you and your wicked brother do not know."

BYRON FROWNED, unsure of what she spoke. "What do you mean? What is it that I do not know?"

Nina clasped her hands before her and took a calming breath. "I loathed your brother for so many years, not simply because I believed he took my virtue like a thief in the night and then up and married someone else. Although that is a good enough reason to loathe him, it wasn't what drove my hate for so long."

"Then what was?" he asked, detesting the fact that he'd done this to her. What a selfish bastard he was.

"I accepted the duke out of sheer fury at your brother's choice, and the fact that my parents had been pushing for a grand match. I figured if I could not have the man I loved, I would therefore marry for money and status. Elevate myself to be higher than Andrew in society and therefore crush him if I chose whenever he dared show his face in London. But I forgot all of that the moment I found out I was with child. A child—two children—I believed to be Andrew's, but which I now know are yours. The girls are not the duke's or Andrew's children. They are yours, Byron."

He stared at her as her unrepentant loathing of his

sibling came into focus. Now it made sense why she'd hated Andrew for so long, years after the fact. Byron thought about the girls, remembered their features, and wondered how he'd not noticed before that they both had his eyes, his dark locks. How they looked nothing like the Duke of Exeter.

The girls were five. He'd missed five years of their lives. A cold annoyance settled in his gut at the realization. "You kept them from me or from Andrew or whoever," he said, more harshly than he ought. He ran a hand through his hair, unable to believe what he was hearing. He was a father. He had two daughters, the sweetest little cherubs, and he didn't know them. At all. "Why did you have to run off and marry the duke like the devil himself was after you? I went looking for you the next day only to find betrothal celebrations happening for both you and Andrew. I didn't have time to court you, to make you see me, for you were already another's."

She stormed over to him, standing as tall as she could before him, which wasn't very high considering he stood a good head above her. "How dare you even say such things! Do not forget I did not know it was you in my bed, not your brother. Count yourself fortunate that I did marry the duke, for he thought the girls were his and he gave them legitimacy. If I had waited I would have been ruined."

"You were ruined the moment you sent a missive to my brother asking him to sleep with you."

She reeled away from him and he went to her, wanting to pull her into his arms and hold her close. Damn it. "I'm sorry, Nina. I didn't mean that."

"Get out," she said, pushing him away. "I don't want to see you. I don't want to know you. I don't want anything to do with you, now or ever."

Panic rose in his gut and he swore. "I will not lose you now. I will not lose my girls."

"You never had us. To society at large they are the deceased Duke of Exeter's children and they will always be known as such."

She shouted for the footman and he entered within a moment. "Escort Mr. Hill outside, Carter, and fetch Digby if he causes you any trouble."

She turned her back on him and Byron watched her for a moment, collecting his thoughts before he did as she bade. He would give her time. Hell, he needed time to think through what had been said this morning.

"I will call on you tomorrow and we will discuss this further when we're both calmer. Good day, Your Grace."

He left her then, striding out onto Berkley Square and fighting to remain calm. A groomsman held his horse and he thanked him before climbing up. Everything would be well. He would give her time and he would calm down and then he could go about setting things to right.

Whatever that right may be.

CHAPTER 13

Nina pushed her horse hard into a gallop across the fields of her Scottish estate, the wind whipping at her hair that had long fallen out of its pinned style.

The day Byron had called on her, a month ago now, she'd packed up the house in Berkley Square and left London. They had travelled at a blistering speed away from town and arrived at Lengrove Hall within a week. Here in Scotland, the home that she had inherited from her paternal grandmother was her safe house. Here she could live free from the ridicule of the *ton*, of seeing her friends look at her with pity once they knew that she and Byron would not be marrying. They didn't need to be privy to the sad details, but it still would not stop them from hovering with concern, something she did not want to endure. Not ever.

She was the worst of people. In a way Byron had been right—she had caused a lot of her problems herself. It was certainly she who had asked Andrew to sleep with her to begin with. Byron had been a pawn in his brother's sick game as much as she was, and she hated to remember what she'd said to him.

But Byron should've told her as soon as he found out the truth of that night. In her anger she'd not asked when he'd been told of his brother's scheme, and it made her wonder if he'd only recently found out himself.

The weeks away from London had given her time to think about what might have happened if she hadn't reacted with such impulsiveness and accepted the duke's offer. What if she had gone to Byron and confessed all to her friend? Would he have shared his part in their sad tale, and thus the outcome might be different today? A terrible ache rose in her heart. He had left a pain so fierce that she wasn't sure she would ever be able to forgive him, or what had been done to them both.

She looked over her lands, wondering what Byron was doing right at this moment. Not even the current Duke of Exeter knew of this estate that her grandmother had owned, and until she returned to town, Byron would never find her here. This home had always had a feeling of safety, been a place where one could heal if they needed. And she so needed it now.

As angry and disillusioned as she was with Byron, she couldn't wedge the pesky emotion of love from her heart. Even after all he'd done to her, and she to him, she loved him. Every moment of every day since she'd been parted from his side she'd thought of him. Was he even thinking of her in return?

Nina pulled her gelding to a slow walk as she started into a glen, the mountains on either side of her making the air cooler than on the open ground. She would have to return to Kent soon. Only today a letter had arrived from her foreman there, saying that the building works had commenced and a new roof would be up within a month or so.

She had hoped Byron would've wanted to be part of her new life, her new direction, but it wasn't to be. His silence over the past month had been deafening, not even a missive. Her housekeeper in London knew her locale, and any correspondence would be forwarded to her here, but nothing had arrived and she could only think of one reason for his silence. And it wasn't a reason she wanted to acknowledge.

In the weeks that they'd been apart, Nina had thought over what had happened all those years ago, and the fact that she'd not been fair. Byron's brother had fooled them both, and although Byron had kept that truth from her, it wasn't his fault.

The thought that Andrew Hill and his scheming had resulted in the loss of her best friend, her lover, her future with Byron, was not a welcome one.

It had taken Byron days to get Nina's whereabouts out of Mrs. Widdle, her housekeeper in London. On his arrival at her home after their heartbreaking quarrel he'd been turned away with no explanation other than that the duchess had shut up the London property and left town.

He'd travelled to Kent only to find Granville Hall also vacant of its mistress. Unsure where to go to next, he'd ridden back to London, and after a lot of coaxing and downright bribery toward Mrs. Widdle, he'd managed to get Nina's address in Scotland.

That she'd travelled to Scotland with the children had come as a surprise. He didn't even know she had property there, not to mention the fact she'd moved so very far away from him didn't give him much hope that she would be willing to hear him out. To listen and let him explain what a complete and utter cod he'd been.

I'm so sorry, my darling…

Now he looked out the carriage window at the passing landscape. They were getting up into the highlands now, the mountains higher and some peaks with snow glistening on their tops. The driver had assured him it wasn't too much longer and he itched to see Nina again. It had been the longest month of his life.

He cringed as he recalled what he'd said to her. He looked up toward the heavens and prayed to the Almighty that she would forgive him his stupidity. He couldn't lose her. No matter what either of them had done, he loved her and he was sure she loved him in return.

The carriage came out of a darkened forest and he glimpsed the roof of a large Georgian home nestled at the base of a small hill, sitting before a fast-moving river.

The home was well cared for, and as night was almost upon them, some lights shone from the windows. Nerves pooled in his gut at the thought of seeing Nina again. It had been a month. Would she still be angry with him? Would she send him away?

The carriage made its way down the hill and pulled up before the house's double doors that faced the gravel drive. A footman opened the door, and Byron caught a glimpse of the inside of the home, a grand central staircase and a flash of children as they ran up it in haste, as if they were playing a game of chasey or hide and seek.

He stepped down and made his way to the door, and heard Nina yelling out to the girls that she would be up with them shortly. He stood at the threshold, not wanting to interrupt the family moment, but also wanting so desperately to be part of it. He wanted to be beside Nina when she sent the girls upstairs to dress or to get ready for bed with their nurse. He wanted to be their father in the truest sense, not just the man who created them during one night of passion.

He stepped inside, and before the footman had a chance to introduce him, Nina saw him, halting mid step as she headed toward the staircase, a book of some kind in her hand.

"What are you doing here?" she asked.

He couldn't read her features or work out what she was thinking, and he desperately wanted to know what was going on in that intelligent, beautiful mind of hers. He came to stand before her, wanting to touch her, but he refrained. There was time for that, when she'd forgiven him. "You're a hard woman to find."

"That's probably because I didn't want to be found." She turned and headed back toward the room she'd come from and he followed, shutting the door behind them. He watched as she went to stand in the centre of the large space, placing her book on a table that sat behind a three-seat settee.

He took in the room. It was a parlor or a games room, he wasn't sure which, but it had books, a desk, and a billiards table, along with an assortment of children's toys that sat in different spots about the room. It was very homely, and exuded a warm feel, just like Nina did toward those she loved. Not toward him so much at the moment.

"I've been trying to find you. It took some inducement to get your whereabouts out of your housekeeper, Mrs. Widdle, but as soon as I knew your location I came. We have to talk, Nina."

She sighed and gestured toward a chair before the hearth. He sat and a little piece of him died when she sat across from him and not beside him.

"Then talk."

Other than throwing himself at her feet, he wondered what else he could do to make her forgive him. Make her look at him again with love and respect. "I'm sorry. I'm sorry for everything. For loving you so much that I kept the painful truth of that night from you, when I knew you didn't know it was me. For not speaking out the next day and telling the world you would not be marrying the duke, but marrying me instead. I'm sorry for not being there when you carried our girls in your belly, when you gave birth to them, and while you cared for them these past years. I'm sorry for hurting you. You are the love of my life. I adore you, Nina. Please forgive me."

She sat back in her chair and glared at him. Her silence made panic claw at his throat and the option of throwing himself at her feet reared in his mind. It may work. It was certainly worth a try.

"You were my friend, Byron. I never saw you as anything other than that, and in my youthful foolishness I thought myself in love with your brother. I've done a lot of maturing since that night I threw myself at a man who did not want me. And over the last few weeks I've come to realize that perhaps you ending up as the man in my bed was fate playing its hand. Because what I feel for you is nothing like what I felt for your brother. What I feel for you is so much more. What I feel for you is true."

His heart burst with joy, and for the first time in a month he felt as though he could breathe. "Are you saying that you love me still? That there is a possibility for you and me, even with all the things we've hidden and done to one another?"

Nina stood and came to stand before him. She reached out a hand and pushed away the lock of hair that had fallen over his eye. "I am saying that. In fact," she said, sitting on his lap and wrapping her arm about his neck, "I want to make you and me permanent."

"So you'll marry me then?" he asked, grinning.

"Is this your way of asking me?" She raised her brow and he laughed. He supposed he could do a lot better than that when it came to proposing. But right now, he didn't want either of them to move. He wanted to stay exactly where they were.

"Marry me?" he asked, meeting her gaze and reveling in the love that shone back at him. A love that was solely for him and no one else.

She nodded. "I will marry you, Byron Hill, my oldest and dearest friend. And then we can raise our girls, and God willing our other children, together. No more wasted time. I don't want to spend another minute out of your company."

The idea sounded perfect to him as well. "Well, we're in Scotland. Perhaps a trip to Gretna is in order."

Nina chuckled. "I'll make arrangements and we'll leave tomorrow."

And they did.

EPILOGUE

12 Months Later

"Are you disappointed, Byron?" Nina asked, grinning at him over the stable door. "I know you were hoping for a boy," she said.

Byron looked down at his daughters dog Bentley, that had just become the proud father of five girl puppies. Not long after their marriage the girls had persuaded them to get another wolfhound—a female one—and now it would seem his destiny was to be surrounded by females of all species.

He patted Bentley, who sat at his side looking in on the makeshift bed that the girls had made the dogs in the barn. Not that they would be here for long. Soon all would be living indoors with them again. There was little that Byron wouldn't allow his daughters, and over the past twelve months they had successfully wrapped him about their little fingers and he was powerless against their charms. And the charms of his wife, who grinned over at him from the other side of the stable door.

"I'm not disappointed. You, my Nina, ought to stop your teasing."

She threw him a mischievous glance and his want of her increased. Hell, he loved her, so much more with every day that passed. They had married in Gretna within a week of his arrival in Scotland, and then returned to Kent to complete the building of Nina's school.

The past year had been the best of his life, and to know that his future held more of the same only increased his love of living.

"I think we'll call this one Bessie," Molly said, stroking the puppy on its ear with the lightest of strokes.

"You shouldn't touch the puppies," Lora said with authority. "They're only new and should be left alone." Lora threw her sister a knowing look, but Molly merely rolled her eyes.

"You are not an expert, Lora. Bentley and Bernadette don't mind me patting their babies and so you shouldn't either." Molly turned toward Nina. "Tell her, Mama Tell her that I'm right."

"I think, girls, it's time for lunch, so hurry up inside and clean up before we dine." Nina opened the stable door, and with begrudging moans the girls headed indoors. Byron also came out of the stall, pulling his wife up against his side before they followed the children.

He reached down and ran his hand over the small bump on Nina's stomach. "Maybe this will be a boy. Not that I care either way—you know I adore all my girls."

She smiled up at him, chuckling a little. "I know you do, but I would like a little boy, if only to replicate the wonderful man who'll be his father and role model."

"You're happy then?" he asked, kissing the top of her head and holding her close.

"The happiest. But then you already know that."

He did, for he was too. And when the time came, seven months later in fact, Nina did birth them another healthy child. A girl.

TO MARRY A
MARCHIONESS

Lords of London, Book 6

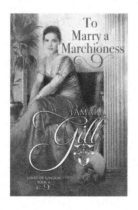

Lady Henrietta Zetland is definitely not looking for love again after being widowed so young. She cannot provide the heirs most husbands desire, so is quite happy to abandon the trappings of the ton and London Season for country life. Yet the moment she meets Marcus Duncan, the new Marquess Zetland, the passion she has long suppressed returns to life and overwhelms all good sense and propriety.

. . .

Becoming a Marquess is just what Marcus Duncan needs to save his crumbling Scottish estate. His travels to England to oversee his newly acquired estates, throws him into the path of his cousin's widow. Marcus is instantly charmed by Henrietta and a passionate love affair ensues. The last thing he expects is to lose his heart and when he pushes for more, it is revealed they both have secrets that could separate them forever.

CHAPTER 1

Lady Henrietta Nicholson, Marchioness of Zetland, sat before her bedroom dressing table and stared at her reflection. Her eyes were bloodshot and puffy, the tip of her nose was red, and her hair had somehow refused to be appropriate on this sombre day and stay confined under her hairpins.

Behind her, her maid bustled about the room, making her bed that now looked too large, empty, and cold, much like her life as she would know it from this day forward. Her mother, the Duchess of Athelby, was downstairs and not willing to leave Henrietta alone in this large estate that was now hers. The property had not been entailed, and she was free to live out the rest of her days in Surrey if she wished. How wonderful that idea sounded. Having laid her husband to rest in the cold, damp soil not an hour before, Henrietta needed something to look forward to.

She swiped at the tears that fell down her cheeks. How could this be her life? They had only been married twelve short months, it wasn't possible for Walter to be gone. His sickness had been so fast, a trifling cold that had settled in his lungs and then would not budge. No matter what they tried, or how many doctors they'd seen on Harley Street, his cough and his breathing steadily became worse until he passed in his sleep.

Henrietta thought back to the day she'd come upon him in their bedroom fighting for breath, and she'd known with sickening dread that he wasn't long for this earth. That the ailment that had wrought carnage on his body would win the war. Wanting to be strong for him, she'd not broken down until alone, and she had remained steadfast in her ability to remain calm in his presence, to try and keep him cheerful, when all the while her heart was crumbling in her chest knowing that he was slipping away. That she was going to lose him.

If only it had been a peaceful passing. His chest had rattled fiercely during the last hours and Henrietta had prepared herself as best she could. And now the worst was here and she was alone. The man she loved was no longer of this realm, and no matter how much her mother tried to comfort her, it was not her that Henrietta wanted at her side.

She sniffed and started to pull out what few pins she had left in her hair, placing them on the shallow crystal dish on her dressing table. Her mother wanted her to return to town with her, but Henrietta would stay in Surrey. This was her home now, the place she'd been happiest, and she wasn't willing to leave it only to be bombarded in town with pitying looks from friends and acquaintances, constant attempts to comfort and relay their sadness regarding her loss.

Her closest friends meant well, and she was thankful they'd come to Surrey to pay their last respects, but the social whirl of London no longer drew her like it once had. Over the past year she'd become accustomed to country living, to running a large home of her own. The frivolities of London life seemed empty and silly now. The gossip and scandal. As much as she'd miss her friends, on the morrow she would bid them goodbye and selfishly be thankful for it.

Should she return to town the ton would expect her to marry again, and she would never do such a thing. She would not cheat another husband out of what they rightfully needed upon marriage—children. No, she was a widow. She would become a matron of the ton—if a very young one—when she eventually did return, and that would be her life.

A light knock sounded on the door and her maid opened it, revealing her mother. Even in middle age, the Duchess of Athelby was a beautiful woman. Many said that Henrietta took after her mama more than her dearest papa, but she'd always liked to think that she and her twin brother Henry took after them both.

"Are you alright, dearest? I thought I'd sleep in here with you this evening."

Henrietta smiled, taking in her mother in her night-gown and bare feet. Even if she'd wanted to be alone this evening, it was pointless to argue with her mama. If she thought she needed to stay, to give comfort—even if that comfort was without words—there was little Henrietta could say to persuade her otherwise.

"You may stay, Mama. I do not mind."

Her mother dismissed the maid and climbed up into the bed, arranging some pillows so she could sit upright.

"Have you given any thought to returning to London with me next week? Or perhaps even Ruxton estate? Your father thought it may be good for you to close up Kewell Hall and come home for a while. Henry too. We discussed it this evening after you retired."

Did they just. Henrietta pushed away the flicker of annoyance that her family was arranging her, for they really only meant well. Today had been hard on them too, she reminded herself. They had loved Walter—there were few who did not—and they would miss him. "I have given it some thought," she said, standing and walking over to the bed, playing idly with the linens. "But I'm going to remain here, Mama. I promise I shall be fine," she continued when her mother looked at her with something akin to horror. "I will not do anything silly, but I want…no, I need, time to be alone. To come to terms with the fact that I'm a widow and Walter is gone. You understand, do you not? I shall return to town after my year of mourning, but until then, I want to be here. Near my horses, our pets, our garden and home. I just need to heal before I start running to where I'll never face the truth of my life." The truth being now that Walter was gone, she would be alone. Forever.

Her mama nodded, her eyes hooded with sadness. "You've been so strong throughout this whole ordeal, my dear. It is acceptable to break when we lose someone we love. Fortunately, you've never lost a loved one before, so I worry that you're bottling your emotions up."

Henrietta swallowed the lump in her throat. She had been strong, and now that she no longer needed to be, all she wished was to be alone. To crumble and break by herself so she may put the pieces of her life back together. She'd never been an impractical woman, but something told her she'd be anything but her usual self in the next few months.

"I love you so much, darling," her mama said. "If I could take away this pain, if I could turn back the clock and give you Walter back, I would in a heartbeat. I'll worry for you if you stay here. Maybe I could delay my departure. I'm sure your papa will not mind in the least."

Henrietta climbed up into bed beside her mama, lying down and cuddling into her arms. "I want you to go with Papa. I'm sad, and I shall cry just as we are now, but I shall be fine. In time. I promise I shall write to you every week, but I need to be on my own at present. I promise all will be well again." Henrietta hoped that was true. The estate and the people who depended on its success were relying on her to make it so. The new marquess would take care of Walter's other properties, but Kewell Hall was her responsibility and she would not fail these people. She would give herself a month at best to grieve and then she would have to rally and push herself into everyday duties. It was what Walter would want her to do. He loved her so very much that he'd never want her to wallow in unhappiness forever.

Her mother ran a hand through her hair, and Henrietta heard her sigh of defeat. "Very well, we shall return to town next week as planned. But I will visit every month or so. Surrey is not so far away, and for my own sanity you shall allow me to. I will never rest easy if I do not know that my baby girl is well."

Henrietta smiled, hugging her mama tighter. "I love you."

Her mother reached down and kissed her hair. "I love you too, my darling girl. And I promise you, your grief will lessen in time, and you'll find that life will carry on, even if you do not want it to. But it will, and when you're ready, you'll love again. You're too young, with too much of a beautiful soul, to be a widow forever."

The idea made Henrietta shudder. The thought of marrying again, of being intimate, of sharing any kind of life with someone who was not Walter was too abhorrent to imagine. She would never marry again, for the love of her life was gone, and such a love only came around once. No one was ever lucky enough to find two great loves in their life. Her mother ought to know very well how true that was, since Henrietta's father the Duke of Athelby was her mama's second marriage after her disastrous first one.

"You know as well as anyone that marriage will not happen again for me, Mama. I cannot marry a man knowing that I'm unable to bear children."

"The doctors could be wrong, dearest," her mother said.

Even to Henrietta her mother's tone held a sliver of despair. "A year of marriage and not one child, Mama. I think in my case they were correct, and I need to accept my fate. I will never be a mother." Not wanting to give her any more reason to worry, or to discuss the matter any further, she yawned, tiredness swamping her. "I need to sleep now, Mama."

"Very well." Her mother settled beside her. "Goodnight, darling."

"Goodnight, Mama." At least in sleep she might be oblivious to the pain that ricocheted through her with every breath. A pain that only sleep would relieve. A pain that she doubted would ever go away.

MARCUS DUNCAN SAT before the roaring fire in his library and read the missive notifying him that his distant cousin, the Marquess of Zetland, had passed away suddenly and unexpectedly from some sort of lung ailment.

He shook his head at the windfall that couldn't have happened at a better time. The knowledge that the marquessate was now his, along with all the properties that came with it, filled him with joy, as well as with despair for the late marquess's family. No one wished to come into lands, money, and a title in such a way, and he would write to them and support them in their grief.

It would also mean, ultimately, that he would have to travel from Scotland to England—leave his beloved son and homeland and deal with the legalities of the situation. Marcus looked down at Arthur, who was sitting with his nurse, playing with a wooden horse. Although his boy would not inherit the marquessate, or the unentailed lands and properties, his future would be more secure. The income Marcus would draw from the estates would help rebuild and repair his own here in Scotland, giving his son a solid footing for the future.

Guilt pricked his soul that he'd not been able to give that solid footing himself just by siring the boy. When one was born out of wedlock, the stigma followed like the waft of cow dung. But now that there was the possibility of fortune favouring them, well, that could change things a little for his lad, and that alone made him thankful.

He skimmed through the legal document that accompanied the letter from his solicitor in Edinburgh stating that his cousin's widow, the marchioness, had remained at Kewell Hall, but that there was some sort of trouble regarding who owned this unentailed estate and that further correspondence would be forthcoming.

Marcus supposed he would have to look over the estates, ensure all were in working order, and lease them out before he headed back to Scotland. His solicitor mentioned the possibility of leasing out the London townhouse as well, an income source that was timely due to the repairs required at his castle. Not that he had wished death upon his cousin, never that, but he would have to think in terms of his own financial responsibilities now that the marquisate was his.

Once the weather was better he would travel south,

maybe in a month or two, but first he would have to go to Edinburgh to sign off on the inheritance and officially become the new Marquess of Zetland.

The name Zetland didn't roll off the tongue as well as Duncan did, but he'd never thought to inherit the title. His poor cousin. Dying at such a young age, and without heirs, must be a terrible blow to the family, and as much as they would hate anyone distant inheriting the seat, Marcus would do all that he could to help them with their grief. He may be a hard man, but he was not unkind.

He stood and went over to his desk, sitting down behind the four feet of mahogany. Sliding a piece of parchment closer, he scribbled a note to his solicitor that he would attend his office next week. As for when he'd leave for England, well, he would think of that later. With his own estate to take care of here in Scotland, and preparing for planting, he didn't have time right now to oversee the estates in England. His son needed him, and the windfall of inheriting the marquessate would give him some extra funds so work could commence on the east wing of his home. He couldn't very well leave now that he had an opportunity to complete all of the building repairs he'd longed to do. There were also numerous crofters homes that needed new roofing prior to winter, and other repairs that had only been temporary until his fortunes turned.

He would ensure the steward overseeing the marquess's homes started proceedings to lease out the properties to anyone who was interested, and have his solicitor forward any correspondence to him here. For the time being, this would be where he'd deal with any business at hand.

CHAPTER 2

One year later

The carriage ride from Scotland was long—too long to be doing again anytime soon. Marcus jumped down when the vehicle stopped before the last estate, the very one where the widow marchioness resided. Although since the property was his, he really had thought she would have vacated the home by now.

He glanced up at the Georgian sandstone structure, noting the large rectangular windows that glistened in the afternoon sun. The grounds were well kept and resembled a parkland more than the manicured estates the English were so very fond of. He liked this design much better—it was more natural, more to his tastes.

He stretched and adjusted his cravat, checking his attire would be suitable to meet his cousin's widow. He doubted she'd be very pleased to see him, since he would be broaching the subject of why she was still here and not living somewhere else.

The front door opened, and a footman in red livery stepped out, bowing to him. "May I help you, my lord?"

Marcus walked up to the young man. His height and the fact he was quite broad did often bring out the fear of God on people's faces, and the young servant was no different. The lad peered up at him as if he were facing his demise.

"Please tell Lady Zetland that the Marquess of Zetland is here to see her."

The footman's eyes widened, but he nodded. "Follow me if you please, and I shall notify her ladyship of your arrival."

Marcus followed the lad indoors. The home was clean, well kept, and didn't appear in need of any repairs. Over the last few months he'd ensured the other two properties he'd inherited in England were let to good and upstanding families, and he was happy to do the same with this estate. Once Lady Zetland vacated of course, unless she wished to take up the lease, and then he would be more than pleased to leave her well alone so he could return to Scotland.

"This way, my lord. Lady Zetland is in the library."

Marcus followed the lad into a room that was floor to ceiling full of books. A roaring fire burned in the grate, and the deep green and red leather furniture gave the room a masculine feel. He admired it, and should he wish to keep the home, he could admit to feeling quite content in a room like this. The layout was very similar to how he had his own library set up in Scotland.

The footman gestured for him to enter. He glanced across the room and his steps faltered before he righted himself and continued on to meet her ladyship. "In ainm Dé," he muttered in Gaelic. He'd not expected that! "Lady Zetland, I'm sorry we're to meet under such sad circumstances. May I offer you my condolences."

She was standing behind the desk. Her morning gown of the lightest blue reminded him of Scottish skies in summer. Her hair was half up, the remainder of her coppery brown locks falling about her shoulders, and his fingers itched to see if it was as soft as it looked.

She held out her delicate hand and he took it, bowing over it. "Please, have a seat, Lord Zetland. I wish we were meeting under different circumstances as well, but alas, life is not always fair."

That he could agree with. Taking a seat, he took in the room some more, anything but to stare at a woman he'd not thought would be as attractive as she was. With her large, luminous eyes and unblemished skin, she was a perfect English rose. He could all too well feel sorry for his cousin if he died leaving such a woman behind to go on with her life. It would be enough to kill him all over again at the thought of someone else marrying his widow.

"You requested a meeting today, although I'm not sure as to why," she said. "Was there something you wished to discuss with me regarding the estates you've taken over? I worked with Walter quite extensively prior to his death, so I do have some idea of how things work."

Marcus shook his head, clearing his throat. "Oh no, all the estates have been leased and taken care of. I'm Scottish, if ye hadn't already guessed from my accent, and will be returning north within the week. But I do have a query about this home."

She frowned, and even the little line between her brows didn't detract from her prettiness. No woman should be so discombobulating, but it would seem the marchioness had him at a loss and certainly was wreaking havoc on the speed his blood was pumping about his body.

"What do you wish to know?" she asked, her large blue eyes clear and intelligent.

Did she really not know? "Well, as to that, and I don't mean to be unfeeling, but this was also part of my inheritance upon taking up the title."

Her ladyship paled, and Marcus fought not to expire of shame at having to bring up the matter. He would have a very stern word with his lawyer when he saw him again.

"Forgive me, Lady Zetland, I thought you knew. I gave you time, over twelve months to be exact, as I thought you needed the time to heal, to mourn. But when my solicitor mentioned you were still residing here upon my travelling to England, I wanted to see for myself if there was a reason as to why you've not moved. Did you not know?" he asked, hating that she looked like she'd seen a ghost.

"But this house is mine. Walter left it to me upon his death." She moved over to a large cupboard behind her and pulled one of the drawers open, before clasping a rolled piece of parchment. "Here, this is the document."

She handed it to Marcus and he opened it and straight away saw the glaring error. "He has not signed it, Lady Zetland. The decree certainly states that the home ought to go to you, but it's not signed." At her dejected look, he inwardly cringed. He was never one to take what did not belong to him, and should he not need the funds for his lad he would gladly walk away from the estate. As his financial situation now stood, that option was not open to him.

"Surely not!" she took the document from him and scanned it before slumping back into her chair. "Oh my, this is dreadful. I don't understand. I don't understand why my lawyer did not pick up on this."

Neither did Marcus, and he hated to be the bearer of bad news. But the house was his, and not entailed, so he could do what he wanted with it. He didn't want to push Lady Zetland out, so maybe there was something he could do for her in return, since she was innocent in this mess.

"Let me seek information regarding the legalities of the problem we now face. Mayhap there is another document that is signed that neither of us are aware of."

She threw him a disbelieving look. "I do believe you're being too kind, my lord. But I agree, we should wait to find out exactly what is the situation regarding this estate and then move forward from there."

He nodded, but the dejected slump of her shoulders left him uneasy. "If the home does fall into my hands, my lady, I'm more than willing to gift the estate to you if it means so very much to you." What was he saying? He needed the funds that the estate would bring in to secure the future of his son and his own Scottish estates. Lady Zetland and her wretched visage had made him soft in the head.

"Oh, no, my lord. I could never accept such a gift, but thank you for offering. That was very kind of you."

He wasn't kind—he felt like a brute kicking a lone woman out of her home. No money was worth doing such an underhanded thing and he would not in this case. Not if she did not have anywhere to go.

"I will send for my lawyer straight away to see what has happened. And I suppose," she said, rolling up the document once again, "since this is your home, I should offer for you to stay while we sort out this problem and decide on what I shall do. There are plenty of rooms, it would be no trouble. We're family, after all."

In a way they were family, but still, Marcus didn't like the fact that Lady Zetland made him feel like a green lad before a beautiful woman for the first time. "If it's no trouble. As I said, I'll be leaving in a week or so, once this debacle is dealt with to everyone's satisfaction. I never meant to boot you out on your ass, my lady."

Her eyes widened, and Marcus recalled that his Scottish way of speaking probably wasn't something her lady-ship had ever heard before.

A chuckle floated toward him and he glanced up to see her laughing. Perhaps she wasn't such a proper English miss.

"Apologies, my lady. I've lived on my own for many years, and I'm not used to being around titled gentlefolk."

She smiled, and the breath in his lungs seized. Holy God, she was too beautiful for words. Although he could think of some: angelic, pure, a rose in full bloom...

"Do not trouble yourself, Lord Zetland, do not change yourself on my account. I can assure you that I've heard worse."

"You have?" He highly doubted it. "Where, may I ask?"

"My mother for many years has been part of the London Relief Society, a place that helps children learn and move on into employment, both in London and in the country. The last few years before I married, my mama included me in the meetings, took me out to the schools and shelters which by then also helped women move on from less savoury means of earning a living to a more respectable, safe one. So I have heard worse than ass, I can assure you."

"Your mother sounds like a woman of great kindness."

"She is," her ladyship said, smiling wistfully. "And I'm afraid that once she hears of my losing Kewell Hall, she'll be on the doorstep within a few days demanding to know what it's all about."

"I should be scared then?" Marcus asked, only half seriously.

"Oh yes, you should be terrified. The Duchess of Athelby is not someone even I would like to go up against."

Marcus swallowed. Lady Zetland was the Duke of

Athelby's daughter. Good God, he'd heard of the Duke and Duchess of Athelby all the way up in Scotland. They practically ran the haute ton. He'd heard his distant cousin had married well, but he hadn't known just how well.

"I consider myself duly warned, my lady," he said, standing. "Do you mind if I retire to my room? I've travelled many miles today and I must admit I'd like to freshen up before dinner."

"Of course," Lady Zetland said, standing and walking over to the fire and ringing the staff bell. Within a moment the footman who'd opened the front door was back, standing to attention and ready to do whatever the mistress of the house decreed.

Marcus had to chuckle at the ways of the English, especially compared to how he lived. He was a simple man. He may live in a castle, but half of it was falling down about his ears, although in time the rents from the English properties would help in the restoration of his home. He was titled in his own right in Scotland—the laird of Clan Duncan—but to be laird was nothing like it once was in the Highlands, and the clan today was nothing like it once was either.

"I dine at eight sharp." She walked him to the library door and pointed to a room across the hall. "The dining room is through there, Lord Zetland."

"Please," he said, turning to her. "Call me Marcus. We're family, distant as that may be."

She smiled and again he had to tear his gaze away from her beauty. When he returned to Scotland he would have to find himself a bride, or a tumble. This visceral reaction he had to Lady Zetland was not common, certainly not for him, and it could only mean one thing. He needed a woman.

"I would like that, Marcus. Thank you. In turn, you may call me Henrietta."

He nodded then followed the footman out of the room and upstairs. He liked the name Henrietta, or Hetti as it was shortened to in Scotland. It made him wonder if that was what her close friends called her, or what her husband used to. It suited her, and with time maybe they too would become friends and she would allow him to call her by such a name as well.

CHAPTER 3

Later that evening, Henrietta paced before the fireplace, the pearls about her neck a lovely distraction running through her hands as she thought about tonight's dinner. The idea of having dinner with her husband's cousin wouldn't normally rattle her so, but the man who'd walked into her library—all six foot six of him she was sure, with shoulders that looked strong enough to haul two women upon them to his chamber for who knows what—was not someone she'd thought to be dining with.

Her body had not been her own upon meeting him, and reluctantly she had to admit to feeling a tidbit of attraction to him that was both confusing and complicating in equal parts.

She recalled the dinners she'd had with her husband Walter, and the times he'd mentioned who would inherit if they did not produce a child, which unfortunately in the short year that they were married they had not. Not that Henrietta had any hope of producing an heir. Her one regret about marrying the marquess was having lied to him.

Walter had talked of Marcus Duncan as nothing more than a distant cousin who would never impact on their life. After today his impact was well felt, and Henrietta's heart still hadn't calmed after meeting him. She suppressed the unexpected nerves that fluttered in her stomach and steeled herself for the forthcoming meal.

The dinner gong sounded below stairs and her maid Mary handed her a shawl. Henrietta thanked her and headed downstairs, concentrating on her breathing and ignoring the havoc in her stomach. She'd been out of society for some time, so it was only natural that the first gentleman to call upon her would make her react in such a nonsensical way. His stay was for only a week. He'd be gone soon enough and then her life would be back to normal.

This afternoon she'd sent an express to her solicitor in London to find out if the paperwork Lord Zetland had showed her today was correct, and if so, how they had been so lax in their handling of her affairs.

Had she known this home was no longer hers she would've moved to the estate she owned not far from here —a lovely country manor house that her parents had gifted her upon her eighteenth birthday, a place she could always go to should the need arise.

It had certainly arisen now.

As much as she would miss her home here at Kewell Hall, a residence where she and Walter had created many happy memories, her own home in Surrey also held fond memories. It was after all where she'd met Walter for the first time, when her parents held a ball there during her first season. It was where Walter had proposed. So if she did lose this house, all would be well in the end.

She clasped the railing of the stairs and, picking up her gown, started making her way downstairs. Halfway down the library door opened and Lord Zetland entered the hall before her. Dressed in a Scottish kilt of deep red and blue, the towering Highlander looked like he'd stepped out of the pages of history. His shirt was tucked into his kilt, the sporran about his hips accentuated his narrow waist, and he wore a dinner jacket over his shirt. Never had she seen a Scotsman look so handsome.

Lord Zetland was all man. There were no soft edges or dandy traits about this gentleman—he was hard, strong, capable. His jaw was angular and looked chiselled to perfection, a god in a kilt, and his hair had the slightest hint of gold through his darker locks, but his eyes were his best feature. They were kind, thoughtful, knowledgeable she would bet, and she doubted he ever missed much that went on before him.

"Good evening, Marcus. You look wonderful. Is that your family kilt you're wearing?"

"Aye, Henrietta, 'tis so." He held out his hand to her. His clasp was warm, gentler than she thought it would be, before he placed her hand onto his arm and escorted her in to dine.

"I asked cook to do up a few Scottish dishes, so I hope you like haggis."

He chuckled, holding out her chair before seating himself across from her. Even the expanse of polished cedar that separated them wasn't nearly far enough to stop the blood in her veins from reacting to his nearness.

Maybe her mama was correct and she needed to return to town, throw herself back into the social whirl of the ton, and continue her mourning away from isolation. She'd been here for just over a year, most of that time alone, other than when her parents or brother visited. Her reaction to the Highlander was proof that she needed to leave, if only for a few months.

The first course, a soup called a la Solferino, was placed before them and for a time they ate in silence, before Henrietta looked up and caught Marcus studying her.

She dabbed her mouth with her napkin. "Is something the matter with the soup, my lord?"

"No," he said, grinning at her mischievously. "I was only thinking that I'd not dined with a woman for quite some time, and how much I missed doing so. My home is quite isolated and I do not travel away from there much, so to be dining with you—a duke's daughter, a marchioness in your own right—well, 'tis a novelty I'll not soon forget."

How sweet he was. His heartfelt words made her lips twitch. "You're not alone in your thoughts of how nice it is to dine with someone. I was thinking the same myself, and that perhaps no matter whether I keep this home or retire to my own estate, it's probably time I returned to London to see my family and regain the life I lost when Walter passed away."

"You have your own estate. May I enquire as to where?"

Henrietta notified the servants to take away their first course and bring in the second. "I do, three miles from Kewell Hall in fact. If I do lose this estate I shall make Cranfield my home and travel to and from London from there. It is only a short horse ride from here if you would like to visit it during your stay. I don't mind, truly. I've been meaning to check on it for some days, and I could show you a little of this estate too on our ride. Kill two birds with one stone."

"A good hard ride is just what I need."

Henrietta hid her grin behind her napkin at his words, and as the second course was placed before them, she glimpsed the reddening of Lord Zetland's cheeks. "Are you well, my lord? You look a little flushed."

He cleared his throat. "I'm very well, thank you. The fire behind me is a little warm, 'tis all."

"Is tomorrow too soon for you? Kewell Hall's estate is very beautiful, and should you end up being owner of the property at least you'll know a little of its layout."

"I would like that very much," he said, a half smile tweaking his lips.

Henrietta caught herself a little obsessed with his mouth, his full, soft-looking mouth. Did Marcus kiss with passion or sweet seduction? Passion, she would guess. Any woman in his arms would be devoured, seduced, and made love to wildly. As wild as the Highlands that he hailed from.

The thought shamed her and she turned back to her meal. After Walter's death, she'd not thought to marry again, to allow the opposite sex to impact on her life. It had only been twelve months. Was it too soon for her to be reacting to another man in this way? That she couldn't answer, but deep down she knew Walter would want her to be happy. Not to lock herself away in Surrey and only live half a life.

She glanced down at her wedding band that she still wore. "It's settled then," she said, forking a piece of duck. "I will have the stable staff notified and we'll head off after we break our fast in the morning."

Lord Zetland nodded and the remainder of the meal was pleasant if not a little quiet at times. Not that those pauses of chatter were awkward—on the contrary, they were anything but, and gave Henrietta time to study the new marquess some more.

Who was he? Did he have a young woman in Scotland that he wanted to marry? Had he already been married? He'd certainly not mentioned a wife, so she didn't think that was the case. But he didn't seem to say much about his home, other than it being a castle. He was a mystery, a Scottish one, but one that she would venture to learn more about during his stay here—if only to fulfil her own curiosity, that wanted to know everything, and now.

CHAPTER 4

The grounds and surrounding property of Kewell Hall were magnificent, and the more Marcus saw of the estate, the more he liked what he saw—including the woman who rode alongside him showing him what could possibly be his.

For a woman who looked to have lost the estate, she was being a good sport about it all. Maybe it was simply because she had an estate not far from here and was a duke's daughter, and so Kewell Hall wasn't of such great importance to her. Although, taking in the grounds and the property, he could see she was one widow who took great care to ensure both the home and lands were well tended.

They stopped before a running stream. A little way along, Marcus could see where carriages made the crossing, and the road leading toward the estate.

"This is where Kewell Hall's lands end, and my estate begins. This stream isn't deep, but if it storms it does become so, so always be careful."

He smiled, liking the fact that she needed to warn him

against such things. It was nice to be fussed over, even if only in a little way such as a warning about floods. He'd not been fussed over for a few years, and the emotion it evoked within him, warm and comforting, was a feeling he could get used to.

"Duly noted, my lady."

"Henrietta, please." She threw him a marked gaze and pushed her horse on to cross the stream.

Marcus followed and kicked his mount a little to get him to trot up the slight incline on the other side. They rode to the top of a hill, and the view that opened out onto the valley beyond was magnificent. Acres and acres of trees and grassland where sheep and deer roamed. Marcus took in the vista, admitting to himself that it was pretty good, even if it was England. And then he saw her home. Nestled within a copse of trees sat Cranfield.

If he had been expecting a small estate, he was sorely mistaken. This home was bigger than Kewell Hall. Hundreds of windows glistened in the morning sunlight, and from here he could see two gardeners working in the grounds.

"Your estate is magnificent, Henrietta," he said, settling his mount as it dug at the soil, impatient to continue. "Seeing it, I'm surprised that you don't live there. It is much bigger than Kewell Hall."

She looked back at her estate and shrugged. "It's too large, and although Walter did give me the choice whether to live here or at his estate, I wanted our life to be at Kewell Hall."

"You wanted your children to be raised under the same roof as their father was. There is nothing wrong with your choice."

At the mention of children her gaze shuttered and all of a sudden she seemed sad. Of course he knew they had no children, or he wouldn't be exactly where he was now, a marquess, but maybe they'd just not had enough time to produce an heir. Walter had after all died very young and only a year into their marriage.

"One day perhaps it'll be filled with the sound of children's laughter," he added.

"Perhaps. Now," she said, once again smiling and at ease with him. "Shall we continue? I always give my horse a run from here. Do you wish to do the same?"

Marcus was never one to turn down a challenge. "Aye, of course."

Before he had a chance to prepare himself, Henrietta had spurred her horse into a canter that soon turned into a full-fledged gallop down the hill. He watched her, forgetting for a moment that they were supposed to be racing. Then he started after her, and his horse, a well-bred gelding that had won a few Scottish derbies, was soon only a few paces behind her.

Her laughter floated to him, and he looked ahead only to see her checking his whereabouts.

"You'll have to do better than that, Lord Zetland, to catch me."

He smiled, enjoying himself way too much considering he was supposed to be concentrating on the lands, not racing about the fields with an English marchioness. Even with the lack of highlands to make the view more pleasing, the sight of Henrietta's perfect derrière in her riding attire did compensate well enough for his liking.

They slowed as they crossed a shallow stream and then, following Henrietta's lead, he pulled his mount into a slow trot then a walk. "Your horse is fast, I will give you that, but had you not cheated and taken off before I was ready, I would've had you beat."

She grinned, patting her horse's neck. "I need no head start to win, do not fool yourself, my lord."

He chuckled. "I shall not argue with you, my lady. I see you're not ready yet to listen to common sense on the matter." He grinned at her affront and laughed when she understood his mirth. To be happy, carefree as she was right at this moment, suited her very well, and never had he seen a prettier woman.

They came clear of a copse of trees and her home rose before them. Built in a similar style to Kewell Hall, the Georgian property's sandstone all but glowed in the morning sun, inviting and homely. And yet no footman came to greet them, no servants. Only the yard staff walked about, going about their duties.

Marcus dismounted and came about to help Henrietta, but found her already beside her horse. She caught his gaze, shrugging. "Thank you for thinking of me, but I've been dismounting on my own for some time now. I'll even surprise you in a little while and climb back on without assistance as well."

He bowed. "You'll have my full attention so I may see that."

They tied the horses to a nearby tree, and started toward the front door. "There isn't any staff within the house itself. They're employed at Kewell Hall now, but the housekeeper does send over maids to keep the dust at bay." She pulled a key out of a pocket in her riding habit and unlocked the door, swinging it wide.

"And this is Cranfield." She turned toward him. "What do you think?"

Marcus entered and looked about. The home was similar to Kewell Hall, except this home was cloaked in dust sheets, the window shutters closed, the sound of life, of people living within the walls, not echoing around them.

Outside the house looked welcoming, inside it looked desolate.

"It is lovely, lass. If not a little lonely, I would think. Why did you not let this property out once you were settled at Kewell Hall?"

Henrietta strode through the foyer and started toward the back of the home. He followed. "I don't know. I suppose I wanted to keep it for myself. It was given to me, after all, and I have so many memories here. I'd hate to lease the property out, allow another family to form their own wonderful memories, only for me to turn around in a few years and tell them they must leave. To do such a thing would upset me, and so instead I closed it up, left her waiting for me when I was ready to return."

The home seemed to suit her, and as little as Marcus knew the Marchioness of Zetland, even he could see she was relaxed and at ease here.

"This is my favourite room, and it was where my grandmother spent most of her time. It's also rumoured that she was proposed to here by King George IV, but she would never confirm or deny the story so it's something we'll never know." She grinned at him and something thumped hard in Marcus's chest. He could well understand his cousin's attraction to the woman—she was certainly likeable in all ways, in temperament, character, and appearance.

"My home in Scotland has many clan stories, dating back to Robert the Bruce, but the Scottish ruler never proposed to anyone in my family. As much as some of my ancestors would've loved to have such a tale to tell around a roaring hearth late at night. My son certainly loves swords and all things medieval."

She sat on a settee that was covered in dust cloths and gestured for him to join her. He did, chucking a little when a poof of dust permeated the air as they made themselves comfortable.

"You have a son? I did not know you were married. Is your wife still in Scotland?"

"Arthur is his name, a fine strapping lad of two years of age. His mother is no longer with us," he said, shying away from the brutal truth that the boy's mother had left without a by-your-leave. Or the fact that he'd not had the chance to marry the lass and bring some respectability to his son's birth.

"I'm very sorry for your loss," she said, touching his hand quickly. "Tell me then, what is your Scottish home like?" she asked, changing the subject, which he was glad of. "My mother has a property there which I love visiting. I haven't been for two or so years, but intend to make the journey before next season."

"My home, Morleigh Castle, sits upon the mountain range overlooking Loch Ruthven. I can see the loch from two sides of the castle and in winter, the peaks are covered in snow. The area is marshy, so 'tis hard to travel at certain times of the year. The castle itself is cold, full of passageways and ghouls, or so my servants say. You're more than welcome to stay should you travel up that far within the country. I'd love the company." And he would love *her* company above anything else. A light blush stole across her cheeks and for the life of him he could not look away.

She sighed, leaning back and laying her head against the settee's back, staring at the ceiling. "I think I shall take you up on that offer, Lord Zetland. The thought of traveling to London and taking part in another season does little to tempt me. I miss my friends, but they can survive some more months without my company. I should so like to travel a little more before the endless nights and days of socializing take up my time and a holiday to the Highlands becomes nothing but a dream."

The thought of Henrietta returning to town, or being courted by eligible gentlemen, left him somewhat annoyed. He didn't want to think about it, and that in itself was worth pondering. Even his son's mother had not brought forth in Marcus this uneasy feeling that should he pursue this woman, she could turn out to be part of his future. Part of his lad's future. He'd always wanted a wife, and Henrietta with her calm and generous nature would make a wonderful mother to his child and any that they would have together.

Marcus looked out toward the back gardens from where they sat and shook the thought aside. He'd only known the woman two days and already he was planning to make her into his brood mare. Did he have rocks in his head? She may not ever wish to marry again, let alone marry him.

Marriage! He really needed to get a grasp on his wayward imaginings.

"Morleigh Castle will always welcome ye, Lady Zetland. You need not even announce your impending arrival."

She turned and met his gaze. "You're being too kind." She studied him a moment. "I have to ask, Lord Zetland. You're an eligible gentleman now—is there not someone pining for you at home?"

"Dinna worry about that, I have no lass waiting for me."

Henrietta frowned. "I find that hard to believe."

He chuckled. How wrong she was. "Do ye think me handsome enough then to tempt the ladies? I shall take that as a compliment."

"You're putting words into my mouth, my lord, as well you know."

He was indeed, and yet he liked sparring with her. She was a worthy opponent.

"Your son, is he well behaved? I should imagine being away from him all these weeks is difficult?"

"He's very well and much loved. I miss him more than I thought I would, and it was one of the reasons why I didna travel from Scotland after Lord Zetland's death. The lad was only a year old then, and I didna feel it was right for me to leave him alone to travel so very far away. But I only have a week left here, so not too much longer before I see him again."

"Does he look like you?" she asked. "I bet he's handsome."

Marcus raised his brow, unable to let such a question pass him by. "There ye go again, hinting at my good looks," he teased. He looked at her and their gazes locked. Held. And a tension that simmered between them, had done so since the moment they met, thrummed hard, and it took all of Marcus's control not to lean across the small space that separated them and take her lips.

Damn, he wanted to kiss her.

"I'm not a green miss, my lord. I can admit when a gentleman is handsome or no, and you sir are as handsome as any I've seen. Terribly shocking for a marchioness and a duke's daughter to say, but my upbringing was not conventional and my parents always taught us to speak our minds and stand up for what we believe in."

"I like those traits. They do you justice."

"I hope so," she said, slapping her hands on her knees and standing. "Now, we'd best return to Kewell Hall before luncheon. I have a surprise for you today."

Did the sweetness of the woman never end? She was a

marvel and he couldn't help but be charmed by her proper English manners. "You do not have to go to any lengths to please me. I'm content just to visit, get to know you and those who live and work at Kewell Hall. You need not go out of your way for me."

"Oh, I haven't, I've simply had a special meal prepared for you for lunch. I think you'll enjoy it."

Please don't be haggis again. As Scottish as he was, the thought of boiled lungs, heart and liver stuffed into a sheep's gut was more than enough to make his stomach roil. It had been bad enough having to eat it the previous evening. "Can you tell me what it is?" If it was haggis, he would have to mentally prepare himself for the torture that was about to unfold.

"No, you'll see soon enough. Now come, I want to show you an old monastery nearby that is fascinating and also supposedly haunted. Since your castle seems to be also, maybe you could give me your professional opinion on this."

He chuckled. "Lead the way, my lady. If there are sprits or ghouls to be found, I'll know it."

The remainder of the day was a day worth living—good company, great conversation, a picnic luncheon of cold meats and wine down beside the river, and an outing that was worth Marcus's time. He could not remember the last time he'd enjoyed himself so much with a woman, and a woman that he wasn't courting. Not that Henrietta wasn't a bonny lass, for she certainly was that, but with her being a new widow, twelve months may be too soon for her to really move on from the loss of her husband. And Marcus wasn't really sure he wanted a wife at this stage in his life.

He was still young, only eight and twenty. As much as he'd like to have more children someday, he also didn't want to rush into anything simply because Lady Zetland encompassed all that he'd ever wanted in a partner.

No, he would return to Scotland, and if their paths happened to cross again, then he'd know fate had stepped in and pushed their hand. Otherwise, mayhap they were not meant to be.

CHAPTER 5

H enrietta lay on her bed late that night and all that
she saw before her was Lord Zetland—Marcus, as
he'd asked her to call him—and his delectable backside as
he'd climbed up the old monastery ruins, reaching back
down to help her join him on the little lookout created by a
crumbling wall.

She smiled recalling the enjoyment of the day, the
carefree conversation that was not stilted or hard fought.
They seemed to talk quite naturally together, found similar
things amusing, and his love for the land, even if Kewell
Hall turned out to be hers after all, was genuine. He
showed that he cared for her discussions about planting,
harvest, and the tenant farmers. Wanted to know her
plans, what the yield was like and the local community.

Even the thought of losing this home and property
wasn't so upsetting if she knew it would go to a man who
would care for it as much as she had. The fact that they
would be neighbors as well was not disturbing either. In
fact, she could ride over to Kewell Hall very easily, to visit,

help his lordship out if he needed, and see the servants again, make sure they were happy.

She rolled over, shaking her head at her own musings. Who was she kidding? The only reason she'd come over to Kewell Hall would be to see Marcus, and the possibility of seeing him in his breeches, perhaps bending over before a fire while he stoked it.

She really shouldn't be thinking about him in such a way—he was her husband's distant cousin, and heir. Although Walter had been gone over a year, was she being callous, disrespecting her marriage vows, to be thinking about another man in such a way? Not that she would marry him. He'd not shown one morsel of attraction to her, except perhaps that one look they shared in her library at Cranfield, but otherwise he'd been the perfect gentleman.

He was a young man, and although they were similar in age, he would no doubt wish for more children one day, and that she could never give him. It was her one shame that she carried with her and had not even been able to tell Walter of, even after their marriage.

To be barren, unable to conceive—as her London doctor had told her—had been a devastating blow, but not one that she did not see coming. She had known since she started to grow into a woman that something was not quite right, and had asked her mother for advice. That she would never bear children was not what they'd expected to hear. Still, she'd had her season, caught the eye of a marquess and married him, all the while hoping the doctors had been wrong. But after a year of marriage, she'd not once had her menses, and so it would seem nor would she have a child.

She pushed back her blankets and slipped out of bed, wrapped a shawl about her shoulders and left her room.

The house was dark, besides the few candles left burning that would soon flicker out due to their own wax burning down to nothing.

Picking up a small candlestick, she started down the stairs and made for the kitchen, intending to pour herself a glass of milk and maybe see if her cook had any freshly baked bread she could snack on.

Entering the kitchen she stifled a scream as she saw the shadowed figure of Lord Zetland sitting at the table, a cup with some sort of beverage clasped tight in his hands. He stood quickly, the scrape of the chair on the slate floor loud in the room, and she cringed, not wanting to wake the staff and have them find them alone.

"You could not sleep either, lass?" he asked, gesturing to a chair for her to sit and join him. Henrietta checked the pantry first for bread, and smiled when she spotted a freshly baked loaf. Cutting a slice, she placed it on a plate and set it on the table before pouring herself a cup of milk and joining his lordship in his midnight snack.

"I could not. I do not know why, since we had such a busy day, but for whatever reason sleep eludes me."

She shot his lordship a quick glance and thanked the shadowed room they were in. Her cheeks burned with what she saw. Lord Zetland wore nothing but a shirt and breeches, but the shirt was open at the neck, so much so that she could see the outline of his chest and the light frosting of dark hair.

She'd not seen a man in such a state of dress for over a year. But looking at this Lord Zetland was so different than looking at her own dearly departed husband's body. Although the late Lord Zetland had been tall, he was also of a wiry figure. He'd had muscles of course, but the current Lord Zetland, who was slowly sipping his coffee, his muscles...well, they were quite profound and filled out his shirt with ease.

Henrietta slipped another bite of bread into her mouth and chewed, anything to keep her eyes from darting back to his marvellous figure that she could see quite well now that her eyes had adjusted to the room.

"You can look at me, Henrietta. I will not bite." He grinned at her and her cheeks heated further.

"I am looking at you," she said, wishing she could pull the words back as soon as she said them. "That is to say, what an odd thing to say, for I have been looking at you. Why do you think I've not been?" But she already knew why he'd asked, because she'd been peeping at him like a delicious naughty novelty before her, as if looking at him was forbidden to her even though she kept sneaking glances.

"You usually can meet my gaze, and yet right now you can barely lift your eyes past my chest."

Henrietta did meet his gaze then, and she didn't miss the simmering heat that lurked in his blue orbs. She'd thought he'd been making light of their situation, of them being in a darkened kitchen, half dressed and alone. But he wasn't. Instead, he was looking at her in a way that she'd not even seen Walter look at her in the depths of night when they were alone. His gaze dropped to her lips and then further over her person, and a shiver stole over her body, making her breasts feel heavy and tight beneath her shift. Her heart was beating too fast to be proper.

"And yet I find right at this moment that your eyes too are not meeting mine, my lord. Do you like what you see?" What was she saying? What on earth was she doing? Never had she been so forward, or scandalous. A little voice whispered that her mother would be so proud of her right at this moment. The duchess was a woman who lived life to the fullest, wanted her children to also, but Henrietta had always been proper, comported herself as the correct daughter of a duke. But in the company of Lord Zetland, something niggled within her to be naughty, to play and laugh for once instead of the opposite.

His gaze darkened further and he placed down his cup. "Very much so." His voice was deep, just above a whisper, and she shivered and then started when he pushed back his chair. "Good night, Lady Zetland."

She watched him go, shutting her mouth with a snap as he closed the kitchen door behind him. Well, she wasn't quite sure what had just happened, and she wasn't entirely sure that she liked Lord Zetland leaving without continuing the enlightening conversation they were just partaking in. Not to mention that the thought of him liking what he saw left her nerves frazzled.

The idea that she would have to speak to him upon the morrow would be awkward and not something to look forward to now. After what they'd said to each other, if he thought her meeting his gaze right now had been a problem, he had not seen anything yet.

MARCUS RODE HARD toward the river that ran about Kewell Hall. The day he and Henrietta had ridden out to her estate, she'd told him that Kewell Hall sat surrounded by a waterway that forked off and ran about the estate, making it almost surrounded by a moat.

The sky bore ominous clouds, and in the distance he could hear the rumbling of thunder, even with the thumping of hooves beneath him. He crossed the stream and had just started up the other side of the embankment when the heavens opened, the heavy, cold rain making his vision less than he'd like. He pulled his horse up, planning to return home to be safe.

Out of the corner of his eye a flash of blue caught his eye and he looked over to see Henrietta pulled up under an old oak, trying to find what little cover she could during the storm.

Lady Zetland looked a treat atop her horse, her figure to full advantage, her seat straight, her chin held high with authority, no doubt from being brought up under a ducal roof.

He started over toward her. He'd not looked forward to seeing her today, not after his atrocious behaviour the night before. What had come over him to have asked her what she thought of him he'd never know. That she'd not looked at him with any yearning since he'd been under her roof had been driving him to distraction, and the more time he spent with her, the more he wanted her to see him. To want him as much as he was fearing that he wanted her.

Henrietta being the daughter of a duke meant that before he even thought of courting a woman of such rank, he had better be sure that she was the woman for him and open to such pursuits—two points that he was not certain of. Which made his taunting words the night before wicked and completely unacceptable.

He pulled up his mount beside her and threw her a half smile. "Lady Zetland, I must apologize for last night. I should never have teased you so, questioned you about where your gaze was situated. It was very wrong of me, and I'm sorry, lass."

She smiled at him and it went some way to dispel his shame. "Do not be embarrassed, Lord Zetland. Your question when all told was on point. I was looking at you, scandalously so, thinking of what lay beneath your shirt and what it would be like to kiss you. So you see," she said, looking back at the weather that continued to gather in strength and ferocity, "I'm not embarrassed or angry at your words and I do not want our open and honest conversations to end because of them."

Marcus stared at her a moment, the breath in his lungs awfully shallow. Did that mean... "You imagined kissing me, Lady Zetland?"

She nodded, biting her lip a little. A small droplet of rain dripped off her chin and her words broke what little restraint he had. Moving his horse to come up beside her, he reached across the space, clasped her cheeks, and kissed her. Hard.

Her cool lips met his, and instead of a woman of rank who did not know how to kiss, he was met by a woman who clasped the lapels of his coat, held him close, and kissed him back with such passion, such need, that it made his head spin.

He shouldn't be doing this. A warning went off in his mind. Henrietta was his deceased cousin's wife. A duke's daughter, a woman who may not want him when she learned of his shame. That his son was illegitimate and birthed from a woman who was in his employ. If she could not accept his son, then he could not make her his. It was one absolute truth that could not be broken in his life.

The kiss went on, their tongues meshed, teased. The kiss slowed and sped up, provoked and beseeched them both for more wonderful things that could be had in bed if they ended up there.

His mount shifted under him and broke them apart. The distance made him relinquish his hold but for the life of him he could not stop looking at her. Her cheeks were flushed, her lips a little swollen from their embrace, and the need in her eyes pulled at a part of him he'd not thought existed. He rubbed his chest, trying to calm his racing heart.

"I suppose now I need to apologize for that kiss, and yet, as much as I should say I'm sorry for taking you in my arms and kissing you, I'm not sorry at all. I've wanted to kiss you since the moment I arrived."

Her lips twitched and again her gaze dipped to his chest, just as it had the night before. "I've wanted to kiss you as well."

A crack of thunder sounded and the rain started down heavier than before.

Henrietta kicked her mount a little to leave the shelter of the oak. Marcus followed. "We'd better cross the river again before it's flooded and we have no way of returning to the estate."

"Of course." They rode as fast as the sodden ground would allow, and only slowed as they came to the river. Although it was a little faster in its flow, it was still passable at this time from the looks of it.

"Follow me here, Lord Zetland, and the horse will keep its footing."

He did as she bade, starting to wonder whether he would comply with whatever she asked of him. The Lady Zetland was a woman worth following anywhere.

CHAPTER 6

Henrietta sat at her desk and scribbled a note to her mother, leaving out the tidbit of information that she'd kissed a man who was not her husband, boldly, wantonly, and with little regard to what anyone thought.

When he'd instigated the kiss she'd thought for a instant to pull away, but the moment his lips touched hers, all thoughts of denying him faded away. Now all that she'd thought of since was doing it again, of when she'd see him privately, and where this newfound intimacy may lead. The idea of him sharing her bed, his strong, capable hands running over her body. Why even now, when he was out with the estate's steward looking over the tenant farms, her stomach fluttered at the thought of bedding him.

To think of what they could do if she allowed such liberties made the breath in her lungs seize. To picture him above her, bare of clothes, his strong muscles flexing with the effort to bring her pleasure… She shut her eyes, liking the imagining more than any well-bred young woman should.

A knock at the door startled her and she jumped in her

chair, the sound of a footman requesting admission bringing her thoughts back to her duties. Henrietta folded her missive and pulling out the top drawer, placed the letter to her mama inside.

"Come in," she said, shutting the drawer and locking it.

"The new housemaid has arrived, Lady Zetland. Did you wish to meet with her now, or at another time?"

"Send her in, thank you." Henrietta stood as the young woman entered, her bright red hair hardly tamed by her hasty tying back. The maid bobbed a quick curtsy, but didn't venture to smile.

"Lady Zetland, thank ye for your employment. I will not disappoint ye."

Henrietta smiled, coming around her desk to lessen the space between them. "Have your duties been explained to you, and what I expect from all the staff here at Kewell Hall?"

The young woman nodded. "The housekeeper has told me of my duties and where I shall sleep."

She was a pretty woman, and Scottish. It would seem that this week she was to be surrounded by those that hailed from the northern region.

"Your name?" she asked.

The woman met her gaze. "Miss Emma Campbell, my lady."

"And what part of Scotland are you from, Miss Campbell?"

The young woman looked about the room a little before answering. "The Highlands, my lady."

Henrietta smiled. "A lovely part of the country if ever there was one." She walked the new maid toward the library door. "Mrs. King will take you from here. I wish you well with your employment here."

The woman dipped into a neat curtsy. "Thank you, my lady. I feel it shall be."

Henrietta watched Mrs. King take her toward the kitchens where no doubt she'd be put to work once the staff had partaken in their luncheon.

The front door opened and in strolled Lord Zetland from his outing with the steward. His hair was mussed from riding all morning, and a shiver of delight stole over her at seeing him again. After their kiss, one that had encompassed more passion than she'd ever experienced before, all her thoughts were consolidated to when they would do it again.

By the looks of his gaze, dark and full of promise, their time to kiss would happen sooner rather than later.

"Lord Zetland. Did you find the tenant farms well tended?"

He handed his grey redingote to a waiting footman, along with his hat and gloves.

"I did, Lady Zetland. They all seem to be in good hands and well tended, just as you said they were." He strode past her, but surprisingly, he clasped her hand and pulled her into the library.

He shut the door behind them, and the moment the door slammed closed he pushed her up against the door, her face clasped between his capable hands as his mouth, hot and insistent, took her lips, pulling forth in her a hunger she'd not known she had.

No sooner had their kiss started than it ended, and for a moment Henrietta held the door handle to steady her feet.

He ran a finger down her cheek, tipping up her chin to meet his gaze. "All day, the entire time that I rode about the estate, all my thoughts were on you. Of seeing you again, of kissing you. I find that from the moment I wake, to the moment I fall asleep, my mind is occupied with nothing but your sweetness."

Henrietta bit her lip, delighted at his sweet words. Had she the ability to speak, she would've told Marcus that she'd done little other than think of him as well. Counting down the hours until he returned to the estate so they might pick up where they'd ended their tryst the day before.

"Your kisses are wicked, my lord, and worse than that, you know how much they affect me."

"They affect ye, do they lass? How so?" he asked, dipping his head and kissing his way along her cheek, her ear, paying attention to her lobe for a moment before kissing down her neck. Oh dear lord. She swallowed as her body yearned with hunger for him to do more. How was she ever to concentrate on his question and answer it when his lips teased her so?

She pushed at his chest a little so she could see him and not be so unfocused. "I loved my husband, I truly did, but although the marriage bed was enjoyable—or at least I thought it was—it wasn't long into our marriage that Walter became ill. So you see, Lord Zetland, I'm at a disadvantage compared to you. I'm not as worldly about such things."

He grinned and she went back into his arms, needing to be close to him again. "I'll not rush you, lass. We're only kissing after all."

Henrietta nodded, wanting more than to kiss the man. A scandalous way of thinking, but in his arms she couldn't think of any place she'd rather be. There was little chance of her falling pregnant should they end up lovers and so nothing ruinous could occur if she did take him to her bed.

A pang of sadness swamped her that falling pregnant wasn't a concern when it really ought to be. Had she grown correctly as the doctor told her, then Lord Zetland would need to be careful. "You're all gentlemanly behavior, my lord," she said, running her hand through the hair at his nape.

"I'm no gentleman. Far from it, lass."

She bit her lip, the deep tone of his words making her ache in places she'd not known could ache. How enlightening. "How so? Show me," she said, stepping closer still so her breasts touched his chest.

MARCUS SWALLOWED AND, about to claim his prize, inwardly swore when there was a light knock on the door with the accompanying sound of female voices. Whoever it was who'd arrived made Henrietta's eyes widen in shock and panic and she shushed him, gesturing for him to sit on the settee near the fire.

He did as she asked, as quietly as he could, while she fought to right her gown and hair which had become a little mussed after their kiss. He couldn't help but watch and grin at her hasty attempt to make herself proper, when all he wanted to do was make her anything but.

She opened the door, delight crossing her features at the sight of whoever stood there. "Mama, how lovely to see you. I didn't know that you were going to visit me. I was just composing a letter to you."

Marcus stood, clasping his hands behind his back as the Duchess of Athelby and another woman walked into the room. The duchess took in the room, and her gaze, sharp and knowledgeable, fixed on him. He fought not to shuffle on his feet at her cool stare, and was relieved when Henrietta walked toward him after greeting the other woman.

"Mama, Margaret, may I introduce Lord Zetland, the

new marquess. Lord Zetland, this is my mama, the Duchess of Athelby and my cousin, Miss Margaret Bell."

He bowed. "A pleasure to meet you, Your Grace." And he could see where Henrietta gained her beautiful looks, for the duchess was also a handsome woman, even with her age.

"How do you do, Lord Zetland?"

"Very well, thank you, Your Grace," he said, not knowing if her tone was that of friend or foe.

"Lord Zetland is here to see the estate. It seems that I may not be the owner of Kewell Hall after all. Walter didn't sign the paperwork to finalize my inheritance."

Marcus looked to Henrietta as her tone was one of disappointment, and he never wanted that for her. The estate wasn't entailed, and so technically he could gift her the house and lands. But if he did that, the blunt that he could gain by leasing the property to help his son have a more secure future, plus help restore his own Scottish castle, would be gone. But he also didn't want Henrietta to be unhappy. Maybe he should just give it to her and be done with it. He had two other properties to gain income from. He did not need to be selfish.

"About that, my dear," the duchess said, going to sit behind the desk. "You are correct in your assumptions, as Walter did not sign the deed transferring ownership. Our lawyer came to see us, apologizing for the error regarding this matter. You are not the owner of Kewell Hall and its lands or tenant farms. I have come here, with your cousin, to help you shift your things to Cranfield. To open up your home and hire the appropriate staff."

Marcus frowned, not wanting Henrietta to go anywhere, and certainly not three miles away. "There is no rush if what you say is true. Henrietta has been helping me learn how the property and home is run, and to gain trust with the steward and staff. It would be a great impediment if she were to leave now."

The duchess raised one suspicious eyebrow. "Henrietta, is it?" She cleared her throat, throwing her daughter a knowing look. "You have a few days to tie up any loose ends regarding the estate and then my daughter will be moving to Cranfield."

Henrietta sighed, but nodded, and Marcus wanted to swear. He didn't want her to go. The thought gave him pause when something akin to panic took flight in his chest. He'd grown used to seeing her at dinner and break-fast. Their rides about the estate. And now that they were on more private terms, the days of homecomings would be sweeter still. Similar to what had happened this afternoon.

"I shall still be able to help you until you return to Scotland, Lord Zetland. Do not worry."

He nodded, but didn't venture any further words on the matter. The duchess, seemingly pleased with the outcome, stood and walked over to her daughter. "Come, help me to my room and we'll discuss Cranfield."

At the door, Henrietta paused, turning back to Marcus. "See you at dinner, Lord Zetland."

He watched them leave and ran a hand through his hair. There wasn't a lot left for him to learn regarding the estate. Glancing over to the desk, he noted a letter left there. Had the duchess placed it there when she sat? He went over to it and flipped it over. Recognizing his lawyer's scrawl and seal on the back, he broke it open, reading the missive quickly.

It stated what the duchess had just said. Kewell Hall was his in its entirety. His lawyer also stated he would forward the documents proving that was the case to his estate in Scotland. Marcus sat on the chair, having to admit that his time here in England would have to come to an

end. Even if the house was leased or he gave it to Henrietta, either way there wasn't anything left to keep him here.

Except the woman that filled his every waking moment
and dream state.

Henrietta.

CHAPTER 7

Henrietta sat in the back parlor that overlooked the terrace with her cousin Margaret—Maggie to the family—and told her of her growing infatuation with Lord Zetland. Of her scandalous idea that she wanted to act on regarding the Scottish lord who currently resided under her roof.

"He's certainly handsome, Henrietta, but as someone who's been married to a man who was one way prior to our marriage and then someone entirely different afterwards, I have to ask if you are certain he's not a wolf in sheep's clothing. He's Scottish, and they're not widely known to have a liking for the English, need I remind you," she said, nodding for emphasis.

Henrietta chuckled, but her cousin had good reason for saying such things. She'd been married to the Earl of Worncliffe, a man who turned out to be so violent that Maggie had no other option but to divorce him. Even being related to the Duke of Athelby had not been enough to save her reputation, and Henrietta's mother bringing Maggie here meant only one thing—that she would make Maggie her companion and give the woman some sort of financial security and position, little as that was.

Henrietta didn't like the idea at all. Maggie should be allowed to marry again, go to balls and parties and continue the friendships she had during her marriage. Whilst, Lord Worncliffe walked about London able to do as he pleased and without an ounce of scandal marring his name. Maggie had been stripped of her fortune that she'd brought to the marriage, leaving her with very little to live on. The unfairness of it all was maddening, and Henrietta hated the outcome that had befallen her cousin just for seeking her freedom.

"He's not a bad man. Even if we were to marry—and I can promise you that will not happen—I do not believe he would change. He's kind, very sensual, and his kisses... well, I cannot even think that a man who kisses so well could turn about and be a monster."

Maggie frowned, thinking over Henrietta's words. "This may be true. God knows, Lord Worncliffe could not kiss at all. In fact, it was quite unpleasant."

They both laughed. Then Henrietta said, "If I leave to go to Cranfield it'll mean that I'll not see Marcus as often as I'd like. I do not wish to leave, not yet at least."

"Hmm," Maggie said, frowning. "Maybe I could fake an illness and that will convince your mama to let you stay here a little longer."

"I think you're forgetting that Mama is the Duchess of Athelby. She'll see through our little ruse soon enough. No," Henrietta said, standing to emphasise her words. "I will simply tell her I'm not yet ready to leave and that I shall have her return to town. When Lord Zetland does depart, I'll send for Mama's assistance. You of course, Maggie, may stay."

"Will your mama leave, do you think? I know she'd been looking forward to seeing you again."

As much as Henrietta loved her parents, they did sometimes meddle a little too much in her life. She was a widow, a grown woman, more than capable of looking after herself and deciding when it was time to depart Kewell Hall and Lord Zetland's company. "I will break it to her in a kind way this afternoon. She's resting at present. She will understand, I'm sure of it. Now, I must go and change."

Maggie glanced out the window. "You're not going outside in this heat, are you? You'll freckle."

"There is a garden house down near the river on the western side of the estate, do not forget. Walter's parents had it built not long after they were married. I'll be sure to not stay in the sun for too long, but it's hot enough for a swim today, so I may dip my toes. You're more than welcome to join me if you like."

"No thank you, I shall remain here. I've never been fond of deep, murky water," Maggie said, shivering a little.

Henrietta bid her good afternoon, and after changing into her swimming costume that was conveniently hidden beneath her morning gown she made her way towards the river. The walk only took about fifteen minutes, and with the forest that surrounded the estate, the walk was dappled in sunlight. In the distance she could hear water splashing and her steps slowed as she came out of the trees to the clearing. Here a wooden frame with newly planted climbing roses sat beside the river's edge, a neat and convenient path leading to the water.

But it was who was swimming that caught her full attention. She stopped, biting her lip, as Lord Zetland stood waist-deep in the river, his bare back glowing in the sunlight, water droplets dripping off his hair to run down his perfect form.

"Gosh," she mumbled, not wanting him to spy her and end her delightful inspection of him. The idea that she could swim with him, feel his body next to hers, had her taking the steps needed to reach the garden house. She sat upon the wooden bench beside the door and kicked off her boots.

He turned upon hearing her and smiled as he met her gaze, a wicked light within his eyes. "I had to take the opportunity to swim on this hot day. Are you going to join me, lass?" He ran a hand through his hair, and the muscle in his arm flexed.

She sighed, undoing the buttons at the front of her gown, and Lord Zetland's gaze dropped to her chest. "What are you doing, Henrietta?" he asked after a moment, his voice deeper than she'd ever heard it.

She stood and shuffled out of her gown, leaving the shift and pantalets beneath. Then she pulled off her stockings and laid them over the bench along with her gown. "I'm going for a swim, just like you. This is my swimming costume."

He gaze raked her, his chest rising and falling with each breath. Did the sight of her tempt him, make him want to kiss her again? Oh dear lord she hoped it did, for she'd certainly wanted to kiss him since they were interrupted yesterday when her mother arrived with Maggie.

She took a tentative step into the water and was relieved to find it wasn't too cold. The river had a muddy bed, and she took care walking into the water lest she fall over. "Have you never before seen a woman in a swimming gown, my lord?"

"Och, yes, I've seen women in swimming costumes, my lady. But never a woman who makes me want to rip the swimming costume off their person."

She slipped and landed with a splash in the water, then

came out of the water laughing. "You did that on purpose to distract my concentration."

He swam over to her, pulling her hard against his body and settling her legs about his waist. The action allowed her to feel all the corded muscles in his chest, the heat of his skin, the trickle of water off his chin... "No, I did not, but I also cannot deny the fact that to see you here with me, your swimming costume perfectly transparent now that it's wet, is a boon I'd not thought would happen when I first came down here earlier today."

Henrietta glanced down at her body and her face heated at the sight of her nipples peeking out from her shift. She looked up at the same time Marcus did and realized he too had been looking at her person. Her nipples!

He grinned. "Beautiful."

She slid her hands about his shoulders and kissed him softly. "You have a way with words. I fear I'm not myself with you." She shouldn't allow herself to get involved, to become attached to this man. One could only assume that he'd like to marry again and have more children. And although she could be a loving and generous wife to him, she could not give him children.

"The feeling is mutual, lass." He kissed her and she didn't shy away from the need that thrummed through his body. At her core his hardening manhood pressed insistently against her mons. She could sense the restraint within him as his hands cradled her tight, and all the while his mouth devoured her, kissed her with such passion that she forgot herself and simply gave in to the want for this man. To being a woman in a man's arms, not a duke's daughter in a lord's arms.

He walked them out into deeper water so it lapped at their chests and Henrietta broke the kiss, leaning back to wet her hair. The water was so refreshing, and she'd never had such an experience before with a man. Not even with Walter. Come to think of it, they had not even had a bath together, but the idea of having a bath with Marcus left her achy with need.

She pushed the hair from his face, wanting to see his long eyelashes that made her envious, to see his strong jaw and straight aristocratic nose. There was little doubt in her mind that she wanted Marcus in her bed. To lie with a man that was not her husband. A most scandalous, sinful act, but she could not help it.

She steeled herself to ask for what she wanted without the fear of his denial of her halting her words. Surely after being with him as they now were he would not decline to sleep with her. "If I were to ask you to come to my room this evening, would you be in agreement with that?"

He watched her a moment, and the desire she read in his gaze made her heart thump hard. "I'll join you after everyone's abed."

She smiled and then screamed as he picked her up and threw her into the depths. She came up, and kicked further away from him as he chased after her. But her attempt to escape was short-lived, for he was too quick. Clasping her ankle, he wrenched her back toward him.

The action caused her to swallow a gulp of water and she coughed, trying to gain her breath.

He took her toward the shallows a little. "Are you alright, lass? I didna mean to drown you."

She chuckled. "You didn't drown me. I swallowed some water, that's all." She lay back into the water and floated for a bit. "Join me," she asked him.

He stepped over to stand beside her, and the touch of his finger circling one of her nipples made them pucker into hard nubs. "After tonight, we'll return here, and I'm going to make love to you on the bank of this river under the stars."

"Do you promise, Marcus? I'd hate to be let down by a gentleman not following through on his word."

She gasped as his mouth came down over one of her nipples and suckled it. "Aye, I promise, lass. This is one promise I'm not ever going to break."

CHAPTER 8

As Marcus bathed and dressed for dinner later that evening, then tied his cravat before the mirror in his room, he debated with himself over what he should do. How much to tell Henrietta before he slept with her? For tonight there was little doubt he would have her, in every which way he could and multiple times to boot if she would allow.

The idea of having her beneath him, of her calling his name while he pushed her toward release, had him hardening in his breeches. Picking up his glass of brandy, he drank it down in one swallow, needing to control his nerves and his desire.

The dinner gong sounded below and taking a fortifying breath, he left his room. He needed to tell Henrietta the truth about his boy. That his son was the bastard child to a woman who had up and left only days after giving birth to the boy. His shame was doubled by the fact that he'd taken comfort in the arms of a maid, working in his home and under his protection.

Some in Scotland had turned their backs on him due

to this truth, their religion and moral sensibilities not forgiving of his sin. Marcus did not care what anyone else thought, so long as his boy was happy and healthy, but Henrietta did deserve to know and to choose which path she would walk.

A slight pounding started behind his eyes with the knowledge of what he had to do.

He made his way down to dinner, thankfully not meeting either of Henrietta's family that had come to stay. The lass's mother wasn't someone he wanted to spar with too often. In all honesty, he was a little scared of the woman, but Henrietta's cousin Maggie was pleasant enough.

He came into the dining room to find everyone seated. Henrietta smiled when she caught his gaze. He smiled back in return. "Apologies for being late, Your Grace, my ladies. I seem to have a slight headache. Too much sun today perhaps."

Henrietta placed down her glass of wine and summoned a footman. "Have a tisane made for Lord Zetland, please, and bring it in here before serving him his first course."

The footman did as she bade, and thanking her, Marcus soon drank down the cloudy liquid and started on his turtle soup.

The courses came and went, along with conversations about the ton and what scandals were happening in London, including what Henrietta's brother—a twin no less, that Marcus had not known about—had been up to of late.

A couple of times Marcus caught Henrietta studying him, and with the pounding behind his eyes gaining strength, he hated the fact that he would disappoint her yet again by crying off their rendezvous.

"When do you intend to leave, Lord Zetland?" the duchess asked, slicing into her pork and placing a delicate piece into her mouth.

"I've been here a week already, so I shall not trespass too much longer on Lady Zetland. Winter will arrive soon enough in the Highlands and I'll need to be home preparing for the season before I'm snowed in and unable to leave."

Marcus met Henrietta's gaze and held it. What a wonderful week it had been. He could not remember a better time he'd had with a woman, or better company. Henrietta had been the perfect hostess, and just as knowledgeable as the steward who oversaw the everyday running of the estate. Marcus took a sip of his wine, admitting to himself that he would miss her.

"Is your home large, my lord?" Maggie asked him, seemingly genuinely interested.

"It's a castle, and overlooks Loch Ruthven. Of course it's in need of many repairs, but I'm hoping to have those completed within a year or two."

"It sounds lovely, my lord. I should like to see it one day," Henrietta said.

Marcus glanced up and didn't miss Henrietta's mother's curious expression at her daughter's words. Henrietta didn't seem to mind that her mother was looking at her. She simply kept looking at him, her beautiful blue orbs full of expectation and warmth.

"Talking of travel, Mama. There are still some details about Kewell Hall and the estate that I have to go over with Lord Zetland prior to my departure for Cranfield. It is probably best that you return to Papa in town and I shall send for you when I'm in need of assistance. Maggie can stay and keep me company until then."

The duchess wiped her mouth with her napkin, before

placing it back onto her lap. "I was meaning to speak to you about this, my dear. I had a letter from your father today wanting to know when I shall return. I think I will travel back to London, tomorrow even, and await your missive."

Marcus continued to eat, not wanting the duchess to see that her forthcoming departure left him relieved. Not that he didn't like Her Grace, but he did want more time with Henrietta, and with the duchess here, pushing Henrietta to leave for her own estate...well, that didn't tie in well with his plans.

"I should imagine a castle in the Highlands of Scotland would have to be haunted, Lord Zetland," Maggie said, grinning at him.

He chuckled. "If you ask my housekeeper she would say yes. But alas, I myself have never seen anything to cause alarm, and nor do I want to."

Henrietta sat back in her chair as the next course was served. "So your castle doesn't have any scandalous, dark, and hidden secrets that it wishes to hide? I thought all castles had some kind of mystery or story to tell."

Marcus choked on his wine and coughed, placing down his crystal glass. "No," he murmured, shaking his head. "There are no secrets at Morleigh Castle."

He turned back to his meal and concentrated on spooning a little bit of brown gravy over his pork. The claim that his home held no secrets was like weight of lead that lodged in his gut. He hated to lie to Henrietta, but he also wasn't sure what she would think if she knew the truth about him. That he had a son, a child out of wedlock, and not with a woman of noble blood, but a housemaid under his protection. It made him look like a vile cur, even though their relationship, as short as it was, was mutual.

A duke's daughter may not understand that he'd been

lonely, and his son's mother had offered herself first as his friend and then his lover. It was only after she'd thickened with his child that he came to know what a deceitful, money grabbing vulture she really was. She never wanted the boy, only her way out of servitude. Which he could not blame her for, but mayhap there were other ways to remove oneself from household employment.

HENRIETTA HAD BATHED after dinner and cheekily had ordered Lord Zetland one as well, but had asked the servants to send his in a little after ten. If her staff thought her illogical for doing so they would hardly say to her face, and with the knowledge that his lordship had a megrim, she'd used that excuse and asked the valet she'd assigned to him to pour a little lavender oil into the water to try to alleviate his pain.

With strict orders that the bath was to be cleared away the next day, she paced in her room before the unlit hearth and waited for the valet to be dismissed. Not that she'd taken up spying on her servants, but it was normally around this time that the staff finished their duties to the family and went downstairs to have their supper.

Footsteps and the unmistakable slam of the servant staircase door closing made her smile. Lord Zetland was alone. And possibly, right at this moment, naked in a bath.

The idea of seeing his toned, sun-kissed skin glistening in water again caused her nipples to tighten under her shift. She walked to the door and, opening it just a crack, looked out into the passage. No one lingered there, so pulling together all the determination and confidence she could, she started toward his room, making sure to close her own bedroom door before going.

She came to his door and with her hand paused over

the handle, a wave of nerves shot through her. Would he wish for her to come to him? Of course they had planned for Marcus to join her in her room tonight. But with his mentioning of having a headache, maybe tonight was no longer possible.

Dropping her hand to her side, she bit her lip in thought before the sound of Lord Zetland's voice inside his room made her start.

"Are you going to stand outside the door all night, Henrietta? If ye do not come in soon, the water will be cold."

She bit her lip, stifling a laugh, and entered, ensuring when she turned to shut the door that the lock slid home. Taking a deep breath she turned, and fought not to gape. He lay back in a bath before a small fire in the grate, just enough to take the chill out of the air.

Just as she remembered, his toned abdomen glistened with water, and he was at present rubbing soap against his skin in a manner that she would love him to do to her. The idea of feeling his work-roughened hands skim across her breasts made her ache between the legs and she swallowed a groan of need. It had been so long since she'd been with a man. Even before Walter's death.

"How did you know I was standing outside your door?" she asked, not moving.

He grinned, placing the soap on a chair that was beside the tub. "Some of the candles must be still burning in the passageway and I could see a shadow beneath the door. I took a guess it may be you."

"And if it hadn't been me?"

"Who else would it be?" he asked, raising his brow.

She had to concede his point. Shrugging, she stepped away from the door, slipping out of her dressing gown and letting it fall to the floor.

His eyes darkened and he paused from washing the soap off his body to watch her. "Are ye going to join me, lass? The water is still warm."

Oh yes, she was going to join him, but first she needed to take control of this situation. He was such a character, so confident, and a true rogue if she were honest. She needed to take back a little of his power and make him wrapped about her finger.

She looked down at her shift, saw her darkened nipples pushing against the fabric, and started to untie the ribbon that held the top of the gown closed. Untying it slowly, she met his gaze, then held it as she let her shift drop to the floor, leaving her as naked as a newborn babe.

In a flash he sat forward, taking her hand and pulling her to step into the bath with him. For a moment she stood before him, her mons at the height of his face. Stifling her mortification over that fact, she held her ground and didn't move.

"Do you like what you see, my lord?"

His hands ran up the back of her thighs, twisting inwards to tease her, so close to her core but not close enough. "Aye, I like what I see."

She moaned as he leaned forward and kissed her there, then took one of her legs and placed it on the side of the tub. His tongue flicked out, running along her core, kissing and laving her cunny in a way that she'd never known to be possible.

Certainly Walter had never touched her so. Their love-making had been sweet, and tender, but quick. Afterwards she'd always been left with a longing that was never sated. But right now, as Marcus kissed her in the most private of places as if he were kissing her lips, a little hint of what she'd been missing flickered within her body.

She spiked her fingers through his hair and his tongue

worked her, his lips suckling and kissing her, before slowly, and with so much care, he slid one finger within her core.

It was too much, all of it was more than she could bear, and with this unending torture pleasure rocked through her body, and she found herself grinding herself against his face, his name a breathless plea on her lips.

His other hand gripped her leg, and thankfully so, for without his support she would've collapsed into a heap upon his person.

With one final kiss against her mons he looked up at her, and the raw need etched on his face was enough to spike her desire for him all over again.

She sat, sitting astride his lap, and clasped his face. "I want you. I want you to take me. Now."

He growled, and lifting her a little, he guided himself into her. And for the first time in Henrietta's life, she was lost.

AT THE SIGHT of Henrietta in his room, all thoughts of his headache dissipated and Marcus's mind became occupied with more pleasurable musings. He had thought their dance into lovemaking would've been slower than what it was, but when Henrietta stood before him, a little unsure but full of unsated need, he'd not been able to stop himself from tasting her sweet nectar.

Just one lick and she'd opened for him, had accepted the pleasure he could give her and allowed him his way. She'd been sweet and wet, and having her grind herself against his mouth, well, he'd almost spilled his seed into the bath like a green lad.

Damn, she was beautiful.

Now Henrietta straddled his body, and with very little finesse he clasped his cock and guided himself into her tight, hot core. She shuddered in his arms and he kissed her deep and long, needing her to relax if she were to find their joining as pleasurable as his mouth on her cunny was.

He didn't force their joining, didn't clasp her hips and grind her atop him, as much as he wanted to. Instead, he simply kissed her, teased her into wanting more, and eventually, at an almost painfully slow pace, she moved, started to undulate atop him and take him fully into her body.

"Mmm," she breathed against his lips. "This is nice."

Nice… It was more than nice. Nice was a too tame a word for what they were doing, what he wanted to do. He wanted her with such a need that he physically had to stop himself from wrenching her from the bath, laying her atop the bed and taking her hard. Fast.

There would be more opportunities to make her scream his name in such a position, but tonight, in the warm soapy water, this location would have to do. "Blast, lass, you make me want you so much that even now, this isn't enough."

She increased her pace, and he couldn't help but reach around her, holding her hard against his chest. Her breasts rocked against him, their tight, hard beaded peaks rasping his chest with each movement.

He kissed his way down her neck, gliding his tongue along her collar bone. She was so small and delicate, her skin perfectly creamy with the slightest hint of blush marring her cheeks at their exertion. Tonight would never be enough for him. He wanted to taste her again, kiss her senseless more often than not, seduce her to be his, not just while he was in England, but forever.

She threw back her head and allowed him his way with her body, and for a moment he fucked her harder than he'd meant to, pushing up in her with fast, hard pumps that left him moaning her name as his balls hardened near release.

"Oh yes," she gasped, helping him to keep up the pace. She did not shy away from the rougher ride, if anything it heightened her pleasure which in turn made his double.

"Come for me, lass." As he continued his onslaught of their joining, water splashed onto the floor and he was heedless of the noise that they were making.

For the past two weeks they had danced around the attraction, and now, alone and together like this, that attraction burst into flame and they were both consumed. He wanted her to shatter in his arms, to take her pleasure, and he wanted to see her mouth open on a gasp as she peaked. He needed to see her eyes darken in enlightenment and enjoyment as tremor after tremor thrummed through her body.

She kissed him and he groaned as her core tightened to the point that he could not stop his own climax. They came, and he pumped hard into her wet heat, lost his self-control and his ability to think straight as his seed spent into her. All the while she rode him, took her pleasure, his name a whisper against his lips as she alternated between kissing him senseless and coming in his arms.

She slumped against his chest, her small kiss upon his neck making him feel things for this woman that he'd never felt for anyone before. He rubbed her back as they both caught their breath.

After a time, he clasped her face in his hands and made her look at him. He took in her beauty, that wasn't only on the outside. The woman in his arms had loved and lost, was a wonderful landlord and employer. A sensual, independent woman that he wanted. Needed for more than one night.

Her brightened eyes shone with newfound knowledge,

and he couldn't help but grin that she would be a woman to be reckoned with from this day on. There would be no holding her back from getting what she wanted. Hopefully him.

"You're so beautiful. I hope ye enjoyed our little rendezvous."

She smiled, and again his heart did a little flip. "I did. More than I ever thought possible. You brought pleasure to me twice, my lord. Is that common?"

He growled, the talk of what they had just done only ensuring that it would occur again, and soon. "Not always, but if you're sleeping with me, then yes. I like to give pleasure as much as I take it."

She studied him a moment, a little shadow crossing her eyes before she blinked, and it was gone. "Do you sleep with many women? I can only assume for you to say such a thing that this is a common occurrence for you."

He chuckled, shaking his head. "Nay, lass. Not common, but I'm no angel, dinna mistake me for one of those. I'm no virgin and I always set out to be pleasing in bed."

Henrietta looked away, biting her lip, and he waited to see what she would say. When she ventured no further conversation, he said, "Are ye jealous, lass?"

She shrugged, and for the longest moment she didn't do a thing. Then she met his gaze, trepidation in her blue orbs. "Maybe I am. I don't like to share, Lord Zetland. I usually get what I want, and I find that I want you." She slid against him and his cock, semi-hard but still within her, stirred at her movement. "While you're here at least. I want to enjoy our time together as much as possible before I return to my widowhood and you return to Scotland."

He didn't want to return to Scotland without her, and now he was determined more than ever to ensure that didn't happen. "We have some time before I depart, and now that your mama is leaving, we'll not have to be too careful about the estate."

"Maggie will still be here," Henrietta said, somehow clenching her core about him and making him lose his breath a moment.

He gasped. "Ah, lass. Do that again," he said, pulling her into a quick kiss.

She did and he moaned. "But I look forward to sneaking about, especially if it's you who is finding me."

And each time he did find her he'd have her, if she allowed. One taste and he was lost, and something told him that in this case, he never wanted to be found.

CHAPTER 9

The following morning Henrietta saw her mama off to London. Standing on the front gravelled drive of Kewell Hall, she waved until the carriage was out of sight.

Maggie, standing beside her, sighed. "Well, now that the duchess is gone, are you going to tell me why when I came to your room last night you were not there? In fact, I waited for you thinking you'd gone downstairs for a late-night snack or to get a book, but when you didn't come back, well, I had to wonder."

Heat rose on Henrietta's cheeks before she grinned. It was the most absurd reaction to such a question, but she could not help herself. When it came to Lord Zetland, she seemed to have the silliest reactions. Not to mention that after their bath last evening, she'd never look at the bath in the same way ever again.

"Do you really wish to know?" Henrietta asked, biting her lip.

Maggie's eyes widened with realization. "You slept with the marquess didn't you?"

Her friend pulled her to walk onto the path that circled

the house, and Henrietta went willingly. The fresh air may help her think straight. God knows after having Lord Zetland in his bed for the remainder of the night, she needed to gain her common sense back.

She nodded, wrapping her arm around Maggie's and smiling. "I did, cousin, and I must admit, it was more than I'd hoped for. He was so caring, so wonderful, in a way I've never known before. Even though mama did say sexual relations with one's husband could be so, I'd never experienced it myself."

"You found pleasure in his arms. Oh," Maggie said, a wistful look on her face. "How wonderful."

"It was the most wonderful thing that has ever happened in my life, other than my marriage to Walter of course." She sighed, recalling Marcus's touch, the reactions he brought forth in her body that even now, simply thinking about them, made her ache with need. "I'm going to be his lover while he's here. I want him, even now. I cannot stop thinking about him." The reactions she was having to this man were so unlike her. She'd not thought to look at another gentleman for the remainder of her life. But with Marcus, her steadfast resolve crumbled into ash. She simply could not stay away.

"Well," Maggie said, fanning herself mockingly. "You make me almost jealous. But know that I'm happy for you, Henrietta. I know you never do things so spontaneously, or without careful planning, so to take Lord Zetland to your bed must mean something."

Did it mean something? She certainly was attracted to the man, and perhaps because she knew she'd never fall pregnant by him, there really was little risk her reputation would ever be tarnished. As much as she would've loved not to be a widow, being one through no fault of her own meant she could take a lover, so long as she was discreet. A lot of women in the ton did so, and there was no bringing Walter back. God rest his soul, he was gone forever. Had been gone for a year now. When she'd received Lord Zetland into her library on the day of his arrival, she had not planned for them to end up so, as lovers and friends. But it would seem that fate had other ideas...

"I do like him. We seem to get along quite well, and he's caring and thoughtful. But do not read into our liaison any more than that. He's to return to Scotland and I shall eventually return to town. Our lives are vastly different, and he's not interested in staying south of the border. Not even for me." Not that Henrietta had asked him his wishes, but she did not want to overcomplicate their liaison. They were two adults enjoying each other, and nothing more.

"Have you asked him?" Maggie queried, looking at her.

"No," Henrietta said, "but I know he wishes to return to Scotland, and soon. He has a son to take care of and the castle is in need of repairs before the winter months. He cannot postpone his trip home just because there is someone willing to share his bed."

They turned around the corner of the home, and on the terrace Henrietta could see Lord Zetland sitting at an outside table that was shaded by a trellis with climbing roses over it. Also with him was the new maid that she'd hired, who was busy tidying away his breakfast dishes.

Beside her Maggie started talking about what she planned to do now that she was Henrietta's companion, and what Henrietta would allow her to do since they were cousins. Which was correct, for Henrietta would never order Maggie about or tell her she could or could not do something. They were like sisters more than cousins and Maggie deserved a happy and easy life, not one of servitude. She'd had enough of that when married to the earl.

Lord Zetland was looking over his paper at the maid, nodding every now and then, and even from where Henrietta stood she could see he looked a little bored as he listened to the young woman, who was speaking with great speed and gesturing hands. What on earth were they talking about?

The young woman spotted Henrietta and, bobbing a quick curtsy, headed indoors.

They walked the remainder of the way and Henrietta took a moment to admire his person. For the first time since Walter's death she had laughed, had fun, and had not been so concerned with the everyday running of the estate. Marcus made her remember that life was for the living and not to waste it by being cosseted away like a mourning recluse.

"I see you've met my new maid. Was she lost? The footmen usually serve the family."

Marcus stood and pulled out a chair for both Henrietta and Maggie. "She was lost, kept going on to me about the size of the home and how the layout of these estates are so different to the previous homes in Scotland she's worked in."

"Really?" Maggie said, looking up at the house. "Most houses of this size are all the same, I find."

"I believe she said she worked in smaller homes, my lady," he said, meeting Henrietta's eyes. "You look very beautiful today, Lady Zetland. You seem quite well rested."

Henrietta threw him a warning glance and Maggie looked at them with annoyance.

"I think I shall return inside. There is a new piece of music that your mama gave me that I want to learn."

"I will catch up with you directly," Henrietta said, turning her attention back to Marcus. "Behave, my lord," she said when Maggie had left. "You cannot speak with such openness even if my cousin is privy to our affair."

"She is?" he said sitting up and, as quick as a flash, leaning over and kissing her soundly. Her breath caught at the sensations his kisses, his touch, always brought forth in her and she clasped the lapels of his coat. "Did you tell her what I did to you last evening?"

Heat bloomed on Henrietta's cheeks and she pushed him away and back into his chair. "Not the details, you rogue, but I did tell her that I'd never in my life felt what you made me feel last evening. Even now, seated not three feet from you I find it too far away. I want you even now."

His lordship's eyes darkened with hunger and a shiver stole down her spine. The man could seduce her with one look, so it was only fair that she tease him in return. She found him attractive in every way, wanted him with a hunger that was never sated. Why should she hide her regard for him? During the time he'd been here they had become friends, and then that friendship had flittered into being lovers. She was a grown woman with needs, and if she wanted those needs met by the man seated beside her, then that is what she would declare.

There was no threat of them having a child, so the risk to her reputation was almost non-existent.

He reached out and ran a finger along her gloveless arm. "From the moment you left my room this morning I've thought of nothing but you. Tell me when I can kiss you once more."

She grinned. "You kissed me not two minutes ago. You cannot be so deprived."

"Oh no," he said, leaning forward to place his hand upon her leg, pulling it apart a little from her other. The action made her heart race and warmth pool between her thighs, but it was what he did next that left her breathless.

Thankfully the outdoor table had a long tablecloth over it, so anything they did behind the table was relatively masked from view. Lord Zetland reached down and placed his hand beneath her gown, running his touch up her leg, over her knee to slide up her thigh.

She placed her hand atop his on her thigh and stopped his course. "You cannot do that here, my lord. It is too precarious."

He shuffled his chair closer still and looked about. "There is no one to see."

Henrietta didn't venture to stop him again when his hand slid the remainder of the way, and touched her core through the slit in her pantalets. She clasped the table, spreading her legs further as he slid his touch against her mons until one finger slid within her.

She bit her lip and fought not to undulate on his hand. To do such a thing was not becoming or at all ladylike and yet she wanted to ride his hand, wanted his mouth where his fingers currently stroked.

"This is too much," she gasped, clasping his nape and forgetting that to anyone who could see that they would look awfully close. Lord Zetland leaned toward her, his hand beneath her skirts, his eyes burning with need and hunger. "You should stop," she begged, not meaning a word. She never wanted him to stop.

"But I will not, lass," he countered, his voice honeyed and brittle with need. "I want to see you, I need to see you shatter at my touch once again. 'Tis a sight that I will never tire of."

Henrietta moaned and throwing all decorum aside she kissed him, took his mouth with all the need that he evoked in her. He groaned and thrust his finger deeper, but slower, and the crest of pleasure that she sought curled more tightly within her but didn't peak.

He took her mouth without restraint and later Henrietta would curse the fact she had allowed such a public display of emotion. Such a public display of two people all but having coition before anyone who bothered to look outside.

"We should stop."

Marcus wrenched out of her hold and pulled her to stand, dragging her into the morning room just off the terrace. Thankfully the room was empty, but he did not stop, no, he continued on into the library where he shut the door, the snip of the lock loud in the empty space.

"Come here, marchioness," he said, his Scottish burr more accentuated with his desire. His chest rose and fell with each breath and she bit her lip in expectation of what was to come.

She edged back toward the settee, bumping into the table that sat behind it and ran the length of the chair.

"Perfect," he said, striding to her and hoisting her to sit atop it before he wrenched up the front of her skirts to pool at her waist. Henrietta all but thrummed with the expectation of what he was about to do. She'd never made love with a man on a table before, and her excitement doubled.

He ripped open his frontfalls, and his penis sprang to attention, thick and hard. She reached out and slid her finger along the silky, smooth shaft. He gasped, growling a little at her action.

Then he took himself in hand and rubbed the tip of his penis against her core, and she moaned, having no idea she could long for a man as much as she now did. How wonderful that women could enjoy a man in such a way. It was something that she could get used to and crave too often to count.

He clasped her hips and she watched, fascinated with

how he guided himself within her. Marcus met her eyes when he was fully sheathed and placed small, sweet kisses across her cheek. He moaned when she lifted her legs to sit about his hips.

In the bath last evening he had allowed her to pick the pace of their lovemaking. Allowed her to get used to his size, take her pleasure. But today, here and now, this was not the case.

His fingers dug into her hips as he thrust, hard and deep, his repetitive strokes causing her breath to catch. Her body was not her own, he owned her at present, and she threw her fisted hand against her mouth to stop herself from screaming his name as with one final thrust she spiralled into pleasure, her core thrumming and contracting against his ever-insistent phallus, before he too took his pleasure, her name a whispered rasp against her ear.

They stayed like that a moment, both lost within each other, before he said, "That, my lady, was not what I expected to do to you upon seeing you walking outdoors. But I must admit, I cannot regret having ye so."

She clutched at him, not wanting the moment to end as the final spirals of pleasure disappeared from her body. "I'm glad you did. It was most enjoyable."

He kissed her one more time, before pulling away from her and helping her to stand. He repaired his clothing and she watched as he tied his frontfalls back up. Something as simple as watching him now made her need of him spark to life. The idea that he would return to Scotland soon, back to his son and the duties as a new marquess and laird to his own tenants in the Highlands, left a pang of regret that he wouldn't be here anymore. It felt wonderful to have someone to laugh and converse with. How had she not realized how alone she'd felt after Walter's death?

Of course, one day he would remarry, have more children just as he should, and their time here at Kewell Hall would be nothing but a fleeting memory, a time of awakening—on her behalf at least—and a lovely rendezvous for his lordship while in England.

He tipped up her chin, a slight frown upon his brow. "What is wrong, lass? You dinna look very happy of a sudden."

She shook the depressing musing away and slid off the desk, righting her gown. "Nothing is wrong. I was merely woolgathering." She started toward the door, not welcoming the emotion that had caused a lump to form in her throat and unshed tears to blur her vision. "I'm going upstairs to freshen up and change for lunch. I'll see you directly."

MARCUS WATCHED Henrietta flee the library as if the hounds of Hell were after her. He allowed her space, but she wasn't quick enough to depart that he hadn't noticed her eyes had filled with tears. He too started for his room, and went over their interlude, every action he'd made, every move, kiss, and touch. Surely he'd not hurt her. He continued to his room and thought over what else could be bothering her.

Their lovemaking had been spontaneous. When he'd touched her leg out on the terrace he'd not meant for it to go as far as it did, or end up with them in the library making love with such passion, such unsated need that even now he wanted to be with her again. Even if to be simply near her, to talk and laugh as they did.

He sighed, walking over to the jug and bowl on a side table and pouring some water into the bowl to clean his face. He splashed water over his face, then using a cloth cleaned himself up as much as he could. Tonight he would go to Henrietta and ensure she was well, that she didn't regret their actions. He had never, and nor would he ever, force anyone to continue an affair if they did not want.

The more time he spent with the lass, the more he liked her. So much more than he thought he would when they'd tumbled into an liaison. He could see her beside him always, the stepmama to his son, mistress of both his Scottish estate and those in England.

He pulled off his cravat, laying it over a nearby chair. Henrietta had not hinted at marriage—she merely spoke about his impending departure as inevitable and with little emotional response. It did not make his reading of her easy. Did she wish to marry him?

He rubbed a hand over his jaw. For God knows he liked her, beyond any other woman before her, and forever seemed not long enough.

CHAPTER 10

After a quiet dinner, Henrietta retired to her room, and after a long, hot bath, she dismissed her maid and prepared herself for bed. She sat at her dressing table, brushing her hair, and wondered when Lord Zetland would leave. Tomorrow they were due to look over the crops to the north, and then return via the estate's flour mill. It was the last of the estate and the working farm that he'd not seen. After that, he would know exactly what he'd inherited, how it worked, who worked it, and what he earned from it each year.

With winter getting closer each day, he would probably leave within the week, and then her dalliance with him would be over.

She threw her hairbrush onto the table and started when her bedroom door opened and Lord Zetland entered quickly, locking the door behind him.

She met his reflection in the mirror and her stomach twisted into knots at the hunger in his eyes. How was it that he could look at a woman so, and even without words, tell her she was wanted, what he would do.

She licked her lips at the thought of having him in her bed, the delicious slide of his body against hers that she would miss terribly when he left.

"Bold, my lord. I did not know we had planned to be together this evening," she said, raising her brow.

He did not move, simply leaned against the door, a Scottish warrior out of a history book. And one she wanted to conquer.

"I came to wish you a good night, nothing more, lass."

She twisted on her dressing table chair, pulling the shawl about her shoulders. "Really? Merely a goodnight."

He pushed away from the door, and the muscles on his thighs caught her attention with each step he made. The buckskin breeches were really a very helpful article of clothing with being tight and allowing others to view all the assets that lay beneath.

He stopped before her, glancing down. "I've had ye today, lass. I'm not a beast. I will not push myself onto ye yet again."

Unable to resist, Henrietta reached out and laid her hand against his hip. He was so warm beneath her touch. Running her finger down the side seam of his breeches, she let her hand drop when she reached his knee. He stilled under her touch. He may say he would not have her again, but he did want her, and that truth filled her with a heady amount of control.

She stood, reaching up to wrap her hands about his neck. She kissed him, slow and deep, flicking out her tongue to mesh with his, and sighed when he gave way to his desire and wrenched her fully against him.

She went willingly, but slowly and deliberately pulled back before stepping out of his hold. "We have a big day tomorrow, my lord. You should probably get a good night's rest."

He studied her a moment and then nodded, willing to do as she bid, no matter that his breathing was as ragged as her own.

"Aye, of course. Goodnight, lass." He went to the door but paused before opening it. "This afternoon, you were upset. Please tell me you're not upset with me or what we're doing. Just say the word and we'll stop our liaison if that is the case."

There were many things wrong. One of which was how much she'd started to feel for the man who stood looking at her with such tenderness that it made her heart ache. But there wasn't any future for them, and if they were both to go on with their lives, forge new ones apart, she didn't need Marcus to form any feelings for her either.

She could not give him what he wanted. What all men of influence, titled gentlemen, needed for their names and great estates. She'd not been able to give her husband a child, and had they had the opportunity to be married longer, it would've only been a matter of time before Walter grew disappointed in her. Learned the truth that she was barren and unable to conceive. Marcus deserved to have more children, and as much as she'd love to give him another one, she could not and never would.

There was no future for them and so the constant bedding, the touches that left her yearning for more, the kisses and sweet words whispered in her ear, had to be lessened.

"There is nothing wrong, I'm merely tired, but I'll see you at breakfast. Goodnight, Marcus."

He frowned and looked as if he wished to say something further, but thinking better of it, nodded and left.

Henrietta slumped onto the chair before the hearth and sighed. What she was doing was for the best, for both of them. One day he would thank her, when he was surrounded by his children.

She smiled at the thought of it. He seemed to love his child very much, and the small boy deserved siblings. Henrietta adored having a brother, as much as her brother Henry revered having a sister. Marcus was a strong, capable, and moral man, perfect in all ways to bring up respectable, honorable children. Just how they all should be.

Marcus looked out over the newly turned fields and listened as the head farmhand talked of yields and what they were preparing to sow. As much as the information interested him, the woman who sat atop her mare, quiet and distracted, interested him more.

Something was up, and he'd be damned if he'd allow another night to go by not knowing what it was. Mayhap her monthly courses had arrived and that was why she pushed him away. But if so, being out on a horse for hours on end would not be the most comfortable for her, so he dismissed the idea.

No, she was fretting about something else and in turn, he was fretting about her.

"And how many bags per acre do you harvest?"

The farmhand went on with the information and Marcus half listened. He tried to catch Henrietta's eye, but she would not look at him. His stomach turned at the thought that she had tired of him, that when he'd taken her in the library the other day, his lack of restraint had disgusted her in some way. Mayhap she thought him a brute.

The farmhand stopped talking and, thanking him for the information, Marcus turned toward where they would head to next, the flour mill. "Lady Zetland, the mill I think. If you're ready?"

She looked at him as if surprised by the question, but nodding once, turned her mount and started east on the estate.

"The mill is quite large, I understand," he said, coming up beside her on his horse.

"Um, yes, that's right. One of the largest in Surrey, in fact. We produce flour for the surrounding counties."

Marcus was impressed. Looking ahead, he could see the pitched roof of a building along with the top of a breastshot wheel that turned as the water poured over it. "Do you have many men working the mill?"

"There are five men. I'll introduce you to them all once we arrive."

A clap of thunder above them startled his mount, and he cooed to his horse to settle him. Henrietta did the same to hers, but for a few steps it pranced with nervousness.

"There is a storm coming from behind us. We should make the mill before it hits," she said. It was more than she'd said to him all morning.

"We should pick up the pace, my lady, or I fear we'll not make it."

Pushing their mounts into a canter, they rode the rest of the way, but with the mill in sight, the first cold and heavy raindrop splashed against his cheek. They shared a look of understanding, and then the heavens opened above them.

By the time they arrived at the mill only minutes later they were drenched. The men who worked there were busy with their duties, and ensuring any wheat that was outside was moved out of the weather's way.

Henrietta introduced him, but said to the foreman that she would give Lord Zetland a tour of the mill. They started through the building, and walking behind her, Marcus couldn't help but admire the view—the sway of her hips beneath her sapphire riding habit and the straight line of her back.

"This is one of the mill stones in use here," she said, pointing it out to him. "Upstairs the grain is stored. We usually produce about 25 loads of wheat a week." As they continued the tour, the pride in her voice over the mill and how successful it was pleased him. It seemed this daughter of a duke enjoyed her duties, and all that she did as the Lady Zetland. "Are you pleased with your inheritance, my lord?"

She smiled up at him, and looking about to ensure they were alone, he pulled her into his arms. "Do you come with the inheritance, my lady?"

Her cheeks pinkened at his words and she grinned. "I'm afraid I do not. But I'm sure in time you'll still be pleased with what you have acquired."

He wanted her, so he doubted he'd be very pleased unless she stayed in his arms, forever. "And if I want more?"

She wiggled out of his hold and started off through a room that held stacked bags of grain. He followed and looked about as they came to an office with a large window overlooking the delivery yard below. The other wall sported a small fireplace. The desk had papers on it, along with a small bank of books on shelving behind.

"This is your office here at the mill. No one else is to come in here unless you're present. The foreman normally takes care of most day-to-day running of the place, but sometimes you're required to look over things. You can of course send your steward if you do not have the time."

"Did you work in here?" he asked, turning back from looking out into the yard. Henrietta sat at the desk, tidying up some of the notes that were before her. "I always did, because that's what Walter did prior to his death. We have a steward of course, but to be a good landlord one must know what's happening with one's own estate and people." She shrugged. "I simply continued in the same way."

"I shall ensure that all important things are brought to me for approval, even if I'm in Scotland. I shall not let down the people who rely on the produce of this estate, or those who earn their living working on it. That I promise ye, Henrietta."

"I'm glad," she said leaning back in her chair. "When do you think you'll leave? I'll work my own departure around the same time."

He sighed, coming to sit on the desk before her and crossing his arms. "I need to leave soon, under a fortnight I'm afraid. I have stayed longer than I intended as it is. There are some pressing matters in Scotland that I have to attend to, and I cannot be away from Arthur too much longer."

She didn't look at him, simply nodded. "Are you going to lease out Kewell Hall?"

"I will," he said, having decided to do that already. "But only when I know that whomever leases the property understands the importance of those who live here. Even so, I shall request monthly reports on the mill and farm to ensure everything is going as it should. I will not let you down, Henrietta."

She did look at him then, and the sadness in her blue orbs gave him pause. "I do not doubt you will be a good marquess."

"Henrietta," he said, reaching down and taking her hand. "Do you regret our dalliance? You are not your happy self, and I fear that I may have forced you into a situation that you did not want." Hell, he hoped that wasn't true, but he needed to know why she was so down-cast the last two days.

She stood and came to stand between his legs, wrapping her arms about his shoulders. "I've enjoyed our time together, but I'm sad that you're leaving. I think I shall miss you."

"You could always come with me." Marcus started at his own words before he thought over them and heartily agreed. He didn't want to leave any more than she did, it seemed, but his son needed him, and his Scottish estate was not in good working order such as those he'd inherited in England. He had to return home.

"I cannot come with you. For one, it would not be proper, and my life is here, in Surrey. I'm not ready for anything else at this time."

Did anything else mean husband? Well, he had two weeks to change her mind, and mayhap once he did leave, her longing and missing of him would have her arrive at his Scottish door one day soon.

"I understand, lass. But know the offer stands." And should she not come to Scotland, well, once the snow thawed on the highland ground, he would travel south again and win her hand and heart.

"Your son will be missing you, I should imagine. More so than I. It would be selfish of me to ask you to stay for a little time longer when you have so many other more important things to occupy your time."

Marcus took in her features, her perfect nose and wide almond-shaped eyes that had the longest lashes he'd ever seen. Her lips were supple, with the slightest hint of rouge upon them. His heart ached at the thought of leaving her behind. He wanted to tell her that she too had become important to him. That his time here in England had been one of the happiest and most enjoyable trips of his life.

"I had a letter from his nurse only yesterday, and he's been asking about the horses. I suppose when I return I shall start taking him out for rides, weather permitting. A Scottish lad is never too young to learn to ride."

"That is very true for English boys as well. My father also had me and my brother riding from the age of three. Only little ponies, you understand, but we're competent riders because of it."

Marcus pulled her closer, nuzzling her neck and breathing in the sweet scent of jasmine that permeated her skin. He could picture their own children learning to ride, of enjoying days out on the land, enjoying life together as a family. He kissed a little freckle that sat beneath her ear and she shifted her head to the side.

"Come to Scotland with me. I won't ask you for any promises, but spend winter in the Highlands with me, and after that, we'll see. Mayhap marriage with a Scottish lord will be to your liking after all." A future, children, and love...

He pulled back and caught her mouth in a searing kiss, taking all that he could from her while she remained in his arms. She did not pull away or deny him and a little flicker of hope sparked in his mind that she would think on his proposition.

She ran her fingers through his hair and pulled back. "I will consider your invitation, but I cannot promise any more than that."

"That's all I ask," he said, holding her tight and not wanting to let her go. Not now or ever. "Should we continue the tour?"

They'd been lucky no one had interrupted them or seen them, since neither of them had remembered to shut the door upon entering the room.

Henrietta pulled him away from the desk and, holding

his hand, dragged him out of the office. "Yes, there are a few more things I want you to see before we return to the hall, and I don't want to return too late just in case the rain decides to settle in."

The remainder of the afternoon went quickly, and just before they arrived home the heavens opened up and they were drenched yet again. Dropping the horses at the stable, they ran into the house, laughing at their unfortunate wet circumstances. Marcus loved the fact that this English beauty, a duke's daughter, was able to see the funny side of life, was not so serious and important to be lofty and aloof.

She was real, and a part of him warned him that he was getting too attached. Should she say no to coming to Scotland, he'd ask her to be his wife. He didn't wish to scare her away, but if she refused to come with no strings, perhaps if there was something tying them together then that would change her mind.

All that was left for him to do was wait and see what she would decide. He just prayed she would decide on him.

CHAPTER 11

Henrietta sat in the parlor that overlooked the terrace and sifted through the mail she'd received that morning. The morning light streamed into the room, and since the storm had passed them the previous night, she had opened up the doors to allow the cooling breeze to enter.

She picked up a letter from her mama, and read it quickly as it spoke of her brother, her father, and some of the latest improvements she was doing at the London Relief Society's Cheapside location.

There was a letter from her childhood friend who was traveling abroad at present, full of pleas for Henrietta to meet her in Spain. Henrietta looked out the open doors and contemplated it for all of a minute. Spain would be lovely, but Scotland was drawing her more if she were to go anywhere…

Since Marcus asked her yesterday about going back to the Highlands with him, her mind had been filled with little else. They had made love last night, and the tender way in which he took her, each kiss a promise, each touch heavily dosed with reverence, left her with little doubt that he was growing attached to her as she was to him. With each joining she couldn't help but feel her heart grow ever fonder of the possibility of a life together.

She put aside a letter for Lord Zetland that looked to have come from Scotland. There was one for her cousin Maggie, who had yet to wake up. She picked up her cup of tea and took a fortifying sip. As much as she wished she could go with him, throw caution to the wind and be his for a little while longer, it would not be fair for her to do such a thing. To give him hope where there was no hope to give.

She would have to tell him the truth as to why her decision would be no. To disappoint him would not be easy. The future he hinted at sounded perfect, but it would never come to pass. Not when she could not be everything that he wished.

He deserved to have children, to give his son a sibling.

"Good morning, Henrietta. I hope you slept well."

Henrietta started at her cousin's greeting and turned on the settee to smile at her. "Good morning, Maggie. Or should I say late morning, almost midday."

Maggie laughed and flopped onto a nearby chair, sighing in relief. "Oh, I'm positively famished. I've asked for my breakfast to be brought in here. I hope you don't mind."

Henrietta shook her head. "Of course not. In fact," she said, looking down beside her on the settee to find Maggie's letter, "this came in the post for you this morning." She handed her cousin the note, not missing the fear that crossed her visage when reading the address.

"Is it from the earl?" Henrietta asked, fairly certain it was.

"Yes. Probably another letter saying how much he

wants us to reconcile." Maggie met her gaze, and the fierce determination Henrietta read in her brown orbs was telling. Maggie meant what she said, and was steadfast in her decision. "The marriage was annulled, and I will never go back to him. He's brutal, and cruel."

"You're welcome to stay with me forever if you wish. You know I shall never turn you away."

"I know," Maggie said, reaching out to touch her arm. "And I'm thankful for it, for I'm not in any way looking to gain a husband ever again. One was quite enough."

"Talking of husbands...I need to confide in you about something, and I need you to give me your honest opinion."

"Of course," Maggie said, before thanking a footman who brought in a fresh pot of tea along with a plate of toast and fried eggs. Waiting for the footman to leave and close the door, Maggie said, "What is it you want to discuss?"

"You must promise not to tell a soul, ever." Henrietta threw her cousin a pointed glance and picking up a piece of toast, took a bite.

"I won't say anything," Maggie insisted. "Tell me before I expire of curiosity."

"Very well," Henrietta said, taking a fortifying breath. "The marquess has asked me to travel with him to Scotland. I think he is considering asking for my hand in marriage."

Maggie's eyes widened, before she jumped up from her chair and pulled Henrietta into a fierce hug. "Oh, my darling, I'm so happy for you. I have been watching the marquess this past week, and after talking to him numerous times, I can see that he's the loveliest of men. Warm and caring and I think possibly as nice as the late Lord Zetland."

TO MARRY A MARCHIONESS

Tears blurred Henrietta's eyes. "It isn't as simple as that, Maggie. I wish it was. But what I haven't told anyone —although my parents know of course—is that I'm unable to bear children."

"Pardon?" Maggie said, frowning. "What makes you think such a thing?"

"Because it's true. I never got my courses like other women. I've never bled at all. I thought that the doctor may be wrong, and I was so in love with Walter that I prayed they were wrong with their diagnosis. But not once in the year we were married did I fall pregnant. I sometimes think it was a blessing that Walter passed away so he never grew to know my shame. That I married him knowing the possibility that having children may never happen."

"Oh, Henrietta. I'm so sorry." Maggie clasped her hand. "And you think Lord Zetland will change his mind once he knows you cannot have children?"

Of course he would. A man of his status had to have heirs. His son would inherit, but what if something dreadful happened to him? Other children were always welcome with great families. She cringed at the unfeeling reasoning behind the choice. "Even if he does not change his mind, in time he may come to regret that choice and I will not enter another union without the truth being known. At the moment we're enjoying each other, and there are no rules. But if I go to Scotland, and the feelings he's evoking in me only grow, it'll be hard to not have a broken heart at the end of this affair. I cannot continue with this business knowing I'm barren and he wants children."

"Surely that is for him to decide. While I agree," Maggie continued, sitting back and picking up her cup of tea, "that the best thing for you to do is tell his lordship, he does have a son—an heir to the marquess title—already, so he may just surprise you and tell you that he is content. You're not the first nor the last to face this heartache."

Henrietta sniffed, thankful her cousin was here so she may discuss such matters. "You're always so forthright and honest. I suppose I'm scared that even if he's content now, he may not be in the years ahead."

"No one can know the future, but that is where I gauge the person's character, and if it's noble, kind and honest, then he will not lead you astray. Give you false hopes of a happy ever after when in truth, it is only a happy ever after for now, not five years from now."

"You make it sound so simple." Henrietta smiled, a little shimmer of hope lighting within her that maybe, just maybe, Marcus would not send her packing once he knew the truth. He was a good man, as Maggie said. Surely he would not lie to her and tell her what she wanted to hear, not what he wanted to say. "But you're right, I will give him the choice and we'll see. And I'll do it soon. He's leaving within a fortnight, so that gives me plenty of time to gather my courage and disclose my secret."

"I think that's best," Maggie said, nodding. "You'll see, cousin. He'll not be a disappointment to you."

Had not Marcus said the same thing to her only yesterday? She held onto his words and the hope it gave her and prayed he wouldn't fail her, or worse, break her heart.

CHAPTER 12

The following morning Marcus sat at breakfast and listened as Henrietta and Maggie discussed the latest scandal that the Duchess of Athelby had written to her daughter about. A debutante running off to Gretna wasn't in Marcus's eyes the worst thing—at least they intended to marry—but he absently smiled as Henrietta and Maggie seemed positively scandalized over the situation.

"Why are you grinning?" Henrietta asked him with a bemused gaze. "This is terrible. The Honourable Edith Feathers is throwing herself before a man with no fortune and therefore her parents have disowned her. What will they live on? She's only eighteen, and has no experience with the real world."

"Maybe he'll make something of himself and the lady's past fortune will not be missed. Not everyone marries for financial gain. I commend her choice. She was brave to follow her heart."

Maggie scoffed. "When they're living in flea-infested housing on the banks of the Thames I doubt very much that Edith will be thankful she followed her heart."

"You dinna know that is what will happen to them," he said, sipping his coffee.

Henrietta shook her head. "Their children will never be accepted into society. Even if they're married, they will be marred by speculation and tarnished by association. The children may even be termed bastards. Baron Feathers will certainly never accept them and therefore society will not either. How dreadful for the baroness to have her daughter do such a thing. One cannot recover from that."

Marcus narrowed his eyes, the mention of bastard children and the ostracising of them making his breakfast sour in his belly. "The English are too judgemental. The couple obviously love each other and should've been allowed to marry. That they married in Gretna ensures their children are not illegitimate. I should hope you, Lady Zetland, would be supportive of their plight."

She looked at him with something akin to shock and the thought of telling her that he had an illegitimate son left dread pooling in his gut. Would she be accepting of his boy? Would she cut anyone who talked down to or ridiculed the lad simply because of a situation not of his making?

"Well of course I would support her should I see her again, but it still does not change the fact that I think she's being very silly. The life Edith has been used to will be very different to the one that she will live going forward. I don't condemn her choice to marry a man she loves, but I fear she will find living conditions so very different that their love may not last under such circumstances."

Relief poured through Marcus like a balm and he released a breath he'd not known he was holding. "I can agree with that. She may find her life much changed, but mayhap in time the family will come around and enfold them back into their life."

"I hope you're right, my lord," Maggie said, taking a bite of her toast. "But if I know the Feathers at all, they will never forgive their daughter and they will make sure everyone she's ever known will follow their lead. I fear Edith's life will be hard."

"What is the boy's crime, as it were?" Marcus asked, curious. "Did he work? Or is he the penniless son of nobody knows who?"

"He was Baron Feathers' steward and was paying his way to becoming a minister with the church," Henrietta said. "He is not legitimate himself, hence why the family were so against the match."

Marcus had heard enough. Pushing back his chair, he walked from the room. He could not stand to listen to anyone talk down about a lad—even a respectable steward and a man of faith—and label him with such a derogatory term.

He walked to the library and, finding his own steward going over the books, he shut the door. "Malcolm, I need ye to find a gentleman who goes by the name of Mr. John Smith. He was working as the steward for Baron Feathers. The lad is also newly married to the Honourable Edith Feathers, and they've travelled to Gretna by all accounts. I want to finish paying for his studies in the church and have the living at Norbery House held for him until he's able to take up the position." If he could help but one man misjudged by society, then damn it, he would do it.

"Of course, my lord," Malcolm said, scrawling on a piece of parchment what Marcus was saying. "Is he expecting this offer, my lord?"

Marcus shook his head. "He is not, but they've been poorly treated in my estimation and they deserve better. Give him the offer and see if he accepts. I should think he will."

"Of course, my lord."

Marcus left the room, heading outside and toward the stables. He needed a hard ride to clear his head. To hear Henrietta speak so casually about a couple's downfall, and that of their children, didn't sit well with his conscience. Nor did it leave him with much hope that she would be accepting of Arthur.

And if she could not see past the fact his son was illegitimate, then there would be no future for them. No matter how much he feared he was falling for the lass. Or worse, how much he'd already fallen for her.

DINNER CAME and went and so too did nightfall and still Lord Zetland had not returned from his ride. Her maid busied herself getting Henrietta's room prepared for the night, but as she stood at the window, looking out over the grounds of Kewell Hall, the pit of her stomach churned that something was wrong. That something bad had happened to Marcus.

After leaving breakfast, she'd thought over their conversation that had made him react in such a way. The plight of Edith Feathers and Mr. Smith had hit a nerve with him, and she couldn't help but wonder why.

The sound of horse's hooves on gravel sounded below and she glanced out to see him finally returning to the hall. Where had he been all these hours, and why was he so upset over a little town gossip? She watched as he rode around the back of the house, then lost sight of him.

Dismissing her maid for the night, she grabbed her shawl and started downstairs. She met him in the hall that led to the back of the house. "You're back. I've been anxious about you."

He swayed and clasped the wall for support. "Ye have? Why?"

The smell of strong liquor permeated the air and his unfocused gaze and mussed hair hinted at what he had been doing all day. "Are you drunk, Lord Zetland?"

He chuckled and pushed past her, walking toward the foyer. She followed him as he made his way upstairs. At least if he fell down the staircase she could make some sort of effort to catch his sorry self.

"'Tis true, I am. Did ye know the Red Lion in Betchworth is well stocked of the finest Scottish whisky? I may have had a dram or two."

His words were slurred and a couple of times she thought she may have to try and catch him when his step faltered on the staircase. She took his arm when he made the first floor landing and helped him to his room.

His valet was waiting for him in his room, and Henrietta dismissed the man for the night so as to have Marcus alone. The older gentleman cast her a confused glance on his way out the door, before closing it quietly behind him.

Henrietta had not been in this suite since she'd walked in on him in the bath, and the idea of seeing him like that again had her cheeks heating. "Let me help you get into bed. You're quite drunk by the smell of you."

"Whereas you, my dear," he said, bending down and smelling her hair, taking a big gasping breath of it, "smell delicious."

"Well." Henrietta helped him to sit on the bed and started to untie his cravat. "Whether I smell delicious or not, I think it's best that you sleep off your little excursion today."

He nodded, seeming to understand, but all the while his eyes were glassy and unfocused. "What if I dinna want to sleep?" His hand reached out and clasped her hip.

Henrietta chuckled. "What do you want to do instead?" The moment she asked the question she regretted her words. Lord Zetland's gaze turned molten. His eyes, unfocused a moment ago, met hers and darkened with hunger.

"You."

Henrietta came back over to him, slipping his coat off his shoulders and unbuttoning his waistcoat. She could feel him watching her, and her blood beat fast in her veins at the thought of being with him again. Surely even drunk he may know what he was doing. And it wasn't like they'd not slept with each other before... She wouldn't be taking advantage of him...

"That is quite a forward statement, my lord. Do you think you're up to it?"

He took her hand away from untying his shirt and placed it on his groin. Henrietta's mouth dried at the feel of him, large and hard in his breeches. He was completely up to *it*, it would seem.

"Does that answer your question, my lady?" His attention snapped to her lips and Henrietta fought to calm her beating heart.

It certainly did. Even so, she wanted to tease him a little before she did anything. "You're drunk, my lord. You may be physically ready, but that does not mean you'll have the stamina."

He wrenched his shirt over his head and threw it on the floor. With him naked from the waist up, she cast her eyes over the corded muscles on his chest, the slight dusting of hair that ticked her breasts when they made love. Her hands itched to feel his warm skin. "I'll not disappoint ye, lass. Come here."

The deep, gravelly command made her sex ache. "You still have your breeches and boots on."

"And you're still dressed, but I can work with ye, even clothed such." He reached out to drag her closer and she let him, unable to deny him even herself.

His strong, capable hands slid up the back of her legs, lifting her gown before he found the hem of her pantalets. He slid them down, his hands leaving a trail of heat as he pushed her unmentionables to the floor.

She stepped out of them and kicked them away, before coming to stand before him again. "Now what?" she asked, hoping it was something wicked and naughty.

He reached under her gown again, and clasping her ass pulled her onto the bed to straddle him. He reached between them and flicked open his frontfalls, sighing when his member sprang free.

Wanting to feel him again, she reached down and stroked him. A bead of moisture sat on the tip of his manhood and she ran her thumb over it, watching his reaction cloud further with the want of her.

His breathing increased, yet he didn't look away from her, and the intense focus on her left her heady and alive.

"What are ye going to do now, Lady Zetland?" His voice was teasing.

What wouldn't she do would be a better question, after the numerous times they'd been together. The past weeks had been the most instructive and carefree of her life— certainly she hadn't known coupling could be so energetic or varied. Not to mention pleasurable.

She lifted herself up and, taking him in hand, lowered herself upon his phallus. He was large and felt even more so in this position, but where she thought there would be pain, she was only met with pleasure, and delectable fullness.

"God, Henrietta," he gasped, kissing her hard. "I canna get enough of you."

It was the same for Henrietta, and she rocked upon him, liking more and more this new position. "And I you," she said, meaning every word. To have Marcus leave, to not have him beside her at breakfast, or for a casual ride about the estate, not to mention in her bed, would be a severing she wasn't looking forward to.

He let her have her way with him, let her pick her own pace, and with that freedom the slow burn to climax was a torturous climb worth the wait. And then it burst within her. She called out his name as tremor after tremor radiated about her body, hard and fast, and somewhere in the chaos of her release she could no longer hold back the truth of her emotions. "I love you, Marcus," she gasped, kissing him.

He kissed her back, hard and deep, and flipped her onto her back, thrusting deep inside, shooting the last of her climax to peak in little tremors. "I love ye as well, lass. So much," he said as he found his own release.

His declaration made her vision blur, and he kissed away her tears before slumping to her side and pulling her into the crook of his arm. "Which leaves us with a problem, do you not think?" he asked, looking down and meeting her gaze.

"It does, doesn't it," Henrietta said, knowing that on the morrow she would have to tell Marcus the truth. Tell him that even though she loved him, loved him so much, she could not give him the future he wanted.

CHAPTER 13

Henrietta lay back in her bath and tried to ignore the fact that her maid was fussing about the room. The girl disappeared into her dressing room and Henrietta jumped in the bath when an almighty crash occurred.

"Is everything okay?" Henrietta called tentatively, wishing to be alone and to have some peace and quiet.

"Everything is well, my lady," her maid answered, before strolling back into the room with a handful of clothes. "I'll just take these downstairs to be laundered."

Henrietta nodded and sighed in relief when she was gone. Today she was determined to tell Lord Zetland the truth. What he did with that truth would be anyone's guess, but before they started any type of future together, they had to be honest. It had been a week since they had professed their love, and even though she'd planned on telling him the day after about her inability to have children, Henrietta had never found the right time.

But no more. Today she would do it. She washed herself quickly and got out, wanting to go downstairs and breakfast with Marcus. The past week had been day after day of bliss, of dining together, picnics, and long horse rides about the estate. She'd not wanted it to end, and fear that he would not want her after he knew she would never bear his children had stopped her from confiding in him.

She shook the painful thought aside, not wanting to imagine such a thing—that Marcus could be capable of pushing her away. He was kind, loving. He would understand, she was sure of it.

She went into her dressing room and chose a light pink morning gown. Then she slipped on a pair of slippers and headed down stairs. Just as she hoped, Marcus was already at table, a large plate of bacon, poached eggs, and two muffins along with a steaming cup of coffee before him. He'd poured her a cup also, and she smiled at the sweet gesture. "Good morning," she said, dismissing the staff from the room and waiting for the door to close before she leaned over the table and kissed him.

He grinned back at her. "Good morning, lass. You look sweet enough to eat."

"Maybe later," she teased, smiling at his chuckle as she spooned some scrambled eggs onto her plate. They ate in silence for a time, before Henrietta said, "If you're free after breakfast, there is something that I'd like to discuss with you if you have time."

He searched her face, but nodded. "Aye, of course lass."

She smiled, and changed the subject to the weather and the possibility of them going for a ride this afternoon. If Marcus noticed her change of subject he didn't say, and she was thankful for it. Telling him the truth would be hard enough as it was, let alone trying to explain why she wanted to talk to him in private.

. . .

Marcus waited in the chair across from Henrietta, who was sitting at her mahogany desk. He supposed the desk was really his now and he should be sitting where she was, but he liked seeing her there, in charge, lady of the house, strong and capable.

"You're nervous, lass. What is it you wanted to talk to me about?"

She fiddled with a paperweight, her long, delicate fingers shaking a little, and he reached over, stilling her hold. "Henrietta, tell me what's wrong."

She schooled her features. "There is something that I need to tell you. It's important and you ought to know before anything is decided between us regarding a future together."

An overwhelming sense of relief poured through him and he sat back in his chair. "I will admit that I'm happy to hear ye have something to tell me, lass, as I have also something that ye ought to know."

"Really? What is it that you wanted to tell me?"

He waved away her request. "You first," he argued. She had after all asked him to come into the library and discuss her matter, so it must be somewhat of importance.

"No, I insist." She settled back in her chair and watched him.

Marcus took a fortifying breath, hoping like hell she'd forgive him his actions. "You know I have a son, a fine, beautiful lad that I love and cherish." He frowned, the words harder than he thought to bring forth. "What ye don't know is that his start to life is not what one hopes for, and there will be repercussions for him for the remainder of his life. That my boy will face such censure is my fault and the blame lies with me." He should've told Henrietta the truth of his situation long before, and it shamed him that he had not.

"What are you trying to say?" she asked in a small voice.

"My son is illegitimate, Henrietta."

She recoiled from the news and Marcus winced. "Before I inherited the title of marquess, I had very little. The Scottish estate does not produce enough funds to keep Morleigh Castle running, let alone complete the repairs that I have planned. My estate is isolated and during the coldest winters becomes inaccessible. During one of these hard winters I sought the solace and company of a woman, a servant. She is the mother of my child."

Henrietta gasped, her mouth agape. "Tell me this isn't true, Marcus. You slept with your servant?"

Damn, hearing her state it aloud made it sound even more underhanded the more she stated it aloud, the more underhanded and seedy. "I was lonely, Henrietta, and I sought comfort in the arms of a willing woman. But if you're willing to accept Arthur, I know you'd be a wonderful mother for him and, God willing, to the children we'll have together."

She was silent a moment, and he cringed. What was she thinking? Did he disgust her now? "This happened a long time before I met you, and after the birth of Arthur, his mother wanted nothing to do with the babe even though I offered her marraige. She left and we've not seen or heard from her again." He leaned forward to take her hand and she recoiled further into her chair. "Please Henrietta, say something." Put him out of the hell he was currently living.

HENRIETTA FOUGHT FOR CALM. Marcus had had a child with his maid! Nor had he ever been married like she'd assumed since he was a father. All her dreams of them shattered like a glass mirror that had been dropped. Had Arthur been legitimate, she would've gladly been his mother, but with the boy illegitimate it changed things. Not that she cared either way if the child was born in or out of wedlock, but that she couldn't give Marcus any children that the law would allow to inherit his English estates. His title.

She sat for a moment, unable to fathom what she'd heard. She had come in here today to tell Marcus she could not give him children, never expecting to be told that he'd fathered an illegitimate child who could not inherit. Why had he not told her?

"How did you come to sleep with one of your maids? One that is under your protection?" She held his gaze and noted the shame that crossed his features.

"This is no excuse, but it had been a hard winter. No one had been able to leave the estate for weeks, and somewhere in between the cold days and even colder nights, I sought company. I know it was wrong, but it is in my past, lass. I want you to be my future."

The idea that his son was illegitimate settled on her shoulders like sack of flour. "You have no heir for the title of marquess."

He nodded once. "The Scottish estate will be his and I've already had a Will drawn up to state so. The English title and properties will be inherited by the eldest male child that I sire with my wife. I want that to be you, Henrietta."

Her stomach roiled at the truth of his words. If only she could give him one. She didn't care that the boy had a less than perfect start to life, but she did care that the situation now changed everything regarding what she hoped. If the boy was legitimate, there was a chance for them. If not, there was no hope.

She steeled herself, willing herself not to break down in a fit of tears. "I will speak frankly, and please let me finish before saying anything. The fact that you slept with your servant is distasteful and ill advised, but I do understand loneliness and what that can make someone do." *Such as fall in love with a man you cannot keep.* "As you said, your son, although born out of wedlock, will inherit the Scottish estates. But what of your English ones? Who will carry on the family tradition here? What will become of the people who work and live on the farms the estate owns if there is no lord to pay their wage?"

Marcus leaned forward in his chair. "We're young, Henrietta. I was hoping that you would marry me. That we could have children—an heir to take over the English title. I dinna wish to propose to ye when you're still angry with me—this is not how I imagined my proposal to be— but I love you. I want ye to be my wife. I want ye to be the mother of my children."

Tears pooled in her eyes and she swiped angrily at a tear that ran down her cheek. "I would like that too, but..." She shook her head, wishing she'd never started this affair that threatened to break her in two. "I'm unable to give you children, Marcus. There is no possibility, nothing I can take or do to change that fact. If you married me, your son Arthur would be the only child you would ever have."

He frowned, running a hand through his hair and leaving it on end. "But surely. You said yourself you'd only been married a year. Having children sometimes takes longer than that I think. You just need time."

She shook her head. "I don't need time. I've known this for a while now, and what I wanted to speak to you about today was this point. I was about to tell you the truth of my situation."

"But surely—"

"No, there is no 'but' in this case. I will not marry you knowing how much you want children. You deserve to have more, and I'm not going to be the one to stop you from doing that."

"We dinna have to have children, lass. I love you and you love me, surely that is enough."

Henrietta read the panic that flared in his eyes, hating that she was the one doing this to him. For all his past mistakes, he was a good man, and deserved only wonderful things to happen to him. He wanted more children, a brother or sister perhaps for Arthur. She had been wrong to allow their understanding to grow into so much more than sporadic tumbles into bed. Now both of them had their emotions engaged, and parting from him would not be easy.

"You mentioned at times your wish for more children. You not only need an heir, but you want one. It's quite clear to me that you're a caring and loving father. I will not deny you what you wish for most."

Marcus stood and came around the desk, pulling her to stand. He clasped her upper arms in a fierce hold, firm but not painful. "I want you more. Dinna send me away, not unless you're in the carriage right alongside me."

How he tempted her, but no. "You may say these things now, but in months to come, years even, you will grow to regret your choice and in doing so, regret me." She shook her head. "I will not be coming with you, Marcus, nor will I marry you." She reached out and ran her hand along his waistcoat. "Please do not make this any harder than it already is. Think of our time here with pleasure only. That is how I'll think in the months and years to come."

He stepped back as if she'd slapped him. "It's because

my son's illegitimate, isn't it? You dinna want to be associated with me because of the scandal that would be attached to our name should it become public what I'd done. We both know that in London, nothing stays a secret."

Henrietta gasped. "It has nothing to do with the circumstances surrounding the birth of your son. I do not care that he was born out of wedlock."

"You may not, but your family will, your friends. And dinna say that isn't so, for the letter from the duchess the other day about Edith Feathers running off with the family steward was proof of that."

"That is unfair. My decision has nothing to do with your son, and if that is what you think of me, you don't know me at all."

Marcus walked over to the unlit hearth and clasped the marble mantle. He sighed, shaking his head a little. "Mayhap 'tis best that I return home tomorrow instead of next week. If I cannot make ye change your mind, we cannot continue in the way that we have been."

Henrietta swallowed the lump that formed in her throat at his words. She didn't want him to go, not really. Even if it was for the best, to allow him to have a wife and more children, she wanted to be selfish. To tell him to stay. To bring his child to England and raise the boy here with them as a family. But she could not. She'd never thought only of herself, and she wouldn't start now. "I'll ensure the carriage is prepared for your departure." He looked over at her, and the pain etched on his features broke her in two. "I'm sorry, Marcus. I wish things could be different."

He nodded and strode for the door. "Aye, so do I."

CHAPTER 14

Six months later

M arcus had returned to Scotland determined to forget his few weeks in England in the bed of one of that country's most beautiful women. He thought it would be easy to forget Lady Zetland, to move on, but damn it all to hell, it was not.

Even with the knowledge that she wanted him to forget her. Had all but demanded he marry another and produce children by the dozen.

He shook his head and slammed the axe down hard on the fallen log just outside his keep. He could no sooner forget her than the Highlands could forget they were Scottish. She was in his blood, had wiggled her way under his skin, and damn it, he loved her.

Loved her wildly.

All that was left for him to do now was win her back. Prove to her that it didn't matter that he had no more children, for to have children with anyone else wasn't an option. He loved *her*. Wanted only *her*.

Couldn't the lass see that?

With winter coming to an end, just this week he'd had word that the roads were passable again, and so in the coming days he'd leave Morleigh Castle and travel to London. He would seek Henrietta out in town and see if he could convince her that she belonged with him. That she didn't belong alone simply because she wasn't able to bear children.

He wouldn't allow her to suffer such a fate. They deserved to be happy. Together.

HENRIETTA HAD RETURNED to town for the Season and regretted the choice immediately. Her mother, sensing her unhappiness, had thrown her into town events with such vigor that within the first week of being back in London, Henrietta was exhausted.

She stood beside her father at the De Veres' ball and watched the dancers partake in a minuet. Not that she really saw anyone at all, for her mind's eye only imagined someone else. Missing Lord Zetland so very much, she'd even a couple of times thought he'd been at a party or ball. The straight line of a gentleman's back, strong muscular shoulders, or hair that was of similar colouring and cut would catch her eye, and her heart would miss a beat.

But it was never him. She had herself to blame for that. She'd pushed him away, told him he'd be happier without her, and six months after Marcus had left Kewell Hall he'd not returned. So it would seem that her banishment of him had been what he wanted after all.

She shook the thought aside. This was for the best. He'd only gone because she'd forced him to, which she needed to do if he was ever to have more children. No one wanted a barren wife. No matter how wealthy or connected with the upper ten-thousand they were, at the end of it all, children ensured a family's survival.

"Father, I think I'll return home."

The duke turned to her, a frown marring his brow. "Let me find your mother and we'll come with you."

Henrietta lay her hand upon his sleeve, stalling him. "I'm perfectly capable of finding my way home, Papa. I'll send the carriage back for you."

"Are you alright, my dear?" he asked, always having a knack of sensing when one of his children were upset.

"Truly, I'm well. I'm just very tired."

Her father watched her for a moment before he said, "Your mother told me of Lord Zetland's visit to Kewell Hall, and that she thought you may have become close while he was there."

Close was not the term Henrietta would use. It was so much more than that. That her mama had picked up on the attraction, as new as it was when she was there, was telling. The pain of losing him, of letting him go, ate at her soul every day, and sometimes she wondered if the pain would ever ease.

She composed herself before she said, "We were close, Papa, but it was not to be."

He threw her a disbelieving look. Her father, even if he were a little grey about the edges, and had smile lines that were a little more pronounced, was still an attractive man for his age. And one of the best men she knew, even if he was her father and she was biased.

"Why was it not to be? I've remained quiet for some months, but I refuse to allow you to pine away and not live. This whole time you've been in London you've not had your heart here. And I think I know why."

Henrietta blinked back the tears that talking of Marcus

brought forth. "Why do you think that?" she asked, not willing to divulge her heartache just yet.

"You fell in love with him, did you not? When you returned to town it wasn't long before your mother and I figured out what was wrong." He took her hand and placed it on his arm, patting it a little. "Tell me, Henrietta, why Lord Zetland has returned to Scotland without you."

She sniffed, and swallowing hard wondered how she would get the words out without breaking down before the ton. "He has a child, Papa. One that was born out of wedlock."

"So?" the duke said, raising his brow. "I did not think we raised you to be so judgemental. Especially as we've had you working at the London Relief Society since you were a child."

Henrietta shook her head. "No, Papa, that's not it. I do not care about that. But his lordship wishes for more children. I could not allow him to go on believing there was a future for us, when there was not. He wants children. I cannot have them." A stray tear ran down her cheek and she dabbed at it with her gloved hand.

"Henrietta," her father said, placatingly. "Did I ever tell you why your mother and I never had any more children after you and Henry were born?"

"No, we just assumed you had all that you desired."

He smiled, patting her hand once again. "We did, never doubt that. We adore you and Henry, but we would've loved to have more children. But your mama almost died during childbirth, and the thought of losing her, the risk we would be taking should she be with child again, was not worth her life. And so we were grateful for what we did have. Two wonderful children, and each other. Having children is all very good, a wonderful gift, but people do survive, live full and rich lives, if they are unable or choose not to have them."

Henrietta had not known that about her parents. Looking across the ballroom floor she spied her mama, laughing with her good friend the Marchioness of Aaron. To have lost her mama, possibly never having her while they grew up, was a sadness she did not want to even contemplate. "But he wishes for children, Papa. I will not be the reason his wishes are not met."

"Was he in agreement with you? Was he happy and thankful that you told him to return to Scotland?"

"No," she said, thinking back on the day. "He argued the point with me."

"That's because he loves you, I think. You're present, alive now. A child, even if you did not have the medical issue you have, may never come. Sometimes that happens also. Women who are in perfect health can still be unable to conceive. But you, my dearest girl and flesh and blood, you're alive, in his life. Why would he not choose you over something that may never come to pass?"

The more her father spoke about her choice to send Marcus away the more she wondered if she'd done the right thing. Was he happy without her? Or did he miss her as much as she missed him?

"You think I made a mistake?" she asked, looking up at her father.

He smiled. "You were only doing what you thought was right. And even after all that I've told you, you may still hold to your choice. But I will tell you this, Henrietta. I love your mama. She is my life. The love of my life. And I would've forsaken the ducal line had I known we would never have children. She means more to me than a title. And if your Scotsman is as dejected, reserved, and pitiful as you have been these last few months, then I think you'll find that you are the love of his life. That you mean more to him than any title he may have inherited."

Henrietta bit her lip to stop it shaking. She had to go and see him. Find out once and for all if he regretted leaving or was thankful. Sitting in London any longer, feeling sorry and sad for herself, was not an option. "I have to go to Scotland."

Her father leaned down and kissed her cheek. "I think you do too, my dear."

Henrietta bade him goodnight and made her way into the entrance hall, where she asked for her shawl from the cloak room footman and ordered the Duke of Athelby's carriage.

The drive to her parents' London home was short. Henrietta alighted from the carriage full of eagerness to pack and be gone, just as a shadow stepped away from the home. She stifled a scream as a man in a dark redingote walked into the light afforded them from the street lamplight.

"Marcus?" she queried, and the driver, content that she knew the gentleman, drove off toward the mews.

"Yes, 'tis me," he said, coming to stand before her.

Her heart skipped a beat at seeing him again. She'd forgotten how tall he was, how much he reminded her of a Scottish warrior of old. "What are you doing in London?" she asked, not believing he was here, really before her, and not some figment of her pining, self-inflicted mind. She stopped herself from throwing herself at his head, begging him to love her just as she was, forever and a day.

"Is there someplace we can speak?" he asked, looking about.

"Of course," she said, realizing they were still standing on the street. She started up the steps. "Come into the parlor. I'll have tea sent in."

"Forget the tea. I just need to speak to you. Alone."

His tone, deep and with a brittle edge, was pleasure and pain all in one. Was what he had to speak to her about good or bad? Maybe he was here to tell her he loved her still. Or, the worst case, he was here to give her thanks, and tell her that he was to marry.

The idea left a sour taste in her mouth.

Without speaking, they walked to the parlor at the rear of the house, and Henrietta locked the door behind them to ensure privacy. They sat on a settee and, fighting the need to know right now what he wanted, she waited as patiently as she could for him to tell her his reasons for being in town.

He took in her features and gown with a look akin to adoration. "You look very beautiful this evening. Have ye been to a ball?"

She looked down at the golden embroidered gown with silk underlay, the diamond necklace about her neck. She nodded, keeping her gaze lowered so he would not see how much she'd missed him. How hearing his voice again was a balm to her aching soul. "I have, the De Veres' annual ball. When did you arrive in London?"

He threw her a sheepish look. "About an hour ago. I came straight here and have been waiting for you since the butler said the family were out for the evening. I took a chance and hoped you'd not stay out all night, but come home at a reasonable hour. Seems my luck is turning."

"So it would seem." She met his gaze and for a moment they just stared at one another. Her body thrummed with expectation, with wanting him as much as ever, and if he did not speak soon she would expire.

"I've missed ye, lass." He took her hand, kissing the inside of her wrist. "I should not have left Kewell Hall all those months ago. I should not have listened to you.

Instead, I should've demanded ye marry me. I dinna care that we'll not have children. I have a son, I'm perfectly content, I promise ye. But I'll only be perfectly *happy* if you'll be mine. Be my wife. Marry me, marchioness."

Her father's words floated through her mind and she blinked to clear her vision. "I should not have let you go and I'm sorry for pushing you away. I simply did not wish for you to miss out on what you wanted."

Marcus shifted closer to her, and as she caught the scent of sandalwood all was right in the world. "I'll only miss out if you send me away. I love you, Henrietta. I want to spend the rest of my life beside ye. I promise you nothing but joy. Just say yes."

She nodded and then chuckled as Marcus pulled her into a fierce hug. His strong arms and warmth enfolded her and she sighed in relief that he was here, that they would never be parted again. She hugged him back, never wanting to let go.

"We will be married in four weeks, and then we'll do whatever you wish," he said. "A trip abroad, a stay at your country house, or we could travel to Scotland where you'll see my beloved Highlands."

"I think first I need to meet your son."

"*Our son*, and if he loves you half as much as I do, you'll be adored."

Tears sprang to her eyes. She didn't think she'd ever cried so much since meeting Lord Zetland, but here she was, a sniffling watering pot. "I would love that. Please tell me you've brought him to London."

"I have, and he's at the Zetland townhouse." He tipped up her chin and feathered her lips, her chin and cheeks with kisses. "Stay with me tonight and meet our son tomorrow. I dinna want to be parted from ye again."

Henrietta stood, pulling him to stand. "Let me get my

shawl and we'll leave directly," she said, laughing at the wicked determination that entered his eyes. For the first time in months she felt alive again, her mind clear, unworried, and her heart filled with joy.

Her Scotsman followed her and soon they were ensconced in the marquess's carriage. The night was filled with joy, and wickedness, and everything she'd ever hoped for. And the following morning, Henrietta met her child.

EPILOGUE

Twelve years later

Henrietta sat atop her mount on the side of the Scottish mountain range that overlooked Loch Ruthven and watched as her son, Arthur, crawled along the ground trying to get a better vantage point to shoot the deer that was just over the ridge.

"How is he doing?" Marcus whispered, coming to stand beside her, his horse's reins loose in his hands.

"I think he has one in his sight. He's become very quiet and still." Henrietta looked down at Marcus, the love she had for the man standing at her feet having never lessened over the years they'd been married. If anything, it had only grown.

He'd kept to his promise—had loved her wildly, devoted his every spare minute to ensuring she was happy, and cared for her and Arthur with a ferocity that was unmatched. He was truly the best of men, and even though they'd never had any children of their own, Henrietta never felt as though she'd missed out.

Marcus's son—her son—meant the world to them, and she was so proud of the young man he was growing into.

A shot rang out and Arthur lifted his head to look above the gun's scope. He turned toward them, a large smile across his handsome features. "A clean shot, Mama."

Henrietta sighed, smiling with pride at her boy. "Well done, Arthur."

Marcus clasped her thigh, rubbing it a little. "Have I told ye today how bonny you look up on that horse, the Highlands behind you, your hair askew, and your cheeks pinkened with cold?"

She chuckled, pushing at his hand. "You, sir, are no gentleman. I look like a fright."

"And you love me for that," he said, winking at her.

She leaned down, clasping his kilt that he had thrown up over one shoulder for extra warmth, and pulling him in for a kiss. "Aye, I do love you, don't I," she said, in the best Scottish brogue she could muster. "And I always will."

He reached up and pulled her off the horse. She laughed before he took her lips and kissed her with such passion that she was left breathless. The sound of their son complaining about them met her ears and she smiled.

Marcus grinned. "And I love you, lass. Always and forever." *My love…*

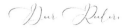

Dear Reader,

Thank you for taking the time to read my Lords of London box set! I hope you enjoyed the final three books in this series.

I adore my readers, and I'm so thankful for your support. If you're able, I would appreciate an honest review of *Lords of London, Books 4-6*. As they say, feed an author, leave a review!

If you'd like to learn about my, Kiss the Wallflower box set, books 1-3, please read on. I have included chapter one of, A Midsummer Kiss for your reading pleasure.

Tamara Gill

A MIDSUMMER KISS

Kiss the Wallflower, Book 1

Orphaned at a tender age, Miss Louise Grant spent her life in servitude to care for her younger siblings. Now, no longer needed as a duchess' companion, Louise has procured employment in York. But on her last night in London, her reputation is shattered when the drunk and disorderly Marquess mistakes Louise's room for his lover's.

. . .

Luke, the Marquess Graham is determined to never torment himself again by daring to love. Stumbling into Miss Louise Grant's room destroys his days of bachelorhood when he is pressured into marrying her. However, the cold and distant Marquess knows they'll never have a happy marriage; his new and fetching wife will never crack the protective barrier around his heart.

Trying to make the best of a bad marriage Louise attempts to break through the icy visage of the Marquess. But when misfortune strikes and Luke reverts to his cold, distant former self, Louise is not willing to give up on the possibility of love. After all, ice will melt when surrounded by warmth.

PROLOGUE

Miss Louise Grant folded the last of her unmentionables and placed them into the leather traveling case that her closest friend and confidante the Duchess of Carlton—Mary to her close friends—had given to her as a parting gift. Louise slumped onto the bed, staring at the case, and fought the prickling of tears that threatened.

There was little she could do. Mary was married now and no longer in need of a companion. But it would certainly be very hard to part ways. They'd been in each other's company since Louise was eight years of age, and was sent to be a friend and companion for the young Lady Mary Dalton as she was then in Derbyshire.

The room she'd been given in the duchess's London home was now bare of trinkets and pictures she'd drawn over the years, all packed away in her trunks to be soon shipped north to a family in York. Six children awaited her there, in need of teaching and guidance and she just hoped she did well with the new position. She needed to ensure it was so since her own siblings relied on her income.

TAMARA GILL

Surely it should not be so very hard to go from a lady's companion to a nursemaid and tutor. With any luck, perhaps if they were happy with her work, when Sir Daxton's eldest daughter came of age for her first Season, perchance they may employ her as a companion once more.

Certainly, she needed the stability of employment and would do everything in her power to ensure she remained with Sir Daxton's family. With two siblings to care for at her aunt's cottage in Sandbach, Cheshire, it was paramount she made a success of her new employ.

Mary bustled into the room and stopped when she spied the packed trunks. Her shoulders slumped. "Louise, you do not need to leave. Please reconsider. Married or not, you're my friend and I do not want to see you anywhere else but here."

Louise smiled, reaching out a hand to Mary. "You do not need me hanging about your skirts. You're married now, a wife, and I'm sure the duke wants you all to himself."

A blush stole over Mary's cheeks, but still she persisted, shaking her head. "You're wrong. Dale wants you to stay as much as I. Your brother and sister are well cared for by your aunt. Please do not leave us all."

Louise patted her hand, standing. As much as Louise loved her friend, Mary did not know that her aunt relied heavily on the money she made here as her companion. That without such funds their life would be a lot different than it was now. "I must leave. Sir Daxton is expecting me, so I must go." Even if the thought of leaving all that she'd known frightened her and left the pit of her stomach churning. Mary may wish her to stay, but there was nothing left for her here. Not really. Her siblings were

432

settled, happily going to the village school and improving themselves. Sir Daxton's six children were in need of guidance and teaching and she could not let him or his wife down. They had offered to pay her handsomely, and with the few extra funds she would procure from the employment, she hoped in time to have her siblings move closer than they now were. A place that no one could rip from under them or force them to be parted again.

The memory of the bailiffs dragging her parents onto the street...her mother screaming and begging for them to give them more time. Even now she could hear her mother's wailing as they threw all their meager belongings onto the street, the townspeople simply looking on, staring and smirking at a family that had fallen low.

None of them had offered to help, and with nowhere else to go, they had moved in with her mother's sister, a widow with no children in Cheshire. The blow to the family was one that her parents could not tolerate or accept and her father took his own life, her mother only days later. Their aunt had said she had died of a broken heart, but Louise often wondered if she'd injured herself just as her papa had done.

Within days of losing her parents, Louise had been placed in a carriage and transported to Derbyshire to the Earl of Lancaster's estate. Having once worked there, her aunt still knew the housekeeper and had procured her a position through that means.

She owed a great deal to the earl's family, and her aunt. She would be forever grateful for the education, love and care they had bestowed upon her, but they had done their part in helping her. It was time she helped herself and started off in a new direction, just as Mary had done after marrying the Duke of Carlton.

"Very well." Mary's eyes glinted with unshed tears and Louise pulled her into a hug.

"We will see each other again and I will write to you every month, to tell you what is happening and how I am faring."

Mary wiped at her cheek, sniffing. "Please do. You're my best friend. A sister to me in all ways except blood. I would hate to lose you."

Louise picked up her valise and placed it on top of one of her many trunks. "Now, should we not get ready for your first London ball this evening? As the newly minted Duchess of Carlton, you must look simply perfect."

"And you too, dearest." Mary strode to the bell pull and rang for a maid. "You're going to look like a duchess as well this evening. I have not lost hope that some gentleman will fall instantly in love with you as soon as he sees you and you will never have to think of York or Sir Daxton and his six children ever again."

Louise laughed. How she would miss her friend and her never-ending hope that someone would marry her. But the chances of such a boon occurring were practically zero. She was a lady's companion, no nobility in her blood or dowry. Perhaps she would find a gentleman's son in York, a man who would love her for the small means that she did possess—a good education and friends in high places. A man who would welcome her two siblings and their impoverished state and support them as she was trying to do.

"One can only hope," she said, humoring her. "I will certainly try, if not for my own sake, then definitely for yours, Your Grace."

Mary beamed. "That is just what I like to hear. Now, what should we do with your hair…"

Want to read more? Purchase, Kiss the Wallflower, Books 1-3 today!

TO TEMPT AN EARL

TO VEX A VISCOUNT

TO DARE A DUCHESS

TO MARRY A MARCHIONESS

LORDS OF LONDON - BOOKS 1-3 BUNDLE

LORDS OF LONDON - BOOKS 4-6 BUNDLE

To Marry a Rogue Series

ONLY AN EARL WILL DO

ONLY A DUKE WILL DO

ONLY A VISCOUNT WILL DO

ONLY A MARQUESS WILL DO

ONLY A LADY WILL DO

A Time Traveler's Highland Love Series

TO CONQUER A SCOT

TO SAVE A SAVAGE SCOT

TO WIN A HIGHLAND SCOT

Time Travel Romance

DEFIANT SURRENDER

A STOLEN SEASON

Scandalous London Series

A GENTLEMAN'S PROMISE

A CAPTAIN'S ORDER

A MARRIAGE MADE IN MAYFAIR

SCANDALOUS LONDON - BOOKS 1-3 BUNDLE

ABOUT THE AUTHOR

Tamara Gill is an Australian author who grew up in an old mining town in country South Australia, where her love of history was founded. So much so, she made her darling husband travel to the UK for their honeymoon, where she dragged him from one historical monument and castle to another.

A mother of three, her two little gentlemen in the making, a future lady (she hopes) and a part-time job keep her busy in the real world, but whenever she gets a moment's peace she loves to write romance novels in an array of genres, including regency, medieval and time travel.

www.tamaragill.com
tamaragillauthor@gmail.com

Made in United States
North Haven, CT
28 April 2022

18677216R00245